Time's
Convert

VIKING

ALSO BY DEBORAH HARKNESS

A Discovery of Witches

Shadow of Night

The Book of Life

The World of All Souls

Time's Convert

Deborah Harkness

⊰ VIKING ⊱

VIKING

An imprint of Penguin Random House LLC

375 Hudson Street

New York, New York 10014

penguinrandomhouse.com

ISBN 9780399564512 (hardcover)

ISBN 9780399564529 (ebook)

ISBN 9780525561347 (international edition)

Printed in the United States of America

1   3   5   7   9   10   8   6   4   2

Set in Adobe Garamond Pro

DESIGNED BY LUCIA BERNARD

A long habit of not thinking a thing *wrong*,
gives it a superficial appearance of being *right*,
and raises at first a formidable outcry in defense of custom.
But the tumult soon subsides.
Time makes more converts than reason.

—Thomas Paine

Time's Convert

⇥ 1 ⇤

Naught

12 MAY

On her last night as a warmblood, Phoebe Taylor had been a good daughter.

Freyja had insisted upon it.

"Let's not make a fuss," Phoebe had protested, as though she was just going on holiday for a few days, hoping to get away with a casual farewell at the hotel where her family was staying.

"Absolutely not," Freyja said, looking down her long nose. "De Clermonts do not skulk around—unless they are Matthew, of course. We shall do this properly. Over dinner. It is your duty."

The evening party Freyja put on for the Taylors was simple, elegant, and perfect—right down to the weather (a flawless example of May), the music (could every vampire in Paris play the cello?), the flowers (enough Madame Hardy roses had been brought in from the garden to perfume the entire city), and the wine (Freyja was fond of Cristal).

Phoebe's father, mother, and sister showed up at half past eight as requested. Her father was in black tie; her mother wore a turquoise and gold *lehenga choli*; Stella was in head-to-toe Chanel. Phoebe wore unrelieved black with the emerald earrings Marcus had given her before he left Paris, along with a pair of sky-high heels of which she—and Marcus—was particularly fond.

The assembled group of warmbloods and vampire first had drinks in the garden behind Freyja's sumptuous house in the 8th arrondissement—a private Eden the likes of which had not been carved out of space-starved Paris for over a century. The Taylor family was accustomed to palatial surroundings—Phoebe's father was a career diplomat, and her mother came from the kind of Indian family that had married into the British civil service since the days of the Raj—but de Clermont privilege was on an entirely different scale.

They sat down to dinner at a table set with crystal and china, in a room with tall windows that let in the summer light and overlooked the garden. Charles, the laconic chef whom the de Clermonts employed in their Parisian homes when warmbloods were invited to dine, was fond of Phoebe and had spared no effort or expense.

"Raw oysters are a sign that God loves vampires and wants them to be happy," Freyja announced, raising her glass at the beginning of the meal. She was, Phoebe noticed, using the word "vampire" as liberally as possible, as though sheer repetition might normalize what Phoebe was about to do. "To Phoebe. Happiness and long life."

Following that toast, her family had little appetite. Aware that this was her last proper meal, Phoebe nevertheless found it difficult to swallow. She forced down the oysters, and the champagne that accompanied it, and picked at the rest of the feast. Freyja kept up a lively conversation throughout the hors d'oeuvres, the soup, the fish, the duck, and the sweets ("Your last chance, Phoebe, darling!"), switching from French to English to Hindi between sips of wine.

"No, Edward, I don't believe there *is* any place I haven't been. Do you know, I think my father might have been the original diplomat?" Freyja used this startling announcement to draw out Phoebe's circumspect father about his early days in the queen's service.

Whether or not Freyja's historical judgment was accurate, Philippe de Clermont had clearly taught his daughter a thing or two about smoothing over conversational rough edges.

"Richard Mayhew, you say? I believe I knew him. Françoise, didn't I know a Richard Mayhew when we were in India?"

The sharp-eyed servant had mysteriously appeared the moment her mistress required her, tuned in to some vampiric frequency inaudible to mere mortals.

"Probably." Françoise was a woman of few words, but each one conveyed layers of meaning.

"Yes, I think I did know him. Tall? Sandy haired? Good-looking, in a sort of schoolboy way?" Freyja was undeterred by Françoise's dour remark or by the fact that she was describing roughly half the British diplomatic corps.

Phoebe had yet to discover anything that could put a dent in Freyja's cheerful resolve.

"Good-bye for now," Freyja said breezily at the end of the evening, kissing each of the Taylors in farewell. A press of cool lips on one cheek, then the other. "Padma, you are always welcome. Let me know when you will be in Paris next. Stella, do stay here during the winter shows. It is so convenient to the fashion houses, and Françoise and Charles will take very good care of you. The George V is excellent, of course, but *so* popular with tourists. Edward, I will be in touch."

Her mother had been characteristically dry-eyed and stoic, though she held Phoebe a bit more tightly than usual in farewell.

"You are doing the right thing," Padma Taylor whispered into her daughter's ear before releasing her. She understood what it meant to love someone enough to give up your whole life in exchange for a promise of what it could become.

"Make sure that prenup is as generous as they claim," Stella murmured to Phoebe as she crossed the threshold. "Just in case. This house is worth a fucking fortune." Stella could view Phoebe's decision only through her own frame of reference, which was entirely concerned with glamour, style, and the distinctive cut of Freyja's vintage red gown.

"This?" Freyja had laughed when Stella admired it, posing for a moment and tilting her flaxen topknot to one side to show the gown and her figure to greater advantage. "Balenciaga. Had it for ages. Now, there was a man who understood how to construct a bodice!"

It was her normally reserved father who had struggled with the farewell, eyes filled with tears, searching hers (so like his, Freyja had noticed earlier in the evening) for signs that her resolution might be wavering. Once her mother and Stella were outside the gates, her father pulled Phoebe away from the front steps where Freyja waited.

"It won't be long, Dad," Phoebe said, trying to reassure him. But they both knew that months would pass before she would be allowed to see her family again—for their safety, as well as for her own.

"Are you sure, Phoebe? Absolutely?" her father asked. "There's still time to reconsider."

"I'm sure."

"Be reasonable for a moment," Edward Taylor said, a note of pleading in his voice. He was familiar with delicate negotiations, and was not above using guilt to tilt matters in his favor. "Why not wait a few more years? There's no need to rush into such a big decision."

"I'm not going to change my mind," Phoebe said, gentle but firm. "This isn't a matter for the head, Dad, but the heart."

Now her birth family was gone. Phoebe was left with the de Clermonts' loyal retainers Charles and Françoise, and Freyja—who was her fiancé's maker's stepsister, and therefore in vampiric terms a close relation.

In the immediate aftermath of the Taylors' departure, Phoebe had thanked Charles for the fine dinner, and Françoise for taking care of everyone during the party. Then she sat in the salon with Freyja, who was reading her e-mail before responding to it in longhand, writing on creamy cards edged in lavender that she slid into heavy envelopes.

"There is no need to embrace this godforsaken new preference for instant communication," Freyja explained when Phoebe asked why she didn't simply hit reply like everyone else. "You will soon discover, Phoebe dearest, that speed is not something that a vampire requires. It's very human and vulgar to rush about as though time were in short supply."

After putting in a courteous hour with Marcus's aunt, Phoebe felt she had done her bit.

"I think I'll go upstairs," Phoebe said, feigning a yawn. In truth, sleep was the furthest thing from her mind.

"Give Marcus my love." Freyja licked the adhesive on the envelope with delicate laps of her tongue before sealing it shut.

"How do you—" Phoebe looked at Freyja, astonished. "I mean, what are you—"

"This is my house. I know everything that happens in it." Freyja stuck a stamp on the corner of the envelope, making sure it was properly aligned with the edges. "I know, for instance, that Stella brought three of those horrible little phones here tonight in her bag, and that you removed them when you went to the toilet. I presume you hid them in your room. Not among your underclothes—you are too original for that, aren't you, Phoebe?—nor under the mattress. No. I think they are in the canister of bath salts on the window ledge. Or inside your shoes—those rubber-soled ones that you wear on walks. Or perhaps they are on top of the armoire in the blue-and-white plastic sack you saved from your trip to the grocer on Wednesday?"

Freyja's third guess was correct, right down to the plastic bag that still smelled vaguely of the garlic Charles had used in his triumphant bouillabaisse. Phoebe had known Marcus's plan to flout the rules and stay in touch was not a good idea.

"You are breaking your agreements," Freyja said matter-of-factly. "But you are a grown woman, with free will, capable of making your own decisions."

Technically, Marcus and Phoebe were forbidden to speak to each other until she had been a vampire for ninety days. They had wondered how they might bend this rule. Sadly, Freyja's only phone was located in the entrance hall, where everyone could hear your conversations. It seldom worked properly, in any case. Every now and again it gave a tinny ring, the force of the bells inside the ancient device so strong that they rocked the handset in its brass cradle. As soon as you picked up the receiver, the line usually went dead. Freyja wrote it off to a bad wiring job courtesy of a member of Hitler's inner circle during the last war; she was not interested in fixing it.

After considering the challenges of the situation, Marcus had, with the help of Stella and his friend Nathaniel, come up with a more secretive means of communication: cheap, disposable cell phones. They were the kind used by international thieves and terrorists—or so Nathaniel had assured them—and would be untraceable should Baldwin or any other vampire want to spy on them. Phoebe and Marcus purchased them in a shady electronics shop located on one of the 10th arrondissement's more entrepreneurial streets.

"I am sure, given the situation, that you will keep your conversation brief," Freyja continued. She glanced at her computer screen and addressed another envelope. "You don't want Miriam to catch you."

Miriam was hunting around the Sacré Coeur and was expected to return in the small hours of the morning. Phoebe glanced at the clock on the mantel—an extravagant affair of gilt and marble with reclining male nudes holding up a round timepiece as though it were a beach ball. It was one minute before midnight.

"Good night, then," Phoebe said, grateful that Freyja was not only three steps ahead of her and Marcus, but at least one ahead of Miriam, as well.

"Hmm." Freyja's attention was devoted to the page in front of her.

Phoebe escaped upstairs. Her bedroom was down a long corridor lined with early French landscapes. A thick carpet muffled her footsteps. After closing the bedroom door, Phoebe reached up onto the top of the armoire (Empire style, circa 1815) and snagged the plastic bag. She pulled out one of the phones and switched it on. It was fully charged and ready for use.

Clutching the phone to her heart, Phoebe slipped into the attached bathroom and closed that door, also. Two closed doors and a broad expanse of thick porcelain tile was all the privacy this vampire household afforded. She toed off her shoes and lowered herself, fully clothed, into the cold, empty tub before dialing Marcus's number.

"Hello, sweetheart." Marcus's voice, usually lighthearted and warm, was rough edged with concern—though he was doing his best to disguise it. "How was dinner?"

"Delicious," Phoebe lied. She lay back in the tub, which was Edwardian and had a magnificent high back with a curve to cradle her neck.

Marcus's quiet laughter told her that he didn't entirely believe her.

"Two bites of dessert and a nibble here and there around the edges?" Marcus teased.

"One bite of dessert. And Charles went to so much trouble." Phoebe's brow creased. She would have to make it up to him. Like most culinary geniuses, Charles was quick to take offense when plates were returned to the kitchen with food still on them.

"Nobody expected you to eat much," Marcus said. "The dinner was for your family, not you."

"There were plenty of leftovers. Freyja sent them home with Mum."

"How was Edward?" Marcus knew about her father's reservations.

"Dad tried to talk me out of our plan. Again," Phoebe replied.

There was a long silence.

"It didn't work," Phoebe added, in case Marcus was worried.

"Your father just wants you to be absolutely sure," Marcus said quietly.

"I am. Why do people keep questioning me?" There was no keeping the impatience from her tone.

"They love you," Marcus said simply.

"Then they should listen to me. Being with you—that's what I want."
It wasn't all that she wanted, of course. Ever since Phoebe met Ysabeau at
Sept-Tours, she had craved the inexhaustible supply of time that vampires
possessed.

Phoebe had studied how Ysabeau seemed to fully extend herself into
every task. Nothing was done quickly or for the sake of getting through
and checking it off one's endless to-do list. Instead there was a reverence
to Ysabeau's every move—how she sniffed the blossoms in her garden, the
feline stealth of her steps, the slow pause when she reached the end of a
chapter in her book before she went on to the next. Ysabeau did not feel
that time would run out before she had sucked the essence from whatever
experience she was having. For Phoebe, there never seemed to be enough
time to breathe, dashing from the market to work to the chemist's for cold
medicine to the cobbler to have her heels fixed, and back to work.

But Phoebe hadn't shared these observations with Marcus. He would
learn her thoughts on the matter soon, when they were reunited. Then
Marcus would drink from her heart vein—the thin river of blue that
crossed the left breast—and learn her deepest secrets, her darkest fears,
and her most cherished desires. The blood from the heart vein contained
all that a lover might conceal, and drinking from it embodied the sincer-
ity and trust that their relationship would need in order to succeed.

"We're going to take this one step at a time, remember?" Marcus's
question reclaimed her attention. "First, you become a vampire. Then, if
you still want me—"

"I will." Of this, Phoebe was absolutely certain.

"*If* you still want me," Marcus repeated, "we will marry and you will
be stuck with me. For richer and poorer."

This was one of their routines as a couple—rehearsing the marriage
vows. Sometimes they focused on one line and pretended that it would be
hard to keep. Sometimes they made fun of the whole lot and the smallness
of the concerns the vows addressed when stacked up against the size of
their feelings for each other.

"In sickness and in health." Phoebe settled deeper into the tub. Its
coolness reminded her of Marcus, and its solid curves made her wish he
were sitting behind her, his arms and legs enfolding her. "Forsaking all
others. Forever."

"Forever is a long time," Marcus warned.

"Forsaking *all* others," Phoebe repeated, putting careful emphasis on the middle word.

"You can't know for sure. Not until you know me blood to blood," Marcus replied.

Their rare quarrels erupted after just this kind of exchange, when Marcus's words suggested he'd lost confidence in her and Phoebe became defensive. Such arguments had usually been settled in Marcus's bed, where each had demonstrated to the other's satisfaction that although they might not know *everything* (yet), they had mastered certain important bodies of knowledge.

But Phoebe was in Paris and Marcus was in the Auvergne. A physical rapprochement wasn't possible at the moment. A wiser, more experienced person would have let the matter drop—but Phoebe was twenty-three, irritated, and anxious about what was about to take place.

"I don't know why you think it's me who will change my mind and not you." She intended the words to be light and playful. To her horror, they sounded accusatory. "After all, I've never known you as anything but a vampire. But you fell in love with me as a warmblood."

"I'll still love you." Marcus's response was gratifyingly swift. "That won't change, even if you do."

"You might hate the taste of me. I should have made you try me— before," Phoebe said, trying to pick a fight. Maybe Marcus didn't love her as much as he thought he did. Phoebe's rational mind knew that was nonsense, but the irrational part (the part that was in control at the moment) wasn't convinced.

"I want us to share that experience—as equals. I've never shared my blood with my mate—nor have you. It's something we can do for the first time, together." Marcus's voice was gentle, but it held an edge of frustration.

This was well-covered ground. Equality was something that Marcus cared about deeply. A woman and child begging, a racial slur overheard on the tube, an elderly man struggling to cross the street while young people sped by with their headphones and mobiles—all of these made Marcus seethe.

"We should have just run off and eloped," Marcus said. "We should have done it our way, and not bothered with all this ancient tradition and ceremony."

But doing it this way, in slow, measured steps, was a choice they had also made together.

Ysabeau de Clermont, the family's matriarch and Marcus's grandmother, had laid out the pros and cons of abandoning vampire custom with her usual clarity. She started with the recent family scandals. Marcus's father, Matthew, had married a witch in violation of nearly a thousand years of prohibitions against relationships between creatures of different species. Then he nearly died at the hands of his estranged, deranged son, Benjamin. This left Phoebe and Marcus with two options. They could keep her transformation and their marriage secret for as long as possible before facing an eternity of gossip and speculation about what had gone on behind the scenes. Alternatively, they could transform Phoebe into a vampire before she was mated to Marcus with all due pomp—and transparency. If they chose the latter course, Phoebe and Marcus would likely suffer a year of inconvenience, followed by a decade or two of notoriety, and then be free to enjoy an endless lifetime of relative peace and quiet.

Marcus's reputation had played a factor in Phoebe's decision, too. He was known among vampires for his impetuousness, and for charging off to right the evils of the world without a care for what other creatures might think. Phoebe hoped that if they followed tradition in the matter of their marriage, Marcus would enter the ranks of respectability and his idealism might be seen in a more positive light.

"Tradition serves a useful purpose, remember?" Phoebe said firmly. "Besides, we're not sticking to *all* the rules. Your secret phone plan is no longer secret, by the way. Freyja knows."

"It was always a long shot." Marcus sighed. "I swear to God, Freyja's part bloodhound. There's no getting anything past her. Don't worry. Freyja won't really mind us talking. It's Miriam who's the stickler."

"Miriam is in Montmartre," Phoebe said, glancing at her watch. It was now thirty minutes past midnight. Miriam would return soon. She really had to get off the phone.

"There's good hunting around the Sacré Coeur," Marcus commented.

"That's what Freyja said," Phoebe replied.

Silence fell. It grew heavy with all the things they couldn't say, wouldn't say, or wanted to say but didn't know how. In the end, there were only three words important enough to utter.

"I love you, Marcus Whitmore."

"I love you, Phoebe Taylor," Marcus replied. "No matter what you decide ninety days from now, you're already my mate. You're under my skin, in my blood, in my dreams. And don't worry. You're going to be a brilliant vampire."

Phoebe had no doubts that the transformation would work, and blissfully few that she wouldn't enjoy being ageless and powerful. But would she and Marcus be able to build a relationship that would endure, like the one Marcus's grandmother had known with her mate, Philippe?

"I will be thinking of you," Marcus said. "Every moment."

The line went dead as Marcus hung up.

Phoebe kept the phone to her ear until the telephone service disconnected the call. She climbed out of the tub, smashed the phone with the canister of bath salts, opened the window, and threw the lump of plastic and circuitry as far as she could into the garden. Destroying the evidence of their transgression had been part of Marcus's original plan, and Phoebe was going to follow it to the letter even if Freyja already knew about the forbidden phones. What was left of the device landed in the small fishpond with a satisfying *plonk*.

Having rid herself of the incriminating evidence, Phoebe took off her dress and hung it up inside the armoire—making sure that the striped plastic bag was once again out of sight on top of it. Then she put on the simple white silk dressing gown that Françoise had laid out for her on the bed.

Phoebe sat on the edge of the mattress, quiet and still, resolutely facing her future, and waited for time to find her.

PART 1

Time Hath Found Us

❖

*We have it in our power
to begin the world over again.*

—Thomas Paine

⇥ 2 ⇤

Less Than Naught

Phoebe stepped on the scale.

"My God, you are tiny." Freyja read the numbers to Miriam, who recorded them on something that looked like a medical chart. "Fifty-two kilograms."

"I told you to gain three kilos, Phoebe," Miriam said. "The scale shows an increase of just two kilos."

"I did try." Phoebe didn't see why she was apologizing to these two, who were on the equivalent of a raw-foods-plus-liquids diet. "What difference does one kilo make?"

"Blood volume," Miriam replied, trying to sound patient. "The heavier you are, the more blood you have."

"And the more blood you have, the more you will need to receive from Miriam," Freyja continued. "We want to be sure that she gives back as much as she takes. There are fewer risks of rejection with an equivalent exchange of human blood for vampire blood. And we want you to receive as much blood as possible."

The calculations had been going on for months. Blood volume. Cardiac output. Weight. Oxygen uptake. If Phoebe didn't know better, she would think she was on trial for the British national fencing team, not the de Clermont family.

"Are you sure about the pain?" Freyja asked. "We can give you something for it. There's no need to experience any discomfort. Rebirth need not be painful, as it once was."

This, too, had been a topic of much discussion. Freyja and Miriam had recounted hair-raising tales of their own transformations, and how agonizing it was to be filled with the blood of a preternatural creature. Vampire blood was thuggish, beating out every trace of humanity in its effort to create the perfect predator. By taking blood in slowly, a newborn vampire could adjust to the invasion of new genetic material with little or no pain—but there was evidence that the human body also had a greater opportunity to reject the maker's blood, preferring to die rather than change into something else. The rapid transfusion of vampire blood had the opposite effect. The pain was excruciating, but the weakened human body didn't have the time or resources to mount a counterattack.

"I am not bothered by the prospect of pain. Let's just get this over with." Phoebe's tone indicated that she hoped to put an end to this conversational avenue—forever.

Freyja and Miriam exchanged glances.

"How about a local anesthetic for the bite?" Miriam asked, turning clinical once more.

"For God's sake, Miriam." When not feeling like a potential Olympian, Phoebe was convinced she was in the most thorough preoperative consultation ever conducted. "I don't want anesthesia. I want to feel the bite. I want to feel the pain. This is the only birthing process I'm ever going to have. I'm not going to miss it."

Phoebe was quite clear on this score.

"No act of creation has ever been painless," she continued. "Miracles should leave a mark, so that we can remember how precious they are."

"Very well, then," Freyja said, brisk and efficient. "The doors are locked. The windows are locked. Françoise and Charles are standing by. Just in case."

"I still think we should have done this in Denmark." Even now, Miriam couldn't stop reanalyzing the procedure. "There are too many beating hearts in Paris."

"Lejre has nearly fifteen hours of daylight this time of year. Phoebe wouldn't be able to stand so much sunshine so quickly," Freyja argued.

"Yes, but the hunting . . ." Miriam began.

What would follow, Phoebe knew, was a long comparison of French and Danish fauna, in which the nutritive benefits of both would be considered, taking into account variability in size, freshness, farmed versus wild, and the unpredictable appetites of the infant vampire.

"That's it," Phoebe said, headed for the door. "Maybe Charles will change me. I cannot go over these arrangements one. More. Time."

"She's ready," Miriam and Freyja said in unison.

Phoebe pulled the loose neck of the white dressing gown aside, exposing rich veins and arteries. "Then do it."

The words were barely out of her mouth when Phoebe felt a sharp sensation.

Numbness.

Tingling.

Suction.

Phoebe's knees buckled and her head swam as the shock of rapid blood loss overtook her. Her brain registered that she was being attacked and was in mortal danger, and her adrenaline rose.

Her field of vision narrowed, and the room dimmed.

Strong arms caught her.

Phoebe floated in a velvet darkness, sinking into folds of quiet.

Peace.

A SEARING COLD BROUGHT HER back to awareness.

Phoebe was freezing, burning.

Her mouth opened in a terrified scream as her body caught fire from the inside.

Someone offered a wrist, wet with something that smelled—delicious.

Copper and iron.

Salt and sweet.

It was the scent of life. *Life.*

Phoebe snuffled at the wrist like a baby seeking her mother's breast, the flesh held tantalizingly close to her mouth without touching her lips.

"You choose," her maker said. "Life? Or death?"

Phoebe used all of her energy to move closer to the promise of vitality. In the distance, someone was knocking, slow and steady. Understanding followed.

Heartbeat.

Pulse.

Blood.

Phoebe kissed the cold flesh of her maker's wrist, reverent and blindingly conscious of the gift being given.

"Life," Phoebe whispered before taking her first mouthful of vampire blood.

As the powerful substance surged through her veins, Phoebe's body exploded in pain and yearning: for what was lost, for what was to come, for all that she would never be, and for everything that she would become.

Her heart began to make a new music, one that was slow and deliberate.

I am, Phoebe's heart sang.

Naught.

And yet.

Now.

Evermore.

⇥ 3 ⇤

The Prodigal Returns

"If the ghosts are making that racket, I'm going to kill them," I murmured, clinging to the disorientation of sleep in hopes of prolonging it for a few more moments. I was still jet-lagged after our recent flight from America to France and had piles of exams and papers to grade following the end of the spring semester at Yale. Pulling the covers closer to my chin, I turned over and prayed for silence.

Heavy pounding echoed through the house, bouncing off thick stone walls and floors.

"Someone's at the front door." Matthew, who slept very little, was at the open window, sniffing the night air for clues as to their identity. "It's Ysabeau."

"It's three in the morning!" I groaned and slid my feet into a pair of waiting slippers. We were no strangers to crisis, but even so, this was unusual.

Matthew relocated in a flash from the bedroom window to the stairs and began his swift descent.

"Mama!" Becca wailed in the nearby nursery, capturing my attention. "Ow! Loud. Loud."

"Coming, sweetie." My daughter had her father's keen hearing. Her first word had been "mama," her second "papa," and her third "Pip" for her brother Philip. "Blood," "loud," and "doggy" had followed quickly thereafter.

"Lightning bug, lightning bug, make me a match." I didn't flick on the lights, choosing instead to gently illuminate the tip of my index finger with a simple spell inspired by a song from an old album of show tunes I'd found in a cupboard. My gramarye—the ability to put my knotted magic into words—was coming along.

In the nursery, Becca was sitting up, tiny hands clapped to her ears and her face twisted in distress. Cuthbert, the overstuffed elephant Marcus gave to her, and a wooden zebra named Zee were prancing around her heavy, medieval cradle. Philip stood inside his own, gripping the sides and looking at his sister with concern.

In dreamtime, the magic in the twins' half-witch, half-vampire blood bubbled to the surface, disturbing their shallow sleep. Though I found their nocturnal activities a bit worrying, Sarah said we could thank the goddess that thus far the twins' magic had been confined to rearranging the nursery furniture, making white clouds out of baby powder, and constructing impromptu mobiles out of stuffed animals.

"Owie," Philip said, pointing to Becca. He was already following in Matthew's medical footsteps, minutely inspecting every creature at Les Revenants—two legged, four legged, winged, or finned—for scrapes, blemishes, and insect bites.

"Thank you, Philip." I narrowly avoided collision with Cuthbert and headed for Becca. "Would you like a cuddle, Becca?"

"Cuthbert, too." Becca was already a skilled negotiator thanks to spending time with her two grandmothers. I feared that Ysabeau and Sarah were bad influences.

"Just you and Philip, if he'd like to join us," I said firmly, rubbing Becca's back.

Cuthbert and Zee hit the ground with petulant thuds. It was impossible to know which of the children was responsible for the flying animals, or why the magic had left them. Was it Becca who had set them aloft, and the backrub had brought her enough comfort that she didn't need the animals anymore? Or was it Philip, who was quieter now because his sister was no longer in distress? Or was it because I had said no?

In the distance, the pounding stopped. Ysabeau was in the house.

"Gam—" Becca began. Then she hiccupped.

"Mer," Philip finished, his expression brightening.

Anxiety wove a tight knot in my stomach. I suddenly realized that something had to be very wrong for Ysabeau to come in the middle of the night without a phone call.

The soft murmurs downstairs were too faint for my witch's ears to catch, though the twins' cocked heads suggested that they could follow the conversation between their father and grandmother. Unfortunately, they were too young to relay its substance to me.

I eyed the slick steps as I shifted Becca to one side and picked up Philip with my free arm. Normally, I clung to the rope that Matthew strung up on the curved wall to keep warmbloods from falling. I'd been limiting the magic I used in the children's presence for fear that they would try to imitate me. Tonight would have to be an exception.

Come with me, the wind whispered, snaking around my ankles in a lover's caress, *and I will fulfill your desire.*

The elemental call was maddeningly clear. Why, then, couldn't it carry Ysabeau's words to me? Why did it want me to join Matthew and her?

But power could be sphinxlike. If you didn't ask the right question, it simply refused to respond.

Cuddling the children closer, I surrendered to the allure of the air, and my feet lifted from the floor. I hoped the children wouldn't notice we were inches above the stone, but something ancient and wise had sparked to life in Philip's gray-green eyes.

A silver moonbeam sliced across the wall, making its way through one of the tall, narrow windows. It captured Becca's attention as we floated down the stairs.

"Pretty," she crooned, reaching for the slash of light. "Pretty babies."

For a moment the light bent toward her, defying the laws of physics as humans understood them. Gooseflesh rose on my arms, followed by letters that shone under the surface of my skin in red and gold. There was magic in the moonlight, but even though I was a witch and a weaver, I did not always see what my mixed-blood children were able to perceive.

Happy to leave the moonbeam behind, I let the air carry me down the rest of the stairs. Once we were on terra firma, my warmblood feet covered the remaining distance to the front door.

A brush of frost on my cheek, the indication of a vampire's glance, told me that Matthew had spotted our arrival. He was standing in the open doorway with Ysabeau. The play of silver and shadow made his cheekbones stand out and his hair appear even darker while, through some strange alchemy, the same light made Ysabeau look more golden. There was dirt on her tawny-colored leggings, and her white shirt was torn where a tree branch had snagged it. She acknowledged me with a nod, her breath ragged. Ysabeau had been running—fast and hard.

The children sensed the strangeness of the moment. Instead of greeting their grandmother with their usual enthusiasm, they clung to me tightly, tucking their heads into the curves of my neck as if to hide from whatever mysterious darkness was impinging on the house.

"I was talking to Freyja. Before we finished, Marcus said he was going to the village," Ysabeau explained, a splinter of panic in her tone. "But Alain was concerned, so we followed him. Marcus seemed fine, at first. But then he bolted."

"Marcus ran away from Sept-Tours?" It didn't seem possible. Marcus adored Ysabeau, and she had specifically requested he stay with her over the summer.

"He took a path west, and we assumed he was coming here, but something told me to stay with him." Ysabeau drew another serrated breath. "Then Marcus turned north, toward Montluçon."

"Toward Baldwin?" My brother-in-law had a house there, built long ago when the area was known simply as Lucius's Mountain.

"No. Not toward Baldwin. Toward Paris." Matthew's eyes darkened.

Ysabeau nodded. "He was not running away. He was running back— to Phoebe."

"Something went wrong," I said, stunned. Everybody had assured me that Phoebe would make the transition from warmblooded human to vampire without a problem. So much care had been taken, so many arrangements made.

Sensing my rising concern, Philip began to squirm and asked to be put down.

"Freyja said it all went according to plan. Phoebe's a vampire now." Matthew lifted Philip from my arms and put him on the floor beside me. "Stay with Diana and the children, *Maman*. I'll go after Marcus and find out what's wrong."

"Alain is outside," Ysabeau said. "Take him with you. Your father believed in having a second pair of eyes in such a situation."

Matthew kissed me. Like most of his farewells, it held a note of ferocity, as though to remind me to not let my guard down while he was gone.

He smoothed Becca's hair and pressed his lips far more gently to her forehead.

"Be careful," I murmured, more out of habit than actual concern.

"Always," Matthew replied, giving me one last, long look before he turned to go.

AFTER THE EXCITEMENT of their grandmother's arrival, the children took nearly an hour to get settled back to sleep. Wide awake myself with nerves and unanswered questions, I went down to the kitchen. There, as expected, I found Marthe and Ysabeau.

Usually, the sprawling set of connected rooms was one of my favorite places. It was unfailingly warm and cozy, with the old enameled iron range fired up and ready to bake something delicious and bowls of fresh fruit and produce waiting for Marthe to transform them into a gourmet feast. This morning, however, the room felt dark and cold, in spite of the illuminated sconces and the colorful Dutch tiles that decorated the walls.

"Of all the things I dislike about being married and mated to a vampire, waiting at home for news has to be the worst." I plunked myself onto one of the stools that surrounded the enormous, pitted wooden table that was the center of gravity in this domestic sphere. "Thank God for mobile phones. I can't imagine what it was like with nothing but handwritten messages."

"None of us liked it." Marthe put a steaming mug of tea before me, along with a croissant filled with almond paste and dusted with powdered sugar.

"Heaven," I said, sniffing the aroma of dark leaves and nutty sweetness that rose from the cup.

"I should have gone with them." Ysabeau had made no effort to twist her hair back into place or remove the smudge of dirt from her cheek. It wasn't like her to be anything less than impeccable.

"Matthew wanted you here," Marthe said, dusting flour on the table with a practiced gesture. She removed a lump of dough from a nearby bowl and began to knead it with the heels of her hands.

"You cannot always get what you want," Ysabeau said, with none of Mick Jagger's irony.

"Can someone tell me exactly what happened to set Marcus off?" I sipped at my tea, still feeling I'd missed something crucial.

"Nothing." Ysabeau, like her son, could be miserly with information.

"Something must have," I said.

"Truly, nothing happened. There was a dinner party with Phoebe's family," said Ysabeau. "Freyja assured me it all went very well."

"What did Charles make?" My mouth watered. "Something delicious, I'm sure."

Marthe's hands stilled and she scowled at me. Then she laughed.

"Why is that funny?" I demanded, taking a bite of the flaky croissant. There was so much butter in it that it melted on my tongue.

"Because Phoebe was just made into a vampire, and you want to know what she ate for her last supper. For a *manjasang*, this seems like an odd detail for such a momentous time," Ysabeau explained.

"Of course it does. You've never had one of Charles's roasted chickens," I said. "All that garlic. And the lemon. Divine."

"There was duck instead," Marthe reported. "And salmon. And beef."

"Did Charles make *seigle d'Auvergne*?" I asked, eyeing Marthe's work. The dark bread was one of Charles's specialties—and Phoebe's favorite. "And for dessert, was there *pompe aux pommes*?"

Phoebe loved her sweets, and the only time I'd seen her waver in her determination to become a vampire was when Marcus took her to the bakery in Saint-Lucien and explained that the apple pastry in the window would taste revolting if she went through with her plan.

"Both," Marthe replied.

"Phoebe must have been thrilled," I said, impressed with the scope of the menu.

"According to Freyja, she has not been eating much lately." Ysabeau caught her lower lip in her teeth.

"So that's why Marcus left?" Given that Phoebe would never eat a proper human meal again as a vampire, this seemed like an overreaction.

"No. Marcus left because Phoebe called him to say one last good-bye." Ysabeau shook her head. "They are both so impulsive."

"They're modern, that's all," I said.

It wasn't surprising that Phoebe and Marcus had grown impatient with the Byzantine labyrinth of vampire rituals and dos and don'ts. First,

Baldwin, the head of the de Clermont clan, had been asked to formally approve Marcus and Phoebe's engagement and her wish to become a vampire. This was considered an essential step, given Marcus's colorful past and Matthew's scandalous decision to mate with me—a witch. Only with Baldwin's full backing could their marriage and mating be considered legitimate.

Then, Marcus and Phoebe chose a maker from a very short list of possible candidates. It could not be a member of the family, for Philippe de Clermont had been strongly against any hint of incest among members of his clan. Children were to be cared for as children. Mates were to be sought outside the family. But there were other considerations, as well. Phoebe's maker needed to be an ancient vampire, one with the genetic strength to make healthy vampire children. And because the vampire chosen would be forever linked to the de Clermont family, their reputation and background had to be above reproach.

Once Phoebe and Marcus had decided upon who would transform her into a vampire, Phoebe's maker and Baldwin made the arrangements surrounding the precise timing, and Ysabeau oversaw the practicalities of housing, finances, and employment, with help from Matthew's daemon friend Hamish Osborne. It was a complicated business to abandon your life as a warmblooded human. Deaths and disappearances had to be arranged, as well as leaves of absence from work for personal reasons that would turn into resignations six months later.

Now that Phoebe was a vampire, Baldwin would be among her first male visitors. Because of the strong connections between physical hunger and sexual desire, Phoebe's contact with other males would be limited. And in order to forestall any possible hasty decisions made in the first flush of vampire hormones, Marcus would not be allowed to see Phoebe again until Baldwin felt she could make a prudent decision about their future together. Traditionally, vampires waited at least ninety days—the average time required for a vampire to develop from a newly reborn infant into a fledgling capable of some degree of independence—before reuniting with prospective mates.

To everyone's shock, Marcus had gone along with all of Ysabeau's intricate plans. He was the family's revolutionary. I had expected him to protest, but he did not say a word.

"Two days ago everybody was completely confident about Phoebe's change," I said. "Why are you so worried about her now?"

"We are not concerned for Phoebe," Ysabeau replied, "but Marcus. He has never been good at waiting, or obeying rules set down by others. He is too quick to follow his heart. It always gets him into trouble."

Someone flung the kitchen door open, entering the house in a smudge of blue and white. I seldom saw vampires moving at unregulated speed, and it was startling when the inchoate blur resolved into a white T-shirt, faded jeans, blue eyes, and thick head of blond hair.

"I should be with her!" Marcus shouted. "I've spent most of my life wanting to feel like I belonged, wanting a family of my own. Now I have one, and I turned my back on her."

Matthew followed Marcus like a shadow chasing the sun. Alain Le Merle, Philippe's former squire, brought up the rear.

"Traditionally, as you know—" Matthew began.

"Since when have I cared about tradition!" Marcus exclaimed. The tension in the room rose another notch. As head of his family, Matthew expected obedience and respect from his son, not an argument.

"Everything all right?" In my life as a professor, I'd learned the usefulness of rhetorical questions that gave everyone a chance to stop and reflect. My question cleared the air, if for no other reason than that it was patently obvious that everything was *not* all right.

"We didn't expect to find you still awake, *mon coeur*," Matthew said, coming to my side and giving me a kiss. He smelled of fresh air, pine, and hay, as if he'd been running through open fields and thick woods. "Marcus is concerned about Phoebe's well-being, that's all."

"Concerned?" Marcus's eyebrows lowered into a scowl. "I'm out of my mind with worry. I can't see her. I can't help her—"

"You need to trust Miriam." Matthew's tone was mild, but a muscle ticked in his jaw.

"I should never have agreed to all of this medieval protocol." Marcus's agitation rose. "Now we're separated, and she's got no one to rely on except for Freyja—"

"You specifically asked for Freyja to be there," Matthew observed calmly. "You might have had anyone from the family serve as Phoebe's supporter during the change. She was your choice."

"God, Matthew. Do you have to be so fucking reasonable all the time?" Marcus turned his back on his father.

"It's infuriating, isn't it?" I said sympathetically, putting a hand at my husband's waist to keep him near me.

"Yes, Diana, it certainly is," Marcus replied, stalking to the refrigerator and flinging open the heavy door. "And I've had to put up with it for far longer than you have. Jesus, Marthe. What have you been up to all day? There's not a drop of blood in the house."

It was impossible to say who was the most shocked by this criticism of the revered Marthe, who took care of every family member's needs before we were even aware of them. It was clear who was the most furious, however: Alain. Marthe was his sire.

Matthew and Alain exchanged a look. Alain inclined his head an inch in recognition that Matthew's need to discipline his son outweighed his own right to defend his mother. Gently, Matthew disentangled my hand.

In the next moment, Matthew was across the room and had Marcus pinned to the kitchen wall. The move would have been enough to break an ordinary creature's ribs.

"That's enough, Marcus. I expected Phoebe's situation to bring back memories of your own rebirth," Matthew said, holding his son in a firm grip, "but you need to exercise some restraint. Nothing will be gained by your flying around the countryside and storming into Freyja's house."

Matthew captured his son's eyes, waited, and released them only when Marcus broke their mutual gaze. Marcus slid several inches down the wall, drew a shuddering breath, and finally seemed to recognize where he was and what he'd done.

"Sorry, Diana." Marcus looked at me briefly in apology, and then went to Marthe. "God, Marthe. I didn't mean—"

"Yes, you did." Marthe cuffed him on the ear—and not gently, either. "The blood is in the pantry, where it always is. Get it yourself."

"Try not to worry, Marcus. No one could look after Phoebe better than Freyja." Ysabeau put a reassuring hand on her grandson's shoulder.

"*I* could." Marcus shook off his grandmother's hand and disappeared into the pantry.

Marthe cast her eyes heavenward as if seeking deliverance from vampires in love. Ysabeau held up a warning finger, which silenced any further

comment from Matthew. As the only person present who was not fully in-
culcated into the de Clermont pack rules, however, I ignored my mother-
in-law's command.

"Actually, Marcus, I don't think that's true," I called into the next
room, pouring myself some more tea.

"What?" Marcus reappeared in a flash, holding a silver julep cup that
I knew held neither bourbon, sugar, water, nor mint. His expression was
indignant. "Of course I'm the best person to look after her. I love her.
Phoebe's my mate. I know what she needs better than anyone."

"Better than Phoebe?" I asked.

"Sometimes." Marcus's chin was now jutting at a belligerent angle.

"Bullshit." I sounded like Sarah—blunt and impatient—and attrib-
uted it to the early hour rather than to any genetic predisposition to
forthrightness among Bishop women. "You vampires are all the same—
thinking you know what we poor warmbloods *really* want—especially
the females. In fact, *this* is what Phoebe wanted: to be made a vampire the
old-fashioned way. It's your job to make sure her decision is honored and
that the plan works."

"Phoebe didn't understand what she was agreeing to. Not entirely,"
Marcus said, unwilling to concede the point. "She could get bloodsick.
She could have trouble making her first kill. I would be able to help her,
support her."

Bloodsick? I nearly choked on my tea. What on earth was that?

"I've never seen anyone so well prepared to become a *manjasang* as
Phoebe," Ysabeau reassured Marcus.

"But there are no guarantees." Marcus couldn't let his worries go.

"Not in this life, my child." Ysabeau's expression was pained as she remembered when life still held the promise of a happy ending.

"It's late. We'll talk more after sunrise. You won't sleep, Marcus, but
try to rest." Matthew touched his son's shoulder as he passed by.

"I might take a run instead. Try to wear myself out that way. Nobody
but the farmers will be awake at this hour." Marcus looked at the brightening light beckoning through the windows.

"You shouldn't attract any notice," Matthew confirmed. "Do you want
me to come with you?"

"No need," Marcus replied. "I'll get changed and head out. Maybe take the route toward Saint-Priest-sous-Aixe. There are some good climbs along the way."

"Should we expect you for breakfast?" Matthew's tone was a touch too casual. "The children are early risers. They'll want a chance to order their older brother around."

"Don't worry, Matthew." A ghost of a smile touched Marcus's lips. "Your legs are longer than mine. I'm not going to run away again. I just need to clear my head."

WE LEFT THE DOOR of our room ajar in case Philip or Becca woke, and got back into bed. I crawled between the sheets, grateful on this warm May morning that my husband was a vampire, and tucked myself into his coolness. I knew when Marcus set out for his run because Matthew's shoulders settled fully into the mattress. Until then, he had been slightly braced, ready to get up and go to his son's aid.

"Do you want to go after him?" I asked. Matthew's legs really were longer than Marcus's, and he was fast. There was plenty of time for him to catch up to his son.

"Alain is following along, just in case," Matthew said.

"Ysabeau said that she was more worried about Marcus than Phoebe." I drew back to look at Matthew's face in the dawn light. "Why?"

"Marcus is still so young." Matthew sighed.

"Are you serious?" Marcus had been reborn a vampire in 1781. Two-hundred-plus years seemed plenty grown up to me.

"I know what you're thinking, Diana, but when a human is made a vampire, they have to mature all over again. It can take a very long time before we are ready to strike out on our own," Matthew said. "Our judgment can be faulty when we're in the first flush of vampire blood."

"But Marcus has already sown his wild oats." The family was quick to tell tales of Marcus's early years in America, the scandals and scrapes in which he became entangled, the difficulties from which he'd had to be extracted by senior members of the de Clermont family.

"Which is precisely why he can't be allowed to supervise Phoebe's transformation. Marcus is about to take a newly reborn vampire as a mate. It would be a major step under any circumstances, but given his youth . . ."

Matthew paused. "I hope I'm doing the right thing, letting him take this step."

"*The family* is doing what Marcus and Phoebe wanted," I said, making sure that my emphasis registered. "They're old enough—be they cold-blooded vampire or warmblooded human—to know their own minds."

"Are they?" Matthew adjusted his position so that his eyes could meet mine. "That's a very modern notion you have, that a man just turned four-and-twenty and a young woman of about the same age would be sufficiently experienced to determine the course of their future lives." He was teasing, but his lowered eyebrows indicated that part of him believed what he said.

"It's the twenty-first century, not the eighteenth," I observed. "Besides, Marcus is not a man of 'four-and-twenty,' as you so charmingly put it, but two hundred and fifty plus."

"Marcus will always be a child of that earlier time," Matthew said. "If it were 1781, and it was Marcus who was experiencing his first day as a vampire and not Phoebe, he would have been considered in need of wise counsel—and a strong hand."

"Your son has asked every member of this family—and Phoebe's, too—for advice," I reminded him. "It's time to let Marcus determine his own future, Matthew."

Matthew was silent, his hand moving along the faint scars that had been left on my back by the witch Satu Järvinen. Over and over he traced them, lines of regret that reminded him of every time he had failed to protect those he loved.

"It will all be fine," I assured him, snuggling closer.

Matthew sighed. "I hope you're right."

LATER THAT DAY, a marvelous air of quiet descended on Les Revenants. I looked forward to these rare moments of peace—often a mere twenty minutes, occasionally a blissful expanse of an hour or more—from the moment I awoke.

The children were in the nursery, tucked in for naps. Matthew was in his library working on a paper he was co-writing with our Yale colleague, Chris Roberts. They were scheduled to reveal more of their research findings at conferences this autumn and were already gearing up to submit an article to a leading scientific journal. Marthe was in the kitchen canning fresh beans in peppery brine while watching *Plus belle la vie* on the television Matthew had installed there. Marthe had insisted she had no interest in such technological fripperies, but she was soon hooked on the escapades of the residents of Le Mistral. As for me, I was avoiding my grading in favor of my new research into the connections between early modern cooking and laboratory practices. But I could spend only so much time bent over images of seventeenth-century alchemical manuscripts.

After an hour of work, the glorious May weather called to me. I made myself a cold drink and went upstairs to the wooden deck that Matthew had constructed between the battlements atop one of Les Revenants' crenellated towers. Ostensibly it was built to provide views of the surrounding countryside, but everybody knew its primary purpose was defensive. It provided a good lookout, and would give plenty of advance warning if a stranger approached. Between our new rooftop aerie and the cleaned and refilled moat, Les Revenants was now as secure as Matthew could make it.

There I found Marcus, wearing dark glasses and lounging in the midday heat, the summer sun streaking his blond hair.

"Hello, Diana," Marcus said, putting aside his book. It was a slender volume, the brown leather cover stained and pitted with age.

"You look like you need this more than I do." I handed him my glass of iced tea. "Lots of mint, no lemon, no sugar."

"Thanks," Marcus said. He took an appreciative sip. "Delicious."

"May I join you, or are you up here to escape?" Vampires were pack animals, but they definitely liked their alone time.

"This is your house, Diana." Marcus drew his feet from the seat of the nearby wooden chair that he was using as an impromptu ottoman.

"This is the family's house, and you are welcome in it," I replied, quick to correct him. The separation from Phoebe was going to be hard enough without Marcus feeling like an intruder. "Any more news from Paris?"

"No. *Grand-mère* told me to not expect another call from Freyja for three days at the earliest," Marcus replied, sliding his fingers again and again through the moisture collecting on the outside of the chilled glass.

"Why three days?" Perhaps this was some kind of vampiric Apgar test.

"Because that's how long you wait before you give a vampire infant any blood that doesn't come from their sire's veins," Marcus replied. "Weaning a vampire off their maker's blood can be tricky. If a vampire ingests too much foreign blood too soon, it can trigger deadly genetic mutations. Sometimes, vampire infants die.

"It will also be Phoebe's first psychological test, to make sure that she can survive by taking another creature's blood," Marcus continued. "They'll start with something small, of course—a bird or a cat."

"Um-hmm," I said, trying to sound approving while my stomach flipped.

"I made sure Phoebe could kill something—before." Marcus stared into the distance. "Sometimes it's harder to take a life when you have no choice."

"I would have thought the opposite," I said.

Marcus shook his head. "Oddly enough, when it's no longer a question of sport, you can lose your nerve. Instinctive or not, it's a selfish act to survive at some other creature's expense." He tapped his book against his leg, an anxious thrum.

"What are you reading?" I asked, trying to change the subject.

"An old favorite." Marcus tossed the volume to me.

Usually, the family's cavalier attitude toward books earned them a lecture from me, but this one had obviously seen worse treatment. Something had nibbled one corner. The leather was even more stained than it had appeared at first glance, and the cover was covered with ring-shaped marks left by glasses, tankards, and cups. There were traces of gilt in the stamped decorations, and their style indicated the book had been bound sometime in the early nineteenth century. Marcus had read the book so often that the binding had split and there were multiple repairs—one made with yellowing cellophane tape.

A cherished item like this held a specific magic, one that had nothing to do with its value or condition and everything to do with its significance. Carefully, I cracked open the tattered cover. To my surprise, the book inside was decades older than the binding suggested.

"*Common Sense.*" It was a foundational text of the American Revolution. I'd expected Marcus to be reading Byron, or a novel—not political philosophy.

"Were you serving in New England in 1776?" I asked, noting its date and Boston publication. Marcus had been a soldier and then a surgeon in the Continental army. That much I knew.

"No. I was still at home." Marcus took the book from me. "I think I'll take a walk. Thanks for the tea."

It seemed Marcus was not in the mood for further confidences.

He disappeared down the stairs, leaving a trail of discordant threads shimmering in his wake: red and indigo tangled up with black and white. As a weaver, I could perceive the woven strands of past, present, and future that bound the universe together. Normally the clear tones of blue and amber that made up the sturdy warp were visible, and the colored threads of individual experience provided bright, intermittent notes in the weft.

Not today. Marcus's memories were so powerful, and so distressing to him, that they were distorting the fabric of time, creating holes in its structure to make way for some forgotten monster to emerge from the past.

The gathering clouds on the horizon and the pricking in my thumbs warned me that stormy times lay ahead. For all of us.

⇥ 4 ⇤

One

13 MAY

Phoebe sat before the locked windows in her bedroom with the plum-colored drapes fully open to the view of Paris, satiated with her maker's blood, devouring the city with her eyes, hungering only for the next revelation afforded by her new sense of sight.

The night, she discovered, was not simply black but a thousand shades and textures of darkness, some gossamer, others velvet, ranging from the deepest purples and blues to the palest of grays.

Life would not always be so easy. Now there was a knock on the door before the gnawing had a chance to start eating away at her belly. Phoebe would have to feel her hunger eventually so that she could understand what it was to covet the lifeblood of a creature and manage her urge to take it.

Her only urge now, however, was to paint. Phoebe hadn't done so for years, not since a casual remark from a teacher—cutting, dismissive—had sent her into the historical study of art rather than its practice. Her fingers itched to pick up a brush and dip it into thick oil paint or delicate watercolor pigments and apply them to canvas or paper.

Could she capture the precise color of the tiled roof across the garden—blue-gray touched with silver? Was it possible to convey the inky blackness of the sky high above, and its sharp metallic gleam at the horizon?

Phoebe understood now why Matthew's great-grandson, Jack, covered any surface he could with chiaroscuro renderings of his memories and experiences. The play of light and shadow was endless, a game that you could watch for hours without ever feeling bored.

She'd learned this from the single candle that Freyja had left burning in a silver holder on the dressing table. The undulating light and the darkness at the heart of the flame were mesmerizing. Phoebe had begged for more candles, wanting to surround herself with the pinpricks of brightness that dazzled and dipped.

"One is enough," Freyja said. "We don't want you light-struck on your first day."

So long as Phoebe was fed regularly, sensory assault was the greatest danger to her as a newly made vampire. To prevent any mishaps, Freyja and Miriam carefully controlled Phoebe's environment, minimizing her chances of getting lost in feeling.

Immediately after her transformation, for example, Phoebe had wanted a shower. Freyja judged the needlelike fall of water too severe, so Françoise drew her a warm bath instead—strictly timed so that Phoebe didn't become consumed by the soft slip of water against her skin. And all the windows in the house, not just those in Phoebe's bedroom, were locked against the alluring scents of warmbloods, the neighbors' pets, and pollution.

"I'm sorry, Phoebe, but an infant male went mad in the Paris Metro last year," Freyja explained when she asked if one window might be opened just a crack to let in the breezes. "The fumes from the old braking system were irresistible to him, and we lost him along Line Eight. It caused no end of delays for morning commuters and made the mayor very cross. Baldwin, too."

Phoebe knew she could break the glass with ease, along with the window frames, and even punch a hole in the wall if escape became necessary. But resisting these temptations was a test of her control, her obedience, and her suitability as Marcus's mate. Phoebe was determined to pass the test, so she sat in the airless room and watched the colors flicker and drift as a cloud crossed the moon, or a faraway star died in the heavens, or the turning of the earth brought the sun fractionally closer.

"I would like some paint." Phoebe said it in a whisper, but the sound echoed in her ears. "And brushes."

"I'll ask Miriam." Freyja's reply came from far away. She was, based on the endless scratching that tickled Phoebe's nerves ever so slightly, writing in her journal with a fountain pen. Occasionally, Freyja's heart gave a slow thump.

Even farther away, in the kitchens, Charles was smoking a cigar and reading the newspaper. Rustle. Puff. Silence. Thump. Rustle. Puff. Silence. Just as a Paris night had its own colorscape, so every creature had his or her own rhythmic accompaniment—like the song Phoebe's heart had made when she first drank from Miriam.

"Do you need something else, Phoebe?" Freyja's pen paused. In the kitchen, Charles stubbed out his cigar in a metal ashtray. Both waited attentively for Phoebe's response. It would take her some time to get used to holding conversations with people in different rooms, never mind entirely separate floors of a large house.

"Only Marcus," replied Phoebe, wistful. She had grown accustomed to thinking of herself as part of a *we*, not as a solitary *me*. There was so much she wanted to tell him, so much she wanted to share about her first day of being reborn. Instead, they were separated by hundreds of miles.

"Why not practice walking?" Freyja asked, capping her pen. Moments later, Marcus's aunt was at the door, the key turning smoothly in the lock. "Let me help you."

Phoebe blinked at the change in the room's atmosphere as the soft glow of the candlelit house seeped across the threshold.

"The light is a living thing," Phoebe said, awed by the realization.

"Both wave and particle. It is astonishing it took warmbloods so long to figure that out." Freyja stood before Phoebe, hands outstretched in a gesture of assistance. "Now, remember not to push on the chair with your hands, or against the floor with your feet. Getting up is simply a matter of unfolding for a *draugr*. It is not necessary to exert oneself."

Phoebe had been a vampire less than twenty-four hours and had already broken several chairs and put a sizable dent in the tub.

"Float up. Just think *up* and rise. Steady. Good." Freyja gave constant feedback, like Phoebe's childhood ballet mistress, a similarly draconian figure though only a fraction of Freyja's Valkyric height. It was Madame Olga who had helped Phoebe understand that size has nothing to do with stature.

The memory of Madame Olga snapped Phoebe's spine straight, and she instinctively took hold of Freyja's hands as if they were a wooden barre. She heard a crack and felt something give way.

"Oh, dear, there goes a finger." Freyja released Phoebe's hand. Her left index finger was hanging at a strange angle. Freyja aligned it with a quick tug.

"There you are. Everything's in working order again. You'll probably break other bones before summer's end." Freyja linked her arm through Phoebe's elbow. "Let's stroll around the room. Slowly."

It was evident why warmbloods thought vampires could fly. All a vampire had to do was think of the destination and she was there in a blink, with no memory of putting any effort into locomotion.

Phoebe felt like the newborn she was, taking one trembling step at a time and then pausing to regain her equilibrium. In addition to everything else, her center of gravity seemed to have shifted. It was no longer in her pelvis but in her heart, which made Phoebe feel tipsy and strange, as if she'd had too much champagne.

"Marcus told me he was a fast learner when it came to being a vampire." Phoebe began to relax into Freyja's stately pace, which felt more like waltzing than walking.

"He had to be," Freyja said with a touch of regret.

"Why?" Phoebe frowned. The sudden turn of her head to study Freyja's expression sent her tumbling toward her companion.

"You know better than to ask, Phoebe darling." Freyja gently set her back on her feet. "You must save your questions for Marcus. A *draugr* does not carry tales."

"Do vampires have a thousand names for themselves, like the Sami have a thousand names for reindeer?" Phoebe wondered, taking mental note of the latest entry in her expanding lexicon.

"More, I think," replied Freyja, her brow creased. "Why, we even have a name for the tattletale vampire who tells someone's mate about their past without permission."

"You do?" Phoebe was eager to know it.

"Absolutely," Freyja said solemnly. "Dead vampire."

Phoebe was worn out with the effort it took to move slowly like a warmblood, without cracking a floorboard or breaking a bone, after making it safely around the perimeter of the room just twice. Freyja left her to recover in peace and returned to her morning room, where she would continue writing in her journal until sunrise.

Phoebe snuffed out the candle to better see night give way to the day, her cold fingers barely registering the heat of the burning wick, and climbed into bed out of habit rather than any hope of sleeping. She drew the coverlet up to her chin, reveling in the smooth fabric and crisp finish.

She lay in the soft bed, looking out at the night, listening to the music of Freyja's pen, and the muffled sounds from the garden outside, and the street beyond the walls.

I am.

Evermore.

Phoebe's heart song had changed. It was slower and steadier, all the extraneous effort of her human heartbeat removed and perfected into something simpler and more compelling.

I am.

Evermore.

Phoebe wondered what Marcus's heart song would sound like. It would be melodic and pleasing, she felt sure. She longed to hear it and commit it to memory.

"Soon," Phoebe told herself in a whisper, a reminder that she and Marcus had all the time in the world. "Soon."

⇥ 5 ⇤

The Sins of the Fathers

It was late morning and I was at my desk transcribing Lady Montague's recipe for a healing balsam—a remedy that could be used for "short-windedness in man, or horse"—from an online image of the Wellcome Library's manuscript. Even without having the actual text before me, I loved tracing the seemingly nonsensical swirls and whorls made by seventeenth-century pens. Gradually, the manuscript displayed digitally on my laptop was yielding a pattern of evidence that showed deep connections between cooking and modern chemistry, one that I would write about in my new book.

Without warning, my work space was invaded by a video call from Venice that reduced my manuscript page down into a corner of the screen. Gerbert of Aurillac and Domenico Michele, the other two vampire representatives on the Congregation, wanted a word.

Though a witch, I occupied the third vampire chair—the one that belonged by custom to a member of the de Clermont family. Though I was a blood-sworn daughter of Philippe de Clermont, my brother-in-law Baldwin's decision to give the chair to me was still a matter of controversy.

"There you are, Diana," Gerbert said once I allowed the connection. "We've left messages. Why aren't you responding?"

I bit back a sound of frustration. "Is it possible that you could handle this situation—whatever it is—without me?"

"If it were, we would have done so by now." Gerbert sounded testy. "We must consult you on matters that pertain to our people—even though you are a witch and a warmblood."

Our people. That was the heart of the problem facing daemons, humans, vampires, and witches. Matthew's work with Chris and the teams of researchers assembled at Oxford and Yale had proved that, at a genetic level, all four hominid species were more alike than different. But it was going to take more than scientific evidence to change attitudes, particularly among the ancient, custom-bound vampires.

"These Hungarian and Romanian clans have been at war for centuries in the Crişana region," Domenico explained. "The land has always been contested. But this latest outbreak of violence is already in the news. I've made sure that the press have interpreted it as simply another escalation in organized crime."

"Remind me who planted that story?" I asked, searching for my Congregation notebook on the crowded desk. Leafing through it, I found no mention of anyone attached to the media. Once again, Gerbert and Domenico had failed to inform me of crucial developments.

"Andrea Popescu. She's one of us, and her current husband—a human, regrettably—is a political reporter for *Evenimentul Zilei.*" Gerbert's eyes gleamed. "I'm happy to travel to Debrecen and supervise the negotiations, if you'd like."

The last thing we needed was Gerbert in Hungary, working out his ambitions in an already volatile situation.

"Why not send Albrecht and Eliezer back to the negotiating table?" I suggested, naming two of the more progressive vampire leaders in that part of the world. "The Corvinus and Székely clans are simply going to have to work out a reasonable solution. And if they don't, the Congregation will have to take possession of the castle in question until they do."

Why anyone wanted the ruinous heap was beyond me. No one could walk inside its hollow walls for fear of being crushed to death by falling masonry. We'd gone there on a diplomatic mission in March, during Yale's spring break. I'd expected something grand and palatial, not piles of moss-covered stone.

"This is not some real estate dispute to be solved according to your modern standards of fairness and equity," Gerbert said, his tone patronizing. "Too much blood has been spilled, too many vampire lives lost. Holló Castle is sacred ground to these clans, and their sires are willing to die for it. You lack the proper understanding of what's at stake."

"You must at least try to think like a vampire," Domenico said. "Our traditions must be respected. Compromise is not our way."

"Slaying each other in the streets of Debrecen hasn't worked, either," I pointed out. "Let's try it my way for a change. I'll speak to Albrecht and Eliezer, and report back."

Gerbert opened his mouth to protest. Without warning, I disconnected the video link. My computer screen darkened. I sat back in my chair with a groan.

"Bad day at the office?" Marcus was leaning against the doorframe, still holding his book.

"Did vampires skip the Enlightenment?" I asked. "It's like I'm trapped in some medieval revenge fantasy, one in which there's no chance of a solution that doesn't involve the total destruction of the opponent. Why do vampires prefer to kill each other rather than have a civil conversation?"

"Because it's not as much fun, of course." Matthew entered the room and kissed me, slow and sweet. "Let Domenico and Gerbert deal with clan warfare for now, *mon coeur*. Their troubles will still be there tomorrow—and the day after that, too. It's the one thing you can rely upon with vampires."

AFTER LUNCH I TOOK the twins into the library and set them up in front of the empty fireplace with enough toys to keep them occupied for a few minutes while I did some more research. I had a working transcription of Lady Montague's recipe in front of me and was noting what ingredients were being used (oil of turpentine, flowers of sulfur, hay), what equipment was needed (a large glass urinal, a deep skillet, a pitcher), and the processes used (mixing, boiling, skimming) so I could cross-reference them with other early modern texts.

The library at Les Revenants was one of my favorite rooms. It was built into one of the towers, and was ringed with dark walnut bookcases that stretched from floor to ceiling. Ladders and staircases spanned the distances at irregular intervals, giving the place the crazed appearance of an Escher drawing. Books, papers, photographs, and other memorabilia that Philippe and Ysabeau had collected over the centuries filled every inch of space. I had barely scratched the surface of what was here. Matthew had built some wooden file cases for the piles of papers to go into—one day when I had time to sort them—and I had started the work of combing through the book titles for obvious thematic clusters, like mythology and geography.

Most of the family found the room's atmosphere oppressive, however, with its dark wood and memories of Philippe. The only creatures who spent much time here were me and a few of the castle's ghosts. Two of them were currently undoing my efforts to organize the recently created mythology section, rearranging books with an attitude of bewildered disapproval.

Marcus strolled in, whistling, his copy of *Common Sense* tucked under his arm.

"See!" Becca brandished a plastic figure of a knight.

"Wow. A knight in shining armor. I'm impressed." Marcus joined the twins on the floor.

Not to be outdone by his sister's claim on Marcus's attention, Philip toppled his tower of blocks so that they made a mighty crash. Both twins loved the polished cubes, which Matthew had carved for them from bits of wood culled from around the family's various homes. There were blocks made from apple and hornbeam gathered near the Bishop House in Madison; French oak and lime from Sept-Tours; and beech and ash from the Old Lodge. There were even some freckled blocks made from the limbs of a plane tree that grew near Clairmont House in London, collected when the city had come by and pruned the lower limbs to let the double-decker buses pass. Each block showed subtle differences in grain and tone, which Philip and Becca found fascinating. The primary colors that drew most children were of no interest to our Bright Born twins, who had their father's keen eyesight. Instead, they loved to trace the patterns in the wood with their tiny fingers as if learning the tree's history.

"Looks like your knight will need a new castle, Becca," Marcus observed, laughing at the pile of blocks. "What do you think, sport? Want to build one with me?"

"Okay," Philip said agreeably, holding up a block.

But Philip's older brother was momentarily distracted by the books that were still sliding along the shelves, moved by spectral hands that not even vampires could see.

"The ghosts are at it again, I see," Marcus said with a chuckle, watching the books move to the left, then to the right, then over to the left again. "They never seem to make any progress, though. Don't they get bored?"

"Apparently not. And we can thank the goddess for that," I replied, my tone as tart as vinegar. "As ghosts go, those two aren't very strong—not like the ones who haunt the room off the great hall."

The two chain-mail-clad men clanking around in that tiny, dark enclosure were a terror: flinging furniture around and pilfering items from nearby rooms to redecorate their space. This insubstantial pair in the library was so vaporous that I still wasn't sure who or what they were.

"They always seem to pick the same shelf. What's up there?" Marcus asked.

"Mythology," I said, glancing up from my notes. "Your grandfather adored the subject."

"Granddad used to say he liked to read about the exploits of old friends," Marcus said with the hint of a smile.

Philip held his block toward me now, hoping I'd join in the fun. Playing with the children was far more appealing than Lady Montague. I put my notes aside and crouched down next to them.

"House," Philip said, happy with the prospect of building.

"Like father, like son," Marcus said drily. "You better watch out, Diana, or you'll find yourself in the midst of a massive renovation in a few years."

I laughed. Philip was always erecting towers. Becca, on the other hand, had abandoned her knight and was constructing something around herself that looked like a fortification. Marcus supplied both of them with blocks, willing as ever to be their assistant when it came to fun and games.

Philip put a block in my hand. "Apple."

"*A* is for apple. Good boy," I said.

"You sound like you're reading from one of the primers I had when I was a boy." Marcus handed Becca a block. "It's strange that we still teach children their alphabet the same way, when everything else has changed so much."

"Such as?" I asked, wanting to know more.

"Discipline. Clothing. Children's songs. *'How glorious is our heavenly King / Who reigns above the sky.'*" Marcus sang the words softly. "'*How shall a Child presume to sing / His dreadful majesty?'* That was the only tune in my first primer."

"Not exactly '*the wheels on the bus go round and round,*'" I agreed with a smile. "When were you born, Marcus?"

My question was an unforgivable breach of vampire etiquette, but I hoped that Marcus would excuse it since it was coming from a witch—not to mention a historian.

"In 1757. August." Marcus's voice was flat and coolly factual. "The day after Ft. William Henry fell to the French."

"Where?" I asked, even though I was pressing my luck to be so inquisitive.

"Hadley. A small town in western Massachusetts, along the banks of the Connecticut River." Marcus picked at the knee of his jeans, worrying at a loose thread. "I was born and raised there."

Philip climbed into Marcus's lap and presented him with another block.

"Would you tell me about it?" I asked. "I don't know much about your past, and it might help to pass the time while you wait for news from Phoebe."

More importantly, remembering his own life might help Marcus. From the bewildering tangle of time that surrounded him, I knew that Marcus was struggling.

And I was not the only one who could see the snarled threads. Before I could stop him, Philip grabbed at a red strand trailing from Marcus's forearm with one pudgy hand, and a white strand with the other. His bowed lips moved as if he were uttering a silent incantation.

My children are not weavers. I had told myself this again and again, in moments of anxiety, in the depths of night while they slept quietly in their cradles, and in times of utter desperation when the hurly-burly of our daily routines was so overwhelming I could barely draw breath.

If that were true, though, how had Philip seen the angry threads surrounding Marcus? And how had he managed to capture them so easily?

"What the hell?" Marcus's expression froze as the hands of the old clock, a gilded monstrosity that made a deafening ticktock, stopped moving.

Philip drew his fists toward his tummy, dragging time along with them. Blue and amber threads screeched in protest as the fabric of the world stretched.

"Bye-bye, owie," Philip said, kissing his own hands and the threads they contained. "Bye-bye."

My children are half witch and half vampire, I reminded myself. *My children are not weavers*. That meant they weren't capable of—

The air around me trembled and tightened as time continued to resist the spell that Philip had woven in an attempt to soothe Marcus's distress.

"Philip Michael Addison Sorley Bishop-Clairmont. Put time down. Immediately." My voice was sharp and my son dropped the strands. After one more heart-stopping second of inactivity, the clock's hands resumed their movement. Philip's lip trembled.

"We do not play with time. Not ever. Do you understand me?" I drew him out of Marcus's lap and stared into his eyes, where ancient knowledge mixed with childish innocence.

Philip, startled by my tone, burst into tears. Though he was nowhere near it, the tower he had been constructing crashed to the ground.

"What just happened?" Marcus looked a bit dazed.

Rebecca, who could not bear it when her brother cried, crawled over the fallen blocks to offer him comfort. She held out her right thumb. The left was firmly lodged in her own mouth. She removed it before speaking.

"Shiny, Pip." A violet strand of magical energy streamed from Becca's thumb. I'd seen vestigial traces of magic hanging off the children before, but I'd assumed that they served no particular function in their lives.

My children are not weavers.

"Shit." The word popped out of my mouth before I could stop it.

"Wow. That was weird. I could see you, but I couldn't hear you. And I couldn't seem to speak," Marcus said, still processing his recent experience. "Everything started to fade. Then you took Philip out of my lap and it all went back to normal. Did I timewalk?"

"Not quite," I said.

"Shit," Becca repeated solemnly, patting her brother on the forehead. "Shiny."

I examined Philip's forehead. Was that a speck of *chatoiement*, a weaver's signature gleam, between his eyes?

"Oh, God. Wait until your father finds out."

"Finds out what?" Matthew was in the doorway, bright-eyed and relaxed from repairing the copper gutters over the kitchen door. He smiled at Becca, who was blowing him kisses. "Hello, my darling."

"I think Philip just worked—or wove—his first spell," I explained. "He tried to smooth out Marcus's memories so they wouldn't bother him."

"My memories?" Marcus frowned. "And what do you mean Philip wove a spell? He can't even talk in complete sentences."

"Owie," Philip explained to Matthew with a tiny, shuddering sob. "All better."

Shock registered on Matthew's face.

"Shit," Becca said as she noticed her father's change of expression. Philip took this as confirmation of the gravity of the situation, and his fragile composure disintegrated once more in a flood of tears.

"But that means—" Marcus looked from Becca to Philip in alarm and then in amazement.

"I owe Chris fifty dollars," I said. "He was right, Matthew. The twins *are* weavers."

"WHAT ARE YOU GOING to do about this?" Matthew demanded.

We had retreated—Matthew and I and the twins—to the suite of rooms we used as a bedroom, bathroom, and private family sitting room. A medieval castle did not lend itself to a feeling of coziness, but these apartments were as warm and comforting as we could make them. The large main room was divided into several different areas: one was dominated by our seventeenth-century canopied bed; another had deep chairs and sofas for lounging by the fire; a third was equipped with a writing desk, where Matthew could get a bit of work done while I slept. Small rooms to the left and right had been repurposed to make walk-in closets and a bathroom. Heavy, electrified iron chandeliers dropped from the arched ceiling, which helped keep the rooms from feeling cavernous on dark winter nights. Tall windows, some of them still glazed with medieval painted glass, let in the summer sun.

"I don't know, Matthew. I left my crystal ball in New Haven," I retorted. The situation in the library had thrown me for a loop. I was attributing my slow response to the stoppage of time rather than to blinding panic.

I closed the bedroom door. The wood was stout and there were many thick stone walls between us and the rest of the household. Still, I switched on the music system to provide an extra buffer against acute vampire hearing.

"And what will we do about Rebecca, when she shows signs of having magical talent?" Matthew continued, driving his fingers through his hair in frustration.

"*If* she shows signs," I said.

"*When*," Matthew insisted.

"What do you think we should do?" I turned the tables on my husband.

"You're the witch!" Matthew said.

"Oh. So it's my fault!" I put my hands on my hips, furious. "So much for their being *your* children."

"That's not what I said." Matthew ground his teeth together. "They need their mother to set an example for them, that's all."

"You can't be serious." I was aghast. "They're too young to learn magic."

"But not too young to work it, apparently. We aren't going to hide who we are from the children, remember?" Matthew said. "I'm keeping my end of the bargain. I've taken the children hunting. They've watched me feed."

"The children are too young to understand what magic is," I said. "When I saw my mother cast a spell, it was terrifying."

"And that's why you haven't been working your own magic as much." Matthew drew in a deep breath, understanding at last. "You're trying to protect Rebecca and Philip."

As a matter of fact, I *had* been doing magic—just not where or when anyone else could witness it. I did it alone, under the dark of the moon, away from curious, impressionable eyes, when Matthew thought I was working.

"You haven't been yourself, Diana," Matthew continued. "We all feel it."

"I don't want Becca and Philip to end up in a situation they can't control." Nightmare visions of all the trouble it might cause washed through me—the fires they might start, the chaos that could be unleashed, the possibility that they would lose their way in time and I wouldn't be able to find them. My anxieties about the children, which had been on a low simmer, boiled over.

"The children need to know you as a witch as well as a mother," Matthew said, his tone gentling. "It's part of who you are. It's part of who they are, too."

"I know," I said. "I just didn't expect Philip or Becca to show an inclination for magic so soon."

"So what made Philip try to fix Marcus's memories?" Matthew asked.

"Marcus told me where he was born. And when," I replied. "Ever since he went after Phoebe, he's been surrounded by a thick cloud of remembrance. Time is caught up in it, and it's stretching the world out of shape. It's impossible not to notice, if you're a weaver."

"I'm no weaver, nor am I a physicist, but it doesn't seem possible that one person's individual recollections could have such a serious effect on the space-time continuum," Matthew said, sounding positively professorial.

"Really?" I marched up to him, grabbed a particularly iridescent strand of green memory that had been hanging off him for days, and gave it a good yank. "What do you think now?"

Matthew's eyes widened as I pulled the thread tighter.

"I have no idea what happened, or when, but this has been flapping around you for days. And it's beginning to bug me." I released the strand. "So don't you dare throw physics in my face. Science isn't the answer to everything."

Matthew's mouth twitched.

"I know, I know. Go ahead. Laugh. Don't think the irony is lost on me." I sat down and sighed. "What was bothering you, by the way?"

"I was wondering whatever happened to a horse I lost at the Battle of Bosworth," Matthew said pensively.

"A horse? That's it?" I threw my hands up in utter exasperation. Given how bright the strand was, I'd been expecting a guilty secret or a former lover. "Well, don't let Philip catch you worrying about it, or you'll find yourself in 1485 extricating yourself from a thornbush."

"It was a very fine horse," Matthew said by way of explanation, sitting on the arm of my chair. "And I wasn't laughing at you, *mon coeur*. I was just amused at how far we've come since the days when I believed I hated witches, and you thought you hated magic."

"Life was simpler then," I said, though at the time it had seemed quite complicated.

"And far less interesting, too." Matthew kissed me. "Perhaps you shouldn't stir up Marcus's emotions any further until after he and Phoebe are back together. Not all vampires want to revisit their past lives."

"Maybe not consciously, but there's clearly something troubling him," I replied, "something unresolved." Whatever was bothering Marcus might have happened long ago, but it still had him tied in knots.

"A vampire's memories aren't arranged in a rational timeline," Matthew explained. "They're a jumbled mess—a magpie assortment of happy and sad, bright and dark. You might not be able to isolate the cause of Marcus's unhappiness, never mind make sense of it."

"I'm a historian, Matthew," I said. "I make sense out of the past every day."

"And Philip?" Matthew asked, one eyebrow raised.

"I'll call Sarah," I said. "She and Agatha are in Provence. I'm sure she'll have some advice on how to raise witches."

WE HAD SUPPER UP ON the roof deck so that we could enjoy the fine weather. I had demolished Marthe's roasted chicken served with vegetables picked fresh from the garden—tender lettuce, peppery radishes, and the sweetest carrots imaginable—while Matthew opened a second bottle of wine to see him and Marcus through the rest of the evening. We withdrew from the old dining table to the chairs arranged around a cauldron full of logs. Once the fire was lit, the wood sent sparks and light shooting into the sky. Les Revenants became a beacon in the darkness, visible for miles.

I sat back in my chair with a sigh of contentment while Matthew and Marcus discussed their shared work on creature genetics in a slow, relaxed fashion that was very unlike what occurred between competitive, modern academics. Vampires had all the time in the world to mull over their findings. They had little cause to rush to conclusions, and the honest exchange that resulted was inspiring.

As the light faded, however, it was evident that Marcus was feeling Phoebe's absence with renewed sharpness. The red threads that tied

Marcus to the world turned rosy and shimmered with copper notes whenever he thought about his mate. I was usually able to screen out momentary slubs in the fabric of time, but these were impossible to ignore. Marcus was worried about what might be happening in Paris. In an effort to distract him, I suggested he tell me about his own transformation from warmblood to vampire.

"It's up to you, Marcus," I said. "But if you think it would help to talk about your past, I'd love to listen."

"I wouldn't know where to begin," Marcus said.

"Hamish always says you should start at the end," Matthew observed, sipping his wine.

"Or you could start with your origins," I said, stating the obvious alternative.

"Like Dickens?" Marcus made a soft sound of amusement. "Chapter one, 'I am born'?"

The usual biographical template of birth, childhood, marriage, and death might be too narrow and conventional for a vampire, I had to admit.

"Chapter two, I died. Chapter three, I was reborn." Marcus shook his head. "I'm afraid it's not so simple a tale, Diana. Strange, minor things stand out so clearly to me, and I can barely recall the dates of major events."

"Matthew warned me that vampire memories might be tricky," I said. "Why don't we start with something easy, like your name?" He went by Marcus Whitmore now, but there was no telling what it had been originally.

Marcus's darkening expression told me that my simple question didn't have an easy answer.

"Vampires don't normally share that information. Names are important, *mon coeur*," Matthew reminded me.

For historians as well as vampires—which is why I'd asked. With a name, it would be possible for me to trace Marcus's past in archives and libraries.

Marcus took a steadying breath, and the black threads surrounding him bristled with agitation. I exchanged a worried look with Matthew.

I did warn you, said Matthew's expression.

"Marcus MacNeil." Marcus blurted out the name.

Marcus MacNeil of Hadley, born August 1757. A name, a date, a place—

these were the building blocks of most historical research. Even if Marcus were to stop there, I could probably find out more about him.

"My mother was Catherine Chauncey of Boston, and my father . . ." Marcus's throat closed, shutting off the words. He cleared it and started again. "My father was Obadiah MacNeil from the nearby town of Pelham."

"Did you have any brothers or sisters?" I asked.

"One sister. Her name was Patience." Marcus's face had turned ashen. Matthew poured him some more wine.

"Older or younger?" I wanted to get as much out of Marcus as possible in case tonight was the only chance I had to gather information from him.

"Younger."

"Where did you live in Hadley?" I steered the conversation away from his family, which was clearly a painful subject.

"A house on the western road out of town."

"What do you remember about the house?"

"Not much." Marcus looked surprised that I was interested in such a thing. "The door was red. There was a lilac bush outside, and the scent came through the open windows in May. The more my mother neglected it, the more it bloomed. And there was a black clock on the mantel. In the parlor. It came down to her through the Chauncey family, and she wouldn't let anyone touch it."

As Marcus recalled small details of his past, his memory—which had grown rusty and sepia toned from disuse—began to operate more freely.

"There were geese everywhere in Hadley," Marcus continued. "They were vicious, and roamed all over town frightening the children. And I remember there was a brass rooster atop the meetinghouse steeple. Zeb put it up there. God, I haven't thought about that rooster in ages."

"Zeb?" I asked, less interested in the town's weather vane.

"Zeb Pruitt. My friend. My hero, really," Marcus said slowly.

Time chimed in warning, the sound echoing in my ears.

"What's your earliest memory of him?" I prompted Marcus.

"He taught me how to march like a soldier," Marcus whispered. "In the barn. I was five or six. My father caught him. He didn't let me spend much time with Zeb after that."

A red door.

A lilac bush.

A wayward flock of geese.

A rooster on the meetinghouse steeple.

A friend who played make-believe soldier with him.

These charming fragments were part of the larger mosaic of Marcus's life, but they weren't enough to form a coherent picture of his past, or reveal some larger historical truth.

I opened my mouth to ask another question. Matthew shook his head, warning me not to interfere in the story but to let Marcus take it in whatever direction he needed to go.

"My father was a soldier. He was in the militia, and fought at Ft. William Henry. He didn't see me for months after I was born," Marcus said, his voice dropping. "I always wondered whether things would have been different if only he had come home sooner from the war, or never gone at all."

Marcus shivered and I felt a flicker of unease.

"War changed him. It changes everybody, of course. But my father believed in God and country first, and rules and discipline second." Marcus cocked his head to the side as if he were considering a proposition. "I suppose that's one of the reasons why I don't have much faith in rules. They don't always keep you safe, like my father believed."

"Your father sounds like he was a man of his time," I noted. Rules and regulations were a fixture of early American life.

"If you mean he sounds like a patriarch, you'd be right," Marcus agreed. "Full of bristle and brimstone, with the Lord and the king on his side no matter what daft position he adopted. Obadiah MacNeil ruled over our house and everybody in it. It was his kingdom."

Marcus's blue eyes shattered under the weight of his recollections.

"We had this bootjack," Marcus continued. "It was made out of iron and shaped like a devil. You put your heel between the horns, stepped on the devil's heart, and pulled your leg free of the boot. And when my father picked up that bootjack, even the cat knew it was time to disappear."

Words of one Syllable

THE NEW ENGLAND PRIMER, 1762

Age	all	ape	are
Babe	beef	best	bold
Cat	cake	crown	cup
Deaf	dead	dry	dull
Eat	ear	eggs	eyes
Face	feet	fish	fowl
Gate	good	grass	great
Hand	hat	head	heart
Ice	ink	isle	job
Kick	kind	kneel	know
Lamb	lame	land	long
Made	mole	moon	mouth
Name	night	noise	noon
Oak	once	one	ounce
Pain	pair	pence	pound
Quart	queen	quick	quilt
Rain	raise	rose	run
Saint	sage	salt	said
Take	talk	time	throat
Vaine	vice	vile	view
Way	wait	waste	would

⇥ 6 ⇤

Time

The black clock on the polished mantel struck noon, marking the passage of the hours. It stood out against the whitewashed walls of the parlor, the only ornament in the room. The family Bible and the almanac his father used to note down important events and the changing weather were propped up next to it.

Its piercing chime was one of the familiar sounds of home: his mother's soft voice, the geese that honked in the road, his baby sister's babble.

The clock whirred into silence, waiting for its next opportunity to perform.

"When is Pa coming back?" Marcus asked, looking up from his primer. His father hadn't been there to preside over breakfast. He must be very hungry, thought Marcus, after missing his meal of porridge, eggs, bacon, bread, and jam. Marcus's stomach grumbled in sympathy, and he wondered whether they would have to wait for Pa to return before eating their midday meal.

"When he's finished." His mother's tone was unusually sharp, her face set in lines of worry under a starched linen cap. "Come, read me the next word."

"N-ame." Marcus slowly sounded out the letters. "My name is Marcus MacNeil."

"Yes, it is," his mother replied. "And the next word?"

"Ni-jit." Marcus frowned. That wasn't a word he'd heard before. "Ni-got?"

"Do you remember what I told you about silent letters?" His mother lifted Patience from the wide-planked floor and went to the window, her brown skirts swishing. As she walked, sand came up through the cracks between the boards.

Marcus did remember—dimly.

"Night." Marcus looked up. "That's when Father left. It was raining. And dark."

"Can you find the word 'rain' in your book?" His mother peered out from among the spaces in the shutters. She dusted them every day, sliding a goose feather through each narrow opening. Marcus's mother was particular about such things and allowed no one else to take care of the front room—not even old Ellie Pruitt, who came one morning a week to help with the other chores.

"Oak. Pain. Quart. Rain. I found it, Mama!" Marcus shouted with excitement.

"Good boy. One day you will be a scholar at Harvard, like the other men in the Chauncey family." His mother was inordinately proud of her cousins, uncles, and brothers, all of whom had gone to school for years and years. To Marcus, the prospect sounded drearier than the weather.

"No. I'm going to be a soldier, like Pa." Marcus kicked at the legs of his chair, a sign of his commitment to this course of action. It made such a satisfying sound that he did it again.

"Stop this nonsense. What is a foolish son?" His mother jiggled Patience up and down on her hip. Patience was teething, which made her fractious and soggy.

"A heaviness to his mother," Marcus said, turning to the page of alphabet verses. There was the proverb—right at the top: *A wise son maketh a glad father, but a foolish son is a heaviness to his mother.* His mother was always pointing it out to him.

"Recite the rest of the alphabet," his mother instructed, walking the edges of the room to keep Patience's mind off her discomfort. "And no mumbling. They don't allow boys to attend Harvard College if they mumble."

Marcus reached L—*Liars shall have their part in the lake which burns with fire and brimstone,* his mother intoned when he had trouble reading out the words—when the wooden gate that protected their front garden from the geese and the traffic opened. His mother froze.

Marcus turned in his chair and pressed his eyes to the two holes bored into the top slat. The holes were for hanging the chair up on the pegs by the kitchen door, but Marcus had discovered they were excellent peepholes. He felt like a bandit or an Indian scout whenever he peered through them. Sometimes, when his mother and father were occupied and he was supposed to be doing his lessons or watching Patience, Marcus pulled the chair to the window and watched the world go by, imagining he was on the lookout for heathens or that he was a captain on a ship staring through a telescope, or a highwayman peering through the trees at his next victim.

The front door creaked open, letting in the wind and the rain. A black wool hat, wide brimmed and sodden with moisture, sailed through the air and landed atop the newel post. Marcus's father used the globe-shaped wooden ball to teach him geography. Pa had inscribed the eastern coast of America on it with black ink that stained the wood, as well as an irregular splotch that showed how far across the ocean the king was. Even so, Pa said, he was watching over his people in America. Ellie polished the post on every visit, but the ink never faded.

"Catherine?" His father stumbled over something in the hall and swore.

"In here, Pa," Marcus called before his mother had a chance to respond. Marcus had learned not to fling himself into his father's arms the moment he arrived home. His father didn't like to be taken unawares, not even by someone as small and familiar as Marcus.

Obadiah MacNeil stepped into the room, swaying slightly on his feet. The scent of smoke and something sweet and cloying followed him. He was holding the heavy iron bootjack that normally sat by the front door.

Peeking through the chair slat, Marcus saw that his father wasn't wearing his woolen muffler around his neck as he usually did. It was a jaunty red that stood out like the color of the fruits left on the rose bush when the first snow fell. Today, his linen shirt was open at the neck, the simple cravat askew and stained.

"Chairs are for asses, not knees." Obadiah ran a grimy hand under his long, sharp nose. It left a smear of yellowed earth. "Did you hear me, boy?"

Marcus swung around and slid his feet over the seat, cheeks burning. His father had told him that dozens of times. A rough hand pushed against the back of the chair, sending Marcus toward the table. The edge hit him in the chest, knocking the wind out of him.

"I asked you a question." Obadiah braced his arms on the table, surrounding Marcus with wet wool and that sickly sweet smell. The boot-jack was still in his hand. It was crafted in the shape of a devil, with the prongs of his horned head serving for the heel rest and the long body the brace. The devil's eyes winked up at Marcus, two black holes above a leering mouth.

"I'm sorry, Pa." Marcus blinked back the tears. Soldiers didn't cry.

"Don't make me tell you again." Obadiah's breath smelled of apples. He stood.

"Where have you been, Obadiah?" Marcus's mother put Patience into her cradle by the fire.

"No business of yours, Catherine."

"On West Street, I warrant."

His father didn't respond.

"Was Josiah with you?" his mother asked. Marcus didn't much like Cousin Josiah, whose eyes shifted when he spoke and whose voice echoed against the rafters.

"Leave it, woman." Obadiah's tone was weary. "I'm off to the barn. Zeb is there tending to the animals."

"I'll help, too!" Marcus scrambled off the chair. Unlike Cousin Josiah, Zeb Pruitt was one of his favorite people. He'd taught Marcus how to string a fishing rod, how to catch mice in the barn, and how to climb the apple tree. Zeb had also made sure Marcus understood that the geese in town were more dangerous than the dogs, and could give a person a savage bite.

"Zeb doesn't need your help," said his mother. "Stay where you are and finish your lesson."

Marcus's face fell. He didn't much feel like reading. He wanted to go to the barn and march up and down the center aisle to Zeb's commands, playing at soldier and hiding behind the water trough when the enemy pursued him.

His mother hurried out of the room after his father, who had left the front door open to the elements.

"Mind that Patience doesn't fall out of her cradle," she told Marcus as she took her shawl down from a peg and left the house.

Marcus stared glumly at his sister. Patience sucked on her fist, which was shiny with spittle and bright red from the constant gnawing.

His sister would make a terrible soldier. Marcus brightened.

"Do you want to be my prisoner?" Marcus whispered, kneeling by the cradle. Patience cooed her assent. "All right, then. You stay where you are. No moving. And no complaining. Or you'll be flogged."

Marcus rocked the cradle gently, lessons forgotten, and imagined himself in a cave in the woods, waiting for his commanding officer to arrive and praise him for his valor.

"YOU MUST HAVE BEEN up all night with the commotion, and the traffic between town and the burying ground." Old Madam Porter put a small cup and saucer on the table at his mother's elbow. Marcus could see the wallpaper, blue as the spring sky, through the eggshell-thin cup.

Madame Porter's house was one of the finest in Hadley. It had smooth wooden paneling and brightly colored paint as well as patterned wallpaper. The chairs were carved and padded for comfort. The windows opened up in the new way, not out like the old casements at their house. Marcus loved to visit—not least because there was usually Madeira cake studded with currants and spread with jam.

Marcus counted to five before his mother reached for the tea. Chaunceys didn't gobble their food or behave as though they couldn't remember their last meal.

Something poked Marcus in the ribs.

It was a wooden whirligig, and Miss Anna Porter was at the end of it. She was Madam Porter's granddaughter, and she never let Marcus forget that she was one year and one month older than he was. A roll of her brown eyes and a toss of her red head suggested they leave the adults to their conversation and find amusement elsewhere.

But Marcus wanted to stay where he was and hear what had happened at the cemetery. It was something bad, something nobody would talk about in front of him and Anna. Marcus hoped a ghost was involved. He liked a good ghost story.

"They asked for my help, and I had no one to send but Zeb." Madam Porter sat down with a deep sigh. "It's on stormy nights when there is a pounding at the door that I miss having a husband."

Marcus's mother made a sympathetic noise and sipped at her tea.

Madam Porter's husband had died a hero, in battle. Zeb had told stories about Master Porter, though, that made Marcus wonder whether he had been a nice man.

"Really, Catherine, you should rent a house in town. Living out by the burial ground cannot be salubrious," Madam Porter said, changing the subject. She picked up her needlework and began to stitch a bright pattern on the cloth.

"My grandmother said your pa is a drunkard," Anna whispered, her freckled eyelids narrowed into slits over pale eyes. She was waving the whirligig to and fro, which made the arms move in slow circles. The face on the whirligig, with its curled black hair and dusky skin, looked like Zeb Pruitt.

"Is not." Marcus grabbed at the whirligig.

"Is too," Anna taunted, still in a whisper.

"Take that back!" Marcus wrestled the whirligig from Anna's hands.

Madam Porter and his mother turned, shocked by his outburst.

"Ow!" Anna grabbed at one of her long red curls, lip trembling. "He pulled my hair."

"I did not," Marcus protested. "I never touched you."

"And he took my toy." Anna's eyes welled over, her tears dampening her cheek. Marcus snorted.

"Marcus MacNeil." His mother's voice was low but intense. "Gentlemen do not steal from defenseless women. You know better than that."

Anna had strong arms, ran faster than a scalded cat, and had many hearty male cousins. She was far from defenseless.

"Nor do they torment young ladies with pinches and pulls," his mother said, dashing Marcus's hope of reprieve. "Since you are not fit for polite society, you will beg Anna's forgiveness, and Madam Porter's, too, and wait for me in the barn. And when we get home, your father will hear of this."

And he would be angry. Marcus's lip trembled.

"I'm sorry, ma'am," Marcus said, bowing slightly to Madam Porter, his fists clenched behind his back. "Please forgive me, Anna."

"A very pretty apology," Madam Porter said with an approving nod.

Marcus fled to the barn without waiting for Anna's response, swallowing down his fears about what awaited him at home and his tears at his mother's rebuke.

"You all right, Master Marcus?" Zeb Pruitt was propped up on his pitchfork in one of the stalls. Standing beside him, long of limb and broad of shoulder, was Joshua Boston.

"Something happen at the house?" Joshua spit out a long, thin stream of brown liquid. Unlike Zeb, who was in stained work clothes, Joshua was wearing a wool coat with polished buttons.

Marcus hiccupped and shook his head.

"Hmm. Something tells me Miss Anna has been up to mischief," Zeb said.

"She said my pa is a drunkard," Marcus said. "It's not true. He goes to church every Sunday. God answers your prayers. Pa says so. And now I have to tell Pa what happened with Anna and he's going to be angry with me. Again."

Zeb and Joshua exchanged long looks.

"Just because a man takes himself to Smith's tavern on a rainy night to dry off by the fire doesn't make him a drunkard." Zeb stuck his pitchfork into a nearby pile of hay and crouched down so he was eye level with Marcus. "What's this about Mr. MacNeil being angry?"

"He was out all night, and when he came back I was kneeling on the chair. He told me not to do it, hundreds of times." Marcus quivered just thinking about it. "Pa told me not to disobey him again, or I'd get another beating."

Joshua said something under his breath that Marcus didn't catch. Zeb nodded.

"You be sure you stay away from your pa if he's in a dark mood," Zeb told him. "Hide in the henhouse, or under the willow by the river until you think it's safe."

"How will I know when that is?" Marcus asked, worried he might miss dinner.

"You'll learn," Zeb said.

THAT NIGHT, MARCUS TOOK HIS pillow and arranged it at the top of the stairs. The pain in his backside and legs had gone from a fierce burn to a dull ache. His father had given him the promised beating, and had used a leather strap from the barn this time rather than his hand so that Marcus wouldn't forget the lesson.

His ma and pa were arguing in the kitchen. Marcus couldn't make out what the fight was about, but he suspected it had to do with him. His stomach growled with hunger—there hadn't been enough food at dinner, and his ma had let the bread they were supposed to have with it burn.

"Mind your place, Catherine," his pa said, storming out of the kitchen and grabbing his hat off the newel post. The woolen felt was dry now, but the brim had wilted and it no longer had a familiar, triangular shape.

Marcus opened his mouth, ready to call out another apology in an attempt to end the shouting. But he wasn't supposed to interrupt his father and mother when they were talking, so he waited, hoping that his father would turn around and see him sitting there and ask what he was doing out of bed.

"It's my place to keep this family from ruin," his mother retorted. "We barely have enough to eat. How are we going to manage if you keep drinking away what's left of our money?"

His father whirled around, one hand lifted in the air.

Catherine cowered against the wall, shielding her face.

"Don't you make me give you a beating, too," Obadiah said softly as he walked out the door.

He never did look back.

⇥ 7 ⇤

Two

Phoebe's second day as a vampire did not include the dreamy, rapturous experiences she'd had on the first. While her body was learning how to be still, her mind could not—would not—be quiet. Memories, images from her years studying the history of art, lyrics from her favorite songs—all these and more flitted across her brain in an unsettling film where she played the starring role and also comprised the entire audience. Since she had become a vampire, her memories were weirdly addled and unusually sharp.

Her first bicycle was navy blue with white stripes on the fenders.

Where was it now? Phoebe wondered. She thought she had last ridden it at the house in Hampstead.

There was a pub in Hampstead, perfect for stopping in and having lunch when you took a Sunday walk.

Not that she would ever have a Sunday lunch again, Phoebe realized. What would she do on Sundays in the years to come? How would she entertain friends? Neither she nor Marcus went to church. They would have to create a different Sunday routine after they got married, one that didn't revolve around a big meal.

The church in Devon where her best friend got married had a beautiful window with bits of blue and rose glass in it. Phoebe had stared at its colors and intricate patterns all through the service, marveling at its beauty.

How old was that window? Phoebe was not a glass expert but she suspected it was Victorian—not very old at all.

The celadon glass pitcher downstairs was far more ancient.

Could it be Roman, maybe third century? Its value would be enormous if that were so. Freyja shouldn't keep it where it could be smashed.

Phoebe had spent a summer in Rome, digging in the ruins and learning about tesserae. It had been so hot and dry that the air singed the tiny hairs in her nose and every inhalation scoured her lungs.

Had her nose changed? Phoebe got up and looked in the time-clouded mirror. Reflected there was the room behind her: the elegant curves of the Second Empire bed, the small canopy suspended from the ceiling that turned the bed into a cozy enclosure, the elegant armoire, and a deep armchair expansive enough that you could curl your feet up underneath you when you were reading.

A crease had reappeared in the bedspread.

Phoebe frowned. She had smoothed out that wrinkle. She remembered doing it.

Before she could complete her next thought, she was kneeling on the mattress. Her hands pressed the fabric, over and over. Every fiber of the sheets was palpable, and rough to her touch.

"No wonder I can't sleep. They're too coarse." Phoebe tore at the linens, intending to drag them from the mattress so they could be replaced with something proper, something that wouldn't scratch her skin and keep her awake.

Instead, she reduced them to ribbons, shredding them with nails that had the sharp ferocity of an eagle's talons.

"We've reached the terrible twos, I see." Freyja entered the room, her blue eyes frosty over high cheekbones as she surveyed the damage Phoebe had inflicted on the room.

Phoebe had been warned about her second day, and how it seemed to mimic the trials and tribulations of the second year of human age, but she'd had no context for the warning, having never been a mother. She could not remember her own time as a toddler, and not a single one of her friends had children yet.

"Are you nesting?" Françoise, whose once-miraculous omnipresence had become just another source of irritation, studied the mess Phoebe had made.

"The sheets are scratchy. I can't sleep," Phoebe said, unable to keep the petulance from her tone.

"We have spoken about this, Phoebe dearest." Freyja's voice was reasonable, compassionate. The endearment grated on Phoebe's raw nerves nonetheless. "It will be months before you take your first nap. A deep sleep is still years away."

"But I'm tired," Phoebe complained, sounding like a troublesome child.

"No, you're bored and hungry. A *draugr* must be very precise about her emotions and state of mind, so as not to be caught up in fantasies of feeling. Your blood is far too strong and restless to need sleep." Freyja noticed something in the window, a tiny imperfection. One of the panes was cracked. Her attention zeroed in on the crazed glass. "How did that happen?"

"A bird." Phoebe lowered her gaze. There was a split in the floor—or was that the grain in the wood? She could follow the line forever. . . .

"This crack begins on the inside," Freyja said, inspecting it more closely. "I will ask you one more time, Phoebe: How did this happen?"

"I told you!" Phoebe said, defensive. "A bird. It was outside in the tree. I wanted to get its attention, so I tapped on the glass. I didn't mean to break anything. I just wanted it to look at me."

The bird would not stop singing. At first Phoebe had found the song enchanting, her vampire ears attuned as they never had been to the trills and warbles. As it went on—and on—however, she wanted to wring the bird's neck.

If she drank the blood of a bird, would she understand why they sang all the time?

Phoebe's stomach gurgled.

"I'm too damn old to be a mother. I'd completely forgotten what a pain in the ass children are." Miriam had arrived. She put her hands on her slender hips and adopted her preferred stance: legs slightly separated, usually clad in some sort of boot (today's were high-heeled and suede), and her elbows pushing into the surrounding space at sharp angles, daring someone to dismiss her as insignificant.

The rush of pride in her maker was instantaneous and surprising, engulfing Phoebe. Miriam's blood flowed through Phoebe's veins, strong and powerful. She might be small and worthless now, but in time Phoebe would be a vampire to reckon with, too.

Disappointment crashed down on her. Phoebe's throat tightened.

"What is it?" Freyja asked, concerned. "Is the light too bright? Françoise, close those drapes immediately."

"It's not the sunshine. It's just I've grown only an inch." Phoebe had been marking her progress every ten minutes or so on the frame of the door that led into the bathroom. The mark hadn't risen for the past eight hours. Phoebe had scratched so many lines into that single location with her fingernail that the paint was ruined.

"If height was what you were after, you should have had Freyja sire you," Miriam said tartly, moving into the room past the nearly six-foot-tall Dane. With one sweeping glance she studied the mess Phoebe had made, confirmed that the window glass was indeed cracked, and fixed dark eyes on her daughter. "Well?"

There was no mistaking the demand for an explanation in her maker's tone.

"I'm bored." Phoebe said it quietly, embarrassed by the puerile confession.

"Excellent. Well done." Freyja nodded approvingly. "That is a tremendous achievement, Phoebe."

Miriam's eyes narrowed.

"And," Phoebe continued, her voice increasingly plaintive, "hungry."

"This is why no one should be made a vampire until they are thirty," Miriam told Freyja. "Insufficient inner resources."

"You were twenty-five!" Phoebe said hotly, her defenses rising at the insult.

"Back then, twenty-five was practically old age." Miriam shook her head. "We can't come running every time you feel restless, Phoebe. You're going to have to figure out how to fill your time."

"Do you play chess? Embroider? Like to cook? Make perfume?" Freyja began to rattle off the activities of a medieval Danish princess. "Write poetry?"

"Cook?" Phoebe was bewildered at the prospect—and the mere thought made her empty stomach rise up in rebellion. She hadn't enjoyed cooking when she was human. Now that she was a vampire it was out of the question.

"It can be a very rewarding hobby. I knew a vampire who spent a decade perfecting the soufflé. She said it was very soothing," Freyja replied.

"Veronique *did* have a human husband at the time, of course. He was quite happy with her efforts, though in the end they killed him. His heart was so blocked with sugar and eggs that he died at fifty-three."

"Do you mean Marcus's Veronique, who works in London?" Phoebe didn't know that Freyja and Marcus's former lover were acquainted.

Marcus.

The thought of him was electrifying.

When Phoebe was a warmblood, Marcus's touches had made her veins turn to fire and her fragile human limbs to liquid. Now that she was a vampire . . . Phoebe's restless mind dwelt on the possibilities. Her lips turned up into a slow, seductive smile.

"Oh, dear," Freyja said, a bit of alarm in her tone as she detected the direction that Phoebe's wandering attention had taken. "What about a musical instrument? Do you play something? Can you sing?"

"No music." Miriam's lilting soprano turned thunderous, something only a vampire could manage. "When Jason discovered the drum, it nearly drove his father and me around the bend."

Phoebe had not yet met Jason, the only surviving child of Miriam's long-dead mate.

She began to thrum her fingers on the tabletop in anticipation. Phoebe had never had a brother, only Stella. Sisters were different—younger sisters, especially. What might she do with an older brother? Phoebe wondered.

Miriam's hand closed on hers, bone-crushing and painful. "No. Drumming."

Bored, hungry, and restless, held captive by Freyja and Miriam—how was Phoebe supposed to endure it? She wanted to run outside and breathe fresh air.

Phoebe wanted to chase something that wasn't a thought, run it into the ground and then—

"I want to hunt." Phoebe was amazed by the realization. She'd worried about hunting for weeks before she became a vampire, and for the past six hours she'd been pushing the idea resolutely from her mind. Because after the hunting came the feeding from a live human, and Phoebe wasn't sure she was ready for that.

Yet.

Phoebe instinctively understood that hunting would push her restless thoughts to the background. Hunting would feed some part of her that was hollow and yearning. Hunting would bring peace.

"Of course you do," Freyja said. "Isn't Phoebe progressing marvelously, Miriam?"

"You're not ready," Miriam pronounced, quelling Phoebe's excitement.

"But I'm hungry." Phoebe fidgeted in her chair, her eyes pinned on Miriam's wrist.

Feeding from her maker was like getting a meal and a bedtime story all at once. With every drop of blood Phoebe swallowed, her mind and imagination were suffused with Miriam's memories. She'd learned far more about Miriam in the past two days than she had in the fifteen months they had known each other.

Some of what Phoebe knew felt intuitive, a flood of scattered episodes from Miriam's long life in which pleasure and pain were inseparable partners.

In subsequent feedings, Phoebe was able to focus on the strongest impressions in Miriam's blood rather than being overcome by waves of blurry remembrance.

Phoebe understood now that the tall, rugged man with the wise, wary eyes and the wide, easy grin had been Miriam's mate, and that she alone called him Ori, though others knew him as Bertrand and Wendalin, Ludo and Randolf, and his mother had called him Gund.

Miriam had sired more men than women in the centuries that led to Phoebe's own conversion. She had to in order to survive, back when having men around you was some measure of protection against rape and robbery. Sons could pretend to be brothers, or even spouses in emergencies, and were a deterrent to both grasping humans with their incessant need for more wealth, and vampires with their desire for greater territory. Her sons, like her mate, Ori, were gone now, killed in the violent warfare that ran through Miriam's memories in a dark ribbon of grief.

Then there were the daughters. First, there had been Taderfit, killed by her vampire mate in a fit of jealous rage. Lalla, Miriam's second daughter, had been set upon by her own children, crushed and torn to death in a competition over who would rule their clan once Lalla was gone. After Miriam had disposed of Lalla's feuding children, she stopped making daughters for a while.

But it was not only ancient history that featured in Miriam's blood. More recent events had a place there, too. Matthew de Clermont, Marcus's sire, was in many of Miriam's memories. In the crowded city of Jerusalem, Matthew and Ori had turned heads and cleared paths, one raven dark and the other golden. The two men had been devoted friends.

Until Eleanor. In Miriam's blood, Phoebe saw that the English woman had been a great beauty, with porcelain skin and flaxen hair that testified to her Saxon heritage. But it was her irrepressible enthusiasm for living that had made the vampires flock to Eleanor's side. Vampire blood honed bones and muscles until they reached their greatest potential, so there was no shortage of attractive specimens. Vitality, however, was a different matter.

Miriam had been drawn to Eleanor's joy just like most of the other creatures in the city: daemon, human, vampire, and witch. She had befriended Eleanor St. Leger when she arrived in the Holy Land with her family and one of the waves of crusaders. And it was Miriam who introduced Eleanor to Matthew de Clermont. When she did, Miriam had unknowingly planted the seeds of her mate's eventual destruction.

Bertrand's life had been sacrificed to save Matthew's, a testament to bonds of friendship so deep that they bordered on the brotherly. Most vampires, however, viewed the warrior's death as collateral damage in the de Clermont family's rise to greatness.

Promise me you'll watch over him. Ori had asked Miriam for the boon in the hour before dawn on the morning of his execution, as he belted his brightly colored tunic and donned his knight's sword for the last time.

Miriam had agreed. Ori's request, and her own promise to him, echoed in her blood.

Even now it bound Miriam and Matthew together. Matthew had Diana to watch over him, as well as his mother Ysabeau, Marcus, and all the other members of the Bishop-Clairmont scion of which Phoebe would soon be a member. But that did not lessen Miriam's commitment—she would never disavow her mate's dying wish.

Phoebe was so focused on what she had gathered from Miriam's memories that she barely registered the closing of the door as Freyja and Françoise left them. But she scented Miriam's approach and reached out, grabbing for her wrist.

"You don't *take*." Miriam's voice was glacial.

Phoebe's hand dropped.

Miriam waited for Phoebe's hunger to climb another notch, standing so close that their two vampire hearts came to beat slowly as one. Finally, Miriam offered her child sustenance.

"Tomorrow you can take," Miriam said. "But not from me. Never from me."

Phoebe nodded slightly, her lips latched on to Miriam's wrist now that it had been offered. One face at a time, she took in the story that Miriam's blood told as skillfully as Scheherazade.

Lalla.

Ori.

Lalla.

Taderfit.

Ori.

Eleanor.

Ori.

Matthew.

Marcus.

Names swam to the surface along with the faces, bubbling through Miriam's sea of experiences.

Phoebe.

She was there, too. Phoebe saw herself through Miriam's eyes, her head tilted to one side, a questioning expression on her face, as she listened to something Marcus was telling her.

Just as Miriam was part of Phoebe, she was now a part of Miriam.

After Miriam left, Phoebe focused on that preternatural connection and found she was neither bored nor restless. She organized her thoughts around the central truth of the bond she and Miriam now shared, holding on to the realization as though it were the focal point of a newly discovered solar system.

Had she been a warmblood and not a vampire, the comforting

assurance that she belonged would have been soothing enough to send Phoebe drifting into tranquil sleep.

Instead, Phoebe sat with the knowledge, quiet and still, letting it soothe her restless mind.

It was not sleep, but it was the next best thing.

⊰ 8 ⊱

The Burying Place

15 MAY

Matthew found me in the library, perched on a ladder and rummaging through the shelves.

"Do you think Philippe owned any books about the history of America?" I asked. "I can't seem to find any."

"I doubt it," he replied. "He preferred newspapers for current events. I'm taking the children to the stables. Why don't you come with us?"

I climbed down, one hand on the rungs and the other clutching an old atlas and a 1784 copy of *Lettres d'un cultivateur américain* signed by the author.

"You'll break your neck if you're not careful." Matthew took up a watchful position at the foot of the ladder as I made my descent. "If you need something, you have only to ask. I'm happy to get it down for you."

"Were there a catalog—or even a shelflist—I could pretend I was at the Bodleian and fill out a call slip and send you to the stacks to page it for me," I teased. "But since I have no idea what's here, I'm afraid I'll be the one climbing the ladders for the time being."

One of the ghosts slid two books down the shelf they were rearranging, and offered me a third.

"There's a book floating near your left elbow," Matthew commented. He was unable to see the apparition, but the book that was seemingly hanging in midair was impossible to miss.

"Ghost." I took the book in question and looked at the title stamped in gold on the spine. "*The Persian Letters.* I'm not looking for books of letters, I'm looking for books about America. But thank you for trying."

"Let me have those," Matthew said, reaching up for the books in my arms.

I made much better progress without them—the atlas was quite large—and was soon back on solid ground. I gave Matthew a kiss.

"Why do you want books about America?" Matthew asked, studying the titles.

"I'm trying to develop what Marcus told us last night into a historical narrative." I took the books from Matthew and put them on the table. There was already a flurry of notes there along with a printout of *The New England Primer* from 1762, and an account of the battle of Ft. William Henry was up on my computer screen. "I don't have much grasp of his eighteenth-century context—not beyond what I remember from *The Last of the Mohicans* and the class I took as an undergraduate on the Enlightenment."

"And you think an atlas and de Crèvecoeur's account of life in New York are going to help?" Matthew looked skeptical.

"It's a start," I said. "Otherwise I won't be able to fit Marcus's story into the big picture."

"I thought the goal was to help Marcus cope with his memories," Matthew said, "not write the definitive account of eighteenth-century America."

"I'm a historian, Matthew. I can't help it," I confessed. "I know the small details of life are important, but Marcus lived during an exciting time. There's no harm in trying to see how his experiences illuminate it."

"You might be disappointed by how little Marcus remembers that historians consider important," Matthew warned. "He was still in his teens when the war started."

"Yes, but it was the American Revolution," I protested. "Surely he remembers that?"

"What do you remember about the invasion of Panama, or the first Gulf War?" Matthew shook his head. "My guess is very little."

"I didn't participate in either of those conflicts. Marcus did." So did Matthew, come to think of it. "Wait. Did you write to Philippe while you were in America with Lafayette?"

"Yes." Matthew sounded wary.

"Are the letters here, do you think? I could use those to flesh out the details that Marcus might not remember." The prospect of examining primary sources further sparked my historical curiosity. I specialized in an earlier period, a different country, and was not a military or political historian, but being a student again was thrilling. There was so much to learn.

"I can look, but it's far more likely they're at Sept-Tours along with the records of the brotherhood. I was in the colonies on official business."

The Knights of Lazarus, the de Clermont family's supposedly secret military-slash-charitable organization, seemed to have their fingers in every political pie, even though creature meddling in human politics and religion was strictly forbidden by the Congregation.

"That would be fantastic. If it's here, you'll find it much quicker than I would." I studied my computer screen for a moment before shutting the lid. "The fall of Ft. William Henry sounds horrifying. Obadiah must have suffered for years because of what he witnessed."

"War is always terrible, but what happened to the British army when they left the fort was tragic," Matthew said. "A lack of understanding, followed by miscommunication and frustration, led to unspeakable violence."

The account I'd read had made it clear that the Native Americans who attacked the British army and their followers had expected to take the spoils of war—guns and weapons—back home with them as symbols of their valor. But their French allies were obeying different rules and allowed the British to keep their muskets so long as they surrendered the ammunition. Deprived of the guns, the Native Americans took other prizes instead: captives and lives.

"And Obadiah saw it all." I shook my head. "No wonder he drank."

"Battles don't always end just because someone negotiates a truce," Matthew said. "For some soldiers, the fight goes on for the rest of their lives, shaping everything that happens afterward."

"Was Obadiah one of those soldiers?" I thought of the bootjack, and the wary look in Marcus's eye when he spoke of his father—even though he was a grown man now and not a little boy, even though he was talking about events that had happened centuries ago.

"I think so," Matthew said.

No wonder Marcus's memories were so snarled and angry. It wasn't the red door and the lilacs that were causing him pain, but his forbidding father.

"As for the bigger historical picture," Matthew continued, taking my hand, "I think you're going to have to do a lot more digging before you discover what that is—never mind its significance."

"When we timewalked, I was surprised by what life was really like," I said, thinking back to the time we'd shared in the sixteenth century. "But it was still possible for me to fit what I discovered into what I already knew. I suppose I thought I could do the same with Marcus's story."

"But remembering the past is not the same as timewalking through it," Matthew observed.

"No. They're entirely different kinds of magic," I mused.

I was going to have to be very careful where I asked Marcus to dig into his former life.

SARAH AND AGATHA arrived around midday.

"We weren't expecting you until late this afternoon," Matthew said, giving first Sarah and then Agatha a kiss.

"Diana said it was an emergency, so Agatha called Baldwin," Sarah explained. "Apparently, he has a helicopter on standby in Monaco and was able to send it for us."

"I never said it was an *emergency*, Sarah," I corrected her.

"You said it was urgent. Here we are." Sarah took Philip from Matthew's arms. "What is all this fuss about, young man? What have you done now?"

Philip presented her with a carrot. "Horsey."

"Carrot," I said. Sometimes the twins confused what the animals ate with the animals themselves.

Becca had forgotten the horses and was totally absorbed in greeting Agatha. She had her fists in Agatha's hair and was examining her curly locks with fascination.

"Watch out, Agatha. Sometimes she gets excited and pulls," I warned. "And she's stronger than she looks."

"Oh, I'm used to it," Agatha said. "Margaret is always trying to braid it, and it just ends up in knots. Where's Marcus?"

"Behind you!" Marcus said, giving out hugs of welcome. "Don't tell me you two are here to check up on me?"

"Not this time," Sarah said with a laugh. "Why? Do you need checking up on?"

"Probably," Marcus said cheerfully, though his smile was a touch anxious.

"What's the news from Paris?" Agatha asked. "How is Phoebe?"

"All good, so far," Marcus replied. "But it's a big day."

"Miriam will begin weaning Phoebe today," Matthew explained, wanting to illuminate vampire culture to his witch and daemon guests. If all went according to plan, today Phoebe would get her first taste of blood that didn't come from her maker.

"You make it sound as though Phoebe's a baby," Sarah said with a frown.

"She is," Matthew replied.

"Phoebe's a grown woman, Matthew. Maybe we could say, 'Today Phoebe is experimenting with new foods,' or, 'Today Phoebe is starting her new diet,'" Sarah suggested.

Matthew's face bore an expression of bewildered exhaustion—and Sarah and Agatha had only just arrived.

"Why don't we go into the solarium," I said, steering Sarah and Agatha toward the kitchen door. "Marthe made some lovely shortbread, and we can catch up on all the news while Matthew feeds the twins."

As I suspected, the prospect of sugary treats was irresistible, and Agatha and Sarah settled into the comfortable chairs with coffee, tea, and cookies.

"So what's the crisis?" Sarah said around a bite of shortbread.

"I think Philip wove his first spell," I said. "I didn't catch the words, so I'm not sure. He was playing with time, at the very least."

"I don't know what you think I can do about it, Diana." No matter the situation, Sarah could be relied upon to be perfectly candid. "I didn't have any babies to worry about, witchy or otherwise. You and Matthew are going to have to figure it out yourselves."

"I thought you might remember what rules Mom and Dad set out for me when I was a baby," I prompted her.

Sarah thought for a moment. "Nope."

"Don't you remember *anything* about my childhood?" Irritation and worry made my tone especially sharp.

"Not much. I was in Madison with your grandmother. You were in Cambridge. You weren't in 'how about you drop by for a visit' range." Sarah gave a disapproving sniff. "Besides, Rebecca wasn't exactly welcoming."

"Mom was trying to keep Dad's secret—and mine. She wouldn't have been able to lie to you," I said, bristling at the criticism. Witches could smell another witch's falsehoods with the same ease that Matthew's dogs could track deer. "What did Grandma do with you and Mom, when you were growing up?"

"Oh, she was a fan of Dr. Spock. Mom didn't worry too much about what we did, provided we didn't burn the house down," Sarah said.

This was not what I wanted to hear.

"There's no need to be concerned that your children might develop magical talent, Diana," Sarah said soothingly. "Bishops have been doing just that for centuries. You should be thrilled they're showing signs of aptitude at such an early age."

"But Philip and Becca aren't ordinary witches," I said. "They're Bright Borns. They're part vampire."

"Magic will out, vampire blood or no vampire blood." Sarah took another bite of shortbread. "I still don't see why you interrupted our vacation because Philip engaged in a little bit of time-bending. I'm sure it was harmless."

"Because Diana's anxious, Sarah, and she wanted you to make her feel better," Agatha said, her tone suggesting this was perfectly obvious.

"Goddess save us, not again," Sarah said, flinging her hands in the air in frustration. "I thought you were over being afraid of magic."

"Maybe for myself, but not for the children," I said.

"They're babies!" Sarah said, as though this were sufficient reason to cast worry aside. "Besides, you have lots of space and too much furniture. They may break things. So what?"

"Break things?" I was incredulous. "I don't care about *things*. I'm concerned for their safety. I'm afraid that Philip can see time and manipulate it and can't yet walk in a straight line. I'm afraid that he might disappear and I won't be able to find him. I'm afraid that Becca will try to follow him, and end up in an entirely different place and time. I'm afraid that Satu Järvinen will find out, or one of her friends, and demand the witches investigate this precocious manifestation of magic in my children as a way of getting back at me for spellbinding her. I'm afraid that Gerbert will discover that Philip and Becca are even more interesting than he thought they might be, and will become fixated on them."

My voice rose with each new fear until I was practically shouting.

"And I am deathly afraid that this is only the beginning!" I finished.

"Welcome to parenthood," Agatha said serenely. She held out the shortbread. "Have a cookie. You'll feel better. Trust me."

I was a great believer in the power of carbohydrates, but not even Marthe's baking—spectacular though it might be—was going to solve this dilemma.

LATER THAT AFTERNOON, the twins and I were playing on a blanket under the sprawling willow that was tucked into the corner where the moat curved around Les Revenants. We had collected sticks, leaves, flowers, and stones and were arranging them in patterns on the soft wool.

I watched, fascinated, as Philip selected items according to their textures and shapes while Becca preferred sorting her treasures by color. Even at this young age, the twins were developing their own likes and dislikes.

"Red," I told Becca, looking at a bright leaf from a Japanese maple that was kept in a pot in the courtyard, a tightly furled rosebud, and a sprig of cardinal flower.

She nodded, her face scrunched up in concentration.

"Can you find more red?" I asked. There was a reddish pebble, and some bee balm that was such a dark pink that it bordered on crimson.

Becca handed me a green oak leaf.

"Green," I said, putting it next to the rose. Becca immediately moved it and started amassing another pile.

As I watched the children play under a blue sky, the willow branches sighing gently in the wind above us and the grass making a bright cushion under the blanket, the future seemed less dark than it had inside while talking to Sarah and Agatha. I was glad the twins would come of age in a time when playing was seen as a form of learning. The lessons Marcus had been taught in *The New England Primer* were weighted far more toward control than freedom.

Still, I needed to help them find balance—not just between playfulness and discipline, but between the other opposing tendencies in their blood. Magic needed to be part of their lives, but I didn't want them to grow up thinking of witchcraft as a labor-saving device. Nor did I want them to think of it as a tool of revenge or power to hold over others. Instead, I wanted them to equate magic with ordinary moments like these.

I picked up a sprig of *muguet de bois.* The perfumed flowers of lily of the valley always reminded me of my mother, and their white and pink bells looked like ruffled caps that might hide a smiling face inside.

The breeze set the small flowers dancing on their delicate stems.

I whispered to the wind, and the faint sound of bells could be heard. It was a small bit of elemental magic—so small that it didn't stir up the power I'd absorbed along with the *Book of Life.*

Philip looked up, his attention captured by the magical sound.

I blew on the flowers, and the sound of bells grew louder.

"Again, Mama!" Becca said, clapping her hands.

"Your turn." I held the sprig between her lips and mine. Becca pursed her lips and gave a mighty blow. I laughed, and the sound of bells swelled and grew.

"Me. Me." Philip grabbed at the flowers, but I held on to them.

This time, with three witches blowing on the dancing bells, the peals were even louder.

Worried that the sound might carry to warmbloods who would wonder how they could hear church bells so far away from town, I stuck the stem into the ground.

"*Floreto,*" I said, sprinkling some earth over the sprig. The flowers grew larger, and they craned upward. Inside each bell the pale green stamens seemed to form eyes and a mouth around the longer pistil that made up its nose.

By this point the children were mesmerized, staring openmouthed at the floral creature waving its leaves in welcome. Becca waved back.

Matthew appeared, looking concerned. Then he saw the waving lily of the valley, and his expression turned to surprise, then pride.

"I thought I smelled magic," Matthew said softly, joining us on the blanket.

"You did." The stem was beginning to wilt. I decided it was time for the lily of the valley to take a bow and for my impromptu magic show to end.

Matthew clapped in appreciation, and the children joined in. Working magic seldom inspired me to laugh, but on this occasion, it did.

Philip went back to his smooth pebbles and velvety roses, while Becca continued to amass everything green that she could find, running around on the thick grass with unsteady legs. Neither of them seemed to think what I'd done was cause for concern.

"That was a big step," Matthew said, drawing me close.

"I'll always worry when they do magic," I said, settling into Matthew's arms as we watched the twins play.

"Of course you will. I'll worry every time they run after a deer," Matthew replied. He pressed his lips against mine. "But one of a parent's responsibilities is modeling good behavior for their children. You did that today."

"I just hope that Becca waits before delving into spell casting and playing with time," I said. "One budding wizard is all I can handle at the moment."

"Rebecca might not wait for long," Matthew observed, watching his daughter blowing kisses at a rosebud, her expression intent.

"Today, I'm not borrowing trouble. Neither of them has done anything alarming for almost six hours—not since Philip put Cuthbert in the dog's food bowl. I wish I could freeze this moment and keep it forever," I said, staring up at the white clouds scudding across a sky that was brightly blue with possibilities.

"Maybe you have—in their memories, at least," Matthew said.

It was comforting to think that Philip and Becca might, a hundred years from now, recall the day their mother did magic—just for fun, just because she could, just because it was a beautiful May day and there was room for wonder and delight in it.

"I wish being a parent was always this simple," I said with a sigh.

"So do I, *mon coeur.*" Matthew chuckled. "So do I."

"WAIT—YOU JUST ANIMATED a lily of the valley right in front of the twins?" Sarah laughed. "No warning? No rules? Just—poof!"

We were sitting around the long table in the kitchen where we could be close to the cozy stove. The days of the calendar devoted to *les saints de glace*, which in this part of the world signaled the beginning of spring, had officially ended yesterday, but apparently SS. Mamertus, Pancras, and Servatius had not been notified and there was still a touch of frost in the air. A tumbler of *muguet de bois* sat in the middle of the table to remind us of the warm weather to come.

"I would never say 'poof,' Sarah. I used the Latin word for 'flourish' in my spell instead. I'm beginning to suspect the reason so many spells are written in an ancient tongue is so that children will find them harder to utter," I said.

"The children were enchanted—in every sense of the word," Matthew said, giving me a rare, unguarded smile that came straight from the heart. He took my hand in his and pressed a kiss on the knuckles.

"So you've decided to just let go of the illusion of control?" Agatha nodded. "Good for you."

"Not quite," I said hastily. "But Matthew and I agreed long ago that we weren't going to hide who we were from the children. I don't want them learning what magic is from television and the movies."

"Goddess forbid." Sarah shuddered. "All those wands."

"I'm more concerned about the fact that magic is so often portrayed as a shortcut around something tedious, time-consuming, or both." I'd grown up on reruns of *Bewitched*, and though my professorial mother did sometimes say a spell to fold the laundry while she was reviewing her lecture notes, these were by no means daily occurrences.

"So long as we establish clear rules around doing magic, I think they'll be fine," I continued, taking a sip of wine and picking at the platter of greens that was sitting in the center of the table.

"The fewer rules the better," Marcus said. He was staring into the candle flames and checking his phone every five minutes for news from Paris. "My childhood was planted so thick with rules I never took a step without running into one. There were rules about going to church and swearing. Rules about minding my father, and my elders, and my social betters. Rules about how to eat, and how to talk, and how to greet people in the street, and how to treat women like fine china, and how to take care of animals. Rules for planting, and rules for harvesting, and rules for storing food so you didn't starve in the winter.

"Rules may teach you to be blindly obedient, but they're no real protection against the world," Marcus continued. "Because one day you will knock so hard against a rule you'll break it—and you'll have nothing standing between yourself and disaster then. I found that out when I ran away from Hadley to join the first fighting in Boston in 1775."

"You were at Lexington and Concord?" I knew that Marcus was a patriot because of his copy of *Common Sense*. He might have answered the call to arms when the first shots of the war were fired.

"No. In April, I was still obeying my father's rules. He had forbidden me to go to war," Marcus said. "I ran away in June."

Matthew sent a lump of misshapen metal spinning across the table. It was dark, almost singed in places. Marcus caught it.

"A musket ball—an old one." Marcus looked up with a quizzical expression. "Where did you get this?"

"In the library, among Philippe's books and papers. I was looking for something else, but I found a letter from Gallowglass." Matthew reached into the pocket of his jeans and pulled out a folded packet of paper. The handwriting on the outside was scrawling and went up and down like the waves.

We didn't often talk about the big Gael who had disappeared more than a year ago. I missed his easy charm and wicked sense of humor, but understood why watching Matthew and me raise our children and settle into our life as a family might be difficult. Gallowglass had known his feelings for me were unrequited, but until Matthew and I had returned to the present where we belonged, he had remained devoted to the job Philippe had given him, namely to ensure my safety.

"I didn't know Gallowglass was in New England when I was a boy," Marcus said.

"He was working for Philippe." Matthew passed him the letter. Marcus read it aloud.

"'*Grandsire*,'" Marcus began, "'*I was at the Old South Meeting House*

*this morning when Dr. Warren spoke on the fifth anniversary of the late mas-
sacre in Boston. The crowds were very large, and the doctor draped himself in
a white toga, following the Roman style. The Sons of Liberty greeted this
spectacle with cheers.'"*

Marcus looked up from the page, a smile on his face. "I remember
people in Northampton talking about Dr. Warren's speech. Then, we still
thought the massacre had marked the low point in our troubles with the
king, and that we would be able to mend our differences. We had no way
of knowing that a permanent break with England was still to come."

Here, at last, was some history I could use to properly frame Marcus's
account of his life.

"May I?" I held out my hand, eager to see the letter for myself.

Reluctantly, Marcus parted with it.

"*'The numerous links of small and great events, which form the chain on
which the fate of kings and nations is suspended,'*" I said, reading one of the
lines from the letter. It reminded me of what Matthew had said about a
vampire's memory, and how it was often ordinary occurrences that were
preserved there. I thought back to my afternoon playing with the twins,
and wondered again whether today I had planted some future remembrance for them.

"Whoever would have imagined that little more than a month after
Gallowglass wrote this letter, a shot fired on a bridge in a small town outside Boston would become Emerson's *'shot heard around the world,'*" Marcus mused. "The day we decided that King George had mistreated us long
enough started out just like any other April day. I was coming home from
Northampton. It had been a warm spring, and the ground was soft. On
that day, though, the winds from the east blew cold."

Marcus's eyes were unfocused, his tone almost dreamy as he remembered that long-ago time.

"And with them came a rider."

Les Revenants, Letters and Papers of the Americas
No. 1
Gallowglass to Philippe de Clermont
Cambridge, Massachusetts

6 March 1775

Grandsire:

I was at the Old South Meeting House this morning when Dr. Warren spoke on the fifth anniversary of the late massacre in Boston. The crowds were very large, and the doctor draped himself in a white toga, following the Roman style. The Sons of Liberty greeted this spectacle with cheers.

Dr. Warren stirred the assembly with mention of his bleeding country and calls to stand up to a tyrant's power. To avoid war, Warren said, the British army must withdraw from Boston.

It will take only a spark to set rebellion alight. "Short-sighted mortals see not the numerous links of small and great events, which form the chain on which the fate of kings and nations is suspended," Dr. Warren said. I wrote it down in the moment, for it struck me as wise.

I have placed this letter in the hands of Davy Hancock, who will see it safe delivered by the swiftest route. I have returned to Cambridge on your other business. I await your wishes with respect to the Sons of Liberty, but predict that your response will not arrive in time for me to alter what now seems inevitable: The oak and the ivy will not grow stronger together, but will be torn asunder.

Written in haste from the town of Cambridge by your dutiful servant,

Eric

Postscript: I enclose a curious item that was given to me as a memento by one of the Sons of Liberty. He said it was the remains of a musket ball fired by the British into a house on King Street when the citizens were attacked in 1770. There were many tales of that dreadful day shared by those in attendance at Dr. Warren's oration, which further inflamed the passions of those who desire liberty.

⇥ 9 ⇤

Crown

APRIL–JUNE 1775

Marcus juggled the pail of fish between his hands and pushed open the door to Thomas Buckland's Northampton surgery. Buckland was one of the few medical men west of Worcester, and though he was neither the most prosperous nor the best educated, he was by far the safest choice if you wanted to survive a visit to the doctor. The metal bell that hung over the door tinkled brightly, announcing Marcus's arrival.

The surgeon's wife was working in the front room, where Buckland's equipment—forceps, teeth-pullers, and cauterization irons—lay in a gleaming row on a clean towel. Pots of herbs, medicines, and salves were displayed on the shelves. The surgery's windows overlooked Northampton's main street so that interested passersby could witness the pain and suffering going on inside as Buckland set bones, peered into mouths and ears, drew teeth, and examined aching limbs.

"Marcus MacNeil. What are you doing here?" Mercy Buckland looked up from the table where she was putting ointment into a stone crock.

"I was hoping to trade some fish for a bit of that tisane you gave my mother last month." Marcus held up his pail. "Shad. Freshly caught at the falls south of Hadley."

"Does your father know where you are?" Mrs. Buckland had witnessed the argument that broke out a few months ago when Obadiah caught him talking with Tom about how to make a salve to heal bruises. After that, his father had forbidden him from going to Northampton for cures. Obadiah insisted that the family see the nearsighted doctor in Hadley instead, who was half as good and twice as expensive, but whose age and tendency to overindulge in spirits made him less likely to interfere in MacNeil family business.

"There's no point in asking, Mercy. Marcus won't answer. He's become a man of few words." Tom Buckland joined his wife, his balding head shining in the spring light. "For myself, I miss the boy who couldn't stop talking."

Marcus felt Mrs. Buckland's eyes on him as she studied his thin arms, the piece of rope that cinched his breeches to his narrow waist, the hole in the toe of his left shoe, the patches on his blue-and-white-checked shirt made from coarse cloth his sister Patience had woven from the flax grown on their farm.

But he didn't want the Bucklands' pity. He didn't want anything—except some tisane. Marcus's mother was able to sleep after she had some of Mrs. Buckland's famous concoction. The surgeon's wife had taught him what was in it—valerian and hops and skullcap—but these plants weren't grown in the MacNeil family garden.

"Is there news from Boston?" Marcus asked, trying to change the subject.

"The Sons of Liberty are rallying against the Redcoats," Tom replied, peering through his spectacles at the shelves in search of the right herbal mixture. "Everyone is fired up, thanks to Dr. Warren. Someone passing through from Springfield said more trouble is expected—though God hopes it won't be another massacre."

"I heard the same, down at the falls," Marcus replied. It was how news traveled through to small towns like these—one piece of gossip at a time.

Tom Buckland pressed a packet into his hand. "For your mother."

"Thank you, Dr. Buckland," Marcus said, putting his pail on the counter. "These are for you. They'll make a fine dinner."

"No, Marcus. That's too much," Mercy protested. "Half of that bucket is more than enough for Thomas and me. You should take the rest home. I've moved the buttons on Thomas's breeches twice this winter."

Marcus shook his head, refusing the offer. "Thank you, Dr. Buckland. Mrs. Buckland. You keep it. I've got to get home."

Tom tossed him a small crock. "Salve. For the extra fish. We like to keep our accounts current. You could put some of it on your eye."

Tom had noticed the blackening on Marcus's cheekbone. He thought it was faded enough to risk a trip into Northampton without setting any tongues wagging. But Tom was sharp-eyed and didn't miss much.

"I stepped on a hay rake, and the handle hit me square in the face. You know how clumsy I am, Dr. Buckland." Marcus opened the shop door and tipped his moth-eaten hat at the couple. "Thank you for the tisane."

MARCUS BORROWED A RICKETY RAFT to cross the river rather than take the ferry, and was on the puddled road back home when he narrowly avoided being struck down by a rider on a fast horse headed toward the center of Hadley.

"What's happened?" Marcus snatched at the horse's reins in a vain attempt to hold the animal still.

"Our militia engaged the regulars at Lexington. Blood has been shed," the rider cried out, his lungs heaving with effort. He turned the horse's head, ripping the reins from Marcus's grasp, and shot off in the direction of the meetinghouse.

Marcus ran the rest of the way back to the MacNeil farm. He would need food and a gun if he was going to join the militia on the march east. He slid through the damp grass in front of the garden gate, narrowly avoiding a furious goose that snapped at his breeches as he passed.

"Bloody goose," Marcus said under his breath. If not for the eggs, he would have wrung the creature's neck long ago.

He slipped through the front door with its faded red paint. Old Widow Noble said the split in the door's upper panel was a relic of an Indian raid that had taken place in the last century—but the old woman believed in witches, ghosts, and headless horsemen, too. Inside the house was quiet, the only sound the regular ticking of his mother's old clock on the mantel in the parlor.

"I heard the bell." Catherine MacNeil rushed out from the kitchen, the only other room on the ground floor of the house, drying her hands on a worn towel. His mother was pale, and her eyes were dark-rimmed from lack of sleep. The farm wasn't thriving, his father was always off drinking with his friends, and the winter had been hard and long.

"The army attacked in Lexington," Marcus replied. "They're calling out the militia."

"Boston? Is it safe?" As far as Catherine was concerned, the city of her childhood was the center of the world, and everything that was great or good came from there.

At the moment, Marcus was less concerned with the threat Boston faced than with the one that shared their hearth and home.

"Where's Pa?" Marcus asked.

"Amherst. He went to see Cousin Josiah." His mother's lips tightened. "Your father won't be back anytime soon."

Sometimes Obadiah was gone for days and returned with torn clothes and bruises, his knuckles bleeding and his breath smelling of rum. If Marcus was lucky, he could go to Lexington and be back again before his father sobered up and noticed his son was missing.

Marcus went into the parlor and took the old blunderbuss from the hooks over the fireplace.

"Your grandfather MacNeil owned that gun," his mother said. "He had it when he arrived from Ireland."

"I remember." Marcus ran his fingers over the old wooden stock. Grandfather MacNeil had told him stories about his adventures with the gun: the first time he felled a deer when the family didn't have enough to eat, how he'd carried it when they went out to hunt wolves when Pelham and Amherst were just tiny settlements.

"What will I tell your father when he comes back?" His mother looked stricken. "You know he's worried about what might happen if there's another war."

Obadiah had fought in the last war against the French. He had been the flower of the local militia once, brave and strong. Marcus's father and mother had been newly married, and Obadiah had big plans for improving the farm he had purchased, or so Catherine remembered. But Obadiah had returned from the campaigns weak in body and broken in spirit, caught between conflicting loyalties to kin and king.

On the one hand, Obadiah believed wholeheartedly in the sanctity of the British monarchy and the king's love for his subjects. Yet Obadiah had witnessed atrocities on the frontier that made him question whether Britain had her colonies' best interests at heart. Like most of the militia who fought in the war, Obadiah found little to admire about the British army. He believed the officers had knowingly put him in harm's way with their blind obedience to orders that arrived from London weeks—if not months—too late to be of any use.

Between his divided loyalties, the violent nightmares of war that plagued him, and his taste for strong drink, Obadiah could not decide whether their present fight with the king was legitimate or not. The puzzle was slowly driving him mad.

"Tell him you haven't seen me—that you came in from the henhouse and found the gun was gone." Marcus didn't want his mother or his sister to pay the price for his disobedience.

"Your father isn't a fool, Marcus," his mother said. "He'll have heard the bells."

They were still pealing—in Hadley, in Northampton, in every meetinghouse in Massachusetts, probably.

"I'll be home before you know it," Marcus assured his mother. He kissed her on the cheek, shouldered his gun, and headed into town.

He met up with Joshua Boston and Zeb Pruitt outside the town's burial ground, where Zeb was at work digging a grave. It was ringed with tall trees, and the burial stones popped out from the ground at all angles, moss covered and worn from the weather.

"Hey, Marcus," Joshua called out. "You joining in the fight?"

"I thought I might," Marcus replied. "It's time King George stopped treating us like children. Freedom is our birthright as British subjects. Nobody should be able to take it from us, and we shouldn't have to fight for it."

"Or die for it," Zeb muttered.

Marcus frowned. "Don't you mean kill for it?"

"I said what I meant" was Zeb's quick answer. "If a man drinks enough rum, or someone stirs up enough fear and hate in his heart, he'll kill quick enough. But that same man will run from the battlefield the first chance he gets if he doesn't believe what he's fighting for, body and soul."

"Best think hard about whether you have that kind of patriotism, Marcus—before you go marching off to Lexington with the militia," Joshua said.

"Too late." Zeb squinted into the distance. "Here comes Mr. MacNeil, and Josiah with him."

"Marcus?" Obadiah stopped in the middle of the street, peering at him through bloodshot eyes. "Where are you going with my gun, boy?"

It wasn't Obadiah's gun, but Marcus felt sure this wasn't the time to argue the point.

"I asked you a question." Obadiah advanced on them, his steps irregular but still menacing.

"Town. They've called up the militia." Marcus stood his ground.

"You're not going to war against your king," Obadiah said, grabbing at the gun. "It's against God's holy order to defy him. Besides, you're just a child."

"I'm eighteen." Marcus refused to let go.

"Not yet you're not." Obadiah's eyes narrowed and his mouth tightened.

This was usually the moment when Marcus capitulated, eager to keep the peace so that his mother didn't intervene and get caught between her husband and her son.

But today, with Zeb's and Joshua's words ringing in his ears, Marcus felt that he had something to prove—to himself, to his father, and to his friends. Marcus stood taller, ready for a fight.

His father delivered a stinging slap across one cheek and then the other. It was not the blow you would give a man, but a woman or a child. Even in his anger, Obadiah was determined to remind Marcus of his place.

Obadiah wrested the gun from Marcus's hands.

"Go back home to your ma," Obadiah said contemptuously. "I'll see you there. First, I need to have a word with Zeb and Joshua."

His father would beat him when he got back to the farm. From the expression in Obadiah's eye, Zeb and Joshua might receive a thrashing as well.

"They've got nothing to do with it," Marcus said, his cheeks red from his father's blows.

"Enough disobedience, boy," Obadiah barked.

Joshua jerked his head in the direction of the farm. It was a silent request for Marcus to leave before things got even more heated.

He turned his back on his friends, on the war, and on his father and moved down the road toward the MacNeil farm.

Marcus promised himself it was the last time his father would tell him what to do.

IN JUNE, Marcus kept his word by running away to Boston. He had been beaten, several times, since the Lexington alarm. The violence usually began after Marcus questioned his father about something small and innocuous—whether the cows needed to be milked, or if the well was running dry. Obadiah took his questions as further signs of rebellion.

Each blow that his father gave with the folded leather reins seemed to make him calmer, his eyes growing less frantic and his speech less angry. Marcus had learned long ago not to cry while his father beat him, not even when his legs were covered with excruciating welts. Tears only made his father more desperate to exorcise Marcus's demons. Usually Obadiah kept going until Marcus collapsed with pain. Then Obadiah took to the taverns, moving from one to the other until he collapsed, too, in a drunken heap.

It was after one of those beatings, while Obadiah was still out drowning his sorrows, that Marcus had packed a pail of food and the family almanac that outlined the towns on the Boston road so that he could mark his progress, and started walking east.

By the time Marcus reached Cambridge, Harvard Yard was buzzing like a hornet's nest. The college had been emptied of its students, and militia from all over New England now occupied their rooms. When the college halls were filled up, the soldiers erected tents outside without much concern for their relationship to one another, the cobblestone streets, the lampposts, or the flow of sewage. The result was a makeshift encampment, crazed with narrow footpaths like the cracks in old crockery that wended their way between the flapping sheets of canvas, linen, and burlap.

Marcus entered the tent city and what had been a steady hum of activity became a din that rivaled the pounding of British artillery. Regimental musicians roused the inexperienced soldiers for the coming battle with a steady beating of their drums. Dogs, horses, and the occasional mule barked, neighed, and brayed. Men freshly arrived from towns as far away as New Haven to the south and Portsmouth to the north discharged their weapons at the slightest provocation, sometimes deliberately and more often accidentally.

Marcus was following the scent of burned coffee and roasted meat in search of something to eat when a familiar face turned toward him.

"Damn." Marcus had been spotted by someone from back home.

Seth Pomeroy's shrewd eyes settled on him, dark and deeply set over prominent cheekbones divided by a sharp nose. The Northampton gunsmith's forbidding expression proclaimed that this was not a man to meddle with.

"MacNeil. Where's your gun?" Pomeroy's breath was foul—there was a decayed tooth in the front of his mouth that wiggled when he was angry. Tom Buckland wanted to pull it, but Pomeroy was adamantly opposed to dentistry, so the tooth was destined to rot in place.

"My pa has it," Marcus replied.

Pomeroy thrust a musket at Marcus, one of his own and much finer than Grandfather MacNeil's old blunderbuss.

"And does your father know you're here?" Pomeroy asked. Like Mrs. Buckland, Pomeroy knew that Obadiah ruled his family with an iron fist. Nobody did anything without his permission—not if he valued his own hide.

"No." Marcus kept his responses to a minimum.

"Obadiah isn't going to like it when he finds out," Pomeroy said.

"What's he going to do? Disinherit me?" Marcus snorted. Everybody knew the MacNeils didn't have a penny to bless themselves.

"And your mother?" Pomeroy's eyes sharpened.

Marcus looked away rather than answer. His mother didn't need to be part of this. His father had pushed her out of the way when she tried to stop their last argument, and she'd fallen and injured her arm. It still wasn't healed, not even with Tom Buckland's salve and the ministrations of the doctor from Hadley.

"One of these days, Marcus MacNeil, you're going to find someone whose authority you can't wriggle out from under," Pomeroy promised, "but today isn't the day. You're the best shot in Hampshire County and I need every gun I can get."

Marcus joined a line of soldiers. He filed into line next to a gangly fellow about his age wearing a red-and-white-checked shirt and a pair of navy breeches that had seen better days.

"Where you from?" his companion asked during a momentary lull in the action.

"Out west," Marcus replied, not wanting to give too much away.

"We're both country bumpkins, then," the soldier replied. "Aaron Lyon. One of Colonel Woodbridge's men. The Boston boys poke fun at anyone who lives west of Worcester. I've been called 'Yankee' more times than I can count. What's your name?"

"Marcus MacNeil," Marcus said.

"Who you with, Marcus?" Lyon rooted around in a pouch at his waist.

"Him." Marcus pointed at Seth Pomeroy.

"Everybody says Pomeroy is one of the finest gunsmiths in Massachusetts." Lyon produced a handful of dried apple slices. He offered some to Marcus. "Picked last year from our orchard in Ashfield. None better."

Marcus devoured the apples and mumbled his thanks.

Their conversation dropped away to silence when they reached the narrow neck of land that connected Cambridge to Charlestown. It was here that the scope of what awaited them became visible. Lyon whistled through his teeth at their first good look at the smoke coming from the distant prospects of Breed's Hill and Bunker Hill.

The line drew to a halt as Seth Pomeroy stopped to converse with a rotund man on horseback wearing a powdered wig and tricorn hat that sat on his balding head at opposing angles. Marcus recognized the unmistakable profile of Dr. Woodbridge from South Hadley.

"Looks like you're joining up with us," Aaron said, watching the exchange between Pomeroy and Woodbridge.

Woodbridge rode down the line, calmly surveying the soldiers.

"MacNeil, is that you?" Woodbridge squinted. "By God, it is. Go with Pomeroy. If you can put buckshot through a turkey's eye in my back pasture, you can surely hit a Redcoat. You, too, Lyon."

"Yes, sir." Lyon's *s*'s whistled through front teeth that let as much daylight through as the pickets on Madam Porter's fence.

"Where are we going?" Marcus asked Woodbridge, planting his feet a bit farther apart and cradling the gun in his hands.

"You don't ask questions in the army," Woodbridge replied.

"Army?" Marcus's ears pricked at this piece of intelligence. "I'm fight-ing for Massachusetts—in the militia."

"Shows what you know, MacNeil. Congress, in its wisdom, decided thirteen different colonial militias were too much. We're one merry Con-tinental army now. Some gentleman from Virginia—tall man, good on a horse—is headed up from Philadelphia to manage things." Woodbridge spat on the ground, a damning pronouncement intended to cover south-ern landowners, tall men, equestrians, and city folk. "Do as you're told, or I'll send you back to Hadley where you belong."

Marcus reached the Northampton gunsmith just in time to hear him address the motley company of soldiers.

"We don't have much ammunition," Pomeroy explained, handing out small leather pouches, "so no target practice unless it's got two legs and is wearing a British uniform."

"What's our mission, Captain?" A tall man in a buckskin jacket with sandy hair and the sharp eyes of a wolf weighed the pouch in his hand.

"Relieving Colonel Prescott on Breed's Hill. He's stranded there," Pomeroy replied.

There were groans of disappointment. Like Marcus, most of the men wanted to fire upon the British army, not help fellow colonials who'd got-ten themselves into trouble.

Pomeroy's men began their march in silence, the bombardment from British canon shaking the ground and rattling nearby buildings to their foundations. The king's troops were trying to blast to pieces the fragile strip of land they were walking on, thereby cutting Charlestown off from Cambridge. The land rolled under Marcus's feet. Instinctively, he picked up his pace.

"Even the whores left Charlestown when they saw what was coming this way," Lyon said over his shoulder.

"What was coming" looked to be Armageddon, or at least that was Marcus's conclusion once he saw the number of British ships on the Charles River, the heavy bombardment from guns across the water, and the thick plumes of smoke.

Then he caught sight of the masses of red-coated British soldiers marching briskly toward them from a distance, and his bowels turned to water.

When Pomeroy's troops finally met up with the other colonials, Marcus was surprised to discover that some of the soldiers were even younger than he was, like the freckled Jimmy Hutchinson from Salem. Only a few were as old as Seth Pomeroy. But most of the men were around Obadiah's age, including the hatchet-faced captain whose orders Marcus now followed: John Stark of New Hampshire.

"Stark was one of the first rangers," Jimmy whispered to Marcus as they crouched behind a makeshift protective bulwark. Rogers' Rangers were legendary for their keen eyes and steady hands as well as their long rifles, which were accurate at far greater distances than the muskets most men carried.

"One more word out of you, boy, and I'll gag you." Stark had crept up to the front line, silent as a snake. A red flag ornamented with a green pine tree was wound around one hand. Stark fixed his attention on Marcus. "Who the hell are you?"

"Marcus MacNeil." Marcus fought the urge to jump up and stand at attention. "From Hadley."

"You're the one Pomeroy says can shoot straight," Stark said.

"Yes, sir." Marcus couldn't hide his eagerness to prove it.

"See that stake?"

Marcus squinted through a small gap in the hay that had been wadded between the fence rails piled atop the old wall to provide better cover. He nodded.

"When the British reach it, you stand and shoot. Shoot the fanciest uniform you see. The more brass and braid the better," Stark said. "Every man against this fence will do the same.

"Eyes or heart?" Marcus's question earned a smile from the forbidding marksman.

"It doesn't matter," Stark replied, "so long as one shot is all it takes to bring him to his knees. After you discharge your weapon, hit the ground and keep your head down. Once you're down, Cole will shoot with the second line."

Stark pointed to the sharp-eyed man in buckskin. The soldier nodded and touched his hat.

"Once Cole's down," Stark continued, "Hutchinson and the final line will take aim."

The strategy was brilliant. It took a count of twenty to reload a musket, give or take. Stark's plan meant there would be no lull in the attack, in spite of the relatively small number of colonials behind the fence. The British were walking straight into a barrage of fire.

"And then?" Jimmy asked.

Cole and Stark exchanged a long look. Marcus's racing blood stuttered. He'd weighed the pouch when Pomeroy gave it to him, and suspected it contained only enough powder for one shot. That look proved it.

"You just wait by me, Jimmy," Cole said, patting the boy on the back.

War involved far more waiting than it did shooting. It was nearly half a day before the British came into view. As soon as the Redcoats began to approach the stake, however, everything seemed to happen at once.

The fife and drums struck up a tune. The drummer was a boy of no more than twelve, Marcus saw—no older than Patience.

One of the British soldiers whistled along. The rest of the red-coated line picked up the song with enthusiasm, belting out the words with jeers and catcalls.

> *Yankee Doodle came to town,*
> *For to buy a firelock,*
> *We will tar and feather him,*
> *And so we will John Hancock.*

"Bastards." Marcus's finger quivered on the trigger at the insult to one of his heroes, and the president of the recently convened Continental Congress.

"Hold your fire," Cole whispered from behind Marcus, reminding him of Stark's orders.

Then the first of the British soldiers, his red-and-gold uniform flaming in the hazy air, stepped past the stake.

"Fire!" Stark shouted.

Marcus sprang to his feet, along with the front line of men packed along the fence.

A British boy—someone Marcus's age, who looked so like him they might have been cousins—looked directly at him, mouth round with astonishment. Marcus aimed.

"Don't fire until you see the whites of their eyes!" Stark shouted.

The British lad's eyes widened.

Marcus pulled the trigger.

A dark hole appeared in the soldier's eye socket. Blood trickled out, increasing to a flood.

Marcus froze, unable to move.

"Get down!" Cole pulled him to the ground.

Marcus dropped his gun as he fell, his stomach heaving. He was dazed, his ears ringing and his eyes burning.

The British fixed their bayonets with a loud *snick*. The soldiers roared as they ran toward the wall, a hail of bullets accompanying them, hurtling toward the colonials from behind the British line.

Stark waved the red-and-green flag. Cole stood along with the second line of men.

Lying faceup on the ground, Marcus followed a single bullet as it passed overhead. He watched, dumbstruck, as it hit Cole in the chest just as the man was aiming his long rifle. Cole grunted and fell—but not before discharging his weapon.

The British line shouted in surprise. They had not been expecting a second round of fire so soon. Shouts turned to screams as colonial bullets found their marks.

Marcus crawled over to Cole.

"Is he dead?" Jimmy asked, eyes wide. "Oh, God, is he dead?"

Cole's eyes stared at the heavens, unseeing. Marcus knelt, hoping to feel the breath coming from Cole's lungs.

Nothing.

He closed Cole's eyes.

Stark tossed his flag in the air, deliberately drawing British fire.

Jimmy and the remaining colonials stood, took aim, and shot.

The screams and shouting continued on the other side of the wall.

"Fall back! Fall back!" The British officer's command carried on the wind.

"I'll be damned." Stark propped himself up against the stone wall while the farmers, woodsmen, and hunters of New England—now soldiers in this new "Continental Army"—turned to one another in disbelief.

"Well, lads," Stark continued, mopping his brow with his sleeve, "that was a good afternoon's work. Seems you turned aside the great British army."

Cheers rose from the ranks, but Marcus couldn't bring himself to join in. Cole's gun lay in a pool of his blood. Marcus took it and wiped the grip on his sleeve. It was even finer than the one Pomeroy had loaned him. And he might need another gun before the day was through.

God knew the New Hampshire man didn't. Not anymore.

THE REST OF THE BATTLE passed in a blur of blood, buckshot, and chaos. There was no water, no food, and little respite from the fighting.

Stark and his men turned the British aside again.

When the British attacked a third time, the exhausted colonists had no ammunition to fight back.

The heartiest and the oldest men volunteered to stand at the wall while the rest retreated.

They were almost across the neck and safely back in Cambridge when Jimmy Hutchinson suddenly fell, a piece of shot embedded in his neck. Blood spatters mixed with the freckles on the boy's face.

"Am I gonna die like Mr. Cole?" Jimmy's voice was faint.

Marcus ripped the bloodstained sleeve from his own shirt and tried to stanch the flow.

"Not today." If it gave Jimmy a shred of hope to cling to—though Marcus knew the boy would curse fate before his ordeal was over—how could it hurt?

Marcus took a coat from a dead British soldier. He and Aaron Lyon made a makeshift stretcher out of it. Together, they carried Jimmy toward the camp hospital that had been set up in Harvard Yard.

The area smelled like a charnel house, the scent of blood and singed flesh filling the air. It sounded even worse. Groans and pleas for water were punctuated by screams of soldiers in agony.

"Bless me, is that Jimmy Hutchinson?" A stout woman, fiery headed with a pipe clenched between her teeth, appeared out of the smoky twilight, barring their way.

"Mistress Bishop?" Jimmy said weakly, blinking up at her. "Is that you, ma'am?"

"Who else?" Mistress Bishop replied tartly. "What fool let you come up here and get yourself shot? You're not even fifteen."

"Ma doesn't know," Jimmy explained, his eyes rolling shut.

"I should think not. You should have stayed in Salem, where you belong." Mistress Bishop gestured to Marcus. "Don't just stand there. Bring him here."

Here was not the direction that most of the wounded were being carried. *Here* was a small fire, with a group of makeshift beds arranged around it. *Here* all was quiet, as opposed to *there*, where shouts and cries and utter bedlam proclaimed the location of the surgeons.

Marcus eyed the woman with suspicion.

"You can take him to Dr. Warren if you want to, but Jimmy's chances of surviving are better with me." Mistress Bishop shifted her pipe from the left side of her mouth to the right.

"We left Dr. Warren on Breed's Hill," Marcus said, pleased to show up the woman as a liar.

"Not that Dr. Warren, you dolt. The other one." Mistress Bishop was equally delighted to let Marcus know he was a conceited fool. "I reckon I'm more familiar with the medical men of Boston than you are."

"I want to stay with Mistress Bishop," Jimmy mumbled. "She's a healer."

"That's a polite term for it, Jimmy," Mistress Bishop said. "Now, are you two louts going to carry my patient to the fire, or do I have to do it?"

"He's got a piece of shot in his neck," Marcus hurriedly explained as they lugged Jimmy the last few yards. "I think it cut through the veins. It could be lodged in the artery, though. Some of the flesh around it is black, but that could be a burn. I tied my sleeve around his neck as tight as I dared."

"So I see." Mistress Bishop picked up a pair of nips, a rushlight pinched between them. She peered into the wound. "What's your name?"

"Marcus MacNeil. Here." Marcus fished around in his pocket and pulled out a bit of candlewood he'd brought from home. The resinous pine splinter would cast a brighter glow than the flickering rushlight. He thrust the end of it in the flame. The wood caught immediately.

"I thank you." Mistress Bishop swapped her nips for the candlewood. "You know your way around a body. Are you one of those Harvard boys?"

Her look of derision was reason enough to deny it. Mistress Bishop clearly had no use for the college educated.

"No ma'am. Hadley," Marcus replied, his eyes pinned to Jimmy's pallid face and blue-tinged lips. "I don't think he's getting enough air."

"None of us are. Not with all this smoke." Mistress Bishop contributed to it by drawing on her pipe. She sighed, a fug of tobacco surrounding her, and looked down at Jimmy. "He'll sleep a bit now."

Marcus knew better than to ask whether Jimmy would wake up.

"It took me eighteen hours to bring that boy into the world, and no time at all for some idiot with a gun to steal him away." Mistress Bishop pulled a small bottle out of her pocket. "War is such a waste of women's time."

Mistress Bishop used her teeth to pull the cork from the bottle and spat it into the fire. It popped and sizzled for a moment before igniting in the flames. She took a substantial swig and offered it to Marcus.

"Thank you, no." Marcus still felt as though his stomach could rise up at any moment. Memories of the battle struggled to the surface of his mind.

He had killed a man. Somewhere in England, a mother was waking up without a son—and it was his fault.

"Think about that weeping mother *before* you pull the trigger next time," Mistress Bishop said, returning the flask to her own lips.

Somehow, the woman had divined the contents of Marcus's guilty conscience. Alarmed and overwhelmed, Marcus clapped a hand over his mouth as his guts heaved. Mistress Bishop looked at him sharply, her hazel eyes snapping.

"Don't you dare go all missish on me. I haven't got time for your nonsense. One of the Proctor boys broke his leg running away from the guns. Fell in a hole. First sensible story of battle I've heard today." Mistress Bishop took another swig from her bottle, then lumbered to her feet. She beckoned for Marcus to follow.

Marcus remained where he was until his innards returned to their natural place. It took rather longer than the redheaded healer found acceptable.

"Well?" she demanded, standing over a prone soldier whose eyes were bugged out from pain and fear. "Are you going to faint, or are you going to help me?"

"I've never set a broken leg." Marcus felt that honesty was the best policy with Mistress Bishop.

"You've never killed a man, either. There is a first time for everything," Mistress Bishop said tartly. "Besides, I'm not asking you to set it. You're going to hold him down while I do it."

Marcus stood at the man's head.

"No, not there." Bishop's patience had been spent. "Hold his hip here and his thigh there." She placed Marcus's hands in the proper position.

"You have anything to drink, Sarah?" the man croaked.

Marcus thought a drink was a very good idea, based on the angle of the soldier's ankle relative to his knee. It looked as though the tibia had snapped in two.

She slapped her flask into Marcus's palm. "You have a sip first, then give John a swig. You've gone all green again."

This time, Marcus accepted her offer. The liquid burned a path down his throat. He held the bottle to the soldier's lips.

"Thank you," the man whispered. "You got anything else for the pain, Sarah? Anything stronger, I mean?"

A long look passed between the soldier and the healer.

Sarah shook her head. "Not here, John Proctor."

"It was worth asking." Proctor sighed and laid back. "The rum will have to do."

"You ready, MacNeil?" Sarah clamped her pipe between her teeth.

Before Marcus could respond, or indeed even fully understand the question, Sarah Bishop had pulled the bones back into place, the muscles in her arms rigid with effort.

Proctor howled in agony, then passed out from the shock.

"There, there. All done." Sarah patted Proctor's leg. "Not shy with their feelings, the Proctors."

Marcus thought the patient had been remarkably composed considering the seriousness of the injury, but he held his tongue.

Sarah pointed to the rum. "Have some more of that. And the next time you set a bone, remember to do it just like I did: immobilize the limb, then put your back into one good tug. You'll do less harm that way. There's no point in being so timid with the bones that you shred the muscles to pieces."

"Yes, ma'am." It had been difficult for Marcus to obey Woodbridge's orders, but Sarah Bishop was another matter.

"I've got more men to treat." Sarah's pipe had gone out, but she kept chewing on it anyway, as though it gave her comfort.

"Should I stay and help?" Marcus wondered whether healing some other mother's son would help him feel more at peace with the fact that he had taken a life.

"No. Go back to Hadley," Sarah replied.

"But the fighting isn't over." Marcus looked around at the casualties. Men had been killed, maimed, fatally wounded. "They need every gun they can get. Freedom—"

"There are ways to serve the cause of liberty that don't involve bloodshed. The army is going to require surgeons far more than soldiers." Mistress Bishop pointed the end of her pipe at him. Her eyes were dark, the pupils huge. Marcus shivered at the sight. It must have been the drink and the smoke that made her look so strange.

"Your time has not yet come," she continued, her voice dropping to a whisper. "Until it does, go home where you belong, Marcus MacNeil. Be ready. When the future beckons, you'll know it."

⇥ 10 ⇤

Three

15 MAY

Miriam dropped off the cat early in the morning on Phoebe's third day of being a vampire. It was black and substantial of build, with a white nose, four white feet, and a white-tipped tail.

"It's time you fed yourself," Miriam said, putting the carrier next to the bed. Inside, the cat made plaintive mewling noises. "I need a break from this relentless motherhood. Freyja, Charles, and Françoise are here, but they won't answer calls for food or drink."

Phoebe's stomach growled at Miriam's words, but it was more out of sympathetic habit than hunger. Where Phoebe now felt the gnawing sensation of *want* was in her veins and in her heart. Like her center of gravity, her appetite had moved up from her belly in a way that seemed impossible based on her study of biology.

"Remember, Phoebe. It's best not to talk to your food. Don't dote on it. Leave it in the cage until you're ready to feed," Miriam instructed in the schoolmarm tone that sent Marcus and Matthew scurrying for their test tubes and computers when she was managing their Oxford biochemistry lab.

Phoebe nodded.

"And for God's sake," Miriam added as she went out the door, "don't name it."

Phoebe released the door to the cage immediately after she heard the front door snick closed. The terrible twos were lingering, and her rebellious streak showed no signs of disappearing.

"Come here, kitty," Phoebe crooned. "I don't want to harm you."

The cat, which knew better, plastered itself against the rear of the carrier and hissed, its back arched and its teeth—sharp, white, pointed—exposed.

Impressed by the cat's display of ferocity, Phoebe drew back to study her first proper meal. The cat, sensing an opportunity for escape, ran out from the carrier and wedged itself behind the wardrobe.

Intrigued, Phoebe settled down on the floor and waited.

TWO HOURS LATER, the cat decided Phoebe meant no immediate harm and ventured to the rug in front of the closed door to the hallway, as though planning to bolt at the first opportunity.

Phoebe had grown bored waiting for the cat to make its next move and spent the intervening time examining her own teeth in the cracked windowpane. There were only a few hours when this was possible, Phoebe discovered, when the light hit the glass just right. Everything else that was shiny had been taken away last night for fear that Phoebe would become mesmerized by her own reflection and, Narcissus-like, find it impossible to break the fascination.

Phoebe ached for a mirror again almost as much as she ached for Miriam's blood. The window glass provided some reflection, but she wanted to study her teeth in detail. Could they really have become so sharp that they would be able to bite through fur, skin, fat, and sinew and reach the cat's life source?

What if my teeth aren't up to it? Phoebe wondered.

What if one breaks? Do vampire teeth regenerate?

Phoebe's active vampire mind skittered to life, hopping from question to question.

Can vampires feed without teeth?

Are they like infants, dependent on others for their sustenance?

Is pulling teeth a death sentence as well as a mark of shame, like taking a thief's hand so that he can't steal again?

"Stop." Phoebe said it aloud. The cat looked up and blinked at her, unimpressed. It stretched, kneading the plush surface of the carpet before returning to a wary knot.

"You still have claws." Of course, Miriam had not stooped to providing her with a defenseless cat. Along with the sharp teeth that the cat had already displayed, the claws were proof that this cat needed to be taken seriously.

"You're a survivor. Like me." The cat was missing the tip of one ear, no doubt lost in some alley fight. It was no great beauty, yet something in its eyes touched Phoebe's heart—a weariness that spoke of struggle and a longing for home.

Phoebe wondered whether, one day when Freyja and Miriam finally allowed her to have a mirror again, she would see the same look in her own eyes. Would her eyes have changed? Would they continue to do so, growing hard and haunted, looking older even though the rest of her did not?

"Stop." Phoebe said it loudly enough this time that the word echoed slightly in the sparsely furnished room. After two days of having people run to her aid whenever she so much as sighed in disappointment, Phoebe found the lack of response from the household both disconcerting and strangely liberating.

Miriam and Marcus had assured her, weeks ago, that her first attempt at feeding from a living creature would not be tidy. They had also warned that whatever unfortunate being Phoebe fed from the first time would not survive. There would be too much trauma—not necessarily physical, but certainly mental. The animal would struggle in her grip and probably frighten itself to death, its system flooded with so much adrenaline that the heart would explode.

Phoebe studied the cat. Perhaps she was not as hungry as she thought.

FOUR HOURS AFTER the cat arrived, Phoebe was able to scoop it into her lap when it was sleeping. She picked it up, all four limbs hanging as if they were boneless, and climbed onto the bed with it. Phoebe dropped into a cross-legged position and deposited the cat into the hollow between her thighs.

Phoebe stroked the cat's soft fur, keeping her touch featherlight. She didn't want to break the spell and send the cat, hissing, to its former retreat behind the wardrobe. She was afraid her hunger might overwhelm her and that, in an effort to get to the beating heart of the cat, she might upend the wardrobe and crush the animal to death before she was able to drink from it.

"How much do you weigh?" Phoebe murmured, her hand continuing to work along the cat's spine. The cat started a low purring. "Not much, even though you're being well fed."

The cat couldn't have much blood, Phoebe realized, and her hunger was considerable—and growing. Her veins felt dry and flat, as though her body didn't hold enough life-giving fluid to round them out to their normal circumference.

The cat pushed slightly against Phoebe's legs before forming itself into a slightly more relaxed loop. The cat sighed, contented and warm. These were instinctive gestures of nesting—of belonging.

Phoebe reminded herself that the cat wouldn't survive what she was about to do.

And for God's sake, don't name it. Miriam's warning echoed in Phoebe's mind.

PHOEBE HADN'T BEEN fed for twelve hours, sixteen minutes, and twenty-four seconds. She had done the math and knew that she was going to have to feed soon or risk becoming frenzied and cruel. Phoebe was determined not to be that kind of vampire; she had heard enough stories of Matthew's early days, told with great gusto by Ysabeau, to want to avoid such unpleasant scenes.

The cat was still sleeping in Phoebe's lap. During the hours they'd spent together, Phoebe had learned a great deal about the animal—including her sex, which was female, her fondness for having her tail pulled slightly, and how much she disliked having her paws touched.

The cat still didn't trust her enough to let Phoebe stroke her belly. What predator would? When Phoebe tried, the cat scratched her in protest, but the scratches healed almost immediately, leaving no mark behind.

Phoebe's fingers still moved, repeatedly and rhythmically, through the cat's fur, hoping for some further signs of yielding, of friendship. *Of permission.*

But the contrapuntal sound of the cat's heartbeat and the hollowness in Phoebe's veins had gone from insistent, to alluring, to maddening. Together, they had become intertwined in a song of suppressed desire.

Blood. Life.

Blood. Life.

The song pulsed through the cat's body, one heartbeat at a time. Phoebe bit her lip in frustration, making it bleed for a fraction of a second before it healed. She had been gnawing at her own lips for the last hour, tasting the salt, knowing it would not satisfy her hunger but unable to stop herself.

The cat opened her eyes slightly at the rich scent, her pink nose quivering. Once the cat determined it wasn't fish, or a piece of meat, she fell back into slumber.

Phoebe bit her lip again, harder and deeper this time. The taste of salt flooded her mouth, savory but empty of nutrients. It was a promise of nourishment, nothing more. Phoebe's mouth watered at the prospect of a meal.

Once again, the cat lifted her head, her green eyes fixed on Phoebe.

"Want a taste?" Phoebe ran her finger over her lip, smearing it with a bead of blood. The skin knit together behind her fingertip. Already the blood on her finger had darkened to a rich violet. Moving quickly, before it dried to black, Phoebe offered it to the cat.

Curious, the cat's pink tongue lapped at Phoebe's finger. Its sandy texture made Phoebe shiver with hunger and longing.

Then something extraordinary happened.

The cat's eyes drifted closed, a tiny bit of pink tongue extended.

Phoebe poked at it but the cat didn't stir.

She ran her fingers lightly over the cat's belly.

Nothing.

"Oh, God, I've killed it!" Phoebe whispered.

Phoebe poked it again, trying to rouse it, and felt a sense of panic. No one would come to save her—not for hours or days. Miriam—her maker, the woman who Phoebe had chosen to give her a new life—had made sure of that. Phoebe would pass out from hunger, the dead cat in her lap. She couldn't feed from a dead thing. It was worse than necrophilia, an abhorrence to a vampire.

Blood. Life. Blood. Life.

The pulsing beat of the song continued, though its cadence was slower.

Dimly, Phoebe recognized it.

A heartbeat. Not hers.

The cat wasn't dead.

It was asleep.

No, Phoebe realized, *the cat was drugged.* She looked down at her finger, which still held traces of purple.

Her vampire blood had put the cat into a state of suspended animation. Phoebe remembered Marcus and Miriam talking about this, and how some vampires abused the soporific effects of their blood, doing unspeakable things to warmbloods after they fed from them.

Phoebe lifted the cat to her nose, the animal's body feeling even more boneless and peltlike than it had before. The cat didn't smell particularly appetizing. Its scent was musky and dry.

Blood. Life. Blood. Life. The cat's slow-beating heart sang into the quiet room. The sound was tempting, tormenting.

Phoebe pressed her lips to the cat's neck, instinctively seeking food. Surely the blood was closest to the skin's surface there. Why else would so many human stories about vampires focus on the neck? Freyja and Miriam had gone over the circulatory system of mammals with her, but, in the hunger of the moment, Phoebe wasn't able to recall a single relevant piece of information.

The cat squirmed in Phoebe's hands. Even under the influence of vampire blood, its instinct to survive hadn't dimmed. The cat sensed a predator—one far more dangerous than she.

Phoebe's mouth moved across the cat's shoulder, taking in the texture of the fur. She grasped a tiny fold of skin between her teeth and bit down a fraction of an inch—the tiniest amount possible—and waited for the blood to fill her mouth.

Nothing.

Don't worry about the mess, Phoebe dear, Freyja had said last night when she checked on Phoebe, sounding almost cheerful at the prospect of a bloodbath. *We will clean it up afterward.*

After you destroy this cat, Phoebe thought. *After you feed. After you survive at some other creature's expense.*

Phoebe's civilized mind rebelled at the prospect, and her stomach followed, heaving and clenching in a futile effort to expel its contents—but it was empty.

There had to be something to eat besides the cat, Phoebe thought. She had drained the carafe hours ago, and the two bottles of Pellegrino that Françoise had given her when Phoebe complained that the flat water tasted unpleasantly metallic. Phoebe hadn't been able to stomach wine—not even wine from Burgundy, which had always been her favorite—so Freyja had taken it away.

Phoebe had even downed the water in the vase on the windowsill. She eyed the flowers strewn on the carpet, wondering whether she could snack on the stems as she had once done on celery, but the thought of so much greenery made her stomach revolt.

She got to her feet, placing the cat on the bed, and searched through her purse. There had to be *something* in there to eat—chewing gum, a throat pastille, a piece of stale biscuit that had fallen out of the wrapper. She tipped the contents onto the bed around the slumbering cat.

Tissues, crumpled.

Receipts, folded in half.

Driver's license.

Passport.

Notebook for jotting down tasks.

A single grubby Polo mint, some fluff and a curl of pencil shaving stuck to it.

Phoebe's hand moved like a snake and snagged the mint. She pried a one-cent euro off the back and popped the mint into her mouth. She closed her eyes in anticipation of the rush of peppermint and sugar.

The mint in her mouth turned to paste. Phoebe spat it across the room, where it pinged as it hit the window.

Another crack, Phoebe thought with sorrow.

The cat stretched, sighed, and turned her belly and paws heavenward, filling the room with a musky scent. She no longer smelled dry and unappealing. Now, with Phoebe's hunger mounting, she smelled glorious.

Phoebe took the cat's decision to expose her soft underbelly as the long-awaited sign of permission. Moving quickly, before she lost her nerve, Phoebe bent over the cat and bit decisively into her neck. Phoebe's mouth filled with the coppery tang of blood. It was not as satisfying as Miriam's, but it was fuel and would keep her from going mad.

After three swallows the cat began to stir. Phoebe withdrew reluctantly from the animal, her fingers pressing into the spot in its neck where she had taken its blood, and waited for the cat to die.

But the cat was a survivor. She studied Phoebe with glazed eyes. Deliberately, Phoebe brought her thumb to her teeth. She bit down. Hard.

The cat lapped the blood with the same curiosity as before, and returned to dozing.

Phoebe drank six more swallows of blood before the cat stirred again. The warm drink had taken the edge off her hunger, though Phoebe was far from satiated. She used a bit more of her blood to help the wound on the cat's neck scab over so that a second set of sheets was not ruined. Phoebe could not afford to further annoy Françoise, bringer of Pellegrino and *Hello!* magazines.

The cat woke from her induced slumber when the clocks in the house sounded the half hour. Phoebe removed the tasseled rope that tied back one of the curtains, and she and the cat played with it until the clocks struck the hour.

It was then that Phoebe knew that she and the cat would not be parted. Not by death. Not by another vampire. They belonged together.

"What should I call you?" Phoebe wondered aloud.

IT HAD BEEN TWENTY-FOUR HOURS since Phoebe had fed from Miriam.

A gentle knock on the door announced the arrival of her visitors. Phoebe had heard them coming up the stairs like a herd of elephants, waking the cat.

"Come in," Phoebe called, her body curved protectively around the purring bundle. She pulled on the cat's tail and scratched the bridge of her nose, much to the animal's delight.

"You've done remarkably well, Phoebe," Freyja said, her eyes taking a quick inventory of the room. There was not a speck of blood anywhere. "Where's the body?"

"There isn't a *body*." Phoebe "There's a cat. And she's right here."

"She's not dead," Miriam said, sounding slightly impressed.

"*She* is called Persephone," Phoebe replied.

⇥ 11 ⇤

Liberty and Restraint

"There's a griffin on the second-floor landing." Sarah entered the library in a cloud of bergamot and lavender. Agatha had been in the fragrant stillroom next to the kitchen, experimenting with essential oils. Inspired by their recent trip to Provence, Agatha was considering launching a line of signature scents.

I looked up from my desk, where I was trying to put what Marcus had told us last night into some kind of context. What was available online was little help. Most accounts of the early years of the American Revolution focused on battle strategies or the occupation of Boston. Few focused on western Massachusetts, the socioeconomic effects of the French and Indian Wars, or generational conflicts between fathers and sons. I would need access to a proper research library to learn more.

"It's quite good, isn't it?" I said absently, returning my attention to my notes.

The tapestry that hung on the wall had a rich red background, and the profuse flowers that surrounded the woven griffin brightened up what would otherwise have been a dark space.

"Ysabeau bought it in the fifteenth century. Phoebe thinks it came from the same workshop that produced the unicorn tapestries at the Musée de Cluny in Paris," I continued. "What was the first name of that gunsmith Marcus mentioned? Saul? Stephen? I want to look him up in this encyclopedia of Massachusetts soldiers and sailors I found online."

"Seth. And I am not talking about Ysabeau's old carpet." Sarah held out a bleeding index finger. "I mean a live griffin. It's small, but its beak works."

I scrambled to my feet and dashed toward the stairs.

The griffin who had taken a bite out of Sarah was sitting before the tapestry, cooing and chattering to its much larger woven sister. From beak to tip of the tail, it was about two feet long, with front legs, head, and neck that resembled those of an eagle, and the hindquarters and tail of a lion. Its beak and talons were formidable looking, in spite of its relatively small size.

I approached the beast with caution. It let out a warning chortle.

"Go on. Pick it up." Sarah pushed me toward the griffin.

"You told me never to touch an unfamiliar magical object," I said, resisting her efforts. "I think a griffin qualifies."

"Object?" The griffin let out a raspy squawk of indignation.

"Oh no. It talks." Sarah got behind me.

"*It* talks." The griffin's feathered neck ruffled.

"We should leave it alone," I said. "Maybe it will go back where it belongs."

"*It,*" the griffin parroted back.

"Can you weave a magical leash for it, like the one you made for Philip so that he doesn't fall down the stairs?" Sarah suggested, peering over my shoulder.

"You weren't supposed to notice that." Even when I called my son's magical restraint by the early modern name "leading strings," my discomfort with it remained.

"Well, I noticed. So did Philip." Sarah gave me a push. "Hurry. You don't want it to escape."

The tiny griffin spread its wings, which were surprisingly wide and gloriously colored with tawny shades of eagle and lion.

Sarah and I scrambled back into the library, like two prim Victorian ladies who had spotted a mouse.

"I don't think it likes the idea of being confined," I said.

"Who does?" Sarah asked.

"Well, we can't just let it fly around inside the house. Remember how much trouble Corra caused." I gathered my resources, took a deep breath, and walked calmly toward the creature. Ten feet away from it, I raised a warning finger and addressed the griffin. "Stay."

The griffin hopped in my direction. Mesmerized by the odd sight, I remained where I was. The griffin was so close now that I could have bent down and picked it up—had that sharp beak not deterred me.

"It. Stay." The griffin planted one of its heavy front talons on my foot, one of the points barely piercing my sneaker in warning.

"Not me. You stay!" I said, trying without success to free myself from the sharp claw.

Unimpressed by my attempts to bring him to heel, the griffin puffed out his chest and rummaged around in his own wing feathers.

Sarah and I bent down to watch, fascinated by the bird's grooming ritual.

"Do you think it might have lice?" Sarah whispered.

"I hope not," I replied. "Why on earth did you summon a griffin, Sarah?"

"There are no spells for summoning mythical beasts in the Bishop grimoire. If you spent more time studying your family's heritage, and less time sniffing at it, you would know that," huffed Sarah. "You're the one with the dragon. You must have called it. You were working magic the other day. Maybe you shook something loose."

"I animated a flower!" It was hardly a work of earth-shattering power. "And I never summoned Corra—who was a firedrake, by the way. She just showed up when I worked my first spell."

Sarah blanched. "Uh-oh."

Our heads turned in the direction of the nursery.

"Shit," I said, biting my lip. "The griffin must belong to Philip."

"What are you going to do?" Sarah asked.

"Catch the griffin," I replied. "After that—I honestly don't know."

It took the combined efforts of two witches, a daemon, and a vampire to capture the small but remarkably agile creature.

Agatha lured it toward Tabitha's beat-up plastic pet carrier with bits of duck meat. The griffin's long pink tongue extended like a whip to snatch the succulent morsels from her fingers.

"Come here, baby." Agatha was already half in love with the beast. "What a pretty griffin. Such splendid feathers."

The griffin, feeling properly appreciated, took step after cautious step in the direction of the snacks.

"Is it trapped?" Marthe asked from below. She was both our lookout and our last line of defense in case the griffin made a run for it.

The griffin croaked ominously and lashed its tail. Marthe made the tiny beast anxious. Though the griffin was doubly predatory with its mixed lion and eagle heritage, a vampire represented a higher link on the food chain. Every time Marthe made the slightest movement, the griffin beat its wings and gave a bloodcurdling cry of warning.

"Not yet, Marthe," I called, standing by the open door to the cage. Sarah stood on the other side of the plastic box, ready to clap the metal grill shut. Years of taking Tabitha to the vet had given her considerable experience in catching skittish animals.

Agatha dangled another piece of duck in front of the griffin, who snatched it away and swallowed with gusto.

"You're doing great, Agatha." Sarah was giving Agatha as much encouragement as Agatha was giving the griffin. "It's mesmerized."

"Such a beautiful baby. I love that shade of brown in your tail. Maybe next autumn's clothing line will be griffin themed," Agatha crooned, placing the pieces of duck in a row that led straight to the door of the cat carrier. "What do you think of that idea, my little lovely?"

"It," the griffin said happily, pecking at the duck.

The scent of food woke Tabitha from her nap. The cat shot across the landing, bristling with indignation over the fact that she had not been invited to Agatha's feast. She stopped abruptly, eyes fixed on the griffin.

"Do eagles eat cats?" I whispered.

"They better not!" Sarah said, alarmed.

Tabitha was no ordinary cat, however, but a superior feline who was more than a match for our new arrival. She stalked past the griffin without a backward glance, rubbed herself against Agatha to indicate prior ownership, picked up a piece of duck meat in her sharp teeth, and sailed into the carrier with her tail straight up in the air like a flag. Tabitha circled on the fleecy cushion, twisting herself into a small knot of gray fur before letting out a mighty sigh of contentment.

The griffin ambled in after Tabitha, its front legs hopping like a bird and back legs striding like a lion. Once it had crammed itself in, the griffin lay down, its tail circling Tabitha protectively, and closed its eyes.

Sarah slammed the door shut.

One of the griffin's eyes popped open. It extended its talons through the metal grid in a luxurious feline stretch and settled in for a nap.

"Is it—purring?" Agatha asked, cocking her head to listen.

"That must be Tabitha," I replied. "Surely griffins don't purr. Not with an eagle's neck. Different voice box."

A guttural snoring issued from the depths of the carrier.

"Nope. *That*'s Tabitha," Sarah said with a touch of pride.

ONCE AGAIN, Matthew discovered me in the library. This time I was going through the mythology books in search of information on the care and feeding of griffins. Our ghostly librarians, still determined to help, kept handing me the same book over and over.

"Thank you—again—but all Pliny says is that the griffin is imaginary," I told one nebulous form before returning the book to the shelf. "Since there's one downstairs, I'm not paying much attention to him. Isidore of Seville is far more useful. You would be far more useful, too, if only you would go and arrange the dictionaries."

"I understand there's been some excitement." Matthew was on the floor below, his hand resting on the railing that protected the way to the upper shelves.

"Oh, good," I said, opening the next volume on the shelf. It was ancient. "Another copy of the *Physiologus*, this one from the tenth century, to go with the six other copies I've found. How many of these did Philippe need?"

"Authors can't resist owning multiple copies of their books, or so I've been told," Matthew said, swinging himself up and over the railing to land, catlike, on the stairs. "I can't say for sure, since I've never published one. But you have at least two copies of yours, as I recall."

"Are you suggesting your father was the author of the most influential bestiary in the Western tradition?" I stood, dumbfounded, with the (seventh and counting) copy in my hands.

"You would know better than I about its importance. Philippe was certainly proud of it. He bought every copy he came across. I think he was largely responsible for its success, to be honest." Matthew took the book from me. "Do you want to tell me why there's a griffin in the pantry?"

"Because we can't put it in the barn. Griffins don't get along with horses." I took another book from the shelf and leafed through the pages. "Lambert of Saint-Omer. Who is that?"

"A Benedictine cleric. Friend of Gerbert's, I think. Lived up north." Matthew took that book away from me, too.

"Did everybody write an animal encyclopedia in the Middle Ages? And why does no one cover the important topics, like how large griffins are likely to become, or how to keep them fed and amused?" I continued to scour the shelves, convinced—as I always had been—that the answers to my questions could be found in books.

"Probably because few had ever seen one up close, and those that had were not disposed to think of them as pets." The dark vein in Matthew's forehead pulsed slightly in irritation. "What on earth possessed you to conjure up a griffin, Diana? And why can't you get rid of it?"

"It's not my griffin." I would have kept going, separating out the bestiaries from the books about fabled lands, the books on ancient gods and goddesses, and the accounts of the lives of Christian saints, but Matthew put himself between me and the shelves with the attitude of someone determined to thwart progress.

"So the griffin *is* Philip's familiar," Matthew said. "I didn't believe Sarah when she told me."

"He might be." Familiars appeared when a weaver wove their first spell. They were a set of magical training wheels that helped to guide a weaver's unpredictable talents as they developed. "Except our children are Bright Born, not weavers."

"And how much do we really know about Bright Borns and their abilities?" Matthew asked, one brow raised in query.

"Not much," I admitted. Weavers were witches with daemon blood in their veins. Bright Borns were creatures born to a weaver mother and a vampire father afflicted with blood rage, a genetic condition that could also be traced back to daemon blood. They were as rare as unicorns.

"Isn't it possible that Philip could be both a Bright Born *and* a weaver, or that Bright Borns have familiars, too?"

There was only one way to find out.

"Move slowly," Matthew told Philip. "Keep your hand flat, like you do with Balthasar."

That Matthew let Philip anywhere near his enormous, fickle stallion had always been cause for concern, but I had reason to be grateful for it today.

Our son toddled toward the griffin and me, the fingers of one hand grasping Matthew and the palm of the other bearing a Cheerio. Becca sat between Sarah and Agatha, watching the proceedings with interest.

The griffin chortled and cooed, lending Philip its encouragement—or possibly just begging for the Cheerio.

Philippe's mythology books had been no help at all when it came to the care and feeding of griffins. We had to figure out what the creature liked through a process of trial and error. Thus far the griffin had been satisfied with more duck, generous helpings of cereal, and sporadic visits from Tabitha, who brought it a vole when it was beginning to get peckish.

"Good Lord, it's huge." Marcus studied the griffin's back paws. "And it's only going to get bigger if the size of its feet are anything to go by."

As Philip got closer to the griffin, the griffin began to hop up and down with excitement, clacking its beak and swishing its tail.

"Sit. Stay. Down. G'boy." Philip, who was used to living with dogs and therefore familiar with all the nonsense adults said to them in an effort to curb their behavior, spouted out the commands as he continued to advance.

The griffin sat.

Then it lowered its body between its paws and waited.

"Well, Diana, you wanted proof the griffin belonged to Philip," Sarah said. "I think you have it."

Philip extended the Cheerio to the griffin. All the adults in the room held their breath as the griffin studied the piece of cereal.

"Treat," Philip said.

The griffin leaped up to a sitting position and took the small oat hoop. As he swallowed the cereal down, I counted to be sure that all of Philip's fingers were still attached to his hand. Mercifully, they were.

"Yay!" Philip hugged the griffin with great enthusiasm and pride. Its beak was perilously close to my child's delicate ear. I moved to separate them.

"I wouldn't interfere, Diana," Sarah said mildly. "Those two have something special going on."

"What will you call it, Pip?" Agatha asked our son. "Big Bird?"

"I think that name is taken," Marcus said with a laugh. "What about George, for George Washington? It is part eagle."

"Name not George." Philip was patting the griffin's head.

"What then?" Agatha wondered aloud. "Goldy?"

Philip shook his head.

"Tweety?" Sarah asked. "That's a good name for a bird."

"Not bird." Philip scowled at Sarah.

"Why don't you tell us, Philip?" I didn't like the idea that my son and a creature straight from the pages of a fairy tale were on a first-name basis.

"Secret." Philip put his pudgy finger to his lip. "Shhh."

My thumb pricked in warning.

Names are important. Ysabeau had told me that when she revealed Matthew's many names to me.

You may call me Corra. My familiar, a firedrake who had been summoned when I cast my first spell, had been willing to share one of her names with me, though her phrasing made me wonder if it was her true name, the name that had the power to conjure her up from wherever she called home.

"Tell Daddy," Philip said, bestowing his favor on his father.

Matthew knelt down, ready to listen.

"'Pollo," Philip said.

The griffin beat his wings once, twice, and rose up from the ground, as if he had been waiting for a summons.

Metal hit stone, landing with a peal that seemed to announce something momentous had happened.

I looked down, searching for what had made the noise. A tiny silver arrowhead lay at Philip's feet, its edges sharp.

Once airborne, the griffin hovered by Philip's head, attentive to his master's next command.

"Pollo?" Sarah frowned. "Doesn't that mean chicken?"

"Apollo." Matthew looked at me in alarm. "The goddess Diana's twin."

BECCA AND PHILIP WERE PLAYING on the fluffy sheepskin in our bedroom, content for the moment with blocks, a truck, and a herd of plastic horses.

The griffin was confined to the pantry.

"I think the ghosts have been trying to warn me about Apollo for days, with their constant prowling around the mythology section," I said, pouring myself a glass of wine. I didn't usually drink during the day, but these were exceptional circumstances.

"How much do you know about the goddess Diana's brother?" Matthew asked.

"Not much," I admitted, examining the small silver arrowhead. "There was something in one of Philippe's books about him. Something about three powers."

A luminous green-and-gold smudge by the fireplace took shape and morphed into my dead father-in-law.

"Gamper!" Becca said, showing him a horse.

Philippe smiled at his granddaughter and waggled his fingers. Then his expression turned serious.

"*Constat secundum Porphyrii librum, quem Solem appellavit, triplicem esse potestatem, et eundem esse Solem apud superos, Liberum patrem in terris,*" he said.

"*According to Porphyry's book, where he is called Sol, his power is threefold, and the same as Sol in the sky, the Father of Freedom on earth.*" I translated the Latin as fast as I could. Apparently, I had skirted some unwritten magical law by not asking a direct question and was going to be able to get the rarest of all treasures: information from a ghost.

"Porphyry?" Matthew looked impressed. "When did you memorize that?"

"I didn't. Your father helped me." I gestured toward the children. "He likes to watch over them."

"*Et Apollinem apud inferos.*" Philippe's attention was locked on his grandson.

"*And Apollo in hell,*" I said numbly. The arrowhead gleamed in the sunshine, illuminating the golden and black threads that tied it to the world.

"*Unde etiam tria insignia circa eius simulacrum videmus: lyram, quae nobis caelestis harmoniae imaginem monstrat; grypem, quae eum etiam terrenum numen ostendit,*" Philippe continued.

"*Therefore, three attributes can also be seen in his representations: a lyre, which figures celestial harmony; a griffin, which shows that he also has a terrestrial power.*" The words I spoke sounded like an incantation, their ancient meaning resonating through the room.

"*Et sagittas, quibus infernus deus et noxius indicatur, unde etiam Apollo dictus est,*" Philippe said.

"*And arrows, by which are symbolized that he is an infernal god, and harmful, which is why he is called the destroyer.*" My fingers closed around the silver arrowhead that the griffin had given Philip.

"That does it." Matthew sprang to his feet. "I don't care what it is or how much Philip likes having him for a pet. The griffin goes."

"Goes where?" I shook my head. "I don't think we have any choice, Matthew. The griffin obeys Philip, not you or me. Apollo is here for a reason."

"If that reason has anything to do with destruction, or that arrow point it dropped on the floor, then the griffin can find another home." Matthew shook his head. "My son is not going to be a plaything for the gods—or the goddesses. This is her fault. I know it."

Matthew didn't approve of the deal I'd made with the goddess to save his life in exchange for giving her the use of mine.

"Maybe we're overreacting," I said. "Maybe the griffin is just a harmless gift."

"Nothing she does is harmless. What might the goddess give Rebecca when the time comes for her to make magic? A golden hind? A bear?" Matthew's eyes were darkening with emotion. He shook his head. "No, Diana. I'm not having it."

"You said yourself we can't just pretend the twins don't have magic in their blood," I said, trying to be reasonable.

"Magic is one thing. Griffins and goddesses and hell and destruction— that's something else entirely." Matthew's anger was rising. "Is that what you want for your son?

And the father of freedom on earth. Philippe's voice was nothing but a whisper, his expression sad. *Why is it always the dark with Matthew? Never the light.*

It was a question Philippe had asked me before. There was no easy answer to it. Matthew's faith, his blood rage, and his overactive conscience colored everything. It made his joy, his unexpected smiles, and his forgiveness all the more precious when he was able to rise above his darker feelings.

"Are you asking me to spellbind him?" I demanded.

Matthew looked shocked.

"Because that's what it might take to raise Philip safely if he *is* a weaver and he doesn't have Apollo to rely on," I said. "Apollo can be with Philip even when we can't. They'll be a team."

"Philip cannot take a griffin to school," Matthew retorted. "New Haven is progressive, but there are limits."

"Maybe not, but he can take a Labrador retriever. Provided it goes through the proper training program, of course, and gets certified," I said, thinking aloud. "Apollo should make quite a convincing assistance dog, with the right disguising spell."

"Not doggy, Mama," Philip said, rocking his horse around the sheepskin in something vaguely like a gallop. "Griff'n."

"Yes, Philip," I said, giving him a weak smile.

My son had a pet griffin. My daughter relished the taste of blood.

I was beginning to understand why my parents might have thought spellbinding was a good option.

WHEN WE REJOINED THE REST of the family, they were settled out in the courtyard under a brightly colored umbrella, gathered around a table covered with snacks and beverages, talking a mile a minute. Apollo was with them.

"Yet you listened to my ancestor Sarah Bishop, and went back to Hadley as she told you to do," Sarah was saying. "That took courage—giving up dreams of glory to look after your mother and sister."

"It didn't feel courageous at the time." Marcus was cracking pistachio nuts at a furious pace, and throwing the shells on the ground for Apollo to peck at. "Some people accused me of cowardice."

"Obviously they didn't live with your father." Sarah cut through any tension Marcus might be feeling with her usual combination of complete honesty and compassion.

I gave her shoulders a squeeze and sat down in front of the iced tea pitcher. My aunt looked up at me in surprise.

"Everything okay?" Sarah asked.

"Of course." I poured myself some tea. "Matthew and I have been talking about what to do about Apollo."

"He didn't like being separated from Philip," Agatha said.

"I'm not surprised." Marcus ate a handful of pistachios. "The bond between a familiar and a weaver must be powerful. How's Becca taking it?"

"She doesn't seem at all jealous," I replied thoughtfully.

"Give it time," Marcus said with a laugh. "I imagine she'll feel differently when Philip chooses to play with Apollo and not her."

"Maybe Apollo is the familiar for both of them?" Matthew said hopefully.

"I don't think it works that way," I said, dashing his hopes. He looked so forlorn that I gave him a kiss. "A familiar is a weaver's training wheels, remember? Each one is different, and perfectly suited to the weaver's talents."

"So because Becca and Philip are fraternal twins, they'll have different abilities, and therefore different familiars," Marcus said. "Got it."

"We still don't know if Becca is a weaver, of course," I reminded them.

Everybody looked at me with pity, as if I'd lost my mind.

I sighed. "Let's look on the bright side. At least we'll have some help keeping an eye on them."

Matthew had consumed a full glass of wine by this point and was beginning to look less dazed.

"It's true that Corra was quick to defend you if you were in danger," Matthew said.

"And she was even quicker to come to my aid if I needed help or a bit of a magical boost," I said, taking his hand in mine.

"Don't you think it's fascinating," Agatha said, "that the power you possess comes with its own safety monitor? And in the form of a mythological creature, no less."

"I've always wondered how weavers discovered they were different if there weren't other weavers around to help them, and how they approached the problem of creating spells instead of just learning to work them the traditional way by studying grimoires and the practices of other witches," Sarah said. "Now I know."

"Dad had a heron," I reminded her. "When I saw him in the past, I never thought to ask him how old he was when Bennu showed up."

"It seems to me that familiars are a little like an inoculation," Marcus said. "A bit of magic that prevents greater harm. Makes perfect sense."

"Does it?" I was so used to thinking of Corra in bicycle terms that it was difficult to switch to a different metaphor.

"I think so. A familiar is like a childhood vaccine," Marcus said. "With all this talk of 1775, I've been thinking a lot about inoculation. Apart from the war, it was the main topic of conversation in the colonies. Remembering Bunker Hill brought it all back to me."

"Until the Declaration of Independence was signed, surely." I felt on familiar historical footing now. "That had to have upstaged medicine."

"No such luck, Professor Bishop." Marcus laughed. "Do you know what they were celebrating in Boston on the fourth day of July in 1776? Not something happening in faraway Philadelphia, I can tell you that. The talk of the town—and the whole colony—was the Massachusetts legislature's decision to lift the ban on smallpox inoculations."

Even today, there was no effective treatment for this terrible disease. Once contracted, it was highly contagious and potentially fatal. The infection led to a high fever and pus-filled blisters that left disfiguring scars. Matthew had made sure I was vaccinated against it before we timewalked. I remembered the single blister that had erupted at the vaccination site. I would carry the mark for the rest of my days.

"We were more terrified of that silent killer than all the British guns," Marcus continued. "There were rumors of infected blankets and sick people deliberately left behind when the British withdrew from Boston. Your ancestor Sarah Bishop warned me that surgeons were going to be as necessary as soldiers if we wanted to win the war. She was right."

"So you trained to become a surgeon after Bunker Hill?" I asked.

"No. First I went home and faced my father," Marcus said. "Then winter came, and with it there was a lull in the fighting. When the battles resumed in the summer, and soldiers gathered together again from all over the colonies, the number of smallpox cases rose until we were on the brink of an epidemic.

"We had nothing in our medicine chests that could fight it, and only one hope of surviving it," Marcus continued.

He turned his left palm heavenward, revealing a round, white scar with a dimpled center on the underside of his forearm.

"We deliberately gave ourselves a mild case of smallpox to make us immune. It would be almost certain death if we contracted the disease through incidental exposure," he explained. "Our independence from the king might have been celebrated in Philadelphia, but in Massachusetts we were simply glad to finally have a fighting chance at survival."

Massachusetts Historical Society, Mercy Otis Warren Papers
Letter from Hannah Winthrop to Mercy Otis
Cambridge, Massachusetts

8 July 1776

(EXCERPT FROM PAGE 2)

The reigning Subject is the Small Pox. Boston has given up its Fears of an invasion & is busily employd in communicating the Infection. Straw beds & cribs are daily carted into the Town. That ever prevailing Passion of following the Fashion is as Predominant at this time as ever.

Men Women & children eagerly Crouding to innoculate is I think as modish, as running away from the Troops of a barbarous George was the last Year.

But ah my Friend I have not mentioned the Loss I have met with which lies near my heart the death of my dear Friend the good Madam Hancock, A powerfull attachment to this life broken off, you who knew her worth can Lament with me her departure. Ah the incertainty of all Terristrial happiness. Mr Winthrop joyns me Sincere regards to Coll Warren & you, he hopes we shall be favord with his company with you & your son.

Yours in Affection
Hannah Winthrop

⇥ 12 ⇤

Pain

Zeb Pruitt returned to Hadley after the disastrous Quebec campaign and brought the smallpox with him. News of his infection spread through town with the fingers of August fog that were settling in the valley after the passing of the summer heat.

Anna Porter was flitting around her father's mercantile like a self-important bumblebee. She enjoyed being in the hive of activity around the counter where people met to purchase newspapers, coffee, and flour—the three mainstays of the patriotic diet—and to exchange gossip. The store shelves were not as full of goods from abroad as they once were. The Porters could still find plenty of local suppliers of iron nails and cooking pots, saddles and shoes, and hog-bristle brushes, but there was no tea, little silver, and no porcelain. Writing paper was in short supply, and the few books available were from Boston and Philadelphia, not London. Spices and tobacco were now behind the counter, for fear that desperate shoppers might steal what little stock the Porters could acquire.

Today, Marcus was one of the few customers in the store. It was harvesttime, and much of the town's male population was off fighting, which meant the women and children were in the fields. Marcus had earned some money doing necessary jobs around town to help out, and the coins were heavy in his pocket. He was leaning against the store counter, one foot resting on the lid to a butter churn, surveying the books and newspapers.

Marcus was seriously considering buying a copy of *Common Sense*. These days, everyone was talking about Thomas Paine. Marcus had participated in several heated discussions over his ideas in Pomeroy's tavern, and read snatches of Paine's work in the newspapers before Anna's father shooed him away with complaints that he owned a store, not a library. Marcus had been transfixed by Paine's simple yet powerful words about liberty, freedom, and the king's obligations as father of the nation. He flipped to the chapter on hereditary succession that he had been studying the last time he was in the store.

For all men being originally equals, no ONE by BIRTH could have a right to set up his own family in perpetual preference to all others for ever, Marcus read, *and though himself might deserve SOME decent degree of honors of his contemporaries, yet his descendants might be far too unworthy to inherit them.*

Marcus's eyes swept the shelves. Even with a war on, there were enough creature comforts in the Porter's shop to keep the MacNeils happy and content for months. The contrast between all this abundance and the meager stores of food, cloth, and other essentials waiting for him at home was stark.

"Zeb's face is monstrous," Anna Porter said to Marcus in a low voice, trying to distract him from his reading. "If not for the color of his skin, you wouldn't recognize him."

Marcus looked up, a protest on his lips. But it died away before it was uttered, banished by Anna's superior expression. Not everybody in Hadley admired Zeb's irrepressible spirits and ingenuity as Marcus did.

"Is that so?" Marcus returned his attention to Mr. Paine's pamphlet.

"Yes. Noah Cook says smallpox is destroying the army. He says they aren't taking on any soldiers unless they can prove they've had the disease."

Marcus hadn't had the smallpox, nor had his father or Patience. Marcus's mother was the only person in the household with immunity, since she was inoculated in Boston before she married Obadiah.

"They say Zeb is in Hatfield. At the old Marsh homestead." Anna shuddered. "Zeb's ghost will be next to haunt the place."

"His ghost?" Marcus snorted. Ghost stories no longer frightened him. "And I suppose you believe old Mary Webster really was a witch."

"Half-hanged Mary walks the riverbank on moonless nights," Anna said, solemn as a judge. "My sister saw her."

"Mary Webster was friendless and unlucky," Marcus retorted, "but she was hardly immortal. I doubt very much that she is wandering around the boat landing, waiting for the ferry."

"How do you know?" Anna demanded.

"Because I've seen dead men up close." Marcus's experiences at Bunker Hill were sufficient to even silence Anna—though not for long.

"I'm bored with Thomas Paine." Anna's lower lip extended in a pout. "It's all anyone will talk about—that and the smallpox."

"Paine is willing to say aloud what other men think but are afraid to utter." Marcus went to the counter and left the price of the pamphlet with the clerk.

"Most people only buy a copy because they're afraid someone might accuse them of being a Tory," Anna said. Her eyes narrowed as she gauged how best to wound Marcus with her words. "Your cousin bought one. Just before he fled."

Cousin Josiah had been suspected of harboring loyalist feelings, and the citizens of Amherst had run him out of town. Marcus's mother had wept for nearly a week at the family's disgrace and refused to show her face at meeting.

"I'm no Tory." Marcus's cheeks burned with shame and he moved toward the door.

"It's a good thing you have Mr. Paine's pamphlet, then. You know how people talk." Anna looked disapproving, as though she were not one of Hadley's finest gossips.

"Good day, Anna," Marcus said, taking the time to make a proper bow in her direction before he headed into the August afternoon.

When Marcus reached the turn toward home, his feet stilled. His plan had been to go to the farm and hide his copy of Thomas Paine in the grain hopper. It was his job to feed the livestock, and for years Marcus had kept his treasures buried where his father wouldn't be likely to find them. These prized possessions included the gun he'd taken off the dead New Hampshire soldier at Bunker Hill, his precious collection of newspapers, the medical books Tom Buckland had loaned him, and a small pouch of coins.

Each item was a piece of his future freedom—or so Marcus hoped. He planned to run away to join the army at the first opportunity. But if what Anna told him was true, and the army wasn't taking anyone who could contract smallpox, then Marcus might be turned away the moment he arrived.

Marcus reached into his pocket and found the spool of red thread he'd been carrying around ever since he heard that Zeb was back from the war. He weighed it in his hand, considering his options.

There was no more farm work at present. It would be a few weeks until the next round of crops was ready to be harvested.

His mother and Patience were in good health, with plenty of food in the larder.

His father went to Springfield with the wagon to sell some wood two days ago. Nobody knew what had happened to him, but Marcus suspected Obadiah was spending the proceeds at every tavern between there and Hadley. It might be weeks before he returned.

With his pamphlet in one pocket and his spool of linen thread in the other, Marcus set off across the river to Hatfield.

The Marsh homestead was rickety to the point of collapse, set in fields that hadn't seen a plow for years. Inside, sunshine slanted through the gaps in the rough timber walls and around the empty window frames. The glass panes had long since disappeared, along with the door latch and anything else of value.

Marcus pushed the door open and located his friend in the gloom. Based on the appearance of the shivering form on the bed, Zeb's chance of survival wasn't great.

"You don't look good, Zeb."

"See. Please." The skin around Zeb's s mouth had erupted in pox blisters that had burst and then crusted over, making speech difficult.

Marcus pulled out his hunting knife and shined the blade on the hem of his shirt. "Are you sure?"

Zeb nodded.

Marcus held the knife up to Zeb's face. Hopefully, it was too small to give his friend a sense of what smallpox had done to disfigure him.

"'Nuff." Zeb's hair was gone, and his scalp covered with sores. But it was the soles of Zeb's feet that Marcus couldn't bear to look at. Oozing and raw, they were covered with maggots that feasted on the dying flesh.

The door opened, flooding the room with sunlight. Zeb made an inhuman sound and turned his fevered eyes away.

"Morning, Zeb. I've brought food and water, as well as—what the hell are you doing here?" Thomas Buckland looked at Marcus in horror.

Marcus held up his spool of thread. "I figure I might as well get inoculated."

"You know what the people of Hadley think of that." The town fathers didn't approve of this newfangled craze. If God wanted you to get smallpox, then you took it like a good Christian, suffered, and died.

"It's not against the law. Not anymore," Marcus replied. "The legislature lifted the ban. Everybody's doing it."

"Maybe in Boston, but not in Hadley. And not with an infected Negro." Buckland took some powder out of his box and mixed it with water to form a paste.

"You think if I catch the disease from Zeb it's going to darken my complexion?" Marcus was amused. "I don't remember reading that blackness is contagious in those medical books you gave me."

"You can't just get inoculated on a whim, Marcus." Buckland applied some salve to Zeb's feet with a gentle touch. "There's a diet you must follow. Weeks of preparation."

"I've had nothing but gruel, apples, and vegetables for most of the summer." Thanks to Tom's books, and the glimpses he'd had of the newspapers, Marcus knew what doctors advised. A strict diet that avoided rich foods and meat was recommended—and it just happened to be all that Marcus's family could afford.

"I see." Buckland studied Marcus's face. "Does your father know?"
Marcus shook his head.

"And your ma?" Buckland asked. "What does she think of this plan?"
"She was inoculated when she was a girl."

"I know her medical history, Marcus. What I'm asking is whether she approves of you staying here, locked up with Zeb, for the next three weeks?"
Marcus fell silent.

"She doesn't know." Buckland sighed. "I suppose you're going to want me to tell her."

"I'd be much obliged, Tom. Thank you." Marcus was relieved. He didn't want his mother to worry. Marcus would be back—just as soon as he was recovered. "If you could look in on Patience, too, I'd be grateful."

Patience was withdrawn and wan. She spent too much time on her own, and seemed scared of her own shadow.

"All right, Marcus. I'll do what you ask. But"—Buckland held up one finger in warning—"you must swear you will stay here until your scabs dry up and fall off. You are not to go hunting. Or visit the Porters' store. Or come to Northampton to borrow a book. I have enough problems treating returning soldiers like Zeb without a full-fledged epidemic on my hands."

Because the course of the disease was so much milder when it was contracted through inoculation compared to what happened if you caught it from contagion, some people got complacent and went about their business, not realizing the smallpox was hatching like a chick inside their bodies.

"I promise. Besides, I've got everything I need." Marcus held up his already much-thumbed copy of *Common Sense*.

"You better not let your father catch you reading that," Buckland said. "Paine's calls for equality don't sit well with him."

"There's nothing wrong with fairness." Marcus sat on the floor next to Zeb's pallet of folded blankets. He rolled up his shirtsleeve.

"Folks are always in favor of fairness, until they have to give up something they have to someone else." Buckland drew a lancet from his medicine box. The double-edged scalpel was narrow and razor sharp. Zeb eyed Buckland warily.

"Don't worry, Zeb," Marcus said with feigned cheerfulness. "The knife is for me."

Buckland bit off a piece of thread. Carefully, he drew it through one of Zeb's open pox sores. Yellow-and-white pus soaked the red linen fiber.

Marcus extended his left arm. He wanted the left arm inoculated in case things went badly and he lost feeling in it because of the scars. Marcus would still need a working trigger finger to be a soldier.

Buckland scratched Marcus's forearm with the lancet. He and Marcus had discussed the Suttonian method of inoculation last summer, after Marcus returned from Bunker Hill and smallpox began its sweep through Boston. It was a new technique, one that carried less risk because the inoculation incisions were far shallower than previous methods.

Marcus watched his blood well up in crisscross lines. The marks reminded him of the plaid fabric that Patience wove.

"You're sure, Marcus? Zeb doesn't have a mild case of smallpox. And he caught it through exposure." Ideally, Tom would have administered pus taken from someone who had also been inoculated. But this was a risk Marcus needed to take.

"Do it, Tom." Marcus was quivering inside, but his voice was steady.

Buckland drew the thread through the incisions on Marcus's skin until the red thread darkened with blood, indicating that the smallpox-soaked linen had done its work.

"Lord help us all if this goes wrong," Buckland said, his forehead shining with perspiration.

OVER THE NEXT SEVEN DAYS, the smallpox advanced under Marcus's skin with the deliberation the British army had shown in Boston, changing everything in its path.

The first sign that the inoculation was working had been a crushing headache. Then his kidneys started to ache, the pain spreading across his back. Marcus had vomited up the crust of bread and cup of ale he'd forced down at breakfast. Now the fever overtook him. It felt like the worse ague Marcus had ever experienced.

Marcus knew that the fever would drop temporarily, maybe for a day or even just a few hours. He looked forward to that brief lull in the storm of infection before the disease rallied once more and erupted through the skin in painful blisters. Until then, he was trying to distract himself with *Common Sense.*

"Here's the part I told you about, Zeb." Marcus's head swam with fever, and he had to concentrate to keep the words from squirming all over the page.

"'*In the early ages of the world, according to the scripture chronology, there were no kings,*'" Marcus continued. Sweat ran into his eyes, the salt stinging. He wiped at his nose, and his fingers came away bloody. "Imagine that, Zeb. A world without kings."

The water had run out hours ago. Usually it was Marcus who went outside to fetch the fresh pails left by Tom Buckland. Just the thought of cold, clear water made Marcus run his dry tongue over his parched lips. His throat was painfully constricted, and when he swallowed there was a foul taste in his mouth.

Weary and thirsty, Marcus dropped the book and slid to the floor. Every part of him ached, and he didn't have the energy to find a more comfortable position.

"I'm just going to rest my eyes for a few minutes," Marcus said.

THE NEXT THING MARCUS was aware of was Joshua Boston's dark face floating over him. Marcus blinked.

"Thank God," Joshua said. "You gave us a fright, Marcus."

"You've been senseless for two days," Zeb said. His feet were healing, and though the sores on his face had left scars, he was recognizable now. "Dr. Buckland thought we might lose you."

Marcus tried to sit up, tamping down the nausea that resulted from this simple movement. He studied his left arm. What been a crisscrossing set of red lines was now a large, oozing sore. He would never have to fear smallpox again—but the disease had almost taken his life. Marcus felt as weak as one of Patience's kittens.

Joshua held a dipper to Marcus's lips. Water stung his cracked skin, but the cool liquid washed down his throat like manna.

"What's the news?" Marcus croaked.

"You are. Everybody in town knows you're here," Joshua said. "They're all talking about it."

Marcus knew it would be another five days—four if he was lucky— before the scab fell off.

"Where's my book?" Marcus's eyes searched the barely furnished room.

"Here it is." Joshua handed him the copy of *Common Sense*. "From what Zeb's been saying, it sounds like you've read the whole thing."

"It was a way to pass the time," Marcus said, comforted by the familiar feeling of the slim pamphlet in his hand. It was a solid reminder of why he had subjected himself to inoculation, and why he was risking his father's wrath to follow the cause of liberty. "Besides, Zeb had a right to know we're a democracy now, and people want freedom and equality."

"Some, perhaps. But I don't think the majority of people in Hadley, patriot or not, would ever sit down and sup with me," Joshua said.

"The declaration made in Philadelphia said *all* men are created equal—not *some* men," Marcus said, in spite of his misgivings.

"And it was written by a man who owns hundreds of slaves," Joshua replied. "You better get your head out of the clouds, Marcus, or you're going to have a hard landing when you come back to earth."

It took seven more days for the scab to fall off, days during which Marcus read and reread *Common Sense*, debated politics with Joshua, and began to teach Zeb how to read. Finally, Tom Buckland pronounced him fit to go home.

It was a Sunday, and the meetinghouse bells pealed over the countryside. Marcus stepped out into the crisp autumn air, naked as the day he was born. Joshua and Zeb were waiting for him by the washtub with clean clothes.

There was a tang of woodsmoke in the air, and the soft smell of leaf mold. Zeb tossed him an apple, and Marcus ate it in four bites. After weeks of thin gruel and ale, Marcus had never had anything that tasted so clean and fresh. Everything he saw, everything he felt, and everything he tasted seemed like a gift after the weeks he'd spent in the grip of smallpox. The army would have to take Marcus now, once he ran away to join the fight.

For the first time, Marcus felt that freedom was in his grasp.

Tom came out of the house, bearing a pot with a lid clamped on top.

"I believe this is yours." Buckland held out the pot. The aroma of toasted paper filled the air. Tom had wanted to burn *Common Sense*, but Marcus would not allow it. Tom fumigated the pamphlet instead, lining the old pot with moss and pine needles before putting it in the embers.

"Thanks, Tom." Marcus slipped the pages in his pocket. Paine's words would help to keep him warm on the way back to the farm, just as they had kept Marcus sane during the period of quarantine.

Marcus left Zeb and Joshua to burn the blankets, bedding, and clothing before abandoning the Marsh homestead to prevent the smallpox from spreading to anyone who might use the place for temporary shelter on the cold autumn nights. Tom and Marcus crossed the river to Hadley and parted ways on West Street, outside the gate to the MacNeil farm.

"Take care, Marcus," Tom said. "Someone said Obadiah is back in town."

Marcus felt a trickle of worry enter his blood.

"Thanks again, Tom. For everything," Marcus said, pushing the gate open. The hinge was bad, and the gate hung heavily on the post. He would have to fix that, now that he was home.

Marcus went around to the back of the house to check on the cows. He thought he would bring in some eggs while he was at it. His mother would fry them up in bacon drippings when she returned from meeting, and Marcus could mop them up with some bread—if there was any to be had. His stomach gurgled in anticipation of the feast to come.

A crash came from the direction of the rickety lean-to his father had built on the rear of the house to serve as a storeroom back when he hoped the farm would be prosperous. Either the Kelloggs' hog had escaped again and had broken into the kitchen in search of food, or Obadiah was home and searching for the spirits his mother hid in the eaves. The badly hung door was ajar, and Marcus pushed it open a bit more with his toe. Surprise would be an advantage, be the intruder pig or patriarch.

"Where's the rum?" His father's voice was slurred and angry. Another piece of crockery fell to the floor.

"There's none left." Catherine's voice was low, but there was a tremor of fear in her voice.

"Liar," Obadiah shouted.

His mother cried out in pain.

Marcus turned and set off at a run for the barn. He pulled the long flintlock rifle out of the grain hopper, along with the powder and balls needed to fire it.

An ancient elm stood two hundred yards from the kitchen door. Marcus hid behind the massive trunk and loaded the gun. He had been practicing with it out in the woods. What he had discovered about the gun was that it was slow to load but astonishingly accurate, even at a distance.

"Father!" Marcus called to the house. He looked down the barrel of the gun and aimed it at the door. "Come out here."

Silence fell.

"Marcus?" Obadiah laughed. "Where are you hiding, boy?"

Someone kicked open the door.

Obadiah came out, gripping his mother with one hand and pulling Patience along by the shoulder with the other.

"We thought you'd run off for good this time," Marcus called.

"And where have you been?" Obadiah's eyes searched for Marcus, but didn't find him. "Up to no good, I hear—holed up with Zeb Pruitt at the Marsh place."

Patience's sobs grew louder.

"Keep your mouth shut," Obadiah warned his daughter.

"Take whatever food you want and go, Obadiah." His mother's voice shook. "I want no more trouble."

"You don't tell me what to do, Catherine." Obadiah snatched her closer, shouting into her face. He had momentarily forgotten Marcus. "Ever."

"Let her go!" Patience lunged at her father, her fists landing on his back in a futile effort to interrupt his attention.

Obadiah turned toward Patience with a snarl. He shook his daughter and then pushed her to the ground. Patience cried out in pain, her leg twisting underneath her.

Marcus fired.

The sound of the gunpowder catching light reached his father before the ball did. Obadiah MacNeil's face registered surprise moments before the shot struck him between the eyes. He fell backward.

Marcus dropped the gun and ran toward his mother and sister. His sister was unconscious. His mother was trembling like a birch tree.

"You all right, Ma?" Marcus asked, kneeling next to Patience. He rubbed her hands. "Patience. Do you hear me?"

"I'm f-fine," his mother stammered, swaying on her feet. She removed her blood-spattered bonnet. "Your father . . ."

Marcus didn't know whether the lump of metal had gone through his father's skull or was still lodged within it. Either way, the man was dead.

Patience's eyes fluttered open. She turned her head and stared into Obadiah's unseeing eyes. Her mouth opened into a soundless O.

Marcus covered her lips before his sister screamed.

"Quiet, Patience," Catherine said. There was a red lump under one eye. Obadiah must have struck her in his frustrated search for alcohol.

Patience nodded. Marcus removed his hand from her mouth.

"You killed Pa. What are we going to do now, Marcus?" his sister asked in a whisper.

"We could bury him," Catherine said calmly, "out under the elm." The tree had sheltered Marcus as he made the fatal shot.

Marcus hadn't considered the future when he pulled the trigger and killed his father. The only thing he had been thinking of was his mother, his sister, and their safety.

"Lord save us." Zeb stood by the corner of the house. He took in Obadiah's body, Patience's red-rimmed eyes and torn dress, and Catherine's bruised face. "Go hide in the woods, Marcus. Joshua and I will come find you after dark."

It took Zeb and Joshua until the early hours of the morning to convince Marcus that he had to leave Hadley.

"I don't have anywhere to go," Marcus said numbly. The shock of the day's events had begun to affect him. Marcus felt cold, jittery, and anxious by turns. "This is home."

"You have to leave. You shot your father on a Sunday morning. No one hunts on the Sabbath. Someone will have heard the gun go off. And folks are going to remember seeing Obadiah in town," Zeb said.

Zeb was right. A gunshot on their farm would not go unnoticed. And plenty of Hadley residents had walked by the place on their way to meeting. Even Tom Buckland had heard rumors that Obadiah was back.

"If you stay, you will be arrested. Your ma and Patience might even be accused of being involved," Joshua said.

"And if I run, it will be an admission of my own guilt, and they will be free of responsibility." Marcus put his head in his hands. The morning had dawned so bright and full of promise. He had smelled freedom on the autumn air out in Hatfield. Now he could lose not only his liberty but his life.

"Take the gun and go south, to the army. A man can lose himself in war. If you survive, you can make a new life for yourself. Somewhere else," Joshua said. "Somewhere far away from Hadley."

"But who will take care of Ma? And Patience?" Winters were always difficult, but with the war and the poor harvest it would be an even greater struggle to survive.

"We will," Zeb said. "I promise you."

Reluctantly, Marcus agreed to their plan. Joshua spread goose fat through Marcus's hair, and followed it up with dark-colored wig powder that clung to the oily strands.

"If anybody is looking for a blond boy, they'll look straight past you. Wait until you reach Albany before you brush it out," Zeb said. "And nobody has seen your pockmarks. You only have a few small ones on one cheek, but even so the justices will be looking for someone smooth faced."

Zeb had run away before, and knew a thing or two about how to hide your real identity.

"Stick to the highways for speed, then take less-traveled routes out of Albany until you reach New Jersey and Washington's troops," Joshua added. "That's where the army is now. Once you're that far south, if you haven't read about yourself in the newspaper or been caught, I reckon you're safe."

"What name will you answer to?" Zeb asked.

"Name?" Marcus frowned.

"You can't tell people you're Marcus MacNeil," Joshua said. "You'll be caught for sure if you do."

"My middle name is Galen," Marcus said slowly. "I'll use that. And Chauncey. Ma always said I was more Chauncey than MacNeil."

Joshua placed his own hat on Marcus's powdered head. "Keep your head down and your wits about you, Galen Chauncey. And don't look back."

⇥ 13 ⇤

Nine

Dozens of drinking vessels covered Freyja's expansive mahogany dining room table: shot glasses inscribed with the names of bars around the world; heavy crystal wineglasses favored at the end of the nineteenth century with faceted stems that cast rainbows on the walls; a tiny jam jar from Christine Ferber; a silver julep cup; a Renaissance covered cup more than a foot tall with a horn bowl and gilt stem.

Each was filled with a mouthful of dark red liquid.

Françoise pulled aside the pale blue draperies to let in more light, revealing fine scrims of silk that filtered the sunshine. Even with that veil of protection, Phoebe blinked. The brightness was as mesmerizing as Freyja and Miriam had warned her it would be, and she was momentarily lost among the dancing dust motes.

"Here. Try this one." Freyja, who was serving as vampire mixologist, gave a chased Tiffany cocktail shaker a final jiggle and poured the contents into a waiting silver beaker. A bottle of red wine stood nearby, the cork pulled, along with a ewer of water to dilute the blood if required. Long-handled spoons of silver, horn, and even gold littered the area by her elbow. Françoise scooped these up, deposited fresh ones, and disappeared into the nether reaches of the house.

Miriam had a clipboard and was, as usual, collating information. For Phoebe's maker, life was a collection of data points waiting to be gathered, organized, assessed, analyzed, and regularly augmented with still more data. The development of Phoebe's vampire taste was Miriam's latest project.

Phoebe couldn't help wondering whether this was how Miriam had stayed sane through the centuries without Ori. She had seen in Miriam's blood that her maker had been prioress in Jerusalem. The priory had an extensive ossuary, and Miriam had spent much of her time there counting and recounting bones, arranging and rearranging them in new groups according to type. One year Miriam sorted them by date of burial. The next, she arranged them by size. After that, Miriam assembled whole skeletons out of the constituent parts, only to take them to pieces again and start over with another sorting scheme.

"Number thirty-two. What's in it?" Miriam asked, scribbling a fresh entry into her notes.

"Let's wait until Phoebe decides if she likes it or not," Freyja said, handing Phoebe the small cup. "We don't want her natural taste to be altered by preconceived notions of right and wrong. Phoebe must feel free to experiment and try new things."

Phoebe had vomited up the dog's blood after she'd been told what it was, and even though Freyja had tried to sneak some more past her, much adulterated with Châteauneuf-du-Pape and cold water, the mere thought of consuming it had nauseated her.

"I'm not hungry." Phoebe just wanted to close her eyes and sleep. She didn't want new foods. She was happy with Persephone's blood.

"You have to eat." Miriam's tone brooked no refusal.

"I did." Phoebe had sipped from the cat that morning.

Persephone was curled up in her basket at Phoebe's feet, lost in slumber, the faint paddling of her paws suggesting that she was happily dreaming of chasing mice. Phoebe, on the other hand, was so mentally exhausted that she could hardly string a sentence together. A sharp pang of jealous rage that the cat could be sleeping so peacefully, when she could not, rose in her gorge with startling swiftness. She lunged.

Freyja had the cat by the scruff of the neck in a flash, while Miriam had hold of Phoebe.

"Let me go." Phoebe's words came out in a snarl, the reverberations in the depths of her throat nearly choking her.

"You do not shed blood in someone else's house," Miriam said, her grip tightening.

"I've already shed blood here," Phoebe said, her gaze locking with Miriam's. "Persephone—"

"The cat," Miriam interrupted, still refusing to call it by name, "entered this house for your use and with Freyja's permission—for consumption in your own room, not anywhere you felt like eating. It was certainly not provided for you to kill out of envy or for sport."

For a moment, Miriam and Phoebe faced off. Then, Phoebe looked away. It was a sign of submission. This much she had learned in her four days as a vampire: Don't challenge your elders—and certainly not your maker—with a direct stare.

"Apologize to Freyja." Miriam dropped Phoebe and returned to her clipboard. "She's gone to a great deal of trouble on your behalf. Most infants aren't given this kind of consideration. They feed off what they're given, without complaint."

"Sorry." Phoebe plopped back into her chair with ill grace and such force that the legs cracked ominously.

"It's f—" Freyja began.

"It certainly is not." Miriam's glacial gaze returned to Phoebe. "Stand up, Phoebe. Do so without breaking anything. Once you have, go to Freyja and kneel. Then you will apologize. Properly."

It was hard to know who was more shocked by this set of instructions—Phoebe or Freyja.

"I will not!" The whole idea of making obeisance to Freyja was appalling, even if she was Marcus's aunt.

"It's not necessary, Miriam," Freyja protested, her expression alarmed. She deposited Persephone in her basket.

"I disagree," Miriam said. "Better Phoebe learn here that incivility has consequences rather than on the streets of Paris, where the mere fact that she is to marry a de Clermont will have fledglings lining up to see if they can best her."

"Marcus would never forgive me if his mate took to her knees before me." Freyja shook her head.

"I'm not a great believer in modern parenting." Miriam was quiet, but the warning in her voice was unmistakable. "Marcus knew that when he asked me to sire Phoebe. So did you. If my way of child rearing is a problem, I'll move Phoebe to my own house."

Freyja drew herself to her full height and lifted her chin. Phoebe didn't have much information on Freyja's origins, but the gesture confirmed what little she did know—that Marcus's aunt had royal blood and had murdered her three young brothers rather than allow them to inherit the family lands.

"I promised dear Marcus I would not leave Phoebe's side until she was reunited with him," Freyja said coldly. "He must have had a good reason to ask for such an assurance."

Before war could break out in the 8th arrondissement, Phoebe rose gingerly from her chair, careful not to put any pressure on the finely carved arms as she did so, and walked to Freyja as slowly as she was able to at this stage of her development. It took only two blinks, in spite of Phoebe's best efforts to curb her speed. Gracefully, she knelt.

Actually, it started out gracefully but ended rather abruptly, her knees gouging shallow dents in the wooden floor.

Phoebe would have to work on that.

It was something about the sight of Freyja's knees, bare and sculpted underneath the edge of her bright turquoise linen dress, freckled slightly from exposure to the sun while in the garden tending her beloved roses, that caused Phoebe to lose her senses. Like the rest of her, Freyja's knees were perfect, elegant, and powerful. Freyja's knees would never be forced to bend before another creature.

"I'm sorry, Freyja," Phoebe began, sounding truly penitent. "I'm sorry that I'm being held prisoner in your house, against my will. I'm sorry Marcus didn't tell the de Clermonts to bugger off so that we could do this our way."

Miriam growled.

Freyja looked down at Phoebe with a mixture of astonishment and admiration.

"I'm sorry I don't want to drink this disgusting mess of cold blood you've so carefully laid out for me so that we can determine whether I prefer cat to dog, rat to mouse, Caucasian females to Asian men. And I'm deeply sorry to reflect badly on my esteemed maker, to whom I owe everything," Phoebe continued. "I am not worthy to share her blood, and yet I do."

"That's quite enough." Miriam said.

But Phoebe was not finished making a mockery of her forced apology.

She bolted for the table and began downing the remaining samples of blood with great speed.

"Revolting," she proclaimed, crushing a wafer-thin glass tumbler to dust in her hands. She took up the next. "Gamey." A silver-stemmed goblet snapped in two, the bowl separating from the base. "Putrid, like death." She spat the liquid back into the shot glass, which was inscribed with the warning BAD DECISIONS MAKE GOOD STORIES. "Not bad, but I'd rather drink cat." Phoebe flipped the empty wineglass over so that the bloody residue slid down the sides and made a sticky ring on the table.

On Phoebe went around the table, slurping blood and tossing glassware aside until she had consumed every last drop. In the end, only a single silver julep cup was left standing. Phoebe wiped her mouth with the back of her hand. It was trembling, and dotted with splashes of blood.

"I'd drink that." Phoebe pointed to the small, straight-sided cup with beaded decoration around the rim (made by a Kentucky silversmith around 1850, if she was not mistaken). "But only if there was no cat around."

"Progress, I think," Freyja said cheerfully, surveying the carnage on her dining room table.

A gasp announced the arrival of Françoise—who would, of course, be expected to clear away the mess.

But it was Miriam's dark expression that held Phoebe's attention. Miriam's face promised punishment—and not within any predictable human timeframe.

Miriam banished Phoebe, Cinderella-like, to the kitchens to assist Françoise. It took several trips up and down the stairs just to clear the debris. Phoebe was grateful for her newly enhanced cardiovascular system, not to mention her vampire speed.

Once the table was cleared, the surface wiped, the floor scrubbed by hand with a brush, and the bits of glass plucked out of Phoebe's knees and shins, Phoebe and Françoise busied themselves at the sink. Françoise took charge of all the breakable glasses, just in case, and handed Phoebe the ones made of metal.

"Why do you stay with Freyja?" Phoebe wondered aloud.

"This is my job. All creatures need jobs. Without one, you have no self-respect." Françoise's reply was succinct, as usual, but it didn't really answer Phoebe's question.

Phoebe tried a different tack.

"Wouldn't you rather be doing something else?" Housekeeping seemed very limited to Phoebe. She liked going to the office and keeping up with the latest developments in the art market, testing her knowledge by attributing and authenticating pieces whose value was either unknown or long forgotten.

"No." Françoise snapped her dish towel and folded it in thirds before hanging it on the waiting rail. She turned her attention to a heaping basket of laundry and switched on the iron.

"Wouldn't you rather work for yourself?" Phoebe was willing to entertain the possibility that there were hidden rewards to cleaning and cooking, but she couldn't fathom a life in service to others.

"This is the life I chose. It's a good life. I am well paid, respected, protected," replied Françoise.

Phoebe frowned. Françoise was a vampire, and her arms were the size of small hams. She didn't seem in need of protection.

"But you could study. Go to university. Master a subject. Do anything you liked, really." Phoebe tried folding her own damp towel. It ended up badly, one side uneven, pulled out of shape by her efforts. She hung it on the rod next to Françoise's.

Françoise removed it and snapped the linen open. She folded it properly and rehung it on the rod. It was perfectly matched to the other, and both towels now gave off an air of perfect domesticity, like the pictures in the women's magazines her mother subscribed to: soothing and mildly reproachful at the same time.

"I know enough," Françoise replied. *I know how to fold a piece of cloth properly, which is more than can be said for you*, her expression said.

"Didn't you ever want . . . more?" Phoebe asked with a bit of hesitancy. She wasn't eager to anger another vampire who was older, faster, and stronger than she was.

"I wanted more than a life toiling in the fields of Burgundy, the soil in my hair and between my toes, until I dropped dead at the age of forty like my mother did," Françoise replied. "I got it."

Phoebe sat on a nearby stool, her fingers threaded together. She shifted, nervous, on her seat. Françoise had never uttered so many words at once—at least not where Phoebe could overhear her. She hoped she hadn't offended the woman with her questions.

"I wanted warm clothes in winter, and an extra blanket at night," Françoise continued, to Phoebe's astonishment. "I wanted more wood for the fire. I wanted to go to sleep without hunger, and never again wonder if there would be enough food to feed the people I loved. I wanted less sickness—sickness that came each February and August to take people away."

Phoebe recognized the cadence of her own display of temper before Freyja and Miriam. Of course Françoise had heard everything. She was subtly mimicking Phoebe—to make a point. Or to issue a warning. With vampires it was so very difficult to tell.

"So you see, I already possess all that I have ever wanted," Françoise said in closing. "I would not be you, with your useless learning and seeming independence, for all the world."

It was a startling announcement, for Phoebe felt her life was nearly perfect already and only going to get better with an eternity to do as she pleased and Marcus at her side.

"Why not?" Phoebe demanded.

"Because I have something you will never again possess," Françoise said, her voice dropping to a confiding hiss, "a treasure that no amount of money can buy nor time secure."

Phoebe leaned forward, eager to know what this treasure was. It couldn't be long life—Phoebe had that now.

Françoise, like most taciturn individuals, enjoyed having an attentive audience. She had also mastered the art of the dramatic pause. She picked up her bottle of lavender water and spritzed a pillowcase with it. Then she wielded the hot iron with the same quick expertise with which she did everything else in the house.

Phoebe waited, as unusually patient as Françoise was unusually forthcoming.

"Freedom," Françoise said at last. She took up another pillowcase and let her words sink in.

"No one pays any attention to me," Françoise continued. "I can do as I please. Live, die, work, rest, fall in love—and out of it, too. Everybody is watching you, waiting for you to fail. Wondering if you will succeed. Come August, you'll have Milord Marcus back in your bed, but you'll have the eyes of the Congregation on you, too. After word spreads of your engagement, every vampire on earth will be curious about you. You'll never have a moment's peace or freedom in your life—which, God willing, will be long."

Phoebe stopped her nervous shifting, and the room was so quiet that even a warmblood could have heard a pin drop.

"But you need not worry." Françoise folded the smooth pillowcase into a sharp-edged rectangle before taking another damp one from the basket. "You will not have liberty, but you will succeed at your job—because I will be doing *my* job, protecting you from those who would do you harm."

"Excuse me?" This was news to Phoebe.

"All newly reborn vampires need someone like me to take care of them—and older ones, too, when they are in society. I dressed Madame Ysabeau, and Miladies Freyja and Verin." Françoise took no notice of Phoebe's startled reaction. "I took care of Milady Stasia back in the winter of 802, when she was taken ill with the ennui and would not leave her house, not even to hunt."

Françoise finished her pillowcase and took up a sheet. The hot iron hissed and spit against the damp cloth. Phoebe held her breath. This was more ancient de Clermont history than she had ever heard before, and she did not wish to interrupt.

"I attended on madame when she was in the past with *Sieur* Matthew, and made sure she did not come to harm when he was about town on business. I kept house for Milady Johanna after Milord Godfrey died in the wars, when she was in a rage and wished to die. I have cooked and cleaned for *Sieur* Baldwin, and helped Alain take care of *Sieur* Philippe when he came home from the Nazis a broken man."

Françoise fixed her dark eyes on Phoebe. "Aren't you glad now that this is the life I chose: taking care of this family? Because without me, you would be eaten up, spit out, and ground under the heels of every vampire you meet, and Milord Marcus with you."

Phoebe wasn't *glad*, precisely, although the more Françoise spoke the more grateful she was for the advice the woman was delivering. And she still couldn't understand why anyone with her full faculties—which

Françoise obviously possessed—would *choose* to look after other people. Phoebe supposed it wasn't dissimilar to Marcus's choice of medicine, but he'd gone to years and years of schooling for that and it seemed somehow more worthy than Françoise's path.

The more she considered Françoise's question, however, the less sure Phoebe was of her answer.

Françoise's mouth began to curve upward in a slow, deliberate smile.

For the first time since becoming a vampire, Phoebe felt an unmistakable flush of pride. Somehow, simply by keeping silent, she had earned Françoise's approval. And it mattered to her a great deal more than she might have expected.

Phoebe handed Françoise the lump of sheet that was uppermost in the basket.

"What's 'ennui'?" Phoebe asked.

Françoise's smile widened. "It's a type of sickness—not so dangerous as *Sieur* Matthew's blood rage, you understand, but it can be deadly."

"Does Stasia still have it?" Phoebe settled back onto her stool, watching Françoise's movements and taking in how she managed the lengths of damp linen without letting them drag on the floor. The two of them would be spending a lot of time together. If housekeeping was important to Françoise, Phoebe should at least try to discover why.

"Middle-aged white women," Miriam said as she entered Françoise's territory.

"What about them?" Phoebe asked, confused.

"They were sample eighty-three—the one you claimed to like second only to cat's blood," Miriam explained.

"Oh." Phoebe blinked.

"We'll get you some more. Françoise will have it on hand—but you have to ask for it. Specifically. Unless you do, you'll have nothing but the cat to feed from," Miriam said.

Whatever was the point of that? Phoebe wondered. Couldn't she just say, "I'm hungry," and rummage through the fridge?

Françoise, however, seemed to understand what was going on. She nodded. Phoebe would learn later why this ridiculous rule was being imposed.

"The cat will be sufficient, thank you, Miriam," Phoebe said stiffly.

She simply couldn't imagine being in such need that she would utter the words "give me the blood of a middle-aged white woman."

"We'll see," Miriam said with a smile. "Come. It's time for you to learn how to write."

"I know how to write," Phoebe said, sounding cross.

"Yes, but we'd like you to do it without setting the paper on fire with excessive friction or carving up the desk." Miriam crooked her finger in a way that made Phoebe shiver.

For the first time in her life, Phoebe left the kitchen reluctantly. It seemed a place of comfort and safe harbor now, with Françoise and the laundry, the clean glasses, and the hiss of the iron. Upstairs there was nothing but peril and whatever fresh tests her sadistic vampire schoolmistresses could devise.

As the baize-covered door to the kitchen swung shut behind her, Phoebe finally arrived at the answer to Françoise's question.

"Yes. I'm glad." Phoebe was back in the kitchen before she had fully formulated a plan to return. Miriam and Freyja were right: thinking of where she wanted to be really was sufficient cause to get her there.

"I thought so. Go now. Don't keep your maker waiting," Françoise advised, brandishing the heavy iron in the direction of the door as though it weighed no more than a feather.

Phoebe returned to Miriam's side. As the baize door flapped its way closed, she heard the strangest sound, something between a cough and a chortle.

It was Françoise—and she was laughing.

⇥ 14 ⇤

A Life of Trouble

"Sit. Stay. Wait." My son's piping voice carried through the open window, uttering a stream of nonsense that exactly imitated the instructions I gave Hector and Fallon every time we attempted to get back into the house without my getting knocked over. The kitchen door creaked open. There was a pause. "Wait. Stay. Okay."

Apollo bounded into the room, looking extremely pleased with himself—but not nearly as proud as Philip, who toddled after him holding Fallon's dog leash, hand in hand with Matthew.

Alarmingly, Fallon's leather lead was not attached to the griffin.

"Mommy!" Philip hurled himself at my legs. Apollo joined in the embrace, wrapping his wings around us both, cooing with delight.

"Did you have a nice walk?" I smoothed down Philip's hair, which was inclined to stand straight up at the slightest breeze.

"Very nice." Matthew gave me a lingering kiss. "You taste of almonds."

"We've been having some breakfast." I pointed to Becca, whose face was partially obscured by jam and nut butter. Her smile of welcome for her father and brother was unmistakable, however. "Becca has been sharing."

This was uncharacteristic behavior for our daughter. Becca tracked her food carefully, and had to be reminded that not everything put on the table was solely for her.

Apollo hopped over to Becca's chair. He sat, long tongue lolling expectantly, his beady eyes fixed on the table, where the remnants of her feast remained. Becca narrowed her eyes at him in warning.

"I see that Rebecca and Apollo are still working out their relationship," Matthew commented. He poured himself a steaming cup of coffee and sat down with the paper.

"Come. Sit. Okay." Philip kept rattling off commands to the griffin while jiggling the leash enticingly. "Come, 'Pollo. Sit."

"Let's get your bib on and some breakfast in you." I snagged the leash and put it on the table. "Marthe made oatmeal. Your favorite!"

Philip's preferred breakfast was pale pink goo—a splash of quail blood, some oats, and lumps of berries—with plenty of milk. We called it oatmeal, though food critics might not recognize the dish as such.

"Apollo. Here!" Philip's patience was running out and his tone was decidedly peevish. "Here!"

"Let Apollo visit with Becca," I said, trying to distract him by picking him up and tumbling him upside down. All I succeeded in doing, however, was alarming the griffin.

Apollo screeched in horror and launched himself into the air, clucking around Philip and comforting him with pats of his tail. It was not until Philip was right-side up and in his booster seat that the griffin settled back down to earth.

"Have you seen Marcus this morning?" Matthew cocked his head, listening for a sound from his grown son.

"He came through the kitchen while you were out. Said something about taking a run." I handed Philip a spoon, which he would use to fling the oatmeal around rather than feed himself, and picked up my cup of tea. "He seems on edge."

"He's expecting an update from Paris," Matthew explained.

The phone calls came every few days. Freyja spoke to Ysabeau, and then Matthew's mother relayed the information to her grandson. So far, Phoebe was doing brilliantly. There had been a few hiccups, Freyja acknowledged, but nothing that wasn't expected during a vampire's first weeks. The stalwart Françoise was supporting Phoebe every step of the way, and I knew from my own experience that she would be dogged in her pursuit of Phoebe's success. Still, Marcus couldn't help worrying.

"Marcus hasn't been himself since he told you about Obadiah," Matthew said, attributing his son's anxiety to a different cause.

Obadiah's violent end had been the subject of many whispered conversations between me, Agatha, and Sarah. Over the past few days, Marcus had returned to the events of 1776, adding new details, worrying if there was some way he could have avoided killing his father and still have protected his mother and sister.

"The threads that bind him to the world have changed in color, but they're still tangled and twisted," I admitted. "I've been wondering if a simple charm would help, one woven with the second knot. He's all blue these days."

"I don't think he's that depressed," Matthew said with a frown.

"No, not that kind of blue!" I said. "Though maybe that's where we get the expression. Everywhere Marcus rubs up against time, it seems to register in shades of blue: royal blue, pale blue, purple, lavender, indigo, even turquoise. I'd like to see more balance. Last week there was some red, white, and black in the mix. Not all of them are happy colors, but at least there was some variety."

Matthew looked fascinated. He also looked concerned.

"Second-knot spells rebalance energy. They're often used in love magic," I said. "But that's not their only purpose. In this case, I could weave a spell to help Marcus sort out the emotions that are tied to his past lives."

"For a vampire, coming to terms with our past lives is the most important work we do," Matthew said cautiously. "I don't think magical assistance is a good idea, *mon coeur*."

"But Marcus is trying to ignore his past, not face it," I said. "I know how impossible that is."

Past. Present. Future. As a historian, I was intrigued by the relationship between them. To examine one thread required that you study them all.

"He'll realize that," Matthew said, returning to his paper. "In time."

MATTHEW AND I WERE TAKING the children for a walk when we spotted a convertible approaching the house. It turned in to the driveway and wended its way to the house at a crawl.

"Ysabeau," Matthew said. "And Marcus, too."

It was a bizarre procession. Alain was at the wheel of the car. Ysabeau de Clermont sat in the passenger seat, wearing dark glasses and a sleeveless dress in a pale primrose color. The ends of the Hermès scarf knotted around her head fluttered in the breeze. She looked like the star of a 1960s film about a European princess on summer holiday. Marcus ran alongside, asking if there was news from Paris.

"Jesus, *Grand-mère*," Marcus said when they finally arrived in the courtyard and Alain switched off the ignition. "Why own a car with that much engine if you're going to let Alain drive it at five miles per hour like a golf cart?"

"One never knows when one might have to make a getaway," Ysabeau replied cagily.

The children clamored for Ysabeau's attention. She ignored them, although she did sneak in a wink at Rebecca.

"How's Phoebe?" Marcus was practically dancing in anticipation of the news.

Ysabeau didn't answer her grandson's question, but motioned toward the rear of the automobile. "I brought decent champagne. There is never enough of it in this house."

"And Phoebe?" Marcus asked, renewing his calls for more information.

"Has Becca's tooth come in yet?" Ysabeau inquired of Matthew, still ignoring Marcus. "Hello, Diana. You are looking well."

"Good morning, *Maman*." Matthew stooped to kiss his mother.

Sarah and Agatha joined us in the courtyard. Sarah was still in her pajamas and dressing gown, and Agatha was wearing a cocktail dress. They made an odd pair.

"It is afternoon, Matthew. Have you no clocks in the house?" Ysabeau looked around for her next target and found one in my aunt. "Sarah. What a strange frock. I hope you didn't pay much for it."

"Nice to see you, too, Ysabeau. Agatha made it for me. I'm sure she'd make one for you, too, if you asked nicely." Sarah drew the vivid kimono around her.

Ysabeau looked askance at the garment, then sniffed.

"Are you having a problem with fleas? Why does everything reek of lavender?" Ysabeau asked.

"Why don't we all go inside," I said, shifting Becca to my other hip.

"I have been waiting for an invitation to do just that," Ysabeau said, her annoyance at the delay evident. "I cannot just walk in, can I?"

"You would know better than me," I replied agreeably, determined not to fight with my mother-in-law. "My vampire etiquette is pretty sketchy. Witches—we just barge right in and head for the kitchen."

Her worst fears confirmed, Ysabeau sailed between us lesser beings and into the house that had formerly been her home.

Once she was ensconced in a comfortable chair in the parlor, Ysabeau insisted everyone have a drink, and then she held the twins on her lap and embarked on a long conversation with each of them. A ringing phone interrupted it.

"*Oui?*" Ysabeau said, after drawing her bright red mobile phone out of a slender vintage clutch with a distinctive Bakelite handle shaped like a running greyhound.

Marcus crept closer to listen to the conversation on the other end, during what I, and the other warmbloods in the room, perceived as a very long silence.

"Ah. That is excellent news." Ysabeau smiled. "I expected no less of Phoebe."

Matthew's face relaxed a fraction, and Marcus let out a shout of joy.

"Bee Bee!" Becca sang out her pet name for Phoebe.

"And she is feeding well?" Ysabeau paused while Freyja responded. "Persephone? *Hein*, I was never fond of that girl and her endless complaints."

My eyes narrowed. In the not-too-distant future, Ysabeau and I were going to have a talk about things mythological. Maybe *she* would know the average height and weight of a fully grown griffin.

"Has Phoebe asked for me?" Marcus demanded of his grandmother.

Ysabeau's long fingernail pressed into her grandson's chest in a gesture of warning. I'd seen that same fingernail push its way into a vampire's heart. Marcus grew still.

"You may tell Phoebe that Marcus is in excellent health, and we are finding ways to keep him occupied until she is returned to us." Ysabeau made it sound as if Phoebe were a borrowed book. "Until Sunday, then." She disconnected the line.

"Two whole days!" Marcus groaned. "I can't believe I have to wait two whole days for more news."

"You are fortunate to be doing this in the age of telephones, Marcus. It took more than two days for news to reach Jerusalem from Antioch when Louisa was made, I assure you," Ysabeau replied, giving him a stern look. "You might attend to the Knights of Lazarus, instead of wallowing in self-pity. There are so many of them now, all quite young and inexperienced. Go and play."

"What are you proposing, *Grand-mère*? That I lead them on a quest to the Holy Land? Have an archery tournament? Put on a joust?" Marcus asked, lightly mocking.

"Don't be ridiculous," Ysabeau said. "I hate jousts. There's nothing for the women to do but gaze at the men adoringly and look decorative. Surely there's a country to conquer, or a government to infiltrate, or an evil family to bring to justice." Her eyes sparkled at the prospect.

"This is precisely how we ended up with the Congregation," Marcus said, pointing an admonishing finger. "Think how much trouble *that* caused. We don't behave like that anymore, *Grand-mère*."

"Then it must be very dull to be a knight," Ysabeau said. "And I shouldn't worry about causing trouble. It seems to find this family no matter what we do. Something will happen any day now. It always does."

Matthew and I exchanged glances. Sarah snorted.

"Has Diana told you about the griffin?" my aunt asked.

WITHIN THE HOUR, Apollo was perched on Ysabeau's arm like one of Emperor Rudolf's eagles. Though the griffin was about the same height, I suspected that his leonine hindquarters added considerable weight. Only a vampire could have held him aloft with such elegance. In spite of her modern clothing, Ysabeau handled the creature with the grace of a medieval lady going hawking.

Becca had elected to have Sarah and Agatha read her a story rather than play with the griffin. The rest of us were with Ysabeau to witness the rare sight of a griffin taking to the open air.

Ysabeau had a dead mouse in one hand, and the griffin's complete attention. When Ysabeau lifted her arm, the griffin left his perch and soared above her. Quickly, Ysabeau tossed the mouse into the air.

Apollo swooped down and caught it in his beak, his tail streaming behind him. He returned to Ysabeau, and laid the trophy at her feet.

"Good boy!" Philip cried, clapping for added emphasis.

Apollo chortled something in response.

"Okay." Philip seemed to understand what his griffin had said and picked up the mouse. He threw it with all his might. It landed about two feet behind him.

Apollo retrieved the mouse in several bounds and dropped it at Ysabeau's feet this time.

"I fear that Apollo is not getting enough exercise, Matthew. You must fly him, or he will amuse himself," Ysabeau said, picking up the mouse once more. She hurled it across the moat. "You won't like the results."

Apollo gamboled up to the edge of the water, flew over it, and found the mouse in the reeds on the other side. The griffin took off with it and circled overhead a few times. Ysabeau's piercing whistle brought him back down to earth.

"You seem to know a lot about griffins, *Grand-mère*," Marcus said suspiciously.

"A bit," she replied. "They were never very common. Not like centaurs and dryads."

"Dryads?" I said faintly.

"Back when I was a girl, you had to be very careful walking through the woods," Ysabeau explained. "Dryads looked like perfectly ordinary women, but if you stopped to talk to one, you could be encircled by trees before you knew it and find it impossible to see your way out."

I glanced at the thick forest that bounded the property to the north, uneasy at the thought that the trees might try to strike up a conversation with Becca.

"As for centaurs, you can be glad Philip didn't summon one of them. They can be devious, not to mention impossible to house-train." Ysabeau crouched down by her grandson. "Give Apollo his mouse. He's earned it."

Apollo extended his tongue in anticipation.

Philip picked the mouse up by the tail. Apollo opened his beak, and Philip dropped the rodent into the griffin's craw.

"All done," Philip said, wiping his hands together in a gesture of completion.

"Still think you can weave a disguising spell for him?" Matthew murmured in my ear.

I had no idea. But I was going to have to reconsider the knots so that it could include weighted feet to keep Apollo attached to the ground. The creature definitely liked to fly.

"I'm sorry Rebecca did not stay to watch the hunt," Ysabeau said. "She would have enjoyed it."

"Becca is a bit jealous," I explained. "Right now Philip and Apollo are getting a lot of attention."

Philip let out a mighty yawn. The griffin followed suit.

"I think it's time you took a nap. You've had a lot of excitement today." Matthew swung his son into the air. "Come. Let's go find your sister."

"'Pollo, too?" Philip inquired, looking especially winsome.

"Yes, Apollo can nap in the fireplace." Matthew gave me a kiss. "Will you join us?"

"There was a bucket of cherries on the kitchen counter this morning. I've been thinking about them for hours, and wondering what Marthe is going to do with them," I confessed, leading the way back into the kitchen.

Marcus laughed and opened the door for me, gentlemanly as always. I knew now that it was his mother who had instilled these manners in him. My thoughts returned to Hadley, and to Marcus's story. What had happened to Catherine and Patience, after Marcus fled?

"Diana?" Marcus said, concerned. I had stopped in my tracks.

"I'm fine. Just thinking about your mother, that's all," I said. "She'd be very proud of you, Marcus."

Marcus looked shy. Then he smiled. In the years I'd known him, I'd never seen such unalloyed joy on his face.

"Thank you, Diana," he said with a small bow.

Inside, Marthe was pitting the fruit by boring one slender pinkie into each cherry and popping the seed kernel into a waiting stainless steel bowl with a satisfying *pling*.

I reached into the bowl. Something snapped at my fingers. "Ow!"

"Keep your hands to yourself and nobody gets hurt," Marthe said, glowering. She had a new crime novel, and was learning all sorts of useful English phrases.

Ysabeau poured herself some champagne, and I made myself a cup of tea and cut a slab from a freshly baked lemon loaf to console myself until

Marthe declared open season on the fruit. Sarah and Agatha joined us. They'd finished Becca's first story—and her second—and left her in Matthew's capable hands. He would sing songs from his childhood to send the twins to sleep.

"Matthew really does have a special touch with the children," Sarah acknowledged. She headed over to the coffeepot. As usual, Marthe had anticipated her need for caffeine and the coffee was hot and fragrant.

"The twins are lucky," Marcus said. "They won't have to search for a good father—a true father—like I did."

"So everyone knows about Obadiah now?" Ysabeau asked her grandson.

"Everybody except Phoebe," Marcus replied.

"What?" Agatha was stunned. "Marcus. How could you keep this from her?"

"I tried to tell her. Loads of times." Marcus sounded miserable. "But Phoebe didn't want me to tell her about my past. She wanted to discover it for herself—through my blood."

"Bloodlore is even more unreliable than a vampire's memories," Ysabeau said. She shook her head. "You should not have let her dissuade you, Marcus. You knew better. You followed your heart, and not your head."

"I was respecting her wishes!" Marcus retorted. "You told me to listen to her, *Grand-mère*. I was following *your* advice."

"Part of growing older and wiser is learning which advice to follow and which to ignore." Ysabeau sipped her champagne, her eyes glittering. My mother-in-law was up to something, but I knew better than to try to ferret it out. Instead, I changed the subject.

"What's a 'true father,' Marcus?" Vampire family vocabulary could be confusing, and I wanted to be sure I had it right. "You mentioned it earlier. Obadiah was your birth father—is that the same thing, in vampire terms?"

"No." The colored threads around Marcus were getting darker, the purple and indigo now almost black. "It has nothing to do with vampires. A true father is the man who teaches what you need to know about the world and how to survive in it. Joshua and Zeb were truer fathers to me than Obadiah. So was Tom."

"I found some letters online about the summer of 1776 and the lifting of the inoculation ban in Massachusetts," I said, determined to find a safer topic of conversation than fathers and sons. "Everything you remember fits into what I discovered. Washington and Congress were panicked at the thought that an epidemic would wipe out the entire army."

"Their fears were justified," Marcus replied. "When I finally reached Washington and the army, it was early November. The battles were drawing to a close for the year, but fatalities were destined to increase when the fighting stopped and the army went into their winter camp. Back then, peace was more deadly to the army than war."

"Contagion," I said. "Of course. Smallpox would spread like wildfire in a crowded encampment."

"Discipline was a problem, too," Marcus said. "Nobody followed orders, unless Washington himself gave them. And I wasn't the only young man who'd run away from home seeking adventure. For every runaway who enlisted, though, it seemed that two men deserted. There was so much coming and going that nobody could keep track of who was there and who wasn't, or which regiment you belonged to, or where you'd come from."

"Did you go to Albany, like Joshua suggested?" I asked.

"Yes," Marcus said, "but the army wasn't there. They'd gone east, to Manhattan and Long Island."

"So that's when you joined the medical corps." I was eager to put together the fragments of what I knew.

"Not quite. First, I joined up with a company of gunners. I had been traveling at night for more than a month. I was alone, spooked like a newborn colt whenever anybody spoke to me, and utterly convinced I would be caught and hauled back to Massachusetts to answer for my father's death," Marcus explained. "The Philadelphia Associators took me in without any questions. It was my first rebirth."

But not his last.

"I had a new father—Lieutenant Cuthbert—and brothers instead of sisters. I even had a new mother of sorts." Marcus shook his head. "German Gerty. Lord, I haven't thought of her for decades. And Mrs. Otto. Christ, she was formidable."

Marcus's expression darkened.

"But there were still so many rules, and so much death. And precious little freedom," he continued, before falling silent.

"Then what happened?" I prompted.

"Then I met Matthew," Marcus said simply.

Washington Papers, United States National Archives
George Washington to Dr. William Shippen Jr.
Morristown, New Jersey

6 February 1777

Dear Sir:

Finding the Small pox to be spreading much and fearing that no precaution can prevent it from running through the whole of our Army, I have determined that the troops shall be inoculated. This Expedient may be attended with some inconveniences and some disadvantages, but yet I trust in its consequences will have the most happy effects. Necessity not only authorizes but seems to require the measure, for should the disorder infect the Army in the natural way and rage with its usual virulence we should have more to dread from it than from the Sword of the Enemy. . . . If the business is immediately begun and favoured with the common success, I would fain hope they will be soon fit for duty, and that in a short space of time we shall have an Army not subject to this the greatest of all calamities that can befall it when taken in the natural way.

⇥ 15 ⇤

Dead

Marcus looked down the barrel of the rifle he had taken at Bunker Hill, toward the head of George III. The image was mounted to a distant tree with the point of a broken bayonet.

"Eyes or heart?" Marcus asked his audience, squinting as he took aim.

"You'll never hit it," a soldier scoffed. "He's too far away."

But Marcus was an even better shot now than he had been when he'd taken his father's life.

The face of the king transformed itself into the face of his father.

Marcus pulled the trigger. The gun cracked into life, and bark flew. When the smoke cleared, there was a hole right between King George's eyes.

"Take your best shot, lads." Adam Swift walked around the crowd with his cap like an entertainer at a fair. He was Irish, wicked, clever—and a source of amusement to half the colonial army, with his songs and pranks. "A halfpenny will buy you a chance to kill the king. Do your bit for liberty. Make Georgie pay for what he's done."

"I want to go next!" cried a fourteen-year-old Dutch rigger named Vanderslice who had run away from a ship newly arrived in Philadelphia and joined up with the Associators soon after.

"You haven't got a gun," Swift pointed out.

Marcus was just about to loan Vanderslice his when two uniformed officers came into view.

"What is the meaning of this!" Captain Moulder, the nominal head of the Philadelphia Associators, surveyed the scene with disapproval.

Lieutenant Cuthbert, a rawboned man in his midtwenties of Scottish extraction, was at his side.

"Just some harmless fun, sir," Cuthbert said, glaring at Marcus and Swift.

Cutherbert's assurances might have satisfied the captain, had Moulder not spotted King George.

"Did you take that from a picture in the college at Princeton?" Captain Moulder demanded. "Because if you did, the college would like it back."

Swift pressed his lips together and Marcus stood at attention.

"Captain Hamilton claimed he damaged the painting, sir," Cuthbert said, diverting the possible blame onto someone better able to withstand it. "Shot a cannonball straight through the canvas."

"Hamilton!" Vanderslice was disgusted. "He had nothing to do with it, Cuthbert. It was the three of us who cut it out of the frame."

This was precisely what Captain Moulder had feared.

"In my tent. Now. All three of you!" Moulder barked.

MARCUS STOOD IN FRONT of Captain Moulder, with Swift and Vanderslice on either side. Lieutenant Cuthbert stood at the entrance to the tent, keeping the rest of the regiment safely out of range of the captain's wrath, though within earshot. Cuthbert was greatly beloved. He refused to put up with any nonsense from the men in his charge while ignoring most of the instructions given to him by his superior officers. It was an ideal style of leadership for the Continental army.

"I should have you all flogged," Captain Moulder said. He held up the limp piece of canvas with the defaced image of their former ruler. "What on earth persuaded you to take it?"

Vanderslice looked at Marcus. Swift looked at the ceiling.

"We wanted to use it for target practice. Sir," Marcus replied, looking Moulder in the eye. He struck Marcus as a bully, and Marcus had some experience with them. "It was my doing. Vanderslice and Swift tried to stop me."

Vanderslice's mouth gaped open in astonishment. This was not at all what had happened. At Princeton, Marcus had climbed up on Swift's shoulder and used a British bayonet taken from the battlefield to behead the portrait of the king. Vanderslice had encouraged him every step of the way.

Swift shot Marcus an approving glance.

"And who the hell are you?" Moulder's eyes narrowed.

"Mar—Galen Chauncey." Marcus still tended to blurt out his baptismal name when under stress.

"We call him Doc," Vanderslice volunteered.

"Doc? You're not from Philadelphia. And I don't remember signing you up," Moulder replied.

"No. That was me, Captain." Cuthbert lied with breezy assurance, the mark of someone skilled at fabrication. "Distant cousin. From Delaware. He's a good shot. Thought he could be useful manning a musket in case the cannon were overrun."

This tale of Marcus's origins was complete fiction, but it served to quiet the captain—at least about how he'd become a part of Moulder's regiment.

Moulder spread the piece of canvas wide. There was little left of the face of George III. The eyes were gone, the mouth was nothing more than a gaping hole, and the monarch's powdered hair was peppered with shot.

"Well, at least one thing you've told me is true," Moulder admitted. "The boy is a good shot."

"Doc saved my life at Princeton," Swift said. "Put a ball right through the eye of a British soldier. And he doctored the lieutenant's hand when he burned it. Useful boy to have around, sir."

"And these?" Moulder picked up two brass semicircles, finely engraved, that had been found in Marcus's haversack when the captain searched it for other spoils of battle. "Don't tell me they're medical instruments."

"Quadrants," Swift replied. "Or they will be when we're through with them."

In addition to the head of George III, Marcus had taken the two pieces from the orrery that stood outside the room where he'd found the king's portrait. Other soldiers had smashed the glass and part of the fine mechanism that marked the passage of the planets across the sky. He had pocketed what remained because it reminded him of his mother, and home.

"General Washington is bound to hear about this target practice of yours." Moulder sighed. "What do you propose I tell him, Swift?"

"I'd let him think Captain Hamilton did it," Swift replied. "That pop-injay likes to take credit for everything, whether he's responsible or not."

There was no denying it, and Captain Moulder didn't even try.

"Get out of my sight, all of you," Moulder said wearily. "I will tell the general that Lieutenant Cuthbert has already disciplined you. And I'm docking your pay."

"Pay?" Swift guffawed. "What pay?"

"Thank you, sir. I'll see to it that nothing like this happens again." Cuthbert took Swift by the scruff of the neck. "Enjoy your lunch, sir."

Outside the tent, Vanderslice, Swift, and Marcus were greeted by silence. Then the pats on the back started, the offers of swallows of rum and gin, the proud smiles.

"Thanks, Doc," Vanderslice said, relieved that he was not going to be beaten.

"You lie like an Irishman, Doc," Adam Swift said, clapping his hat on his head. "I knew I liked you."

"The Associators take care of their own," Cuthbert murmured in Marcus's ear. "You're one of us now."

For the first time since leaving Joshua and Zeb in Hadley, Marcus felt that he belonged.

SEVERAL DAYS AFTER being hauled before Moulder, Marcus and Vanderslice were sharing what qualified as a fire in Washington's winter encampment: a pile of damp logs that smoked and gave off very little heat. He had no feeling in his fingers or toes, and the air was so cold that it seared the skin before burning a pathway into his lungs.

The frigid temperatures made conversation difficult, but Vanderslice was undeterred. The only topic that the boy refused to discuss was his life before he became part of the Philadelphia artillery company. This was the root of the friendship that had sprung up between Marcus and Vanderslice. While most of the soldiers talked about nothing but their mothers, the girls they'd left behind, and male relatives who were fighting for Washington in other regiments, it was as though Marcus and Vanderslice had been born in November and only remembered life with the Associators: their retreat from Manhattan following the loss of Ft. Washington, the battle at Trenton at Christmas, and the most recent battle near the college at Princeton.

"'*Two angels came down from the north; / one named Fire, the other Frost; / Frost said to Fire go away, go away; / in the name of Jesus go away,*'" Vanderslice said, blowing on his cold-reddened fingers. He had only one glove, and kept swapping it back and forth between his hands.

"Wonder if we could expel the cold if we said it backward." Marcus burrowed into the woolen muffler he'd taken off a dead soldier after the battle at Princeton.

"Probably. Prayers have power," Vanderslice replied. "Do you know any others?"

"Frostbite in January, amputate in July." It was more of a prophecy than a prayer, but Marcus shared it anyway.

"You can't fool me, Yankee. You didn't learn that in church." Vanderslice reached into his pocket and pulled out a small flask. "Want a nip of rum? It's got gunpowder in it, to give you courage."

Marcus took a precautionary sniff.

"You'll shit your brains out if you drink any more of that," he said, returning the flask to Vanderslice. "It's castor oil."

Lieutenant Cuthbert strode toward the fire, attracting the attention of the other Associators who gathered around to see what was afoot.

"You're in a hurry," Adam Swift remarked in his decidedly Irish drawl. He had been one of the first to sign up when the Associators were established, and was Cuthbert's de facto second-in-command.

"We're going home." Cuthbert quickly hushed the cries of relief. "I heard it from one of the whores, who learned it from one of Washington's aides, who heard the general talking to the other officers."

Conversation burst out between members of the regiment as they began making plans for what they'd do once they were back home. Marcus shivered as the cold whistled through his coat. Philadelphia was no home to him. He would have to find another regiment to join—and soon. Maybe he would have to change his name again. If Washington was breaking up their winter camp and sending everyone back home, Marcus would need somewhere to go.

"You coming with us, Doc?" Swift elbowed Marcus in the ribs.

Marcus smiled and nodded, but there was a cold knot in his stomach.

He didn't have any skills that would be useful in Philadelphia. There wouldn't be farm work until spring.

"Of course Doc is coming. He's going to hang a shingle outside German Gerty's and sell his medical services," Cuthbert said. "I'll stand outside and testify to your skill." He held up his thumb.

"Let me see that." Marcus stood, his cold joints creaking at the change in position. What he wouldn't give for some of Tom Buckland's liniment to soothe the ache in his bones.

Obediently, Cuthbert offered his hand to Marcus. Marcus looked at it closely, pushing up Cuthbert's sleeve to examine the arm as well. At Princeton, Cuthbert had grabbed the wrong end of a gun brush, and some of the wire had become embedded in his thumb. It was still angry and red, but not nearly as swollen as it had been.

"No red streaks. That's good—no infection." Marcus probed the skin around the wound. There was a bit of discharge, but not much. "You must have the constitution of an ox, Lieutenant."

"You there!" A small, elderly man in a wig that was at least forty years out of style pointed in Marcus's direction. "Who are you?"

"Galen Chauncey," Marcus said as confidently as he could. Cuthbert cut him a shrewd glance.

"You are the regimental surgeon for these men?" The longer the man's sentences, the more evident his German accent became, all the *th*'s turning into soft *d*'s.

Sensing a potential crisis, Cuthbert turned on his considerable charm. "How can I help, Mr. . . . ?"

"Dr. Otto," the man said, planting his feet wide. "This is a Pennsylvania company, *ja*?"

"Yes," Cuthbert admitted.

"I am chief surgeon for the Pennsylvania companies, and I do not know this man." Otto sized up Marcus from head to toe. "He does not look like one of us. That shirt is very odd."

"Doc's not odd. He's a Yankee, that's all," said Swift.

Marcus glared at him. That was not something he wanted officers to know.

"Doc?" Otto's voice rose.

"Not exactly," Marcus said hastily. "I learned some tricks of healing from a friend back home, that's all."

"Tricks?" Otto's voice was now as high as his eyebrows.

"Skills," Marcus corrected himself.

"If you are so skilled, then what are the healing properties of mercury?" Otto demanded.

"Treating lesions on the skin," Marcus said, happy to remember some of what he'd learned from Tom's medical books.

"And why would you administer calomel and jalap?"

"To purge the bowels," Marcus replied promptly.

"You know of Dr. Rush's methods, I see. And what do you know of Dr. Sutton?" Dr. Otto's dark eyes fixed intently on Marcus.

"I know he charges too much for ordinary people to afford his services," Marcus said, tired of the inquisition. He pushed up his sleeve. The puckered scar from his own inoculation was still visible on his arm, and likely would be for his whole life. "And I know his method works. Any other questions?"

"No." Otto blinked. "You will come with me."

"Why?" Marcus asked warily.

"Because, Herr Doc, you are going to work for me now. You should not be behind a gun, but in the hospital," Otto said.

"But I belong to them." Marcus looked to the men in his company for support, but Cuthbert just shook his head.

"It will be months before we're on the battlefield again," Cuthbert said. "You can do more for the cause of liberty with the doctor than you can drinking the winter away with Vanderslice and Swift."

"What are you waiting for, Herr Doc?" Dr. Otto demanded. "I gave you an order. Get your pack, and bring your blanket. All of mine are on the sick soldiers."

After Hadley, Marcus's life path had been as twisted and dark as a forest trail. It had led him through New England and into New York, skirting the edges of battle while constantly afraid of being captured as a deserter or a spy or a murderer. Then the Associators had let him join their ranks, and Marcus had been able to see a few miles ahead into December and now January.

But the Associators were all returning to the comforts of home. His life was taking another strange turn, thanks to this odd little German doctor, who was plucking him out of the crowded, smoky conditions of the camp only to thrust him into the bloody world of what passed for hospitals in Washington's army. For Marcus, it was a chance to escape even further from what had happened in his past. He remembered what Sarah Bishop had told him at Bunker Hill: that the army was going to need healers more than it needed fighters.

Still, Marcus hesitated, standing at this unexpected fork in the road.

"Go on," Swift said, tossing Marcus's heavy haversack to him. "Besides, if you don't like it, you can find us at German Gerty's tavern most days. It's down on the Philadelphia docks. Anyone can point the way."

WHEN HE LEFT the Associators' fire, Marcus finally saw Washington's army laid out in all its confusing squalor. Until today, he had not explored the rest of camp for fear that he might see someone from Massachusetts—but that seemed unlikely given the fact that it had a population to rival some big towns, and the layout was just as confusing. Dr. Otto seemed to know every alley and byway, however, and moved with assurance through the troops, their smoking fires, and the torn and stained flags that proudly flew at the center of each company to identify which patch of frozen ground belonged to Connecticut and which to Virginia.

"Fools," Otto muttered, slapping away a standard for a New Jersey regiment that was snapping in the cold wind.

"Excuse me?" Marcus was struggling to keep up with the old man's pace.

"So busy fighting each other, it is no wonder the British have been winning." Otto noticed a soldier sitting on a fallen log, his leg blackened and oozing. "You there. Have that leg seen to by your surgeon or you will lose it, *ja*?"

Marcus shot a quick glance at the suppurating leg. He'd never seen anything so gruesome. What had the man done to cause such an injury?

"Burned with powder, then marched through the cold on poor rations. And no shoes!" Otto continued through the camp, his accent growing thicker with each step. "Idiocy. Sheer madness. Soon the Big Man will have no army left."

Marcus assumed the Big Man was Washington. He had seen the general three times: once on his horse overlooking the Hudson River as Ft. Washington fell to the Hessian troops, again at Trenton when he climbed into a boat to cross the Delaware, and a third time in Princeton when Washington had nearly been shot by one of his own cannon. Washington towered over the rest of his men on foot, but on a horse, he was like one of the heroes of old.

"One army. One camp. One medical service. This is the way to win a war," Otto muttered. "Connecticut has medicine chests, but no medicines. Maryland has medicine, but no bandages. Virginia has bandages, but no chests to store them in, so they have been ruined. Around and around we go. Madness."

Dr. Otto stopped abruptly and Marcus ran into him, almost knocking the doctor off his feet.

"I ask you, how are we supposed to heal these men if Washington will not listen?" Otto demanded. His wig tipped to one side as if it, too, were considering the question.

Marcus shrugged. Otto sighed.

"Exactly," he said. "We must do what we can, in spite of the lunatics."

"That's been my experience, sir," Marcus said, hoping to soothe the irascible German.

Otto looked sour, but they had at last reached their destination: a large tent on the outskirts of the encampment. Beyond it was Morristown. Marcus had noted the town's prosperity and the hum of business that surrounded it, even in the depths of war and winter.

Around the tent, men loaded boxes onto wagons and unloaded more boxes from carts coming in from the countryside. A troop of local boys was splitting an enormous pile of logs into wood for the fires. Women stirred cauldrons of steaming water filled with sodden blankets.

A tired-looking man in a bloodstained apron was sitting on an overturned bucket, smoking a pipe.

"This is my new surgeon's mate, Dr. Cochran," Dr. Otto said. "His name is Margalen MacChauncey Doc. It sounds Scottish, *ja*?"

"Scottish? No, I don't think so, Bodo," Dr. Cochran said with a thick burr that reminded Marcus of his grandfather MacNeil. "Where are you from, boy?"

"Mas—Philadelphia." Marcus caught himself just in time. A slip like that could cost him his life, if someone with an active curiosity were to hear it.

"He sounds foreign to me," Otto said in his thick accent. "Some boys from Philadelphia said he was a Yankee, but I do not know whether to believe them."

"He might well be." Cochran studied Marcus closely. "Yankees do have very strange names. I've heard some called Submit and Endeavour and Fortitude. Does he have any experience? He looks too young to know much, Bodo."

Marcus bristled.

"He is familiar with the methods of Dr. Rush," Otto said, "and how to empty a man's bowels most forcefully."

"Hmph," Cochran replied, drawing on his pipe. "We don't need any help with that. Not in this army."

"The boy has heard of Dr. Sutton, too." Dr. Otto blinked like one of the owls that roosted in their barn in Hadley.

"Is that so?" Cochran's tone was speculative. "Well, then. Let's see if he knows something more useful than one of Dr. Rush's extreme cures. If your patient was complaining of rheumatism and pain in the joints, how would you induce a sweat, boy?"

More questions. Marcus would rather be back among the Associators than be grilled and scolded like a schoolboy by the army surgeons.

"I'd have him examined by a committee of medical officers, Dr. Cochran," Marcus retorted. "And the name is Mr. Chauncey, if you please."

Cochran bellowed with laughter.

"What do you think, Dr. Cochran? Did I not find us a suitable replacement for that frightened young man who ran off at Princeton?" Otto asked.

"Aye. He'll do." Cochran tamped down on the tobacco in his pipe and slipped it into his pocket. "Welcome to the army's medical corps, Doc— or whatever your name is."

For the second time in his short life, Marcus shed one identity and adopted another.

———

TIME PASSED DIFFERENTLY in the medical corps than it had on the farm in Hadley (where nothing seemed to change except the seasons), or in his life as a fugitive (where every day was different), or the brief period among the Associators (when time passed so quickly that you didn't have the opportunity to think). In the army's temporary hospital in Morristown, time passed in a never-ending stream of wounds and illnesses that flowed among tables and cots, crates of bandages, and boxes of medicines. No sooner did a new patient arrive than a former patient left. Some left in pine boxes, destined for the graveyard dug on the outskirts of town. The more fortunate were sent home to convalesce from broken limbs and gunshot wounds or cases of dysentery. Others languished on the wards, poorly fed and poorly housed, unable to die, yet equally unable to heal.

As the newest recruit, Marcus had first been posted to the part of the hospital reserved for men with minor injuries and ailments. There his jobs were menial, requiring no medical knowledge whatsoever. His duties did provide a way for him to learn the rhythms of this new environment and to develop his skills. Marcus was learning how to diagnose patients by carefully watching their restless limbs, the pace of their breathing as they dreamed, and the spots of color that often appeared in the middle of the night and indicated that infection was taking root in the body.

The moonlit hours also provided Marcus with an opportunity to eavesdrop on the senior medical officers, who would gather by the ancient, inefficient stove to talk when the wards were quiet, their patients had sunk into whatever troubled sleep their injuries allowed, and only a skeleton crew of low-ranking surgeons' mates like Marcus were present.

Cochran was smoking his pipe—something he did whenever he had an opportunity, even in the midst of a surgical procedure. Otto was rocking slowly in a chair with uneven runners, which made him look like he was riding a lame hobbyhorse.

"If we are to remain at Morristown, there must be proper housing, with latrines dug farther away from the soldiers," Dr. Otto said. "Dysentery and typhus are more deadly than any British bullet."

"Watery bowels, like the itch, are fixtures of army life. The smallpox, on the other hand . . ." Cochran trailed off into silence. He puffed on his pipe, the smoke wreathing his head. "We will have to inoculate them all, Bodo—every last one of them—or the whole army will be dead by the spring thaw."

"There is nothing quick in army life, except for retreats," Dr. Otto observed.

Marcus snorted in agreement, then tried to cover it up with a fit of coughing.

"We are aware that you can hear us, Mr. Doc," Otto said sharply. "You are like one of the Big Man's dogs, always watching and listening. But these are good traits in a doctor, so we let you do it."

"Washington tells me that I will soon to go into Pennsylvania to open a hospital there. But if the general agrees to inoculate the entire army, as we hope, the burden will fall largely on your shoulders at Trenton, Bodo," Dr. Cochran said, returning to their conversation.

"*Das ist mir Wurst*, my friend," Otto replied. "I have my sons to help—unless you wish to take them with you instead."

All three of Dr. Otto's sons were medical men, carefully trained by their father to treat a variety of common ailments as well as undertake surgical procedures. They could concoct medicines, suture wounds, and diagnose patient complaints. Marcus had seen them working in the wards, following their father like a flock of devoted chicks, and had been amazed by their quiet competence in the face of the most gruesome injuries.

"I thank you, Bodo, but my staff did not abandon their patients and go home, as so many others did. I am well served, at present." Cochran angled his head in Marcus's direction. "What will you do with him?"

"Take him to Trenton, of course, and see if we can make him a doctor in truth as well as in name," Dr. Otto replied.

MARCUS HAD THOUGHT NEVER to see Trenton again. He had nearly frozen to death there, waiting to cross the Delaware River with the rest of Washington's troops during the dark days before Christmas when all had seemed lost.

Trenton was a very different place now where, with utmost secrecy and under direct orders from General Washington, Dr. Otto and his staff were inoculating the entire Continental army.

These days, Marcus's pockets were filled with spools of thread and scalpels rather than ammunition and fuses. Dr. Otto had definite ideas about cleanliness, and the scalpels were boiled in a mixture of vinegar and soap each night. Once a piece of thread was used, it was put into a shallow basin, the contents tossed into the stoves and burned at the end of each day. To keep their clothes from harboring the infection, all of the soldiers were stripped naked and wrapped in blankets. Mrs. Dolly, that indispensable member of Dr. Otto's staff, had come to Trenton along with all three of Otto's sons, his medicine chest, and the laundress's seemingly bottomless iron cauldrons. It was she who had the job of washing the threadbare clothes and (if possible) returning them to the soldiers once they recovered from the pox.

The Trenton barracks housed men from every part of the colonies, all of them undergoing some form of treatment. Southerners with their soft drawls were bedded down next to fast-talking New Yorkers and long-voweled New Englanders. Marcus heard many a soldier's story on those long nights when he was cleaning up after the men. Some were younger than fifteen and had signed up for service in place of an older man who didn't want to go to war. Some were hardened veterans who told harrowing tales of their previous service to while away the hours of confinement as they waited for the pox to take hold.

All of the men—young and old, Southerner and New Englander alike—were anxious about inoculation. Dr. Otto was a good teacher, and patiently explained the process and why General Washington had ordered that the whole army undergo the procedure.

These explanations might have been medically sound, but they did little to ease the soldiers' minds. As the smallpox spread, fear grew alongside it. While many of the Continental soldiers knew of at least one person who had undergone inoculation and survived, most also knew someone who hadn't been so fortunate. Dr. Otto kept careful records of the soldiers he inoculated, noting how the fever progressed in each, how severely they contracted the smallpox, and whether they lived or died. If a soldier refused to be inoculated, Dr. Otto shared his accounts of successful inoculations. If that didn't convince the soldier, he barked that he was following General Washington's orders.

So far, Dr. Otto hadn't lost a single patient through inoculation, though men *were* dying in the hospital from smallpox they'd caught in the camps.

By the end of February, Marcus had been promoted from performing menial tasks on the wards at night to undertaking inoculations on his own. It was evening at the end of a long day, and Marcus had only one more soldier to see to before he could leave the hospital for a few hours of sleep.

"What's your name?" Marcus asked the newest man on the ward as he sat down at his bedside. He was about Marcus's age, smooth of face and wary in his expressions.

"Silas Hubbard," he replied.

Marcus drew out a small knife and tin box. The soldier looked at them with barely controlled fear.

"Where you from, Silas?"

"Here and there. Connecticut. Mostly," Hubbard confessed. "You?"

"New York. Mostly." Marcus lifted the tin lid. Inside the box were whorls of thread, all of them dampened with fluid from the sores of inoculated smallpox patients.

"Is this going to kill me, Doc?" Hubbard asked.

"Probably not," Marcus said. He showed Hubbard the scar on his left arm. "What I'm about to do to you, someone else did to me last summer. And here I am, freezing to death in Washington's army not six months later."

Hubbard gave Marcus a tentative smile.

"Give me your arm. I'll give you a small case of smallpox in return. That way you can survive the winter and get a fierce case of the itch come spring," Marcus said, employing soldiers' humor to lighten the atmosphere.

"And what are you going to do for me when I'm tormented with itching?" Hubbard asked.

"Nothing," Marcus said with a grin. "Unless Washington orders me to scratch it for you."

"I saw Washington. At Princeton." Hubbard settled back against the pillows and closed his eyes. He held his arm out obediently while Marcus examined it for a good place to make the shallow incisions.

Marcus found a spot between two old scars that were puckered and twisted. He wondered how—or from whom—Hubbard had received them.

"I wish he was my pa," Silas said, his voice wistful. "They say he's as fair as he is brave."

"That's what I hear, too," Marcus said, drawing the lancet through Hubbard's flesh. The boy didn't even wince. "God didn't give the general sons of his own. I reckon that's why He gave Washington an army—so that he could be father to us all."

A draft brushed across Marcus's shoulders. He turned, expecting to see the surgeon's mate who was replacing him on the wards.

Instead, he saw something that made his hackles rise.

A tall man in the deerskin hunting shirt and leggings of a Virginia rifleman was stalking silently through the beds. His feet made no sound, though Marcus knew the springy floorboards creaked under the slightest pressure. There was something in the way he carried himself that was familiar, and Marcus searched through his memories, trying to place him.

Then Marcus remembered where he'd seen that wolfish face before.

It was the dead New Hampshire rifleman from Bunker Hill. Except this man was alive. And dressed like he came from Virginia, not New England.

Their eyes met.

"Well, well. I know you." The man cocked his head slightly. "You stole my rifle. At Bunker Hill."

"Cole?" Marcus whispered. He blinked.

The man was gone.

The Pennsylvania Packet
August 26, 1777
page 3

SIXTEEN DOLLARS REWARD.

WAS STOLEN out of the pasture of the subscriber, in North Milford Hundred, Cecil County, Maryland, on the night of the 3d of July last, a light dun Mare, about fourteen hands high, black mane and tail, a natural trotter, newly shod, has a small ace on her forehead, and a remarkable white piece of hair above her foretop which extends across to the root of her ears. Whoever takes up the mare and thief, so that the owner may have his mare and the thief be brought to justice, shall have the above Reward, and for the mare only, EIGHT DOLLARS paid by

PETER BAULDEN

TWENTY DOLLARS REWARD.

DESERTED last night from Capt. Roland Maddison's company, the 12th Virginia regiment, commanded by Col. James Wood, in General Scott's brigade, JOSEPH COMTON, eighteen or nineteen years of age, five feet eight inches high, brown complexion; and WILLIAM BASSETT, of the same age, five feet six inches high, fair complexion, has two of his foreteeth. They carried with them a blanket and other clothing usual for soldiers to wear, and a quantity of cartridges. Whoever takes up said Deserters and takes them to camp at Head Quarters, or secures them in any of the States gaols and gives information thereof, shall have the above Reward and all reasonable expences, or TEN DOLLARS for each.

Rowland Maddison, Captain

Freehold, Monmouth County, New Jersey, Aug. 11

TEN DOLLARS REWARD.

DESERTED from Capt. John Burrowe's company, in Col. David Forman's regiment of Continental troops, on the 6th of July last, a certain GEORGE SHADE, about twenty-four years of age, five feet eight inches high, has light coloured hair and blue eyes, one of his legs thicker than the other occasioned by it being broke. It is supposed he is on one of the vessels of war in the Delaware river. Whoever will apprehend the said deserter and secure him, so that he might be had again, shall receive the above Reward and all reasonable charges.

JOHN BURROWES, Captain

⇥ 16 ⇤

Lame

Gerty's tavern was quiet now that the merchants had finished their mid-day trading, and the men had not yet come off the Philadelphia docks at the end of work to share a drink with friends. It was sweltering at the busy intersection of Spruce and Front Streets, the strong sun casting shadows of the masts of the ships at the wharves. The temperatures would not peak until three o'clock. By then, Marcus suspected Gerty would be able to fry bacon on her doorstep, and the city would be uninhabitable due to the stench coming from the tanneries and the filth in the streets.

He sat in the corner by the open, deeply casemented window next to the articulated skeleton of a man that Gerty had won from the medical students in a game of cards. It had been propped up in the front room ever since, festooned with broadsides and notices tied to his ribs, a pipe clamped between his teeth, clutching used tickets to the anatomy lectures in his bony fingers.

Marcus was reading the *Pennsylvania Packet*. It had become a part of his routine to thumb through the papers Gerty kept on hand and scour them for news from Massachusetts. At first, he had done so out of fear, looking for mention of Obadiah's murder. But nearly a year had passed and there was still no accusation against a blond young man answering to the name of MacNeil. Now he did so out of a more nostalgic hunger for news of home. But there was little of it. These days the papers were filled with rewards for anyone who would turn in an army deserter or return a lost or stolen horse, and news of the latest British maneuvers off the coast.

"Afternoon, Doc." Vanderslice plopped himself on the bench opposite and stacked his feet on the windowsill. "What's going on in the world?"

"Everyone's running away," Marcus said, scanning the columns of print.

"I'd run from this heat if I could." Vanderslice mopped his forehead with the tail of his coarsely woven shirt. Even for Philadelphia, it had been a prodigiously warm summer. "Why hasn't Dr. Franklin invented a way to stop it? I hear he can devise a way around anything."

"Franklin's still in Paris, probably eating iced berries from a spoon," Marcus replied. "I don't think he has any time to worry about us, Vanderslice."

"Iced berries. I feel cooler just thinking about them." Vanderslice plucked a card from the skeleton's hand and fanned himself. "And that spoon is probably held by a fine French lady."

A blowsy woman of indeterminate age with pockmarked skin and orange hair that defied nature came to the table. Her dress was parrot green, stained with wine, and strained over her bosom.

"You'll need to be spoon-fed yourself if you don't get your filthy boots off my wall," Gerty said, knocking Vanderslice's feet to the ground.

"Aw, Gert." Vanderslice gave her a piteous look. "I just wanted to see if I could feel a breeze on my legs."

"Give me a shilling and I'll blow on them for you." Gerty pursed her lips, ready to do just that, but Vanderslice didn't take her up on her offer. "When do you get paid, Claes? I am owed money."

"You'll get it," Vanderslice promised. "You know I'm good for it."

"Hmph." Gerty knew no such thing, but she liked the young Dutchman. "I have windows to fix. If I'm not paid by Friday, you will be up on ropes and working off your beer."

"Thanks, Gert." Vanderslice resumed his fanning. "You're a gem."

"And thanks from me as well, Gerty." Marcus put a copper token on the table. "I have to get back to the hospital. Did you get extra provisions in? Water and fuel? In case the British do come?"

"*Och*, you worry too much." Gerty dismissed his words with a wave. "Now that General Washington has all these handsome Frenchmen to help him, the war will be over before Christmas."

The ladies of Philadelphia were all in love with the Marquis de Lafayette, a nineteen-year-old beanstalk with red hair and a minimal grasp of English.

"Your marquis brought only a dozen men with him." Marcus didn't think that would be enough to turn away the king's troops based on what he'd seen on the battlefield.

"La." That was Gerty's answer to anything annoyingly factual. "The marquis is so tall we could divide him in two and still be left with someone more fit for battle than most of my customers."

"Just remember what I told you. Keep your patriotic opinions to yourself if the British come. Serve anyone who has proper money. Survive." Marcus had been trying to drum this message into Gerty since the Trenton barracks had been emptied of their inoculated troops and Dr. Otto and his staff removed to Philadelphia.

"I will, I will. Now give Gerty a kiss and be on your way." Gerty pursed her rouged lips and waited. Marcus gave her a perfunctory kiss on the cheek instead.

"Tell Dr. Otto that Gerty is always here for him, if he is lonely," Gerty continued, unfazed by the lack of enthusiasm in Marcus's embrace. "We will speak our mother tongue and remember old times."

Marcus had met Mrs. Otto, a buxom woman who spoke little and commanded the entire family and medical staff with nothing more than frowns and her heavy step on the wards. Dr. Otto would no more seek solace from German Gerty—even if he was sorely in need of it—than impale himself on a bayonet.

"I'll pass that along." Marcus clapped his hat on his head, waved his farewell to Vanderslice, and headed out into the summer sunshine.

Marcus's route to the hospital took him across most of the crowded, chaotic city. In only a few months he had grown to love Philadelphia and its inhabitants, in spite of the filth and the noise. The brick market house was filled with produce from nearby farms and rivers, even in wartime. Every tongue was spoken in the coffeehouses and taverns, and the whole world seemed to pass through her docks.

In spite of the August heat (which seemed destined never to break) and the imminent threat of British invasion (which seemed never to come), Philadelphia thrived. The streets were packed with carriages and horses, their wheels and hooves making a racket on the cobblestones. Every inch of space that wasn't a residence or a tavern was taken up by someone making and selling something: saddles, shoes, medicines, newspapers. The air rang with the sound of hammers and the whir of lathes.

He walked west into the quieter residential streets where the rich merchants lived. The heavy summer air further muffled the sounds of servants tending to children in walled gardens, the drone of insects sipping at blossoms, and the occasional call of a delivery boy as he dropped off his wares. Marcus had never crossed the threshold of such a grand house, but he liked to imagine what it would look like: black-and-white polished floors, a curved banister reaching toward the second floor, high windows with sparkling glass, white candles in brass sconces to beat back the twilight, a room full of books to read, and a globe for imagining a voyage around the world.

One day, Marcus promised himself. *One day I will have such a house.* Then he would go back to Hadley and collect his mother and Patience, and bring them to live in it.

Until then, Marcus enjoyed the pleasures associated with simply being near such luxury. He drank in the honeyed scent of the chestnut trees and the tang of coffee that escaped through the windows of elegant drawing rooms. Dr. Otto had bought him a cup of the dark elixir at the City Tavern when they arrived in Philadelphia. Marcus had never tasted anything like it, having drunk only tea and the black sludge that was served in the army. The feeling of elation that accompanied the tiny cup stayed with Marcus for hours. He would forever associate coffee with witty conversation and the exchange of news. Sitting for an hour in the City Tavern with Philadelphia's merchants and businessmen was, in Marcus's estimation, the closest he was likely to get to heaven.

As Marcus walked, the fine houses gradually gave way to the tall brick buildings where more ordinary Philadelphians lived and worked. He traveled a few blocks farther, and the outlines of the city's two hospitals came into view, both topped with cupolas. The Pennsylvania Hospital was attached to the city's college and was where the university-trained physicians performed dissections and gave medical lectures. Dr. Otto, his family, and his staff were in charge of the other hospital: Philadelphia's Bettering House for the indigent, criminal, and insane.

When Marcus stepped into the Bettering House, the entrance was filled with boxes of every size, several large wooden apothecary chests, and more doctors bearing the surname of Otto than any army should have to endure. All four men in the Otto family—Bodo; his eldest son,

Frederick; Bodo's second son and namesake, called "Dr. Junior"; and his youngest son, John, who was usually called "boy"—were busily checking their inventories. Nurses and orderlies rushed around fulfilling the doctors' requests. Mrs. Otto alone remained serene, winding strips of bandage into tight rolls despite a hospital cat's determination to play with them.

"There you are," Dr. Otto said, peering over his spectacles at Marcus. "Where have you been, Mr. Doc?"

"He's been in a tavern reading newspapers," Dr. Frederick said. "His fingers are black, and the smell of beer is overwhelming. You might have at least rinsed out your mouth, Doc."

Marcus bristled, his lips pressed firmly closed. He said not a word but picked up a box of stoppered bottles and took it over to Dr. Otto.

"Here is the camphor! I asked you for it three times, boy. How did you not see it? It was at your elbow this whole time," Dr. Otto exclaimed.

John, who had recently married and was often thinking about more pleasant matters than apothecary chests and jalap, heard his name and looked around in confusion.

Dr. Otto muttered in German, clearly irritated. Marcus's knowledge of the language was growing. He caught the words for "idiot," "lewd," "wife," and "hopeless." John heard, too, and turned pink.

"Where will you go first, Bodo?" Mrs. Otto packed her rolled bandage away in a basket and picked up another length of cloth. "To the hospital in Bethlehem to wait for the wounded?"

"I leave such decisions to the Big Man, Mrs. Otto," the doctor replied.

"Surely we will be going straight to the battlefield," Junior said. "They say the whole British army is at the mouth of the Elk River, and marching north."

"They say many things, most of which turn out to be false," Frederick observed.

"There is one thing that is for sure," Dr. Otto said, his tone sober. "Wherever we are going, we are going soon. The battle is coming. I can feel it, pricking at my soles."

Everyone within earshot stopped to listen. Dr. Otto did have a preternatural ability to anticipate the orders that Washington handed down. No one had realized Dr. Otto was getting his intelligence from his feet, however. Mrs. Otto looked down at her husband's shoes with new respect.

"Don't stand there gawping, Mr. Chauncey!" After her husband's prognostication, Mrs. Otto was seized with anxiety and spurred to greater efficiency. "You heard the doctor. You are not pulling a cannon any longer. There is no time for idleness in the hospital service."

Marcus put down the box of camphor and picked up another. Not every tyrant, he had discovered, was a man. Some wore skirts.

WHEN AT LAST the battle came, at a small town outside Philadelphia on the shores of the Brandywine, the chaos was unspeakable.

Marcus thought he knew what to expect. He had been with Dr. Otto since January, had inoculated hundreds of men, and had seen soldiers die of smallpox, typhus, camp fever, wounds acquired during foraging expeditions, exposure, and starvation.

But Marcus had never been behind the advancing army with the medical service, waiting for the casualties to arrive after the orders to fire had been given. From the rear, it was impossible to tell whether the Continental army was inches from victory or if the British had routed them.

The medical corps set up their first hospital in a mercantile just outside the battle lines, where the surgeons' mates transformed the dry goods counter into an operating table. They stacked the dead in a small room where extra flour and sugar had once been stored. Those awaiting treatment lay in rows on the floor, filling the hall and the porch outside.

As the battle commenced, and the number of wounded and dying men rose, Dr. Cochran and Dr. Otto decided that a dressing station should be set up closer to the action to evaluate the wounded. Dr. Otto took Marcus to his new field hospital, leaving Dr. Cochran in charge at the store.

"Dressings. Why are there no dressings? I must have dressings," Dr. Otto repeated in a low mutter as they set up the treatment areas.

But the dressings and bandages that Mrs. Otto had so assiduously rolled and packed had all been used. Marcus and Dr. Otto were forced to use blotting paper and soiled dressings from dead men instead, the blood wrung out into buckets that attracted the summer's black flies.

"Hold him there," Dr. Otto said, directing Marcus's attention with a shift of his eyes. Underneath their hands, a soldier writhed in agony.

Marcus could see crushed bone and raw muscle through torn clothing. His stomach tightened.

"The patient may faint, Mr. Doc, but not the surgeon," Dr. Otto said sternly. "Go out to the porch and take six lungfuls of air and then come back. It will steel your nerves."

Marcus bolted for the door but was barred from leaving the farmhouse by a stranger who cast a long shadow in the hall.

"You." The shadow pointed at him. "Come."

"Yes, sir." Marcus wiped the sweat from his eyes and blinked.

A man came into focus, one so large he filled the doorway. He was wearing a dark blue coat with a standing collar, few buttons, and no gold braid. *French.* Marcus recognized the cut and style from the parades he'd seen on Market Street in Philadelphia.

"Are you a doctor?" The Frenchman spoke perfect English, which was unusual. Most of his countrymen got by with hand gestures and the occasional English word.

"No. A surgeon. I'll call—"

"There's no time. You'll do." The man reached out a long arm and caught Marcus by the collar. His hands were crusted with blood, and his white breeches were smeared with splashes of red.

"Are you wounded?" Marcus asked his captor. The Frenchman seemed robust enough, but if he were to fall down, Marcus wasn't sure he would have the strength to lift him to safety.

"I am the chevalier de Clermont—and I am not your patient," the Frenchman replied, a sharp edge to his voice. He pointed again, his arm long and his fingers fine and aristocratic. "He is."

Another French soldier lay on a makeshift stretcher, nearly as tall as his friend and covered with enough gold braid to draw the notice of even the most discriminating Philadelphia maiden. A French officer—an important one, by the looks of him. Marcus rushed to his side.

"It is nothing," the fallen officer protested in a thick French accent. He struggled to sit up. "It is a very little hole—*une petite éraflure.* You must see to this man first."

A young private from a Virginia regiment was slung, unconscious, between two friends. Blood poured from his knees.

"A musket ball went through the marquis's left calf. It doesn't appear to have hit the bone," Marcus's captor said. "His boot needs cutting off, and the wound needs cleaning and dressing."

God help me, Marcus thought, staring down at the stretcher. *This is the Marquis de Lafayette.*

If Marcus didn't call Dr. Otto immediately, Mrs. Otto would hold him down while Dr. Frederick beat him senseless. General Washington doted on Lafayette like a son. He was too important for the likes of Marcus.

"Sir, I'm no doctor," Marcus protested. "Let me fetch—"

"That you, Doc? Thank God." Vanderslice was helping Lieutenant Cuthbert hop in his direction. Cuthbert's eyebrows were nearly singed off, and his face was the color of boiled lobster, but it was his bare, bloody foot that captured Marcus's attention.

"Doc?" The tall Frenchman's eyes narrowed.

"*In de benen!*" Vanderslice whistled as he watched a ball pass overhead. He gauged its trajectory with the quizzical attitude of a seasoned artilleryman. "They're getting closer—or more accurate. If we don't get out of the line of fire we'll all be beyond Doc's help."

"Very well, *Meneer Kaaskopper.*" The French soldier's bow was mocking.

"Cheesemonger?" Vanderslice bristled and loosened his hold on Cuthbert. "You take that back, *kakker.*"

"Carry the marquis to the front parlor. Now." Marcus's voice cracked like a gunshot. "Put Cuthbert on the porch, Vanderslice. I'll see to him after Dr. Otto examines the marquis. And for Christ's sake, get that Virginian to the kitchen. What's his name?"

"Norman," one of the Virginians shouted through the rising din. "Will Norman."

"Can you hear me, Will?" Marcus lifted the Virginian's chin and squeezed gently, hoping to rouse him. Dr. Otto didn't believe in striking senseless patients.

"The marquis takes priority." The chevalier gripped Marcus's forearm with a bruising hold.

"Not with me, he doesn't. This is America, *kakker*," Marcus retorted. He had no idea what it meant, but if Vanderslice felt this fellow deserved the name, that was good enough.

"The Virginian," the marquis said, trying to rise from the stretcher. "I promised him that he would not lose his limbs, Matthew."

De Clermont's head angled slightly toward one of the marquis's stretcher-bearers. The man looked miserable, but nodded abjectly before punching Lafayette in the chin. This knocked the French aristocrat out completely.

"Thank you, Pierre." De Clermont turned and strode into the farmhouse. "Do what the Yankee says until I return. I'm going to find another doctor."

"*Vas ist das?*" Dr. Otto demanded of the chevalier de Clermont, who had plucked him off his patient and was dragging him toward Lafayette.

"The Marquis de Lafayette has been wounded," de Clermont said brusquely. "Attend to him. Now."

"You should have taken him to the mercantile," Dr. Otto said. "This is a dressing station. We do not have—"

Dr. Cochran arrived with Dr. Frederick in tow.

"John. Thank God you're here," de Clermont said with visible relief.

"We came as soon as we heard, Matthew," Cochran replied. Behind them were Drs. Shippen and Rush, followed by an anxious flock of aides who usually didn't leave General Washington's side.

"Where is he?" Dr. Shippen demanded in panic, his nearsighted eyes scanning the darkened room. There were two things on which you could rely with Dr. Shippen: He always chose the most aggressive course of treatment even if it killed the patient, and he never had his spectacles with him.

"At your feet," de Clermont said. "Sir."

"That boy needs both legs taken off," Dr. Rush said, pointing at the Virginian. "Do we have a saw?"

"There are less barbaric alternatives." De Clermont's expression darkened.

"Perhaps this is not the best time to discuss them," Dr. Cochran warned. But it was too late.

"We are in the midst of battle!" Dr. Rush exclaimed. "We must take the legs now or we can wait and take them after gangrene has set in and the flesh is putrefied. In either case, the patient is not likely to live."

"How do you know? You haven't even examined him!" de Clermont retorted.

"Are you a surgeon, sir?" Dr. Shippen demanded. "I was not informed that monsieur the marquis was traveling with his own medical staff."

Marcus knew that when doctors fell out over cures, the patients were forgotten. For the moment, at least, Norman's legs were safe. While the rest of them argued, he could at least uncover the Marquis de Lafayette's wound.

"I know my way around a human body," de Clermont said evenly in his perfect English. "And I've read Hunter. Amputation in battlefield settings is not necessarily the best course of treatment."

"Hunter! You overstep yourself, sir!" Shippen exclaimed. "Dr. Otto is extremely fast. The Virginian may well survive the operation."

Marcus examined the marquis's boot. Its leather was soft and pliable, not tough and weather hardened. That would make it much easier to cut through—though it would be a shame to ruin such a fine item of footwear in this army, where so many went poorly shod.

"Here." The man called Pierre held out a small knife.

Marcus glanced around. Other than this French orderly, no one was paying him any notice. Dr. Cochran was trying to soothe Dr. Shippen, who was threatening to throw de Clermont out of the house for impudence. The chevalier had switched to Latin—at least Marcus was fairly sure it was Latin, since Dr. Otto and Dr. Cochran often conversed in the language when they didn't want their patients to understand what they were saying—and was probably continuing his lecture on Hunter's reluctance to amputate. One of the aides was staring at de Clermont with open admiration. Dr. Otto spoke in low tones to Dr. Frederick, who disappeared into the kitchen. Meanwhile the surgeons' mates quietly exchanged bets on the outcome of the argument between de Clermont and Shippen.

Marcus took the knife and neatly sliced the boot from cuff to ankle. He peeled the leather away from the wound. It had clean edges and there was no sign of protruding bone. *No compound fracture*, Marcus thought. An amputation would have been necessary had that been the case, no matter what the chevalier said or Dr. Hunter believed.

Marcus probed the wound with his fingers, feeling for the telltale bump that would indicate that the musket ball was still in the wound, or that the bone had been chipped and a piece was lodged in the muscles. *No lump, no resistance.* That meant there was nothing in the wound that would aggravate the nerves, tendons, or muscles, and no foreign body that might cause the wound to fester.

The marquis stirred. Marcus's touch was gentle, but the man had been shot and the pain must be intense.

"Shall I hit him again, Doc?" Pierre whispered. Like de Clermont, his English was flawless.

Marcus shook his head. His examination had confirmed what he already suspected: The only thing about the marquis's condition that warranted immediate treatment was his aristocratic blood and high rank. The marquis was a fortunate man—far more so than Will Norman.

Marcus felt eyes on him, heavy and watchful. He looked up and met de Clermont's stare. Shippen was sputtering about surgical methods and patient outcomes—the man had an unholy fondness for the knife—but it was Marcus, and not the esteemed doctors, who held the chevalier's attention.

"No." The single word from de Clermont cracked through the room. "You will not treat the Marquis de Lafayette, Dr. Shippen. Ruin the life of the man in the kitchen with your knives and saws, but the marquis will be seen to by Dr. Cochran."

"I beg your—" Shippen blustered.

"It is a minor wound, Dr. Shippen," Dr. Otto interjected. "Let your poor surgeons, Dr. Cochran and me, see to the marquis. Your greater skills are needed elsewhere. I believe the boy with the bad knees was recruited from General Washington's estate."

This got Shippen's attention.

"My son is cleaning his wounds and is waiting to assist." Dr. Otto stepped aside and swept a shallow bow.

"Indeed." Shippen pulled on the edge of his waistcoat and straightened his wig, which he had worn to the field in spite of its impracticality. "A Virginian, you say?"

"He is one of the new riflemen," Dr. Otto said, nodding. "Let me take you through."

As soon as the doctors were clear of the room, everyone who remained swung into action. Cochran asked for lint, ointment, and a probe while he examined the marquis's leg.

"You know better than to bait a quarrelsome animal when he has his dander up, Matthew," Cochran said. "Hand me the turpentine, Doc."

"So you are a doctor, just like the Dutchman said." De Clermont studied Marcus with unblinking eyes.

"He could be," Cochran said, swabbing at the marquis's wounds, "were he given your education, taught Latin, and sent to medical school. Instead, Mr. Chauncey has absorbed more knowledge than most of Dr. Shippen's students through an occult means that he will not divulge."

De Clermont looked at Marcus appraisingly.

"Doc knows his anatomy and basic surgery, and has a good grasp of medicinal simples," Cochran continued, as he carefully cleaned the hole in Lafayette's leg. "His artillery company gave him the title Doc after the army withdrew from New York. Bodo captured him at Morristown and Mr. Chauncey reenlisted for a three-year term in the medical department."

"So you're a New Yorker, Mr. Chauncey," de Clermont said.

"I'm a man of the world," Marcus muttered, trying not to sneeze as Cochran applied fluffy lint to the wound. Man of the world, indeed. He was a cat with nine lives, and nothing more.

"We must get the marquis to safety, John," de Clermont said. "The future of the war might depend on it. Without him advocating for the Americans, it will be hard to get the arms and supplies that you will need to beat the British army."

Marcus's job here was done. There were sick and wounded men outside. And Vanderslice was right: The battle was drawing dangerously near. He headed for the door.

"You'll stay with the marquis, Chauncey," de Clermont ordered, stopping Marcus in his tracks.

"I must see to Lieutenant Cuthbert," Marcus protested. Cuthbert was still waiting for treatment and would not be left behind, even if Marcus had to carry him.

The Marquis de Lafayette stirred. "The Virginian. Where is he?"

Dr. Otto and Dr. Frederick appeared, carrying another stretcher bearing the wounded soldier from Virginia, still with both legs and still unconscious.

"Do not trouble yourself, Marquis," Dr. Otto said cheerfully. "Dr. Shippen and Dr. Rush have gone somewhere out of the range of the British guns. For the better preservation of the wounded."

"For the better preservation of the wounded," Dr. Frederick solemnly repeated, though his lips twitched.

"If we remain here, our next operating theater will be inside a British prison," Cochran warned. "Load those we can transport onto the wagons, Doc. Which way did Shippen and Rush go, Bodo?"

"Back to Philadelphia," Dr. Otto replied.

Marcus wondered how long they would remain there.

Les Revenants, Letters and Papers of the Americas
No. 2
Matthew de Clermont to Philippe de Clermont
Bethlehem, Pennsylvania

23 September 1777

Honored Father:

I am with our friend, who has been shot in battle. He tells me that it was the most glorious moment of his life, to shed blood for liberty. You must forgive him his enthusiasms. If you could tell his wife, madame the marquise, that her husband's spirits are high and that he is in no discomfort, I know that it would ease her mind. She will have heard every sort of account—that he is maimed, that he is dead, that he will die from infection. Assure her that none of these are true.

The medicine is savage here, with few exceptions. I am overseeing Lafayette's care personally, to make sure that they do not kill him with their cures.

I have passed your letters on to Mr. Hancock, who is here in Bethlehem along with most of the Congress. They were forced to leave Philadelphia when the British took the city. Washington needs supplies if he is to succeed—ammunition, guns, horses. More than that, he needs experienced soldiers.

I must go and see to a controversy. The people of this town are very pious, and do not welcome the army and its soldiers.

In haste,

your devoted son,
Matthew

⇥ 17 ⇤

Name

"No, Mr. Adams. It will not do," the chevalier de Clermont said, shaking his head.

Marcus, along with the rest of the medical corps, was standing aside and waiting for the politicians to make a decision about the expansion of the hospital. Congress had decamped north from Philadelphia to the town of Bethlehem to avoid being captured by the British. A flock of women in dark clothing, each one wearing a white ruffled cap on her head, watched the proceedings with open hostility. So, too, did the leader of Bethlehem and its Moravian religious community, Johannes Ettwein.

"We must make sacrifices in the name of liberty, Chevalier. Each one of us, according to our station." John Adams was as sharp-tongued as Ettwein and just as quick to anger.

"There are four hundred sick and wounded soldiers occupying the house belonging to the single brethren." Ettwein was puce with irritation. "You seized our wagons to transport supplies. You are eating the food from our tables. What more must we do?"

As they stood at the corner of Main and Church Streets, Dr. Otto said something in German. One of the women snorted, then quickly disguised it with a cough. De Clermont's lips twitched.

The more time Marcus spent with Lafayette, the more he became fascinated by the chevalier de Clermont. There seemed to be no language the man didn't speak—French, English, Latin, German, Dutch—and nothing he could not do, from taking care of horses to examining wounds to conducting diplomacy. But it was his air of calm authority that made him indispensible at the moment.

"You cannot displace so many women, many of them elderly, Mr. Adams," de Clermont pronounced, as if the decision were up to him and not Dr. Otto, the medical officers, or the members of Congress. "We will have to find another way to house the ill and the wounded."

"It does not seem chivalrous to discommode the ladies, Mr. Adams," the Marquis de Lafayette said from the wheeled chair he called *La Brouette*. The chevalier de Clermont had constructed it out of an ordinary wooden chair he'd found in the Single Brethren's House when it became necessary to move from the Sun Inn. De Clermont had prescribed rest and a good diet for the marquis—neither of which could be found at the tavern, which had been utterly taken over by Congress and couriers ferrying messages. The chevalier had found everything the marquis required a few doors away from the Sun Inn at the house of the Boeckel family—including skilled nurses in the form of Mrs. Boeckel and her daughter, Liesel. When not in use, *La Brouette* was parked by the fire in the Boeckels' parlor, where it received more visitors than Lafayette.

"Chivalry is dead, sir!" Adams declared.

"Not while Gil breathes," the chevalier de Clermont murmured.

"We are fighting a war to loosen the grip of tradition, not to be enslaved by it further," Adams continued, undeterred. "And if the Moravians of Bethlehem will not fight with us, they must prove their loyalty in other ways."

"But it is our duty to protect these women. Imagine if it were your own dear wife, Mr. Adams, or my Adrienne." Lafayette looked genuinely pained at the prospect. He wrote at least one letter a day to his distant spouse, who though not yet eighteen was already the mother of two children.

"Mrs. Adams would not hesitate to take in four thousand wounded soldiers if it were asked of her!" Adams, like Ettwein, did not like to be challenged.

Mr. Hancock, who had a formidable wife of his own by all accounts, looked doubtful.

"If I may," Dr. Otto interjected. "Would it perhaps be better for the surgeons if the soldiers were kept closer together? Already we are stretched too thin, and running all through town for supplies. Perhaps we might use the gardens, and put up tents for the patients who are convalescing so that they might be in the fresh air, away from the fevers that are already spreading?"

"Fevers?" A man with the distinctive drawl of the southern colonies frowned. "Not the smallpox, surely."

"No, sir," Dr. Otto hastened to reply. "The general's orders last winter have spared us from that. But camp fever, typhus . . ." His words drifted into silence.

The members of Congress looked at each other nervously. Ettwein's eyes met de Clermont's, and the two exchanged a meaningful glance.

"These common illnesses threaten the health of the entire community," de Clermont said. "Surely the brethren and sisters must not suffer unduly. Why, Brother Ettwein's own son is nursing the soldiers and risking his life to care for them. What greater form of patriotism can there be, than to put one's own child at risk?"

Marcus eyed the young man standing next to him. The younger John Ettwein was far more amiable than his father but otherwise resembled him closely, with his upturned nose and wide-set eyes. Though John was indeed a skilled nurse, Marcus suspected that Ettwein's son had been seconded to the hospital to make sure that the brethren's house was not harmed during the army's occupation.

"Let us adjourn to the inn," Hancock said, "and deliberate further."

"YOU KNOW HOW TO HANDLE a hoe as well as a lancet, I see," said young John Ettwein.

Marcus looked up from the patch of herbs that they were cutting in anticipation of the tents that would soon spring up on the hillside overlooking the river. The apothecary, Brother Eckhardt, had ordered the two of them to harvest every medicinal simple they could before the soldiers destroyed the gardens.

"And you don't sound like you're from Philadelphia," John continued.

Marcus resumed his task without comment. He pulled a mandrake from the earth and put it in the basket next to the snakeroot.

"So what's your story, Brother Chauncey?" John's eyes were bright with unanswered questions. "We all know you're not from around here."

Not for the first time, Marcus was glad he had been born on the frontier and not in Boston. Everybody knew he was from somewhere else, but no one could place his accent with any precision.

"You needn't worry. Most people in Bethlehem came from elsewhere," John remarked.

But most people hadn't killed their fathers. Marcus had barely spoken a word around the delegates from Congress for fear someone might recognize that he was from Massachusetts and ask difficult questions.

"Cat's still got your tongue, I see." John wiped the sweat from his brow and peered down at the riverside road. "*Mein Gott.*"

"Wagons." Marcus scrambled to his feet. As far as the eye could see, there were wagons. "They've come from Philadelphia."

"There are hundreds of them," John said, thrusting his hoe into the earth. "We must find my father. And the chevalier. At once."

Marcus abandoned his basket of roots and leaves and followed John toward the Brethren's House. They had not made it more than a few yards when they ran into de Clermont and Brother Ettwein. The two men were already aware of the invasion from Philadelphia.

"There are too many of them!" Brother Ettwein was saying to de Clermont, his eyes wild. "We have already unloaded seventy wagons in just two days. The Scottish prisoners are in one of our family houses. Their guards are living in the pumping house. The army's stores have filled the lime kilns and the oil house. The single brothers are displaced. And now more locusts descend! What are we to do?"

The wagons from Philadelphia pulled to a stop in the fields on the southern bank of the river, one after another, flattening the buckwheat planted there. A troop of horse accompanied them.

"So much for our peaceable village!" Ettwein continued, his voice bitter. "When Dr. Shippen wrote, he said the army would be an inconvenience—not drive us out of hearth and home."

Still the wagons came. Marcus had never seen so many at one time. The drivers unhitched their teams and led them to the water. The wagon train's guards dismounted, allowing their horses to graze.

"Shall I speak to them, Johannes?" The chevalier de Clermont looked grim. "There is probably little I can do, but at least we will know their plans."

"We settled in Bethlehem to avoid war." Ettwein's voice was low and intense. "We have all seen enough of it, Brother de Clermont. Religious war. War with the French. War with the Indians. Now war with the British. Do you never get tired of it?"

For a moment, the chevalier de Clermont's composed mask slipped, and he looked as bitter as Ettwein sounded. Marcus blinked and the Frenchman's face became as inscrutable as it was before.

"I am more tired of war than you know, Johannes," de Clermont said. "Come, Chauncey." He beckoned to Marcus.

Marcus scrambled down the hillside in de Clermont's wake, trying in vain to keep up so that he could reason with the man.

"Sir." Marcus struggled to regain his footing. "Chevalier de Clermont. Are you sure—"

De Clermont wheeled around. "What is it, Chauncey?"

"Are you sure you should be interfering in this matter?" Marcus asked, adding, "sir," again as an afterthought.

"You think the citizens of Bethlehem will fare better if John Adams argues their case?" The chevalier snorted. "That man is a menace to international relations."

"No, sir. It's just—" Marcus stopped and bit his lip. "Those are Virginians, sir. I can tell from their clothes. They're wearing buckskin, you see. Virginians don't like being told what to do."

"Nobody likes to be told what to do," de Clermont observed, his eyes narrowing.

"Yes, but they have rifles. Very accurate rifles, sir. And swords," Marcus continued, determined to avert disaster. "We're not armed. And the marquis is alone at Brother Boeckel's house."

"Sister Liesel is with Gil," de Clermont said curtly, resuming his blistering descent of the hill. "She is reading to him about the Moravian missions to Greenland. He says he finds it soothing."

Marcus had seen the fervent glances that the marquis had bestowed on the Boeckels' charming daughter, and was glad that Lafayette was married, as well as that Sister Liesel was a paragon of virtue.

"Nevertheless, sir—"

"For God's sake, Chauncey, stop calling me sir. I'm not your commanding officer," de Clermont said, wheeling around to face him once more. "We need to know why these wagons have arrived. Has Philadelphia fallen to the British? Are they here on Washington's orders? Without information, we cannot determine what must be done next. Are you going to help me, or hinder me?"

"Help." Marcus knew this was his only real option, and followed de Clermont in silence the rest of the way.

When they reached the southern bank of the river, all was confusion.

A man in buff breeches and a blue tunic rode toward them on a horse that was probably worth as much as the MacNeil farm. A long Kentucky rifle—the kind used by woodsmen on the frontier—was jammed through a loop on his saddle, and a fur-trimmed helmet was strapped to his head. Marcus thought his brains must be baking inside it on such a warm day.

"I am the chevalier de Clermont, servant to the Marquis de Lafayette. State your business." De Clermont motioned Marcus to stay behind him.

"I am here to see Mr. Hancock," the man replied.

"He's at the inn." De Clermont jerked his head toward the ford. "In town."

"Doc?" a voice cried out across the clearing. "That you?"

Vanderslice was in one of the wagons, perched atop a pile of hay. He waved.

"What are you doing here?" Marcus said as he approached the wagon.

"We've brought the bells from Philadelphia so that those British bastards don't melt them down and make bullets out of them," Vanderslice explained, launching himself from the pile of hay with a mighty leap. He landed on his feet, like a cat. "I didn't expect to see you here. Still with that French *kakker* and his friend, I see?"

"Washington sent the marquis here to recover—and the rest of the army with him, it seems," Marcus replied. He looked over at de Clermont, who was deep in conversation with a knot of cavalry officers. The chevalier wanted information, and Marcus had pledged to help him. Marcus had to at least try to keep his bargain. "Where are you all headed?"

"Some town west of here," Vanderslice said vaguely. "We've brought along everything we could haul out of Philadelphia. Even Gerty." He looked up at the town of Bethlehem and whistled. "What kind of place is this, Doc? It seems awfully grand to be filled with religious folk. I hear the women are all unmarried and the men live in one big room, together."

"It's like nowhere else I've ever been," Marcus replied honestly.

"Is the food good?" Vanderslice asked. "Are the girls pretty?"

"Yes," Marcus replied with a laugh. "But Congress has ordered us not to disturb the women, so you best keep your fingers in the pies."

THAT EVENING, John Ettwein led Marcus and Vanderslice on a tour of his town. Instead of starting with the large, imposing stone buildings in the center of Bethlehem, John headed straight for the warren of structures that were built along the Monocacy Creek.

"This is where our people first settled," John explained, standing before a small, low structure made of logs. The land sloped down to the water, giving a clear view to the west over the Moravians' mills, tanneries, butchers, and waterworks. Ettwein pointed at one of the buildings. "There's the springhouse. The water never freezes. Not even in winter. And it turns the wheel that sends the water up the hill and into the town."

Marcus had been amazed to discover that water flowed into the apothecary's stillroom, and that he didn't have to run up and down the hill to fetch clean water for the marquis's medicine.

"I'd show you inside," John continued, "but your guards have taken it over."

Some of the colonial soldiers quartered there were congregating outside and watching while stores of ammunition were unloaded into the nearby oil mill.

John showed them the millworks instead. As they neared the workshop, a black couple came into view, climbing the hill from the river. They were about Brother Ettwein's age, and their arms were linked at the elbows. Both wore the dark, simple clothing of the Moravian Brethren, and the woman wore one of their crisp white caps, this one unadorned with ruffles and tied with a blue bow—the sign of a married woman. Marcus regarded the pair with curiosity, as did Vanderslice.

"Good evening, Brother Andrew and Sister Magdalene," John called to them. "I was showing our visitors the millworks."

"God sends us too many visitors," Sister Magdalene said.

"God sends us only what we can handle," Brother Andrew said, giving her a comforting smile. "You must forgive us. Sister Magdalene has been hard at work for many hours, washing the sick soldiers' clothes."

"They were crawling with vermin," Sister Magdalene said, "and worn nearly to shreds. There is nothing to replace them with. If God wants to help us, He should send us breeches."

"We must be thankful for his mercies, wife." Brother Andrew patted her hand. He opened his mouth to speak again, but his body was racked with a deep cough.

"That sounds like asthma," Marcus said with a frown. "I know a tea made of elderflower and fennel that might help your breathing."

"It is only the hill," Brother Andrew replied, stooped over with the effort to clear his lungs. "It always brings on my cough. That, and the cold mornings."

"Doc can fix you up," Vanderslice said. "He healed all of the Associators last winter, when we were fighting together."

Sister Magdalene looked at Marcus with interest. "My Andrew's back aches after a coughing fit. Do you have something that might ease it?"

Marcus nodded. "A liniment, applied with warm hands. The ingredients are all in the apothecary's shop."

"There is no need to concern yourself with me, when you have so many patients already," Brother Andrew said. "All I need is rest."

Brother Andrew and Sister Magdalene preceded them through the open door into the millworks. The scent of wood shavings filled the dusty air, and Brother Andrew's coughing resumed.

"You shouldn't be sleeping here," Marcus protested. "This air will make the cough worse."

"There is nowhere else," Sister Magdalene said, sounding weary. "They took our house from us to accommodate the prisoners. I could go to the sisters' house, but that would mean leaving Andrew, and we are used to being together now."

"Magdalene does not trust the visitors across the river, or the guards in the waterworks," Brother Andrew explained. "She fears they will take me from the Brethren and sell me to a new master."

"You are not free, Andrew," Sister Magdalene said fiercely. "Remember what happened to Sarah. The Brethren sold her quick enough."

"She was not a member of the congregation, as I am," Andrew said, still wheezing. "That was different."

Sister Magdalene did not look convinced. She helped her husband to a chair by a tiled stove. A small mattress was in the corner behind the stove, neatly covered with a clean blanket. A few personal items—a cup, two bowls, a book—were placed nearby.

"I will take care of my husband, Brother John," Sister Magdalene said. "Go back to the hospital, to the sick soldiers."

"I will pray for you, Brother Andrew," John said.

"I am already in God's care, Brother John," Brother Andrew replied. "Pray for peace instead."

MARCUS WAS WORKING alongside Bethlehem's apothecary, Brother Eckhardt, in the small laboratory behind his shop facing the town square known as *der Platz*. Today the army's wagons were moving from their riverside camp and through the town to their next destination, transforming an already busy thoroughfare into a public highway.

When he returned last night from the mill, Marcus had been told he would be staying with the Ettweins and sharing a room with John. De Clermont and Dr. Otto had undertaken a lengthy negotiation with Brother Ettwein to get Marcus removed from the Single Brothers' House and away from the soldiers so that he did not unwittingly carry some contagion to the marquis's bedside. Marcus's new hosts were a pious family, and Brother Ettwein was not only the chief intermediary between the Moravians and the colonial army but also the town's minister. This meant that the rafters echoed with both prayers and complaints. Marcus found the peace and quiet of the apothecary's house soothing in comparison.

He stood at a clean wooden table with an array of pottery jars before him. Each one was labeled with its contents—mallow and almond oil and sal ammoniac. A bottle of spirit of lavender was at his elbow.

"That is not for Brother Lafayette," Brother Eckhardt observed, studying the medicines on the table. He was a tall, elderly man with spindly legs, spectacles perched on a beak of a nose, and stooped shoulders, which gave him the look of a strange marsh bird.

"No. This is for Brother Andrew," Marcus said, mixing some more oil into the brass bowl. "He was coughing last night."

"Put some nightshade in it, too." Brother Eckhardt handed Marcus another pot. "It eases spasms."

Marcus took the pot, grateful for the advice, which he filed away for future reference. He had known Brother Eckhardt for only a few hours, but there was no doubt the man had a prodigious knowledge of medicines.

"A bit more mallow, too, I should think," said Brother Eckhardt after giving the contents of Marcus's bowl a good sniff.

Marcus added more dried pink flowers to the mortar and pounded them with the pestle.

"I will make some salve for Sister Magdalene's hands, and you can take that to the mill when you go," Brother Eckhardt said. "The bleach and soap she uses are very strong, and her hands crack and bleed."

"I noticed." Marcus had seen the evidence of hard labor on the woman's skin. "Sister Magdalene doesn't seem happy, washing for the soldiers."

"Sister Magdalene is often unhappy," Brother Eckhardt said mildly. "She has been since she arrived, I am told. She was a girl then, and sent here from Philadelphia by her master, who later freed her."

"And Brother Andrew?" Marcus asked, his mind as busy as his hands.

"Andrew belongs to the Brethren," Brother Eckhardt replied, "and is a member of our Congregation. He and Sister Magdalene were married some time ago. They are part of our community, and live and work alongside us under God."

Alongside you, Marcus thought, going back to his work, *but still not fully among you.*

Marcus was troubled by the distance between the community's language of brotherly love and equality and the fact that the Brethren owned slaves. It had bothered him in Hadley, too, and in the army, that men could espouse the ideals of liberty and equality in *Common Sense* and yet still treat Zeb Pruitt or Mrs. Dolly like they were lesser beings.

Shouts and a huge crash punctured the quiet of the laboratory.

"What was that?" Brother Eckhardt said, pushing up his spectacles. He ran outside, Marcus following.

A wagon had broken down outside the Sun Inn, just where the road began its descent toward the creek. The Brethren streamed out of houses, workshops, and barns to see what the fuss was about. The last remaining members of Congress stood outside the Sun Inn, surveying the damage. Even the chevalier de Clermont and the Marquis de Lafayette were there to witness the spectacle, thanks to *La Brouette.*

As Marcus and Brother Eckhardt drew closer, one voice could be heard above the noise of the crowd.

"I told you this would happen!" John Adams waved his arms in the air as he approached the listing wagon. "Did I not say you would need a team of oxen to safely move the statehouse bell down the hill, and stouter chains to stop the wheels? No one ever listens to me."

"Should I take the marquis back to the Boeckels?" Marcus asked de Clermont. All of this excitement could not be beneficial for their patient.

"I fear that not even Adams and his oxen could pull Gil away," the chevalier replied with a sigh. "Wait here. I'll go see to the wagon. It will draw all the traffic to a halt, if left where it is."

De Clermont joined the throng around the broken wheel. Marcus could see the chain that had done the damage, a length of it wrapped around one of the spokes and the rest of it lying in the road.

"I fear this is a bad sign," Lafayette said mournfully. "First the crack. Now this. Do you believe in omens, Doc?"

"I do," said a soft voice.

Marcus turned to find Brother Andrew standing at his elbow.

"I was taught to watch for them, when my name was Ofodobendo Wooma and I was still in the land of my fathers," Brother Andrew continued. "Lightning and rain and the winds—these were all signs that the gods were angry and must be appeased. Later, when my name was York and I lived with a Jewish master on the island of Manhattan, he planned on selling me to Madeira in exchange for some wine. I prayed for deliverance, and one of the Brethren bought me instead and brought me here. That was a sign, too—of God's love."

Lafayette listened, fascinated.

"But I do not think this broken wheel should be counted among them, Brother Lafayette," Brother Andrew said with a shake of his head. "God does not need to send his poor servants a message that we misjudged the weight of the bell. The broken chain is sign enough."

"That is what Matthew said," the marquis said, watching his friend argue with John Adams. Over by the wagon, tempers were fraying.

"Fetch Brother Ettwein," Brother Eckhardt murmured to Brother Andrew. "Then go back to the mill. They will have need of you before this day is done."

IT WAS TWILIGHT BEFORE MARCUS had an opportunity to take the medicines to Brother Andrew and Sister Magdalene. The area beside the creek was a hive of activity, even at this late hour, and the lamplight spilled through the windows and illuminated Marcus's path.

The door to the millworks was ajar and Marcus craned his head around it, wanting to see what was going on inside. The sight that met his eyes was astonishing.

The chevalier de Clermont was working alongside Brother Andrew. His shirtsleeves were rolled up, displaying muscled forearms, and his dark breeches were covered in wood shavings. De Clermont's skin was pale and smooth, unmarred by the marks of battle common to the soldiers Marcus treated. Not for the first time, Marcus wondered exactly what kind of knight the chevalier de Clermont was, with his craftsman's skills and preference for the workshop rather than the tavern. The chevalier was a hard man to know—and an even more difficult one to understand.

"I think that's straight," the chevalier said, handing a spoke to Brother Andrew. "What do you think?"

Brother Andrew weighed the spoke in his hand and looked down the length of it with a practiced eye. He coughed as he drew the air of the mill into his lungs. "That will do, Brother Matthew. Shall I take them to the wheelwright?"

"Let Doc do it." The chevalier de Clermont turned and motioned Marcus forward.

"I brought the liniment, Brother Andrew, and the tea," Marcus said. "Brother Eckhardt made something to treat Sister Magdalene's hands."

"She is still down at the laundry," Brother Andrew said. "I told her not to walk home unaccompanied. I will go—"

"No. I will go and escort Sister Magdalene home," de Clermont said.

"The hill is too much for your lungs at present. Doc will make you some of his tea and then come straight back from the wheelwright and put some liniment on your back. By the time I return with Sister Magdalene, you will be as hale and hearty as the day you married."

Brother Andrew laughed, but the laughter soon turned to spasms of coughing. Marcus and de Clermont waited in silence until the fit passed and the man was able to breathe again.

"I thank you, Brother Matthew," Brother Andrew said, "for your kindness."

"It is nothing, Brother Andrew," de Clermont said with a bow. "I will return soon."

Marcus poked at the fire and put the dented kettle on the stove to boil water. Once it was piping hot, he shook out some of the dried herbs from the packet of tea and set it to steep. He made sure Brother Andrew was comfortable and breathing more easily before trotting off with the bundle of wheel spokes. Marcus was saved from having to take them into town by some of the single brethren who were wheeling a metal hoop in that direction, no doubt to go around the new wheel that would carry the state-house bell out of Bethlehem.

When Marcus returned to the mill, Brother Andrew was still coughing but the fits were less severe. Marcus poured some of the tea into the cup he'd noticed earlier. Brother Andrew sipped at it and his coughing abated further.

"This tastes better than most of what Brother Eckhardt makes," Brother Andrew commented.

"I put mint in it," Marcus explained, "just like Tom taught me."

"And this Tom, he was your brother?" Brother Andrew eyed him over the cup.

"Just someone I knew once." Marcus turned away.

"I think you are someone who has traveled far, and been known by many names," Brother Andrew commented. "Like me. Like Brother Matthew."

"The chevalier de Clermont?" Marcus was surprised. "I have never heard him called anything else, except for his Christian name Matthew."

"And yet today he answered to Sebastien, when one of the German soldiers called out to him." Brother Andrew sipped at his tea. "What other names do you answer to, Brother Chauncey?"

Somehow, Brother Andrew had divined that Marcus was not who he seemed to be.

"I answer to Doc," Marcus replied, making for the door. "The liniment is on the table. Have Sister Magdalene warm her hands before she applies it. Twice or three times a day will help to ease the spasms as well as the tightness in your chest."

"Once my wife answered to Beulah. Before that, she had another name—one her mother and father gave her." Brother Andrew's eyes were unfocused, as though he had forgotten Marcus was in the room. "When we were married, I asked for that name, but she said she no longer remembered it. She said the only name that mattered was the name she took when she was made free."

Marcus thought of all the names he had gone by in his life—Marcus and Galen, Chauncey and MacNeil, Doc, and boy, and once even son. If he ever married, and his wife asked him his true name, which one would he share with her?

THE NEXT DAY, Bethlehem had returned to some semblance of its normal routine. Congress had left town, and the windows of the Sun Inn were flung open to air out the rooms. All of the wagons save one had moved on, along with most of the guards and the camp followers—except for Gerty, who had decided to stay in Bethlehem. Marcus had seen her outside the bakery, talking nonstop in her native language. Some of the brethren were already at work in the fields to the south of town, replacing the fence posts the soldiers had burned in their campfires and raking the manure left by the horses in the trampled buckwheat fields.

In *der Platz*, a small group of men were lifting the statehouse bell out of the broken wagon. The spokes that Brother Andrew and the chevalier de Clermont had been working on last night were not for a new wheel but a whole new wagon. How the Brethren had managed to construct it so quickly was a mystery. It stood next to the old one, waiting for its cargo.

Marcus watched as the men strained and struggled with the heavy load. Only one man seemed oblivious to the weight: the chevalier de Clermont. His grip on the bell never loosened, and no groans or complaints issued from his lips.

But it was not only the men who were participating in the work taking place in *der Platz*. A few of the sisters were assisting the process, adjusting ropes and darting to place another block under the wagon's wheels to keep it steady. A group from the children's choir stood nearby while their teacher explained what was happening, highlighting the mathematics and engineering that had been used to figure out the best way to transfer the bell from one wagon to another.

Brother Andrew kept a close eye on the new wagon as the statehouse bell was placed inside and the blocks were removed to allow its slow descent down the road to the creek. The brethren and sisters broke into spontaneous applause when the wagon started to move. Marcus joined them.

"Perhaps you will stay here, *Liebling*, and learn German?" Gerty smiled at Marcus, exposing the gaps where she was missing teeth. "I think you might enjoy life among the single brethren—for a time. Then perhaps you might court Sister Liesel, and start a family."

For a moment Marcus considered what life would be like were he to leave the army and stay in Bethlehem, working alongside Brother Eckhardt in the laboratory, spending more time with John Ettwein, reading the books in the Gemeinhaus.

"To join the Brethren, you have to tell your life's story and how you found God." The chevalier de Clermont was standing only a few feet away, listening to every word.

A sense of danger surrounded the French soldier, as though de Clermont knew Marcus's true name—and what had happened in Hadley.

"La!" Gerty waved her hand. "Doc will make something up. Something so full of sin it will satisfy even the *Brüdergemeine*. I will help you, Doc, by sharing some of my own life history with you." Gerty gave him a salacious wink and strolled away.

"Stay with Dr. Otto and the army, Doc," de Clermont advised. "They're family enough."

For now, Marcus thought. *For now.*

PART 2

'Tis Time to Part

Male and female are the distinctions of nature,
good and bad the distinctions of heaven;

but how a race of men came into the world
so exalted above the rest,

and distinguished like some new species,
is worth enquiring into,

and whether they are the means of
happiness or misery to mankind.

—Thomas Paine

⇥ 18 ⇤

Fifteen

When Phoebe awoke on her fifteenth day as a vampire, she discovered that the world was somehow more sensual than it had been only the day before. The touch of silk on her skin was so arousing, so provocative, that she sought refuge in nakedness, shedding her nightgown so quickly that the straps broke and the seams tore.

That had been a mistake.

The breath of air that caressed her bare neck reminded her of Marcus. The feel of cool sheets took her back to his bed. But the softness of the pillow where she rested her cheek was a poor substitute for his familiar body.

Phoebe had taken a shower to cool down her heated thoughts, but it only made the throbbing between her legs worse. Her slippery fingers had dipped into her cleft to ease the pressure, but her mind would not be still, and her touch brought no relief. She picked up a bar of soap and threw it at the porcelain wall in frustration, unsatisfied.

It had been a very long day.

Françoise delivered a tray to Phoebe's room shortly before midnight. On it was coffee, dark chocolate, and red wine—the only substances she could stomach at this point in her development besides blood.

"Soon, you will have to feed," Françoise said as she slowly plunged the mesh filter down into the glass carafe. "And *not* on cat."

Phoebe was riveted by the suggestive slide of metal against glass. It reminded her suddenly, sharply, of Marcus and sent a ripple of need through her body. Memories flooded her mind.

She was in her flat in Spitalfields. It was the first night Marcus had made love to her. He had been so gentle, never breaking the connection with her eyes as he slowly—so slowly—entered her. They hadn't made it to the bed that first time, or the second.

Phoebe closed her eyes, but the heavenly scent of coffee set her mind racing down another of memory's paths.

It was a warm, languid New Orleans morning in Marcus's house on Coliseum Street. The aroma of chicory and coffee beans was a darkly bitter note in the bright air. Ransome had left them alone after regaling them with tales from last night's business at the Domino Club. Marcus was still chuckling over one of the stories, a cup of steaming liquid before him, his fingers cool in spite of the heat, one hooked into the waist of the pajama bottoms she'd found in the chest of drawers. They were softly worn, the legs rolled up so that she wouldn't trip on their length. Marcus added another finger to the first, both moving in a sinuous pattern on her lower back, and pressed a kiss to her damp neck in a promise of the afternoon pleasures to come.

Phoebe's mouth watered. She swallowed, shifting in her chair.

"You need blood." Françoise's blunt voice broke memory's spell.

"That's not what I want." Phoebe's whole body was a single, focused ache. It originated in her core, from an empty place that could only be filled by another creature.

By Marcus.

"These feelings you are having, they are a sign that you are ready to take human blood," Françoise said, lifting Persephone from her nest in the remains of Phoebe's nightgown and depositing the cat on the armchair. Françoise picked up the tattered silk and tossed it in the laundry basket hidden in the wardrobe.

Insatiable lust is the sign that you've graduated to two-legged food? Phoebe's dark eyes narrowed as she considered Françoise's words, which usually carried hidden meaning.

"Vampires are nothing but desire, you see." Françoise returned to the tray and poured some coffee. "Can you not scratch what itches yourself? Your mate cannot always be around, after all."

But Phoebe wanted Marcus's deft fingers, his soft mouth sucking at her flesh, the nip of his teeth when he wanted her attention, the way he teased her until she was insane with longing and only then gave her the heart-shattering climax she craved. And what Marcus whispered as he brought her to that precipice, over and over, until she was mad and begging—Phoebe wanted those intimate, dark, seductive words most of all.

"No," Phoebe said shortly. She eyed the top of the wardrobe.

"If you call him, it will make everything worse." Françoise sighed.

"Call him?" Phoebe tried to look innocent.

"Yes. With one of the telephones in the bag on top of the armoire." Françoise's expression held disdain, understanding, and a touch of humor. She clapped her hands briskly. "Milady Freyja is dining out tonight, so I suggest you be quick about it."

"I don't think I'm in the mood." Phoebe had no intention of whispering sweet nothings to Marcus (which always turned into very sweet somethings) on someone else's timetable.

"Give it a few minutes," Françoise said as she departed. "You'll be in the mood again in no time."

Françoise was right. Her footsteps had barely faded before the throbbing between Phoebe's legs returned. Before she was consciously aware of formulating a plan, Phoebe had gone to the armoire, leaped for the phone (a surprisingly easy feat, she discovered), and dialed Marcus's number.

"Phoebe?"

The effect of Marcus's voice on Phoebe's raw nerves was electrifying. She pressed her legs tightly together.

"You didn't tell me everything." Phoebe's voice was breathy and rough.

"Just a minute." There was a conversation, muffled and indistinct, and then footsteps. Then Marcus's voice came clearly through the speaker once more. "I take it your vampire hormones have kicked in."

"You should have warned me," Phoebe said, irritation mounting along with her desire.

"I told you, quite explicitly, about the pleasures and problems associated with a vampire's sexual awakening," Marcus said, lowering his voice.

Phoebe racked her brains for the details of this conversation. Dimly, she recalled a few particulars. "You told me it was dangerous—not that I was going to feel an insatiable need to . . . you know . . ."

"Tell me."

"I can't." Pillow talk was not her department.

"Sure you can. What is it you want, Phoebe?" Marcus was teasing—but only in part. Most of him was deadly serious.

"I need . . . want . . . to . . ." Phoebe's words drifted into silence, replaced by startlingly clear images of just what she would do to Marcus if he were to walk through the door. One encounter took place in the shower, where Marcus slipped inside her while the water flowed over their bodies. Another involved pinning him to the wall, dropping to her knees, and taking him in her mouth. And then there was the stunning image of Marcus taking her from behind, fully clothed, while she was splayed, face-down, across the end of his dining room table, which had been set for a romantic meal complete with flowers and a Georgian silver candlestick.

"I want you in every way imaginable," Phoebe whispered, her cheeks red with honesty. There was nothing tender in her first wave of vampire fantasies—just pure, raw hunger.

"And then what?" Marcus's voice turned to gravel.

"Then I want to make love, slowly, for hours, in a bed with white sheets, and curtains that blow in the breeze from the open windows." Phoebe's imagination was now captured by an altogether different image of their coupling, one driven not so much by lust as by longing. "Then I want to swim together, and make love in the ocean. And again, in a garden, under the stars with no moon."

"Summer or winter?" Marcus asked.

She was pleased by his request for further details. It showed he was paying attention.

"Winter," Phoebe said promptly. "The snow melting underneath us as we move."

"I've never made love in the snow," Marcus said, thoughtful.

"Have you made love in the ocean?" Phoebe's erotic dreams were carried away in an undertow of jealousy.

"Yes. It's fun. You'll like it," Marcus said.

"I hate your previous lovers—all of them. And I hate you," Phoebe hissed.

"No, you don't," Marcus said. "Not really."

"Tell me their names," she demanded.

"Why? They're all dead," Marcus said.

"Not Veronique!" Phoebe retorted.

"You already know Veronique's name, and her phone number, and her address," Marcus said mildly.

"I hate that you're more experienced than I am," Phoebe said. "You keep talking about our equality, but in this . . ."

"I sure as hell hope you aren't intending to level the playing field." Marcus's voice held a sharp edge.

Phoebe was slightly mollified. She was not the only one in the relationship who experienced a pang of jealousy when other lovers, real or imagined, came up in conversation.

"I feel like a teenager," Phoebe confessed.

"I remember that phase well," Marcus replied. "I was hard for a solid week in November of 1781. And I was on a ship full of men, all of whom were jerking off at night when they thought the rest of us were asleep."

"It sounds dreadful," Phoebe said with mock sympathy. "But being with your aunt and Miriam is no picnic, I assure you. Tell me what it will be like when we're together."

"I've already told you," Marcus replied with a laugh.

"Tell me again," Phoebe said.

"It will be like a very long honeymoon," Marcus said. "Once you're sure it's me you want, we'll be allowed to go off together."

"Where will we go?" Phoebe asked.

"Wherever you want." Marcus's response was swift.

"India. No, an island. Somewhere we won't be disturbed," Phoebe said. "Somewhere there are no people to bother us."

"We could be in downtown Beijing, surrounded by millions, and we wouldn't care." Marcus sounded very sure. "It's one of the reasons Ysabeau wanted us to wait a full ninety days."

"Because it's easy for newborns to get lost in their mates." Phoebe recalled the conversation that had taken place in Ysabeau's apartments at Sept-Tours, on stiff-backed chairs. Marcus's grandmother had recounted horrifying tales of young lovers who had starved to death in their houses, so intent on the pleasures of the flesh that they forgot to feed. There were tales of jealous rages, too, in which one mate killed the other over a sidelong look at another creature passing by the window, or the mention of a former lover. In such fraught emotional situations between newly mated vampires, even the simple word "no" could bring about death and destruction.

"So they tell me," Marcus replied. It was a reminder that he might have been in love before, but that was very different from what would happen between him and Phoebe, once they were together again.

Just like that, her mood shifted.

"I wish it were August," Phoebe said wistfully, her heart kicking up a notch in excitement.

"It will go by quickly," Marcus promised, "far more so than your first two weeks. There will be so much to do, you won't have a chance to think about me."

"Do?" Phoebe frowned. "Françoise says I will have to feed from a human. She hasn't mentioned anything else."

"You're growing up as a vampire," Marcus said. "You'll feed from a human, go hunting, meet other members of your new family, choose your names, even spend some time outside of the nest."

So much time had been spent getting Phoebe ready for the first weeks of her life as a vampire, Miriam and Freyja had never ventured much beyond that point. It was as if—

"Did they expect me to die?" Phoebe had never seriously considered this outcome.

"No. Not really. But vampire children can be unpredictable, and sometimes there are . . . complications." The slight pause Marcus took before his final words spoke volumes. "Remember how sick Becca was, after she was born and she refused any food other than Diana's blood."

Rebecca had been a wan, frustrated creature. While Philip had thrived on breast milk, Diana's daughter had needed richer food.

"Bloodsickness is rare, but it can be fatal," Marcus continued. "Most vampires develop a broader palate after a few weeks, but not all."

"So that's why they put out so many different kinds of blood." Phoebe had thought it was just Miriam being her usual, overzealous self, but now her thoroughness took on a new, more nurturing tone.

"We all want this to be as smooth and painless a process as it can be, Phoebe." Marcus sounded sober. "Not all of us had that kind of upbringing. But for you, I wanted it to be different."

Phoebe was curious about Marcus's life as a warmblood in the eighteenth century, and his younger years as a vampire. But she also wanted to see them from a vampire's perspective, through Marcus's own memories. So Phoebe kept her lips pressed together, and only when she was sure she had the resolve not to ask any questions, she spoke.

"It's not long now," Phoebe said, her tone brisk.

"No. Not long," Marcus repeated, but he sounded frustrated. "Just long enough to feel like forever."

They said their good-byes. Before the call ended, Phoebe dared to ask one final question.

"What was your mother's name, Marcus?"

"My mother?" Marcus sounded surprised. "Catherine."

"Catherine." Phoebe liked it. It was timeless, as common today as it had been when it was bestowed on a baby daughter in the first half of the eighteenth century. She repeated it, feeling how it sat on her tongue, imagining responding to it. "Catherine."

"It's a Greek name, and it means pure," Marcus explained.

More importantly, it meant something to Marcus. That was all that mattered to Phoebe.

After they hung up, Phoebe took a sheet of paper from the desk drawer.

Phoebe Alice Catherine Taylor.

She looked at the paper critically. Her mother had chosen Phoebe when she was born. Alice was her paternal grandmother's name. Catherine belonged to Marcus. And she wanted to retain Taylor, in honor of her father.

Satisfied with her choices, Phoebe returned the paper to the drawer for safekeeping.

Then she returned to bed, to daydream further about her reunion with Marcus.

Twenty-One

2 JUNE

For Phoebe's twenty-first birthday as a warmblood, her parents had given her a small key-shaped pendant encrusted with tiny diamonds, and a party for a hundred friends. The key was to unlock her future, her mother explained, and Phoebe had worn it every day since. The party, which included a sit-down dinner under a marquee and dancing in the garden, was to launch her into her adult life and give her a memorable day to look back on when she was older.

For Phoebe's twenty-first day as a vampire, she got another key and a much more intimate dinner celebration.

"It's a key to your room," Freyja said when she gave the small brass item to Phoebe.

Like many of the gifts Phoebe had received from vampires thus far, the key was symbolic, a sign of trust rather than a way of ensuring any real privacy in a household where any door could be broken down with a single push.

"Thank you, Freyja," Phoebe said, pocketing the key.

"Now, when you lock your door, we will know that you wish some time alone and we will not disturb you," Freyja said, "not even Françoise."

Françoise had walked in on Phoebe while she was in the bathtub thinking of Marcus and trying to satisfy one of her more persistent itches. Françoise had put down the clean laundry and disappeared from the room without saying a word. Phoebe would prefer to avoid more moments like that one if she could.

"Miriam is waiting for you downstairs in the kitchen," Freyja said. "Don't worry. Everything will be completely fine."

Until that moment, Phoebe had been unconcerned about whatever her maker had planned for her twenty-first, but the combination of Freyja's words and the location of their meeting suggested this was no ordinary present.

Her first glimpse of Miriam's gift confirmed Phoebe's suspicions.

Sitting by the chopping block, a glass of champagne before her, was a middle-aged Caucasian woman. Miriam was with her.

They were talking about *E. coli.*

"Vegetables. I wouldn't have thought they were the culprit," the woman said, reaching for a carrot.

"I know. The cases in Bordeaux came from contaminated sprouts," Miriam said.

"Exciting times for epidemiologists," the woman replied. "Shiga toxins in an EAEC strain. Who would have imagined it?"

"Come in, Phoebe, and meet Sonia," Miriam said, pouring another glass of champagne and offering it to her. "She's a colleague at the World Health Organization. Sonia is joining you for dinner."

"Hello, Phoebe. I've heard so much about you." Sonia smiled and took a sip of her champagne.

Phoebe looked from Sonia to Miriam and back to Sonia again. Her mouth was as dry as dust.

"Sonia and I have known each other for more than twenty years," Miriam said.

"Twenty-three, to be exact," Sonia replied. "In Geneva, remember? Daniel introduced us."

Sonia was old enough to be Phoebe's mother.

"I'd forgotten you've been with him so long," Miriam said. She turned to Phoebe. "Daniel Fischer is a Swiss vampire, and a very good chemist."

"He put me through graduate school," Sonia said, "in exchange for feeding him."

"Oh." Phoebe didn't know where to look. Her wine? Sonia? Miriam? The floor?

"There's no need to feel awkward. This is all quite normal—at least for me," Sonia said. "Miriam tells me I'm your first."

Phoebe nodded, unable to speak.

"Well, I'm ready when you are." Sonia put her glass down and rolled up her sleeve. "The anticipation is worse than the doing of it. Or so I'm told. Once you latch on and get your first taste, it will be instinctive."

"I'm not hungry." Phoebe turned to go.

"That's no way to treat your guest." Miriam barred her way. She gave Phoebe a stern look.

Phoebe turned back to Sonia. She could smell the woman's blood pulsing warmly through her veins, but it wasn't the least bit appealing. Still, she would try. If she couldn't manage it, she would try another time. She waited for Miriam to leave.

"I'm not going anywhere," Miriam said. "You will not become one of those vampires who drinks alone, bolting down your food, ashamed to be seen. That's how problems start."

"You're not going to—*watch*?" Phoebe was horrified.

"Not closely. There's nothing much to see, is there? But I am going to stay here with Sonia until you're finished having dinner," Miriam said. "Feeding is a normal part of vampire life. Besides, you've never done this before. We don't want there to be any accidents."

Phoebe had managed to feed off Persephone without any mishaps, but there was no telling what might happen once she was exposed to the richer blood of a human.

"Fine." Phoebe just wanted to get it over with.

As soon as she got near Sonia, however, her composure dissolved. First, the scent and sound of Sonia's blood was distracting. Second, Phoebe could not imagine how the act could take place, logistically. Sonia was sitting on a tall stool. Phoebe would have to stoop to take the woman's bared elbow into her mouth. Was Sonia supposed to stand? Or was Phoebe supposed to sit? Or was some other arrangement of limbs advantageous?

"Reclining is easiest," Miriam said, following her unspoken train of thought, "but not always desirable, nor practical. Traditionally, the vampire knelt. It was considered a sign of respect, as well as gratitude, to the one who gave them nourishment."

It wouldn't be the first time Phoebe had knelt as a vampire. Something told her it wouldn't be her last, either. Before her knees could hit the floor, however, Miriam had kicked a low, square stool out from underneath the counter. Françoise used it to reach items on high shelves. Apparently, that was not its only use in a vampire's kitchen.

Once she had knelt down, Phoebe was at the ideal height to take blood from the soft skin inside Sonia's elbow. Blue veins were close to the surface. Phoebe's mouth watered.

Sonia rested one hand, palm up, on her knee. She picked up her champagne with the other.

"Did you hear the latest about Christophe?" Sonia asked Miriam.

The adults were going to continue their conversation while she ate. Feeling like a toddler on her low stool, Phoebe waited for some gesture of permission—an acknowledgment of what she was about to do.

It didn't come.

"He's taken up with Jette—again!" Sonia took a sip of her wine. "Can you imagine?"

"No!" Miriam sounded shocked. "But she sold his house while he was away on business. That's not the kind of thing a vampire forgets—or forgives."

Phoebe could hear Sonia's maddening pulse and smell the tang of minerals in her blood. She could wait no longer.

"Thank you," she whispered before closing her eyes.

She lowered her mouth and blindly bit down. Phoebe's sharp teeth cut into Sonia's skin, releasing the fluid of life into her mouth.

Phoebe moaned, the taste intensely pleasurable. This was nothing like sipping blood and wine from a glass. Feeding straight from the vein was intoxicating. She sucked as gently as she could, but the pull was insistent. Someone would surely stop her before she'd had too much.

"And his possessions, too," Sonia said. "Perhaps Phoebe could help him reclaim some of what he's lost. Baldwin told Daniel she is quite good."

Normally the prospect of dealing in fine art would have had her complete attention, but Phoebe could think only of feeding.

"I'll give Christophe a call. It would give Phoebe something to do until her ninety days are up," Miriam said, as though Phoebe were not there.

"Poor thing. It's a long time to wait. Daniel was shocked that you were being so traditional. It's not like Marcus to take the old-fashioned route." Sonia laughed.

Phoebe's skin prickled and her hackles rose. What right did Sonia have to second-guess their plans?

"It was Phoebe's decision," Miriam said. "Ysabeau had a lot to do with it, of course."

"Still at Sept-Tours?" Sonia tried to sound casual, but there was no disguising the curiosity in her tone.

"Yes, she is. Not that it's any business of yours," Phoebe said as she licked the blood from her lips, making sure to get the drop that was pooled in the corner. She bit her thumb and swiped it across Sonia's arm to help the teeth marks heal.

"I meant no offense," Sonia said mildly.

"Sonia's a warmblood, Phoebe, not a vampire," Miriam reminded her. "And your guest. The usual rules about personal information don't apply."

"And Ysabeau is my mate's grandmother." Phoebe's veins were thundering with fresh blood, and she felt a bit tipsy. She eyed the champagne bottle. It was nearly empty.

"She's loyal, I see, as well as polite." Sonia rolled her sleeve down. "She said thank you before she took a bite. And she was able to stop herself from feeding. I'm impressed."

Phoebe stood and poured the last of the wine into the waiting glass. Once again, she had passed some kind of test. She felt that a drink was in order.

After that, Phoebe sincerely hoped there would be an offer of dessert.

TWO BOTTLES OF CHAMPAGNE LATER, Miriam put Sonia in a cab. There had been dessert, thanks to Sonia's generosity and due in no small part to the excellence of Freyja's wine cellar.

Freyja returned home shortly after Sonia left. She cast an eye over her upholstery, saw Persephone was purring by the fire, and let out a sigh of relief.

"It all went according to plan," Miriam assured her, looking over the lid of her laptop.

"Just as we thought." Freyja smiled. "And the other matter?"

"What other matter?" Phoebe said, still glowing from drinking blood laced with champagne.

"Must there really be *five* names, Freyja?" Miriam wondered. "It seems a bit excessive."

"It is common among de Clermonts," Freyja said, "not to mention useful. We are a long-lived family, and it saves trouble later. This way there is no last-minute legal scramble if property needs to change hands."

"I've already picked four," Phoebe said, scrambling in her pocket for the slip of paper. She had anticipated that this all-important matter of names would be sprung on her without warning. "Phoebe Alice Catherine Taylor. What do you think?"

"Alice?" Miriam frowned. "But that's German! What about Yara?"

"Taylor?" Freyja looked shocked. "I don't think that's appropriate, Phoebe dearest. People will think you are in trade. I've been wondering if Maren would suit you. I had a great friend named Maren, and you remind me of her."

"I like Taylor," Phoebe said.

Freyja and Miriam took no notice of her, and continued to argue for the relative merits of Illi and Gudrum and Agnete.

"As a matter of fact, I like all of my names. So does Baldwin," Phoebe said, raising her voice slightly.

"Baldwin?" Miriam's eyes narrowed.

"I wrote him last week," Phoebe said.

"But it's not up to Baldwin," Miriam said, her voice purring in her throat. "You're *my* daughter. Naming you is *my* job."

Wisely, Phoebe kept silent. A few moments passed. Miriam sighed.

"The de Clermont family will be the death of me one day," she said. "Keep your names, then. And add Najima."

"Phoebe Alice Najima Catherine Taylor de Clermont." Freyja considered the string of names. "That's settled, then."

Phoebe pressed her lips together to keep from smiling.

She had won her first battle against her maker.

Now she just had to tell Baldwin, in case Miriam suspected she was lying and called to check up on her story. Phoebe felt sure Baldwin would cover for her.

"And how was your twenty-first day as a vampire?" Freyja asked. It had become part of the household ritual—and part of her education—for Phoebe to share how she had gotten on that day.

"Perfect," Phoebe said, finally able to smile openly without showing her maker any sign of disrespect. "Absolutely perfect."

⇥ 20 ⇤

As the Twig Is Bent

5 JUNE

It was ten days before Matthew's rebirthday, and we were in the library reviewing the arrangements for this summer's party. Although I'd promised him there would be no large event like last year, I couldn't let the day go without some kind of celebration. We had finally settled on having a small family affair—just Sarah and Agatha, Marcus, Ysabeau, Marthe and Alain and Victoire, and Jack and Fernando, in addition to me and the children.

"That's nine other people," Matthew said with a scowl, looking at the guest list. "You promised it was going to be small."

"Ten, if you include Baldwin."

Matthew groaned.

"I couldn't very well leave him out," I said.

"Fine," Matthew said hastily, wanting to stem any additional invitations. "When are they all coming?"

Just then a towheaded young man with long, gangly legs and wide shoulders walked in.

"Hi, Mum," he said. "Hey, Dad."

"Jack!" I said, surprised. "We didn't expect you so soon!"

Jack was, in many ways, our first child. Matthew and I had taken him into our household in Elizabethan London, hoping to give him a life that was not filled with terror, homelessness, and hunger. When we left in 1591, I had put him in the care of Andrew Hubbard, who ruled over London's vampires—then and now. We had not expected to see Jack again, but he had chosen to become a vampire rather than succumb to the plague.

"Something wrong, Jack?" Matthew's expression registered unease as he picked up on unspoken signals of distress coming from Jack.

"I'm in trouble," Jack confessed.

The last time Jack had been "in trouble," he ended up in the newspapers as the mysterious "vampire murderer" who drained his victims of blood before abandoning their corpses.

"Nobody's dead," Jack said hastily, guessing the direction of my thoughts. "I was feeding—on Suki, Dad, not some stranger. I took too much blood too quickly and she ended up in hospital. Father Hubbard told me to come straight here."

Suki was the young woman the family employed to watch over Jack in London and provide him with sustenance when he could no longer make do with animals and bagged human blood. Vampires needed to hunt, and there were humans who were happy to oblige them—for a fee. It was a dangerous business, and one that I thought the Congregation should be regulating. My proposals on the subject had been met with resistance, however.

"Where is Suki now?" Matthew's mouth was grim.

"Home. Her sister is with her. Father Hubbard said he'll check on her twice a day." Jack looked and sounded miserable.

"Oh, Jack." I wanted to give him a hug and comfort him, but the tension in the air between Matthew and our son made me reconsider wading into something I didn't fully understand.

"Suki is your responsibility," Matthew said. "You shouldn't have left her in that state."

"Father Hubbard said—"

"I'm not really interested in what Andrew said," Matthew interrupted. "You know the rules. If you can't put Suki's well-being before your own, your relationship will have to end."

"I know, Dad. But I wasn't—I'm still not—I don't even know what happened. One minute I was fine, and then . . ." Jack trailed off. "When I left her with Father Hubbard, I thought I *was* looking after her."

"There are no second chances, Jack. Not with blood rage." Matthew looked regretful. "I'll settle things with Suki. You won't have to see her again."

"Suki didn't do anything wrong and neither did I!" Jack's eyes got darker and his tone more defensive in response to Matthew's disapproval. "This isn't fair."

"Life isn't fair," Matthew said quietly. "But it is our obligation as vampires to do what we can to take care of creatures who are weaker than we are."

"What will happen to her now?" Jack asked, miserable.

"Suki will never want for anything. Marcus and the Knights of Lazarus will see to that," Matthew assured him.

This was the first time I'd heard that some of the brotherhood's accounts covered payments to humans for services rendered. It was undeniably creepy, but it certainly explained why there weren't even more sensational stories out there about vampires feeding off warmbloods.

"Let's get you something to eat," Matthew said, putting his hand on Jack's shoulder. "And you'll want to meet the newest addition to the family."

"You got Mum a dog?" Jack brightened. He loved his four-legged Komondor companion and was a firm believer that there was no such thing as too many dogs.

"No. The goddess gave Philip a griffin," Matthew said. "It seems he's a weaver like his mother."

Jack didn't bat an eye at this announcement, but gamely followed Matthew into the kitchen. After he'd had something to drink and we'd caught up on Jack's less alarming news, we went in search of Agatha, Sarah, and the twins. They had been playing outside in a brightly colored tent that Agatha made by draping old sheets over some chairs. The four of them were huddled inside, playing with every knight, horse, and stuffed animal that could be found.

Apollo was also there, keeping a beady eye on the rest of the menagerie and occasionally reproaching one of its members for an imaginary infraction with a sharp peck.

Once everybody was free of the tent (which collapsed in the excitement of Jack's arrival), the hellos were exchanged, and the children were cuddled and kissed to their satisfaction, Jack crouched down by the griffin.

"Hello, Apollo." Jack stuck out his hand in greeting. Apollo immediately placed his talon on top of it.

Apollo's long tongue came out, and he touched it to Jack's hair, his ear, his nose, and his cheek as if he was getting to know the newest member of the pack. He began to cluck, bobbing his head up and down in approval.

"Jack!" Becca held up her stuffed parrot. "See. Bird. Mine."

"Nice, Becca. I'll come play with her in a minute." Jack narrowly avoided getting a griffin tongue up one nostril. "Can he fly?"

"Oh, yes," Sarah said. "Ysabeau carried Apollo around like a hawk and trained him to catch mice in midair."

Jack laughed.

Becca, who felt Apollo was getting her fair share of attention, flung her parrot at Jack. It hit him in the shoulder and he reared back in surprise. She snarled, her lip curling.

"Rebecca Arielle," Matthew said, voice firm. He swooped down and picked her up. "We've talked about this. No throwing."

Becca opened her tiny mouth. I thought she was about to yell. Instead, she lowered it toward her father's hand with the quickness of a striking snake. She bit down. Hard.

The silence that followed was absolute as we all stared at father and daughter in astonishment.

Matthew was white as paper and his eyes were black.

The bite had set Matthew's blood rage alight.

"And definitely no biting." Matthew stared down at his daughter with an intensity that caused Becca to raise her blue eyes to his. As soon as she saw the expression on her father's face, she opened her jaws and released him. "Diana, please take Philip and Apollo back to the house."

"But—" I began. One wild, desperate look from Matthew had me swinging Philip into my arms. I headed toward the house without a backward glance.

After a moment, Matthew sent the rest of the family away.

"What's Matthew going to do?" Sarah asked, joining me and Philip in the kitchen.

"Dad's shunning her," Jack said, sounding unhappy.

"Do I smell blood?" Marcus asked, entering the kitchen with Marthe.

"Becca bit Matthew," I replied.

Through the thick, wavy glass, I saw Matthew say something to Becca. He then deliberately turned his back on his daughter.

"Wow," Jack said. "That's harsh."

"When an older, more powerful vampire turns his back on you, it's both an insult and a rejection—a sign that you've done something wrong," Marcus explained. "We don't like to be at odds with the leader of the pack."

"That's an awfully subtle message for a toddler to grasp," Sarah said.

The expression on Becca's face suggested that she understood it perfectly, however. She looked devastated.

"Milady Rebecca must apologize," Marthe said. "Then *sieur* will forgive her and all will be well again." She gave me a comforting pat.

"Becca isn't good with apologies," I fretted. "This could take awhile."

"Sorry," Philip said, his eyes filling with tears. Our son, on the other hand, apologized all the time—even for things he hadn't done.

"Thank God," Marcus reported, sounding relieved. "She apologized."

Matthew picked Becca up and kissed her on the top of her head. Then he carried her into the kitchen.

Becca's expression was worried as she faced her family again for the first time. She knew she had done something terribly wrong, and wasn't sure of her reception.

"Hello, princess," Jack said, giving her a wide smile.

"'Lo, Jack," Becca said, her anxiety evaporating.

Feeling unsure of what to do in the midst of all these vampires and their unspoken rules, I stood with Philip and waited until the rest of the group had welcomed Becca back into the fold. Philip squirmed to be put down and ran off in the direction of the pantry with Apollo, no doubt in search of congratulatory Cheerios for his sister.

Finally, Matthew put Becca in my arms. I kissed her and held her tight.

"Brave girl," I said, closing my eyes for a moment in silent thanks that this episode was over.

When I opened them again, Matthew was gone.

MATTHEW WAS RUNNING THROUGH THE forest beyond the moat as if the hounds of hell were pursuing him. I located him with the help of Rakasa, who was almost as fast as he was, and a magical tracking device I'd been working on to help watch the children. I called it a dragon-eye because the central, shining black orb reminded me of Corra, and the shimmering wings that shot out from each side resembled those of a dragonfly. It was a useful bit of magic, inspired by the drawings in a copy of Ulisse Aldrovandi's *Historia Monstrorum* I'd found among Philippe's books.

I caught up with Matthew only when he stopped to draw breath under a wide oak on the other side of the wood that marked the point where four fields came together. Once it had provided shade for the plow horses and estate farmers when they took their midday break. Today, it was providing a different kind of protection.

Matthew's fingers gripped the rough bark, his lungs working harder than normal. I slid down from Rakasa and tied up her reins.

"Are you and Rebecca all right?" Matthew's voice rasped in his throat. Even in this state, his first concern was for the creatures he loved.

"We're fine," I said.

Matthew put his back to the tree and slid down it, eyes closed. He buried his head in his hands.

"Even warmblooded children bite when they're frustrated, Matthew," I said, trying to comfort him. "She will grow out of it."

"A vampire won't see it that way. A bite is an act of aggression. Our every instinct is to bite back—to fight back. If Rebecca bites the wrong vampire, and they react as their genetics tells them to do, they could kill her in an instant, crush her tiny bones to powder." Matthew's eyes were still dark with blood rage, even though physical exertion usually brought him temporary relief from its symptoms. "It took all of my self-control not to react. Would another vampire exercise the same restraint, if he were in my place? Would Gerbert?"

"She's just a child—" I protested.

"This is why making children into vampires is forbidden," Matthew replied. "Their behavior is unpredictable, and they don't have sufficient self-control. Newly reborn vampires exhibit some of the same tendencies, but at least they have adult bodies that can survive punishment."

A horse and rider approached. It was Marcus. I had never seen him on horseback before, and he rode with the same practiced assurance as the rest of the family. In Marcus's case, he hadn't even bothered with a saddle and bridle. He'd simply thrown one leg over the animal's back and left the rope attached to the horse's halter.

"Just checking to make sure you're both okay," Marcus called to us, trotting closer. "Jack was worried, so I told him I'd make sure you'd found each other."

I was worried, too. Matthew's blood rage wasn't abating as quickly as it normally did.

"You handled that better than most vampires would have," Marcus commented.

"She's my daughter. I love her," Matthew replied, looking up at his son. "But I came close—so close—to lashing out. Like I did with Eleanor."

And Eleanor had died. It had been a long time ago, in a different world and under very different circumstances, but Matthew had discovered in one horrible instant that loving someone was not always enough to protect them from harm.

"Like I did with Cecilia," Matthew whispered, burying his head in his hands again.

Marcus wasn't the only one in the house who was struggling with his memories.

"You aren't the same man you were back then," I said firmly.

"Yes, he is." Marcus's voice was rough.

"Marcus!" I was shocked. "How can you—"

"Because it's the truth."

"John Russell always said you were too sincere to be a de Clermont." Matthew gave a humorless laugh. "He said I was mad to make you a vampire."

"Why did you do it, then?" Marcus asked his father.

"You fascinated me," Matthew replied. "I knew you had secrets, but you were honest and true in so many other ways. I couldn't figure out how you managed it."

"So it wasn't my gift for healing," Marcus said sardonically.

"That was part of it." Matthew's blood rage was being carried away on a tide of recollection. He settled more easily against the tree. "But the question really shouldn't be why I changed you from a human to a vampire, but rather why you accepted my offer."

Marcus took his time before he answered.

"Because I had nothing left to lose that mattered," Marcus replied. "And I thought you might be the father that I had been searching for."

Words of Two Syllables

THE NEW ENGLAND PRIMER, 1762

Absent	abhor	apron	author
Babel	became	beguile	boldly
Capon	cellar	constant	cupboard
Daily	depend	divers	duty
Eagle	eager	enclose	even
Father	famous	female	future
Gather	garden	glory	gravy
Heinous	hateful	humane	husband
Infant	indeed	incense	island
Jacob	jealous	justice	julep
Labour	laden	lady	lazy
Many	mary	motive	musick

⇥ 21 ⇤

Father

The hospital outside Yorktown echoed with the quiet sounds of death. Agitated limbs fought with worn sheets and blankets, making a soft rustle. And every few minutes, sighs floated through the air as the soldiers' ghosts flew free.

Marcus lay on the cot in the corner, his eyes locked shut against the ghosts, unable to respond to calls for help that once would have had him rising to tend and comfort the sick. Tonight, he was just another soldier far from home, dying among his brothers-in-arms.

Marcus swallowed against the dryness in his throat. It was parched and raw from fever, and it had been hours since someone came through with the bucket and dipper. So many men in Washington's army were ill with camp fevers—too many to care for now that the war was nearly over and the able-bodied were on their way home to their former lives.

He heard low voices at the entrance to the ward. Marcus clawed weakly at the sheets, hoping to get the orderly's attention.

"What does this French soldier look like, Matthew?"

Lantern light flickered against Marcus's closed eyelids.

"*Dieu*, John. How do I know?" The voice was familiar, tugging on Marcus's memory. "I barely knew him. It's Gil who wants him found."

Marcus's sticky eyes cracked open. His throat worked to make a sound, but nothing came out but a whisper that was far too low for anyone to hear.

"Chevalier de Clermont."

Booted heels stopped on the dirt floor.

"Someone called my name," the chevalier de Clermont said. "Speak up, Le Brun. We've come to take you from here."

The lantern swung closer, closer. Its brightness pierced the thin skin of Marcus's eyelids, sending rivers of pain through his fevered body. Marcus moaned.

"Doc?" Cool hands touched his forehead, his neck, pulled the sheets from his clawed hands. "Christ alive, he's on fire."

"I can smell death on the fellow's breath," the other man said. His voice was familiar, too.

There was a jostle of water against wood. De Clermont pressed the chipped edge of a dipper, slick from men's spittle, against his lips. Marcus was too weak to swallow, and most of the water ran from the corners of his mouth.

"Take his head—gently, Russell—and hold him, just so, there."

Marcus felt himself raised up. Liquid tipped into his mouth, cool and sweet.

"Tilt his head back. Just slightly," de Clermont instructed. "Come, Doc. Swallow."

But the water dribbled out again. Marcus coughed, racking his body and wasting more of his pitiful strength.

"Why won't he drink?" the other man asked.

"His body is shutting down," de Clermont said. "It's refusing its own salvation."

"Don't be so bloody Catholic, Matthew. Not here, surrounded by all these proper Puritans." Whoever was speaking—when had Marcus heard that voice before?—was trying to lighten the atmosphere with soldiers' humor.

Marcus opened his eyes and saw the dead rifleman from Bunker Hill named Cole—the same man he'd seen at the hospital in Trenton wearing the clothing of a Virginian.

"You're not Russell." Against all odds, Marcus's throat moved to swallow, and a drop of moisture slid down the parched tissues. "You're Cole. And you're dead."

"So, sir, are you—or near enough, by the smell of you," he replied.

"You know Doc?" De Clermont's voice registered his surprise.

"Doc? No. I knew a boy named Marcus MacNeil once, a brave lad from the frontier with a marksman's eye and a reckless disregard for orders," the man from Bunker Hill replied.

"Name's Galen," Marcus croaked. "Galen Chauncey."

The chevalier de Clermont tipped water into his mouth again. This time, a few spoonfuls made their way down Marcus's raw gullet and into his stomach. The effort left him gasping. As quickly as it had gone down, however, the water came back up. His body wanted no part of it.

A cool, damp cloth wiped the crust from his eyes and traveled down to remove the residue of bile and water from his mouth and chin. Someone rinsed the cloth with fresh water before it mopped at his cheeks and stroked softly across his brows.

"Ma?" No one else had ever touched him with such tenderness.

"No. It's Matthew." His voice, too, was tender. Surely this wasn't the same chevalier de Clermont who had cowed Dr. Shippen and silenced John Adams?

"Am I dead?" Marcus wondered aloud. If they were all gone to hell, then tonight would make better sense. Marcus didn't remember that any of the vivid descriptions of the netherworld Reverend Hopkins had shared from the Hadley pulpit on Sundays had included an army hospital, but the devil was nothing if not creative.

"No, Doc. You're not dead." De Clermont pressed the dipper to Marcus's mouth. This time, Marcus sipped and swallowed—and the water stayed put.

"Are you the devil?" Marcus asked de Clermont.

"No, but they're on very close terms," Russell replied.

Marcus saw that de Clermont's companion was no longer wearing a hunting shirt or buckskins. Now the man was dressed in the smart red uniform of a British regimental.

"You're a spy." Marcus pointed a trembling finger.

"Wrong man, I'm afraid. It's Matthew who gathers the intelligence. I'm just a soldier. The name is John Russell, Seventeenth Regiment of Light Dragoons. Death and glory boys. Formerly John Cole, First New Hampshire Regiment." Russell patted the breast of his coat, which gave off a strange crinkling sound like it was full of paper. "Come, Matthew. There's a war to finish."

"Go. You've got the terms of surrender," de Clermont said. "I'll sit with Doc."

"Why did the brotherhood wait so damn long to do something? We might have been spared this whole summer of campaigning—not to mention saved this boy's life."

"Ask my father." De Clermont sounded as weary as Marcus felt. "Or Baldwin, if you can find him among the jaegers."

"Oh, well. It's no matter. If not for war, what would creatures like us do each spring?" Russell asked with a snort.

"I don't know, John. Plant gardens? Fall in love? Make things?" De Clermont sounded wistful.

"You're a sentimental old fool, Matthew." Russell extended his right arm. De Clermont took it, clasping it at the elbow. It was an oddly old-fashioned farewell, one that seemed more appropriate to armored knights and Agincourt than to Yorktown's battlefield. "Until next time."

With that, Russell vanished.

MARCUS'S GRASP OF TIME and place loosened further after Russell's departure. His fevered dreams were filled with odd, sharp fragments of his past, and he found it increasingly difficult to answer the chevalier de Clermont's questions.

"Is there someone I should write to?" de Clermont asked. "Family? A sweetheart you left back home?"

Marcus shuffled through the ghosts of Hadley who haunted his waking hours: kindly Tom Buckland and his caring wife; Anna Porter, probably married by now; old Ellie Pruitt, probably dead; Joshua Boston, who had enough worldly cares without Marcus adding to them; Zeb Pruitt, his hero, who could barely read. His friends in the Philadelphia Associators had moved on with their own lives. For a moment, Marcus considered writing to Dr. Otto, who had given him a chance at a better life.

"No family," Marcus said. "No home."

"Everyone has a family." De Clermont's expression was thoughtful. "You are a curious man, Marcus MacNeil. What made you give up your name? When I met you at Brandywine, you were already Doc. And Galen Chauncey is an assumed name if ever I heard one."

"Am a Chauncey." Marcus found talking exhausting but would force himself to do so on this important point. "Like my mother."

"Your mother. I see." De Clermont sounded as though he understood.

"Tired." Marcus turned his aching head away.

But the chevalier kept asking him questions. Whenever Marcus's delirium abated, he answered them.

"What made you become a surgeon?" de Clermont asked him.

"Tom. He fixed me up. Taught me things." Marcus remembered the lessons in anatomy and doctoring he'd learned in Buckland's Northampton surgery.

"You should have gone to university, studied medicine properly," de Clermont said. "You are already a fine physician. I suspect you might have been a great one, given an opportunity."

"Harvard," Marcus whispered. "Ma says Chaunceys go to Harvard."

"Far be it from me to contradict your mother, but these days the best surgeons go to Edinburgh," de Clermont replied with a smile. "Before they went to Montpellier or Bologna. Before that, it was Salamanca, Alexandria, or Pergamum."

Marcus sighed, wistful at the prospect of so much knowledge, forever out of reach. "I wish."

"And if someone could grant you that wish—could give you a second chance at life—would you take him up on the offer?" De Clermont's face bore a strange, avid expression.

Marcus nodded. His mother would be so pleased if he went to college, even if he didn't attend Harvard.

"And what if you had to wait a time before you could begin your studies—establish a new name, learn a new language, polish your Latin?" de Clermont asked.

Marcus shrugged. He was dying. Polishing his Latin seemed easy in comparison.

"I see." De Clermont's shrewd eyes darkened. "And what if you had to hunt, every day of your life, just to survive?"

"Good hunter," Marcus replied, proudly thinking of the squirrels, fish, turkeys, and deer he'd shot to keep his family alive. Hell, he'd even gotten a shot off on a wolf once, though they were supposed to be gone and Noah Cook said it was just a mangy old dog.

"Marcus? Did you hear me?" De Clermont's face was very close, and his eyes reminded Marcus of that gray and grizzled animal who yelped and ran away, never to be seen again. "You don't have much time to decide."

In his bones, Marcus felt he had all the time in the world.

"Pay attention, Marcus. I asked if you would be willing to kill someone for this chance to live a doctor's life. Not an animal—a man." De Clermont's voice held a note of urgency that cut through Marcus's fever and the fog of disorientation and pain that accompanied it.

"Yes—if he deserved it," Marcus said.

MARCUS SLEPT FOR A WHILE after that. When he woke, the chevalier de Clermont was in the midst of a story that was more fantastic than Marcus's own dreams. He said he had lived for more than a thousand years. That he had been a carpenter and a mason, a soldier and a spy, a poet, a doctor, a lawyer.

De Clermont spoke of some of the men he had killed. Someone in Jerusalem, and others in France and Germany and Italy. And he mentioned a woman, too, someone named Eleanor.

There were frightening parts to the story, elements that made Marcus think he was indeed in hell. The chevalier talked about his taste for blood, and how he drank from living creatures and tried not to kill them. Surely such a thing was impossible.

"Would you drink from a man's veins to survive?" Even in the midst of his story, the chevalier de Clermont kept asking questions.

Marcus was burning up with fever, his mind addled with the heat and the pressure in his veins.

"If I did, would the pain stop?" Marcus asked.

"Yes," de Clermont replied.

"Then I would," Marcus confessed.

MARCUS DREAMED HE WAS FLYING, high and fast above the hospital. The floor below was stained with vomit and worse, and mice foraged for scraps to eat.

Then everything turned green as the hospital tent vanished and the filthy floor became grass, and the grass turned to forest. The forest grew deeper, greener. Marcus moved faster and faster. He never climbed higher, but his rapid progress turned the whole world to a blur of green and brown and black. Marcus felt the air, cold against his fevered body. His teeth chattered like the skeleton in Gerty's front room in Philadelphia.

Day became night, and he was flying on a horse. Someone slapped him. Hard.

"Don't die." A man with dark eyes and pale skin stared down at him. "Not yet. You have to be alive when I do this."

The chevalier de Clermont was in his dream now, and so was Russell. They were in a sheltered glade, surrounded by trees. With them was a band of Indian warriors who obeyed de Clermont's orders.

"What are you doing?" Russell asked de Clermont.

"Giving this boy a second chance," answered de Clermont.

"You have a war to finish!" Russell said.

"Cornwallis won't be in any rush to agree to the terms of surrender. Besides, I have to collect the mail," de Clermont said.

Marcus finally understood why the colonial mail service was so expensive and unreliable: It was run by devils and dead men. He laughed at the image of Beelzebub, mounted on a black horse, carrying a sack of post. But the mirth split his head in two like a rotten apple, and his mouth filled with the bitter tang of blood.

Something had hemorrhaged.

"No more." For Marcus, those three words encapsulated a lifetime of disappointment and broken promises.

"War is a hellishly difficult time to become a *wearh*, Matthew," Russell said, worried. "Are you sure?"

Now Russell was asking questions, too.

"Yes," Marcus and de Clermont said at the same time.

A sudden, searing pain at his neck told Marcus that his carotid artery had ruptured. It was too late. He would surely die now, and there was nothing that anyone could do for him.

With a deep, rattling breath, Marcus gave up the ghost trapped in his body.

Hell, he discovered, was strangely cold now that his soul had flown. There was none of the fire and brimstone Reverend Hopkins had promised, and the heat of his fever was gone, too. Everything was icy and still. There was no screaming, or howls of pain, but only a slow, stammering drumbeat.

Then that faded, too.

Marcus swallowed.

When he did, there a sudden cacophony of sound louder than Washington's band. Crickets trilled, owls bugled. The limbs of the trees beat out a rat-a-tat-tat.

"Christ, no," de Clermont murmured.

Marcus fell from a height and landed with a thud. His skin prickled with awareness, the night air and the rush of the wind sending every hair on his head aloft, every hair on his neck rising along with it.

"What is it, Matthew? What did you see?" Russell asked.

The sound of Russell's voice prompted images to flash through Marcus's mind as though they were printed on Gerty's deck of cards and she was shuffling through them at lightning speed. He seemed to be looking out at the world through a different set of eyes, eyes that saw everything in crisp detail. At first, the images were of John Russell.

John Russell in a dark tunic, his expression bitter and hard.

A sword slicing into John Russell's neck, through a chink in plates of armor—a death blow.

John Russell sitting, hale and hearty, at a table in a dark tavern, a woman on his knee.

John Russell taking blood from a woman's arm—drinking it, devouring it. And the woman liked it. She cried out in ecstasy, her fingers working between her legs as Russell fed.

"His family." De Clermont's voice sounded like broken glass, jagged in Marcus's newly sensitive ears.

At the word "family," the flood of images twisted and turned direction.

A golden-haired woman.

A mountain of a man with critical eyes.

A pale, slender creature with a baby in her arms.

The dark glance of a woman in yellow, her eyes hectic and wandering.

A gentle man who reclined in the eyes of another man—this one dark and handsome.

An old woman with a round, creased face and a kind expression of welcome.

Family.

"His father." Hands took Marcus by the arms and grasped them so hard that he feared his bones might snap.

Father. This time the word shaped the images that followed into a story.

Matthew de Clermont, his hands holding a chisel and hammer, his clothes stained with sweat and covered in gray dust, walking home on a summer night, met on the way by the same woman Marcus had seen before, the one with the child in her arms.

Matthew de Clermont, leaning on a shovel's handle, face damp with effort or tears, his expression bleak, staring into a hole that contained two bodies.

Matthew de Clermont falling to a stone floor.

Matthew de Clermont, covered in blood and gore, exhausted and kneeling.

Matthew de Clermont fighting with a hard-faced young man not much older than Marcus, who gave off an air of bitter malevolence.

"I know why MacNeil changed his name," de Clermont said. "He killed his own father."

FROM THAT POINT on they were constantly moving, and always at night. Marcus's delirium gave way to a desperate thirst that nothing would quench. His fever abated, but his mind was still addled and restless. Marcus's life became a patchwork quilt of jagged impressions and conversations stitched together with bloodred thread. Russell left them to return to the armies at Yorktown. De Clermont's Indian friends led Marcus and Matthew along paths no wider than a deer trail and impossible to follow unless you knew the subtle signs that marked the way.

"What if we get lost?" Marcus asked. "How will we find our way in the dark?"

"You're a *wearh* now," de Clermont said briskly. "You have nothing to fear from the night."

During the day, Marcus and de Clermont took refuge in houses along the road whose doors opened without question when the chevalier appeared, or in caves tucked into the hillsides. The Indian warriors who traveled with them kept their distance from the farmhouses, but always rejoined them after the sun set.

Marcus's body felt unwieldy, both oddly weak and strangely powerful, slow one moment and then quick the next. Sometimes he dropped things, and other times he crushed them with no more than a touch.

While they rested, de Clermont gave him a strong drink that had a medicinal, metallic tang. It was thick and sweet and tasted heavenly. Marcus felt saner and calmer after he had it, but his appetite for solid food did not return.

"You're a *wearh* now," de Clermont reminded him, as if this should mean something to him. "Remember what I told you at Yorktown? All you need to survive is blood—not meat or bread."

Marcus dimly recalled de Clermont telling him that, but he also remembered there was some mention of never getting ill again, and it being difficult for him to die. And de Clermont had told him that he had been alive for more than a thousand years—which was preposterous. The man had a thick head of raven-colored hair and a smooth complexion.

"And you're a *wearh*, too?" Marcus asked.

"Yes, Marcus," de Clermont replied, "how else did you become one? I sired you. Don't you remember agreeing to it, when I gave you the choice of living or dying?"

"And Cole—Russell—is a *wearh* as well, and that's why he didn't die at Bunker Hill?" Marcus kept at his efforts to assemble the events of the past week into something that made sense. No matter how hard he tried, the result was always something more fantastic than *Robinson Crusoe*.

They had reached the border between Pennsylvania and New York when Marcus's powerful thirst gave way to different urges. The first was curiosity. The world seemed a brighter, richer place than it had before Yorktown. His eyesight was sharper, and scents and sounds made the world crackle with texture and life.

"What is this stuff?" Marcus asked, drinking deeply from the tankard that de Clermont offered to him. It was like nectar, fortifying and satisfying at once.

"Blood. And a bit of honey," de Clermont replied.

Marcus spit it out in a violent stream of red. De Clermont cuffed him on the shoulder.

"Don't be rude," the chevalier said, his voice purring in his throat like a cat. "I won't have my son behaving like an ungrateful lout."

"You're not my father." Marcus swung at him, his arm whipping out. De Clermont blocked it easily, cradling Marcus's hand in his own as if there was no force behind it.

"I am now, and you'll do as I say." De Clermont's face was calm, his voice even. "You'll never have the strength to beat me, Marcus. Don't even try."

But Marcus had grown up under another iron first and had no more intention of giving in to de Clermont than he had to Obadiah. In the following days, as they continued to travel farther north and deeper into the woods of New York, Marcus fought with de Clermont about everything, just because he could, just because it felt better to wrestle with him than to keep everything bottled up inside. Marcus now had three powerful desires: to drink, to know, and to fight.

"You cannot kill me, much as you might like to," de Clermont said after a wrestling match over a rabbit left them both temporarily bloodied, the rabbit torn to pieces and Marcus's arms—both of them—broken. "I told you that on the night you were made a *wearh*."

Marcus didn't have the courage to confess that he didn't remember much about that night, and what he did remember made no sense.

De Clermont reset Marcus's right wrist with the practiced touch of a skilled physician and surgeon.

"Your arm will heal in moments. My blood—your blood, now—won't allow sickness or injury to take root in the body," de Clermont explained. "Here. Give me your other arm."

"I can do it myself." Now that his right wrist was working properly again, Marcus pushed his left forearm back together. He could feel the bones fusing, his blood crawling with power. That sense that something was invading his body and taking it over reminded him of being inoculated. Marcus was thinking about what it might be in de Clermont's blood that would make him immune to sickness or harm—when the chevalier asked the question that had hung between them, unanswered, since that night in Yorktown.

"Did you kill your father because he beat you?" de Clermont asked. "I saw what he did. It was in your blood, when I took it at Yorktown. He beat your mother, too. But not your sister."

But Marcus didn't want to think of his mother and Patience. He didn't want to think of Hadley, or Obadiah, or life before. He had killed his father but had always retained a small hope that he might return home again. Now that he drank blood, he knew that was out of the question. He was no better than a ravening wolf.

"Go fuck yourself," Marcus snarled.

De Clermont rose to his feet without a word and stalked off into the darkness. He didn't return until the sun rose. De Clermont brought him a small deer, and Marcus fed on it, better able to stomach the blood of a four-legged creature than another person.

Finally, Marcus and de Clermont reached the hills and valleys of a part of New York that Marcus had never seen before—far north, almost into Canada. It was there that they took shelter with the Oneida. Marcus recalled the spring of 1778, at Valley Forge, when news had swept through camp that the Marquis de Lafayette and his French companions had brought a troop of Oneida allies to fight the British. As the Indians who had guided them here were welcomed home by friends and family, Marcus realized that the Oneida had been ensuring their safety.

In New York, Marcus was at last allowed to hunt. He found relief running after deer and game, and pleasure in taking their blood. De Clermont also encouraged him to compete with the young warriors. Marcus might be fast and impervious to injury, but he was no match for the Oneida when it came to tracking animals in the forest. Next to them, Marcus felt clumsy and foolish.

"He has much to learn," de Clermont apologized to a battle-scarred elder who was watching Marcus's hapless attempts to trap a duck with ill-concealed scorn.

"He needs time," the elder replied. "And as he is your son, Dagoweyent, he will have plenty of that."

THE PUNISHING REGIMENS MARCUS WENT through with the other young men of the tribe did take some of the fight out of him. Marcus wanted to sleep but couldn't seem to shut his eyes and rest. He still didn't fully understand what had happened to him. How had he survived the fever? And why was he now so strong and fast?

De Clermont kept repeating the same information over and over again—that Marcus would heal from almost any wound, that he would be difficult to kill, that he would never be ill another day in his life, that his senses were now far beyond what most humans enjoyed, that he was a *wearh*—but there was something missing in the account, some larger perspective that would explain how all this could be true.

It was the hunting—not the fighting or the questions or even the drinking of blood—that finally brought the fact that he was no longer human home to Marcus. Every day and every night, de Clermont took Marcus hunting. They tracked deer at first, then moved on to other prey. Ducks and wild birds were difficult to capture, and contained only a small amount of the precious blood that kept Marcus alive. Boars and bears were rare, and their size and drive to survive made them formidable opponents.

De Clermont would not let Marcus hunt with a gun, or even a bow and arrow.

"You're a *wearh* now," de Clermont said once more. "You need to run your prey down, catch it with your wits and your hands, best it, and feed. Guns and arrows are for warmbloods."

"Warmbloods?" Here was another new term.

"Humans. Witches. Daemons," de Clermont explained. "Lesser creatures. You will need human blood to survive, now that you are growing and developing. But it's not time to take it—yet. As for the witches and daemons, their blood is forbidden. A witch's blood will eat away at your veins, and the blood of daemons will sour your brain."

"Witches?" Marcus thought of Mary Webster. Had those old legends in Hadley been true after all? "How will I recognize them?"

"They smell." De Clermont's nose flared in distaste. "Don't worry. They fear us and stay away."

Once Marcus could bring down a deer quickly and feed from it without tearing the animal apart, they left the Oneida and traveled east. Along the route they met with fleeing soldiers, some wounded and others perfectly hearty. Some were British soldiers running away from the war. Others were Loyalists trying to escape into Canada and freedom now that they could see which way the fight would end. Many more were Continental soldiers who had grown weary of waiting for a formal declaration of peace and decided to go home to their farms and families.

"Which one do you want?" de Clermont asked. They were crouched in the tall grasses that grew beside a meandering stream, watching a group of British soldiers on the opposite bank. There were four men, and one was wounded.

"None." Marcus was happy with deer.

"You must choose, Marcus. But remember: You must live a long time with your decision," de Clermont said.

"That one." Marcus pointed to the smallest of the lot, a wiry fellow who spoke in a broad, unfamiliar accent.

"No." De Clermont pointed to the man lying by the water, groaning. "Him. Take him."

"Take him?" Marcus frowned. "You mean feed from him."

"I've seen you feed from a deer. You won't be able to stop drinking from a human once you start." De Clermont sniffed the breeze. "He's dying. The leg is gangrenous."

Marcus took in a gulp of air. Something sweet and rotten assaulted his nose. He practically gagged. "You want me to feed off *that*?"

"The infection is localized at the moment. He would smell worse otherwise," de Clermont said. "It won't be the sweetest blood you'll ever taste, but it won't kill you."

De Clermont vanished. A shadow passed over the narrow, pebbled ford. The British soldiers looked up, startled. One of them—the largest, most muscular of the soldiers—gave a frightened shout when de Clermont seized him and bit into his neck. His two companions ran away, leaving their few possessions behind. The wounded soldier, the one with the dying leg, began to scream.

The smell of blood sent Marcus after de Clermont. He arrived on the opposite bank more quickly than he would have dreamed possible—before.

"We aren't going to kill you." Marcus knelt beside the man. "I just need to take some of your blood."

De Clermont's prey was slowly sinking toward the ground as his blood was drained.

"Christ. Please. Don't kill me," the wounded soldier begged. "I have a wife. A daughter. I only ran away because they said we would be put on a prison ship."

It was every soldier's nightmare to be flung onto one of the foul vessels anchored offshore with no food, no fresh water, and no way of surviving the filthy, crowded conditions.

"Shh." Marcus patted him awkwardly on the shoulder. He could see the man's pulse, skittering at his neck. And the leg—Lord, John Russell had been right at Yorktown. Warmbloods did give off a terrible stench as their flesh died. "If you would just allow me—"

Strong white hands reached in and took the soldier by the collar. The man began to weep, his begging now constant as he faced what seemed like sure death.

"Stop talking. Bite him here. Firmly. You'll be less likely to kill him if you latch on to him, like a babe on his mother's breast." De Clermont held the soldier still. "Do it."

Marcus bit, but the man whimpered and moved, and that urge Marcus had been feeling to fight and fight some more roared back to life. He snarled and sank his teeth into the soldier's neck, shaking him slightly to quiet him. The man fainted, and Marcus felt a pang of disappointment. He wanted the man to challenge him. Somehow, Marcus knew the blood would taste better if he did.

Even without the fight, human blood was intoxicating. Marcus could taste a sourness that he supposed was from the gangrene and whatever other illnesses were pulsing through the soldier's veins, but even so Marcus felt fortified and stronger with every sip.

When he was finished, he had taken every drop in the man's body. The soldier was dead, his neck torn open with a gaping wound that looked as though an animal had attacked him.

"His friends," Marcus said, looking around. "Where are they?"

"Over there." De Clermont jerked his head toward a grove of trees in the distance. "They've been watching."

"Those cowards just stood there, and watched while we fed off people they knew?" He would never have let de Clermont feed on Vanderslice or Cuthbert or Dr. Otto.

"You take the little one," de Clermont said, dropping a few coins by his soldier's face. "I'll have the other."

BY THE TIME THEY REACHED the Connecticut River, Marcus had fed from old men and young men, sick men and hale men, criminals and runaways and even a rotund innkeeper who never woke up from his fireside slumbers while Marcus drank. There were a few tragic accidents when hunger got the better of him, and one rage-filled attack on a man who had been raping his way across New England and who even de Clermont agreed deserved to die.

Marcus and Matthew boarded a ferry and crossed the water. When they landed on the other side, Marcus realized that he was close to Hadley. He looked at de Clermont, unsure of why his father had brought him here.

"You should see it again," de Clermont said, "through new eyes."

But it was Marcus's nose that first registered the familiarity of the place. It was filled with the scents of fall in western Massachusetts—leaf mold and pumpkins, cider presses filled with apples, woodsmoke from chimneys—long before the MacNeil farm came into view.

The place was in much better condition than it had been on the day Marcus killed his father.

A woman laughed. It wasn't his mother's laughter—he would have known that silvery, infrequent sound in a heartbeat. He stopped his horse to see who lived here now, and de Clermont stopped with him.

A young woman of twenty or so came from the henhouse. She was blond, sturdy looking and strong, with a red-and-white apron over a blue dress that was simple but clean. She had a basket of eggs in one arm, and a pail of milk slung over the other.

"Ma!" the woman called out. "The hens laid! There are enough eggs to make custard for Oliver!"

It was his sister. This young woman—she was his sister.

"Patience." Marcus kicked his horse and started forward.

"It's your decision whether or not you speak to your family," de Clermont said. "But remember: You can't tell them what you've become. They wouldn't understand. And you can't remain here, Marcus. Hadley is too small to harbor a *wearh*. People will know you're different."

Then his mother came from the back door of the house. She was older, her hair white, and even at a distance Marcus could see the wrinkles that were etched into her skin. Still, she didn't look as tired as the last time he had seen her. In her arms was a baby wrapped in a homespun blanket. Patience kissed it on the forehead, talking to it with the rapt adoration that new mothers lavished on their children.

My nephew, Marcus realized. *Oliver.*

Catherine, Patience, and Oliver formed a small family knot around the door. They were happy. Healthy. Laughing. Marcus remembered when fear and pain hung over the house in a dark pall. Somehow, joy had returned when Obadiah and Marcus departed.

Marcus's heart stopped in a spasm of grief for what might have been. Then it started up again.

This was no longer his family. Marcus did not belong in Hadley anymore.

But he had made it possible for his mother and sister to find a new life for themselves. Marcus hoped that Patience's man—if she still had one and he had not been killed in the war—was good and kind.

Marcus turned his horse's head away from the farm.

"Who is that?" Patience's question floated through the air. Had he not been a *wearh*, Marcus might not have been able to hear her.

"It looks like—" his mother began. She stopped, seeming to consider whether her eyes were playing tricks.

Marcus faced resolutely forward, eyes on the horizon.

"No. I was mistaken," Catherine said, her voice tinged with sadness.

"He's not coming home, Ma," Patience said. "Not ever."

Catherine's sigh was the last thing Marcus heard before he put all that he once was and might have been behind him.

⊣ 22 ⊢

Infant

Portsmouth's harbor was filled with ships waiting to load and unload their cargo. Though it was well past midnight, the docks still bustled with activity.

"See if you can find a ship called the *Aréthuse*," de Clermont told Marcus, passing him the horse's reins. "I'll ask at the tavern to see if anyone's spotted her."

"How big?" Marcus studied the sloops, schooners, brigantines, and whaleboats.

"Big enough to make it across the Atlantic." De Clermont pointed to a ship at the very edge of the harbor. "There. That's her."

Marcus squinted into the dark, trying to make out the name. But it was the French flag flying off the stern that convinced him de Clermont was right.

De Clermont jumped into a small skiff and pulled Marcus in after him. The sailor on watch was horribly drunk and barely noticed that the vessel in his charge had been taken. De Clermont made quick work of reaching the *Aréthuse*, pulling mightily on the oars so that the boat's pointed bow rose up with every stroke.

When they reached the ship, someone flung a rope ladder over the side.

"Climb," de Clermont commanded, holding the skiff steady against the hull.

Marcus eyed the ship's steep side with concern.

"I'll fall off into the sea!" he protested.

"It's a long way, and the water is cold. You're better off taking your chances on the ladder." A disembodied voice floated down to them. Then, a square-jawed, clean-shaven face appeared over the railing, wreathed in shoulder-length golden hair that had escaped from the cocked hat perched, backward, on his head. "Hello, Uncle."

"Gallowglass." De Clermont touched his hat in greeting.

"And who's this with you?" Gallowglass asked, squinting at Marcus with suspicion.

"Let's get him up there before you start questioning him." De Clermont took Marcus by the scruff of the neck and lifted him up the first two rungs of the rope ladder while the skiff rocked underneath them.

When he reached the top, Marcus fell onto the deck in a dizzy heap. He was not, it turned out, very good with heights anymore. He closed his eyes to let the sea and sky return to their proper positions. When he opened them, there was a giant *wearh* hovering over him.

"Jesus!" Marcus scrambled away, afraid for his life. He might be hard to kill now, but he was no match for this creature.

"Christ and his apostles. Don't be daft, boy," Gallowglass said with a snort. "I'm hardly going to attack my own cousin."

"Cousin?" The family connection did nothing to soothe Marcus's fears. In his experience, family members often posed the greatest danger.

An arm the size of a howitzer shot forward, palm open, bent at the elbow. Marcus remembered how John Russell and de Clermont had said their greetings and taken their farewells. *Wearhs* must all be Masons, he thought—or perhaps this was a French custom?

Marcus gingerly clasped the proffered arm, elbow to elbow, aware that his cousin could break it like a twig. Anxious at the prospect of further injury, Marcus's fingers tightened on Gallowglass's muscular arm.

"Easy there, pup." Gallowglass's eyes creased in warning as he lifted Marcus to his feet.

"Sorry. Don't seem to know my own strength these days," Marcus mumbled, embarrassed by his inexperience.

"Hmph." Gallowglass's mouth tightened as he released his grip.

De Clermont swung himself from the ladder to the deck with the lithe self-assurance of a tiger. The man he called Gallowglass turned and, in a blur of fists, landed two blows to de Clermont's jaw.

Cousin or no cousin, Marcus's protective instincts howled to life and he launched himself at the stranger. Gallowglass's paw held him off with lazy ease.

"You'll be wanting to ripen a bit more before you take me on," Gallowglass advised Marcus.

"Stand down, Marcus," de Clermont said once he had realigned his jaw and worked it open and closed a few times.

"What the hell were you thinking, Uncle, making a baby in the middle of a war?" Gallowglass demanded of de Clermont.

"The circumstances of your own rebirth were not so different, as I recall." De Clermont's aristocratic black eyebrows shot heavenward.

"Hugh sired me after the heat of battle was over, when he was picking through the field looking for dead friends," Gallowglass said. "This boy is too young to have seen battle. You found him loafing about on some corner, I warrant, and took the stray in."

"The boy has seen more than you know," Matthew said in a tone that discouraged further conversation on this point. "Besides, the war is all but over. Both armies are riddled with fever and tired of fighting."

"And Gil? You didn't just leave him there?" Gallowglass swore a blistering oath. "You had two jobs, Matthew: see to it the colonials won the war, and return the Marquis de Lafayette to France in one piece."

"Pierre is with him. Baldwin is among the jaegers. And John Russell has a place in Cornwallis's staff and the terms of surrender in his pocket. I've done my job." Matthew straightened the seams on his gloves. "The morning is upon us. To business, Gallowglass."

Gallowglass led them to a small cabin belowdecks that had a view of the water through a wide rectangular window. The room was sparsely furnished with a desk, a few stools, a heavy-bottomed chest, and a hammock strung up between two posts.

"Your letters." Gallowglass opened the chest and drew out a small oilskin pouch. He tossed it to de Clermont.

De Clermont loosened the ties and riffled through the contents. He drew out a few pieces and hid them away in the breast pocket of his coat.

"You missed one." Gallowglass plucked out another that was sealed with a heavy daub of red wax. "Mademoiselle Juliette sends her regards. And here is Granddad's post."

The second bag Gallowglass pulled from the chest was considerably larger than the first and full of interesting bumps and bulges, one of which looked like a bottle of wine.

"Madeira. For General Washington," Gallowglass said, tracking Marcus's wandering attention. "Granddad thought he might share it with Mrs. Washington after he's back home."

Marcus knew that the Marquis de Lafayette was dear to General Washington, but had no idea there was a connection between the chevalier de Clermont and the commander of the Continental army.

"How kind," Marcus said, filing this bit of intelligence away for further reflection.

"Oh, I doubt it," Gallowglass said cheerfully. "Philippe will want something in exchange. He always does."

"And how is Philippe?" de Clermont asked. "And my mother?"

"Davy says they're finer than frog's hair," Gallowglass replied.

"That's it?" de Clermont said. "That's all the news from France?"

"I haven't got time for a saucer of tea and a lengthy reunion, Matthew. I want to catch the tide." Gallowglass sniffed the wind like a hound.

"You're hopeless." De Clermont sighed and handed over a small stack of letters and a silk bag. "These are for Juliette. Don't lose the strand of beads."

"When have I ever lost anything?" Gallowglass's blue eyes widened in indignation. "I've been to the edges of the earth running errands for this family and even got that bloody leopard from Constantinople to Venice so that Granddad didn't leave the sultan's gift behind."

Marcus liked this brawny Scot. Gallowglass made Marcus wonder what his own Scots grandfather might have been like as a young man.

"True. These are for Philippe. General Washington's letters are on top. See he reads those first." De Clermont handed him another parcel of mail. He pointed to Marcus. "And of course, there's him."

Gallowglass was dumbfounded. So, too, was Marcus.

"Oh no. No. Absolutely not." Gallowglass held his hands up in horror.

"Me?" Marcus's head swung from Matthew to Gallowglass and back again. "I can't go to France. I'm staying with you."

"I have to get back to Yorktown to oversee the peace, and you're not ready for that much society," de Clermont said.

"What about my ship? Life at sea is hardly suitable for a newly made *wearh*!" Gallowglass exclaimed. "He'll eat the crew before we reach France."

"I'm sure one of them will feed him, for the right price," de Clermont replied, unconcerned.

"But there's nowhere to hunt at sea. Have you lost your mind, Uncle?" Marcus wondered the same thing.

"Can he even feed himself?" Gallowglass demanded. "Or must he be bottle-fed like a mewling infant?"

"I fed on a man—in Albany!" Marcus replied, indignant.

"Ooh. Albany. Very nice. Had a bit of farmer and a nibble of fur trapper?" Gallowglass snorted. "You'll get naught but stale beer and rat with me. It's not enough to keep a baby alive."

"Baby?" Marcus's arms windmilled toward Gallowglass in a gratifying whirl of speed. Sadly, they never made contact with their target. De Clermont took him by the collar and flung him into the corner.

"No more arguments—from either of you," de Clermont said brusquely. "You're taking him to France, Gallowglass. See to it he gets there alive. I promised him an education."

"We'll need more chickens," Gallowglass remarked. "And what do I do with him once we reach Bordeaux?"

"Deliver him to *Maman*," de Clermont said, making his way to the door. "She'll know what to do. *À bientôt*, Marcus. Obey Gallowglass. I'm putting you in his charge."

"Wait just a minute!" Gallowglass strode after de Clermont.

Marcus watched from the quarterdeck as the two men had a heated argument. When Gallowglass sputtered into silence, de Clermont swung over the rail and disappeared down the rope ladder.

Gallowglass watched him descend. He shook his head, then turned to face Marcus and sighed. Then the giant *wearh* cupped his hands around his mouth and let out a deafening whistle.

"Cast off, lads!"

MARCUS WATCHED THE VANISHING SPECK of shoreline from the quarterdeck and wondered whether it might be wise to swim back to shore after all. The big sailor crouched down next to him.

"We still haven't been properly introduced." One arm shot toward Marcus. "I'm Eric. Most people just call me Gallowglass."

"Marcus MacNeil." He took Gallowglass's arm again. This time the gesture felt right, familiar. "Most people call me Doc."

"Marcus, eh? A Roman name. Granddad will be pleased." Gallowglass's eyes were permanently creased at the corners, which made him look as though he were about to burst into laughter.

"The chevalier de Clermont didn't tell me he had a father," Marcus said, daring to reveal his ignorance.

"The chevalier de Clermont?" Gallowglass tipped his head back and roared with laughter. "Christ's bones, boy. He's your maker! I understand your reluctance to call him Papa—Matthew is as paternal as a porcupine in full needle—but you might at least call him by his first name."

Marcus considered it but found it impossible to view the austere, mysterious Frenchman as anything but the chevalier de Clermont.

"Give it time," Gallowglass said, patting Marcus on the shoulder. "We've got weeks to share stories about your dear dad. By the time we arrive in France, you'll have far more colorful names for him than Matthew. More fitting, too."

Perhaps the journey would not be as tedious as Marcus had feared. He felt the slender, familiar outlines of *Common Sense* in his coat pocket. Between Thomas Paine and Gallowglass, Marcus could spend the entire voyage reading and figuring out what it was going to take to survive as a vampire.

"I saw—felt—some of the chevalier's history." Marcus wasn't sure whether this was something he should discuss.

"Bloodlore is tricky. It's no replacement for a proper story." Gallowglass ran a gloved finger under his nose, which had gone watery in the rising wind.

This was another unfamiliar word—like "*wearh*" and "maker." Marcus's curiosity must have shown.

"Bloodlore is the knowledge that's in the bones and blood of every creature. It's one of the things we crave as *wearhs*," Gallowglass explained.

Marcus had felt that hunger to know—along with the urge to hunt, to drink blood, and to fight. It was comforting to realize that his lively curiosity—a curse, his father Obadiah had called it—was now a normal, acceptable part of who he was.

"Didn't Matthew explain how the world really works and what you were about to become before he made you?" Gallowglass looked concerned.

"He might have. I'm not sure," Marcus confessed. "I had a fever—a bad one. I don't remember much. The chevalier told me I would be able to go to university, and study medicine."

Gallowglass swore.

"I have some questions," Marcus said hesitantly.

"I imagine you do, lad," Gallowglass said. "Fire away."

"What's a *wearh*?" Marcus asked, his voice low in case a member of the ship's crew was nearby.

Gallowglass buried his face in his hands and groaned.

"Let's start at the beginning," he said, rising to his feet with the practiced grace of a man who had spent his life afloat. Gallowglass extended a hand to Marcus and lifted him up. "You've a long journey ahead of you, young Marcus. By the time we get to France, you'll understand what a *wearh* is—and what you've taken on by becoming one."

ONCE THEY WERE ON OPEN seas, Gallowglass had all the flags lowered save one that was black with a silver snake carrying its tail in its mouth. This kept most vessels at a respectful distance.

"The family crest," Gallowglass explained, pointing up at the standard that flapped and crackled in the wind. "Granddad is more gruesome than any pirate. Not even Blackbeard wanted to be on his bad side."

During the voyage, Gallowglass told Marcus a story about what it was to be a *wearh* that finally made sense of the weeks since Yorktown. At last Marcus understood the nature of not only *wearhs*, but witches, daemons, and humans, too. He was fairly sure, looking back over his life, that the healer at Bunker Hill had been a witch. And he knew for certain that John Russell—the man he first knew as Cole—was a *wearh*. As for daemons, Marcus didn't think he knew any, although Vanderslice was the most likely prospect.

Gallowglass also impressed upon him what it was to be a de Clermont.

Oddly, it seemed that becoming a blood-drinking, nearly immortal, volatile, two-legged creature was the easier task. Being a de Clermont seemed to require knowledge of a great many prickly characters and mastery of a list of rules a mile long. Based on Gallowglass's description of the family and how it operated, it did not seem that the de Clermonts had read *Common Sense*. There was certainly no hint that they had embraced the new world of liberty and freedom that Paine outlined in his work. While Marcus lay in his berth, reading and rereading the worn pages of his treasured book, he had time to wonder what his new family would think of Paine's assertion that virtue was not hereditary.

After more than a month of blockade-running, stiff winds, and rough, frigid seas, the *Aréthuse* arrived in the French port of Bordeaux. Gallowglass had made excellent time in the crossing, thanks to a combination of utter fearlessness, an encyclopedic mastery of the currents, and the fact that the de Clermont standard frightened off every privateer and blockade-runner in the Atlantic, as he had promised it would.

As they sailed down the Gironde, Marcus eyed the French countryside with a mixture of relief and trepidation, now knowing what awaited them on terra firma.

Marcus had never strayed much beyond the Connecticut River growing up, and though the varied origins of the Philadelphia Associators had introduced him to a world beyond the colonies, he as yet had no direct experience of it. The air in France smelled different, and the sounds that came from the shore did, too. The fields were bare, except for rows of vines held up by wooden supports that would bear the fruit for the wine *wearhs* drank to quench their thirst when blood was not available. The brilliant leaves that had still been on the trees in Portsmouth were nowhere visible in France in late December.

Marcus had grown accustomed to seeing nothing but canvas and water, and to being in close quarters with only Gallowglass and the crew. Bordeaux was a bustling port like Philadelphia, filled with creatures of every description—including females. Once they had docked and filled out all the paperwork that was required to unload the *Aréthuse's* cargo, Gallowglass led him off the ship. His cousin's hand was firm on his elbow. Even so, the press of warm bodies, along with the bright colors and strong scents of the port, left Marcus dazed and a trifle confused.

"Steady on," Gallowglass said in a low murmur. "Stop and take it all in. Remember what I told you. Don't be following wherever your nose leads, like a boy trailing after every pretty girl."

Marcus swayed on unsteady legs, feeling the ground moving beneath him and his full stomach sliding along with it. Stefan, the *Aréthuse's* plump cook, had fed him that morning while they were anchored outside the harbor, waiting for the customs men to inspect their wares. Stefan not only provided sustenance to the warmbloods in the form of hardtack and grog, but fed the *wearhs* from his veins, too.

"*À bientôt*," Stefan said cheerily as he passed, carrying the ship's last remaining chicken down the ramp, clucking and scolding in its wicker cage.

"Until next time, Stefan." Gallowglass handed him a fat pouch that made a satisfying clinking sound. "For your trouble."

"*Non*," Stefan demurred, though he was already weighing the coins and calculating how much he could buy with them. "I was paid before we set sail, *milord*."

"Consider it a boon, then," Gallowglass said, "for taking care of young Monsieur Marcus."

Marcus's mouth gaped. He had never dreamed of being worth so much money.

"Monsieur Marcus was a gentleman. It was my pleasure to serve him." Stefan bowed low, sending the chicken hurtling forward in his cage with an angry squawk.

Marcus bowed in return. The cook's eyes widened. Had Stefan been a chicken, he would have squawked, too. Gallowglass hauled Marcus upright and steered him away.

"Don't be bowing to the servants, Marcus," Gallowglass muttered. "You are a de Clermont now. Do you want the gossips noticing your strange ways?"

As a *wearh* who drank the blood of living creatures for sustenance, never slept, and could reduce a mizzenmast to splinters with his bare hands, Marcus felt sure that bowing to servants was the least of what warmbloods might notice.

"I suppose we can attribute your oddness to being American," Gallowglass mused, surveying the Bordelaise on the docks. Every last one of them was festooned with ribbons of red, white, and blue. The French were more visibly patriotic than most of the citizens of Philadelphia.

"Great Jesus and his sainted mother! Who is that?" A small, dark *wearh* with a pronounced squint approached them through the crowd with two spirited horses in tow. Marcus could tell what he was from the way the man smelled, which was so much less gamey and ripe than a warmblood. The man was slightly bowlegged, as though he had spent too much time on horseback.

"This is Matthew's latest project," Gallowglass said. "Marcus, meet Davy Gams. We call him Hancock."

"Pleased to meet you, sir." Marcus bowed. Davy's eyes popped.

"He's American," Gallowglass said apologetically.

Davy glowered at him. "You Americans have caused a great deal of trouble and cost a packet, too. You better be worth it."

Not knowing how to respond, Marcus adopted the silent, attentive attitude that he had perfected while working for the doctors Otto.

"How old is he?" Davy demanded of Gallowglass, who was studying the faces of the people passing them.

"Bonjour!" Gallowglass called to one particularly attractive young woman wearing a red, white, and blue rosette on her bodice who was shopping among the hucksters at the wharf. He turned back to Davy. "Somewhere in his fifties, I warrant. Matthew didn't give me exact facts and figures."

"Damn frogs." Davy spat on the ground. "They talk a good game, with their cockades and coffee, but you can't trust them. Not even Matthew."

"I'm only twenty-four, Gallowglass. I was born in 1757," Marcus said, swallowing down the stab of desire that shot through his loins at the sight of that Bordelaise bosom, fair and freckled.

"Gallowglass means days, not years. And don't contradict your elders," Davy said, cuffing Marcus on the chin. Once, it would have broken his jaw; now the blow registered only as an unpleasant reverberation. "It doesn't matter, in any case. You're as useless as a fart in a jam jar."

"Fuck off." Marcus made a rude gesture, one he'd learned on the *Aréthuse* from Faraj, the ship's pilot. He could now curse in Arabic as well as Dutch, French, German, and English.

"I suppose we'll have to take him to Paris." Davy let out an earsplitting whistle. "For that, we'll need a carriage rather than horses. You can't travel on horseback when you've got a baby with you. More needless expense."

"I know, I know." Gallowglass clucked with sympathy and clapped Davy on the shoulder. "I tried to put in at Saint-Malo, but the seas weren't having it."

"Bloody Matthew and his daft ideas." Davy's finger shot up in warning. "One of these days, Eric, I'm going to strangle that boy."

"I'll hold him down while you do it," Marcus said, still smarting from all that he'd discovered about his new life from Gallowglass. "High-handed bastard."

Davy and Gallowglass stared at him, astonished. Then Davy began to laugh in the gasping, unpracticed wheezes of one who hadn't been amused in some time.

"Not yet sixty and already angry with his sire," Davy said, wheezing and coughing some more.

"I know," Gallowglass said fondly. "The lad has real potential."

MARCUS HAD NEVER ridden in a carriage before, only a wagon. He found that he did not like it. Mostly he was able to make it outside before being sick. Hancock soon grew impatient with their frequent stops, and resorted to holding Marcus's head out the open window so that he could continue vomiting while they traveled.

His eyes streaming from the grit from the road, Marcus clamped his teeth shut against the rising bile (his guts were empty of blood and wine by this point), and strained to overhear the conversation in the carriage, before the words were blown away by the wind.

"—Granddad will have a stroke," Gallowglass said.

"Wasn't Matthew strictly forbidden—" Hancock's next words were inaudible.

"Wait until Baldwin discovers." Gallowglass sounded both alarmed and pleased by the prospect.

"—another bloody war will break out."

"At least Granny will—"

"—dote on him like an old woman."

"Watch your tongue around Marthe or she'll—"

"—better idea to take him there if she's in town."

"Auntie Fanny won't be at home. We'll have a devil of a time—"

"—deposit him with Françoise and then have a drink."

"It is a lot to take in—"

"—fucking boat home to his family."

The strange names—Marthe, Fanny, Françoise—swirled through Marcus's swimming brain, along with the realization that he had not only a grandfather but a grandmother as well. After years of being alone in the world, Marcus felt he was now part of a family. Warm feelings of obligation filled his hollow veins with gratitude. Even with his head bouncing on his neck like a pumpkin on a stalk as they careened along the Bordeaux–Paris road, Marcus was aware that he owed this third—no, fourth—chance at a new life to the chevalier de Clermont.

This new life would be his last, Marcus promised himself.

"REMEMBER, DON'T BOW TO ANYONE in this house. They won't like it." Gallowglass straightened Marcus's limp, stained neckcloth. "I'm sure your mother was a lovely woman, but you're in France now."

Marcus put this bit of intelligence into a crowded compartment of his mind that he was reserving for future study.

"Soon, you will meet a woman called Françoise. She is not to be trifled with, no matter how appetizing she smells. Charles will beat you with his rolling pin if you so much as look at her," Gallowglass continued, twitching Marcus's coat into place. "And do not, under any circumstances, play cards with your aunt Fanny."

An arresting combination of aromas, including pastry, lemons, and starch, filled the carriage. Three male *wearhs* sniffed the air like wolves tracking an alluring new animal. Marcus looked out the window, eager to see the creature attached to this irresistible scent.

"*Oh la vache!*" shrieked a rawboned woman of impressive height and lung capacity. "*Qu'est-ce que c'est?*"

"Mademoiselle Françoise. Do not be alarmed," Hancock said, leaping out of the carriage and taking her hand. "He is nothing but a mewling infant, and poses no danger to you."

"Infant!" Marcus exclaimed. He'd killed British soldiers, saved dozens of Americans and French patriots, assisted at several amputations, and fed off a cutthroat thief before accidentally killing him in Newburyport. He was no infant.

Marcus was, however, still a virgin. He eyed Françoise's quivering lips with interest. They were full and moist, and promised pleasure. And the woman smelled heavenly.

Françoise's eyes narrowed, and she pressed those lush lips together into a taut, forbidding line.

"This is Marcus. He belongs to Matthew. We thought we could leave him with Fanny." Gallowglass climbed out of the carriage and gave the woman a dazzling smile.

It might have worked on a warmblood, but not on a *wearh*. Françoise crossed her arms, which made her look twice her already ample size, and snorted.

"You cannot leave him here. Madame Fanny is out," she said.

"That does it. Take him to Philippe. Then we can make a run for it and be as far from Paris as possible when he explodes." Davy wiped his brow with his cuff.

"Where is she?" Gallowglass sailed forth through the front doors, undeterred. Françoise bustled after him. "Denmark? Sept-Tours? Burgundy? London?"

"No, *milord*. Mademoiselle Fanny is at Dr. Franklin's house. Helping him with his correspondence." Françoise glared at Marcus, as if he were somehow to blame for her mistress's absence.

"Correspondence, eh? Why, that old lecher." Hancock began to gasp and wheeze again.

"We'll just wait in the salon for her, if you don't mind, Françoise. And perhaps Charles could fix a bit of something for young Master Marcus," Gallowglass said cheerfully. "He's feeling peaked from all the excitement, poor lamb."

FRANÇOISE DEEMED MARCUS TOO COMMON and filthy for Fanny's salon, and banished him instead to the kitchen.

Charles, the *wearh* who ruled that subterranean lair, was not female and did not smell as appetizing as Françoise did, but within thirty minutes of meeting him, Marcus felt nothing but love for the man. Charles took one look and put Marcus in a wingback chair near the fire. He then began rummaging in cellars, larders, and game pantries for something to tempt his appetite and soothe his stomach.

Marcus was sipping a heady mixture of red wine from Burgundy—he had never tasted anything like it—and blood from a Normandy wood pigeon when a tall blond *wearh* strode into the room. The creature was a bewildering mix of female and male, allure and aggression, sweetness and swagger. The long flaxen curls and frothy skirts indicated it was female. The crisply tailored army coat with brass buttons and braid, the triangular cocked hat embellished with a red, white, and blue rosette, the gun strapped to the hips, the culottes that peeked out from lace petticoats, and sturdy shoes suggested the opposite.

"*Bon sang*, what is that smell? Is Matthew home from the war, his tail between his legs?"

The warm contralto voice settled it. This was a woman.

Remembering his manners, but not that he was now a *wearh*, Marcus shot to his feet to make the necessary courtesies to a member of the fairer sex. His wine went flying, and one of the padded arms of the chair gave a sharp crack.

"It's a baby!" she cooed, blue eyes round in amazement.

Definitely female. Marcus bowed.

"Whyever are you doing that?" she asked in strangely accented English. "You must stop it, at once. Charles, why is he bowing?"

"*Le bébé est américain*," Charles said, his mouth pursed as though he'd bitten into something sour.

"How useful," she declared. "The family doesn't have one of them."

"I'm Mar—Gale—Chaun—" Marcus trailed into confused silence and then regrouped. "I'm Matthew's."

"Yes, I know. You still reek of him." She extended her arm, bent at the elbow, palm open. "I'm Freyja de Clermont. Your aunt. You may call me Fanny."

Marcus took Fanny's elbow, and she took his. Her grip was firm and steely. It was going to take Marcus some time to absorb the concept—never mind the reality—of female *wearhs*. Women were meant to be soft and sweet, in need of nurture and protection. Neither Fanny—Freyja suited her far better, Marcus thought—nor Françoise fit this description. Gallowglass's strict instructions that Marcus never play cards with his aunt made abundant sense now that he'd met her.

"Is Matthew with you?" Fanny asked.

"No. The chevalier is at Yorktown, ending the war," Marcus replied. He still couldn't call de Clermont by his Christian name.

"Oh, the war is over. At least that's what all the papers say." Fanny deposited her hat, crown down, upon a mountain of flour.

Marcus expected this to draw a sharp rebuke from Charles, but the chef was gazing at Fanny with adoration.

"Have you supped, Mademoiselle Fanny?" Charles asked. "You must be famished, working all morning with Monsieur Franklin. Antoine is in the stables. I could send him to your room? Or Guy, if you prefer?"

"I'll have my breakfast in bed." Freyja paused, considering her options. "I believe I would like Josette."

Charles bustled off to make arrangements. Marcus tried desperately to unpick the meaning of Fanny's words. Surely, she didn't plan on—

"I often crave something sweet at this hour," Fanny explained.

Fanny was going to feed off Josette. In bed. What else might happen there stirred Marcus's imagination. Fanny sniffed the air and smiled.

"You can have her when I'm done and she's had a chance to recover. Josette is very generous, dear girl." Fanny sat in the wing chair Marcus had vacated, resting her booted feet on the fireplace's stone surround. This sent her skirts sliding toward her hips, revealing a long, shapely pair of legs. "You're terribly young to be so far from your sire."

"I am just over sixty, mademoiselle." Marcus was trying to think of his age in terms of days rather than years, but it still sounded strange. He sat gingerly on the edge of the bin that held wood for the fire.

"No wonder you are having licentious thoughts. You must explore them," Fanny commented, "if you expect to achieve self-mastery. Thank God you are no longer with Matthew. He would raise you as a monk, and forbid you all congress with women."

That was precisely what had happened in Pittsfield, where Marcus had been slavering for a taste of a young woman but had had to make do with a rum-soaked male instead.

"Matthew says I mustn't feed off women. He says it's too easy to con-
fuse desire with hunger. He says—"

Fanny hushed him with a gesture common to the soldiers of the Philadelphia Associators.

"It is terribly fortunate for you, then, that Matthew is not here. We are
living in a different time, a different world. We must embrace carnality,
not flee from it."

Marcus was now so hard it was painful, his desire fueled by Fanny's
libertine ideas. These days, his lust was as bottomless as his other appetites. On the *Aréthuse*, even the snap of the canvas had prompted lewd
thoughts.

Charles delivered an aromatic cup of black coffee to Fanny. "Josette is
drawing your bath, mademoiselle."

"Have her take a long soak and wait for me." Fanny sipped her coffee
and let out a sultry sigh. "The hot water will bring all the blood rushing
to the surface of her skin, and put her in a more relaxed state."

Marcus filed Fanny's wisdom away for future use, shifting on the edge
of the bin to give himself more room.

"So. Tell me your news. How did it go with *Far*?" Fanny fixed her
frosty blue eyes on Marcus.

Marcus had no idea who *Far* was. He shrugged. Fanny's expression
turned sympathetic.

"Give Philippe time." Fanny reached over and patted him on the knee.
"Once Father has figured out what use you are to him, and given you
names, he will thaw. Until then, you will stay with me. I will teach you
how to be a *wearh*—and do a far better job than Matthew would have
done. Even *Far* will be astonished at what I have achieved."

Marcus bit back a sigh of relief. He wasn't sure Fanny would make a
better parent, but he was confident she would make his education a more
interesting—not to mention pleasurable—experience.

FANNY EMBRACED THE CHALLENGE of Marcus's education with enthusiasm, supplying him with dancing and fencing masters, French and
Latin tutors, a tailor, and a wigmaker. Marcus's days were filled with ap-
pointments, his nights with reading and writing.

Still, Fanny fretted about how Marcus might develop, and aspired to do everything she could to see him become a credit to the family.

"We must occupy your mind with new experiences, Marcus," Fanny declared one night. "Otherwise you might slip into ennui and come out jaded like my sister Stasia. Do not worry. I have sent a message to a friend. She will have marvelous ideas about how to perfect you."

Stéphanie Félicité du Crest de Saint-Aubin, Comtesse de Genlis, received Fanny's cry for help and left the opera at once to lend assistance. She arrived like a spring sunset, swathed in lavender and blue silk, sparkling with tinsel braid, and topped with a powdered, puffed wig that resembled clouds. The comtesse peered at Marcus through a pair of spectacles worn around her neck on a sky-blue ribbon.

"A remarkable creature," she pronounced in perfect English, once her examination was complete.

"Yes, but he is still an infant," Freyja said sadly. "We must spare no effort in preparing Monsieur Marcus to meet his grandfather, Stéphanie. You will move in—straightaway."

Together, Fanny and Madame de Genlis poked and prodded him, firing off questions and comments so rapidly in English (the questions) and French (the comments) that Marcus couldn't keep up. Marcus stopped trying to anticipate whether the next topic would be his experience with women (tragically limited, they agreed), his education (shockingly poor), or his manners (quaintly old-fashioned, but really he *must* stop bowing to servants).

"It is a very good thing Le Bébé doesn't require sleep," Madame de Genlis commented to Fanny. "If we work night and day, he might be ready to meet your father *le comte* at midsummer."

"We do not have six months, Stéphanie," Fanny said.

"You will be lucky to have six days" was Françoise's dour prediction.

"*Six jours!*" Madame de Genlis was appalled. "Françoise, you must do something! Talk to Madame Marthe. She will get Philippe and Ysabeau out of Paris. Perhaps they could go to court?"

"Ysabeau hates Versailles. Besides, news travels between Paris and the palace too quickly," Fanny fretted.

"Surely they would enjoy spending the winter months in Blois, or even at Sept-Tours? You could suggest it, Fanny," Madame de Genlis insisted.

"Father would know I was up to no good," Fanny said. "No, Stéphanie, we must be brave and ruthless, and teach Le Bébé all we can as quickly as we can. The fear of discovery will sharpen our focus and enliven us to new possibilities. Energy and persistence will conquer all obstacles, as Dr. Franklin says!"

Marcus's days and nights passed in a dizzying whirl of activity. He didn't much care for the Latin, the French, or the dancing lessons. The fencing lessons were better. But his favorite moments were discussing politics and philosophy in Fanny's opulent library. Marcus had never seen so many books in one place. Madame de Genlis was quick-witted and well-read, which meant that Marcus had to work hard to keep up with her, even when the subject of their conversation was Thomas Paine. But it was their outings into the city streets that Marcus loved above all else.

"Paris is the best teacher," Madame de Genlis proclaimed as they crossed over the Seine and into the narrow, twisting thoroughfares of the Île de la Cité.

Together, they watched cows being butchered and the prostitutes in Madame Gourdan's brothel taking their afternoon ablutions. Fueled by his unfulfilled desire for Françoise, they spent a glorious morning amid the *bateaux-lavoirs* on the Seine, drinking in the heady scents of starch and soap and giving washerwomen a few sous in exchange for a cup of their blood. Gunpowder was next, after they stumbled across a tense duel while hunting at dawn in the Bois de Vincennes. Print shops followed, the damp pages and tang of the ink drawing Marcus like iron filings to a magnet.

Though Marcus had seen a few news sheets roll off the presses in Philadelphia, Paris's booksellers operated on an entirely different scale. Books in French, Latin, Greek, English, and languages Marcus couldn't recognize were typeset in wooden racks. Sometimes the metal letters were still glistening with ink from their previous jobs. Then it was off to the press to be aligned, inked, and imprinted. Reluctantly, Marcus handed over his copy of *Common Sense* to a bookbinder so that it could be kept from falling apart. He watched the man select the stiff backing for the new leather cover and paste fresh paper down to protect the worn contents. When the bookbinder returned it, now wrapped securely in brown leather stamped with gold, Marcus held in his hands a volume that would not be out of place in the finest of libraries.

Marcus was so entranced by the world of books that Fanny paid a beefy printer with a daughter in need of a dowry half a year's earnings so that he could drink his blood and imbibe a truer sense of what it was to be involved in the book trade.

"*Alors.* It was an experiment," Madame de Genlis said with a tinge of disappointment after Marcus confessed that most of what he'd seen in the man's blood concerned his wife—a real harridan, if he were to be brutally honest—and his futile efforts to get out of debt.

"We shall try again," Fanny said, unfazed by failure.

Nothing was off-limits to him so far as Fanny and Madame de Genlis were concerned—even though Marcus's keen sense of smell led him around by the nose, as Gallowglass had feared. He found the scent of young women irresistible.

"I know just the place to go," Fanny confided to Madame de Genlis. "A brothel where the women are young and enthusiastic."

Then Marcus smelled something even more enticing than a woman.

"Stop. What is that?" Marcus discovered he could slow Fanny's progress by planting his feet so firmly on the street that his shinbone cracked under the stress.

"The Hôtel-Dieu." Madame de Genlis pointed to a vast, fire-scarred building stretched along the banks of the Seine in the shadow of Notre-Dame cathedral. Parts of it had collapsed. The rest of it looked like it might tumble into the river at any moment.

"Hotel?" Marcus asked.

"The hospital," she replied.

"I want to go inside," Marcus said.

"Just like his father." Fanny looked disappointed at Marcus's decision to leave off his pursuit of women in favor of death and disease, but then her face brightened. "Perhaps there is something to be learned from the similarity? What do you think, Stéphanie?"

Aromas of camphor, lint, coffee, and spices assaulted Marcus's nose when he entered, followed by the sweet smell of decay and darker notes of opium and death. He drank it in, along with layers of copper and iron scent.

So much blood, he realized, each person's subtly different.

Marcus trailed through the wards, using his nose—that powerful part of the vampire body—rather than a manual examination to diagnose illnesses and patients' conditions.

The hospital was enormous—larger even than Philadelphia's Bettering House, or the hospital the army had occupied in Williamsburg—and night had fallen before he was through exploring. By then, Marcus's coat was stained with blood and vomit—he hadn't been able to ignore the patients' pleas for water and care. He was also ravenous, and wanted to go to a tavern and order a pint of beer and a piece of well-seasoned beef, even though he knew it would no longer satisfy his hunger.

He got Josette instead.

MARCUS WAS IN THE LIBRARY the next morning, conjugating Latin verbs, when there was a commotion in the front hall.

A petite woman burst into the room, followed by Fanny's footman, a strange-looking fellow named Ulf whose arms were too long for the rest of his body. Trailing behind was another small, elegant female.

A wearh.

"You see! There he is!" the woman cried, clasping a folded piece of paper to her breast. She was draped in yards of red-and-white-striped silk and wore a redingcote along with a ridiculously tiny cocked hat set on her powdered wig at a jaunty angle. The woman was childlike in her appearance, with small features. "He is just as my Gilbert described, is he not? I knew him the moment I spotted him from my carriage, entering the Hôtel-Dieu."

The female *wearh* inspected Marcus through a filmy veil that floated from the brim of her hat and covered her piercing green eyes.

"Madame de Clermont, Madame la Marquise, let me call—" Ulf said, flapping his large hands in consternation.

"Ysabeau!" Fanny arrived in a whirl of pale blue and green. She was followed at a more sedate pace by Madame de Genlis, who continued to sport the colors of the Revolution and was today dressed in naval blue with golden braid. A model of a ship in full sail was pinned to her wig in lieu of a hat.

"And the Marquise de Lafayette." Madame de Genlis swept her skirts into one hand and curtseyed. "What brings us this honor?"

Marcus stared at his former patient's wife. She did not look old enough to *have* a husband, but then again, Lafayette hadn't seemed mature enough to *be* a husband, either.

"I came to thank my husband's savior." Adrienne rushed at Marcus, her lips pursed to bestow kisses on him.

"Please, madame. There is no need—" Marcus's protests were cut off by an enthusiastic embrace.

"How will I ever repay your kindness?" Adrienne wept into his coat, clinging to him for dear life. "Your skill as a physician? Your—"

"I have come to see my grandson," the veiled woman interrupted, clearly out of patience with Adrienne's effusiveness. She lifted the scrap of fabric, revealing her face. It was perfectly formed and exquisitely beautiful, but there was a ferocity to her features that would warn any prudent warmblood to stay away.

"Grandmother?" Marcus whispered, taking a step in her direction.

"Marcus is not yet ready—" Fanny began.

A cold glance stopped her.

"If you insist," Fanny said smoothly, though Marcus could hear that her heart was beating more quickly than usual. "Marcus, this is Ysabeau de Clermont, Matthew's maker—and your grandmother."

His grandmother. Marcus's blood beat out a staccato tattoo of pride and respect. He took one step toward her, then another.

Marcus studied his grandmother as he did, intrigued by the affinity he felt for this stranger. He was struck by the beauty of her face and features, the sharp delicacy of her bones, and the blue-tinged porcelain quality of her skin. Her eyes were the color of jade, and so penetrating that they seemed to flay Marcus to the bone. Her dress was a froth of creamy silk, but the layers of fabric wrapped and puffed around her slender frame did nothing to diminish the woman's presence. Ysabeau de Clermont was powerful—and powerfully intelligent.

Marcus couldn't stop himself. He bowed. His grandmother was the finest lady he had ever encountered. Adrienne cooed and clapped in approval, wiping a tear from her eye at the touching domestic scene unfolding in Fanny's front hall.

Cold, delicate hands touched him on the shoulders, a quiet command to rise.

"Yes. You are Matthew's son," Ysabeau said, her eyes holding his. "I hear his bloodsong in your veins. This will fade in time, as you become your own creature. But you are still too young for such independence. It is important that vampires understand who you are until you can protect yourself."

"Vampire?" Marcus looked to Fanny in confusion.

"We do not use that old-fashioned word '*wearh*' anymore," Fanny explained. "Vampire is fresh—modern."

"It matters little what you are called," Ysabeau said, her voice dismissive. "All that is important is who you are: Matthew's son—and a de Clermont."

Thirty

12 JUNE

"Do you have your phone?"

"Yes, Miriam." Phoebe waited by the window, impatient for her first glimpse of their visitor.

"And some money?"

"In my pocket." Phoebe patted the hip of her jeans, where a mixture of small bills (for taxis) and large bills (for bribes) was neatly folded.

"And no ID?" Miriam said.

The need to go out hunting without any identification, in case the unimaginable happened and someone was killed, had been drummed into Phoebe.

"Nothing." Phoebe had even taken off the diamond key her parents had given her on her twenty-first birthday in case the stones were registered and could somehow be traced back to her. The emerald ring that Marcus had slipped on her finger when they were engaged remained where he had put it, however.

"Stop gawping at the window," Miriam said, sounding peevish.

Phoebe tore herself away from the view of the street. She would be out there soon enough.

She was going for a walk.

In Paris.

At night.

With Jason.

He was a member of Miriam's family—now Phoebe's family—a male, and the son of Miriam's former mate.

Tonight marked Phoebe's next step in becoming an independent vampire. The significance of this rite of passage had been impressed upon her by every member of the household, including Freyja's driver, who had taken Phoebe for a ride along the same streets she would be traveling tonight on foot. Miriam told her that if all went as planned, Phoebe might be allowed to hunt with Jason, though not to feed. She was not yet mature enough for that.

Given that incentive, Phoebe was determined to succeed. She'd pored over the arrangements, rehearsed every moment of going out into the city in the privacy of her room, and felt ready for any eventuality.

A knock sounded at the door.

Phoebe practically leaped into the air with excitement. She was about to meet a member of her new family. Françoise gave her a stern look when it seemed as though Phoebe herself might rush to the door and fling it open. Phoebe stilled her feet, folded her hands before her, and waited in Freyja's salon.

This act of self-control earned her a slightly approving glance from Miriam, and a small smile from Françoise as she left to see to their visitor.

"Milord Jason," Françoise said. A wave of unfamiliar scent washed over Phoebe: fir and the dark scent of mulberries. "*Serena* Miriam is in the salon."

"Thank you, Françoise." Jason's voice was low and pleasing, accented in a way that Phoebe—traveled as she was—had not heard before.

When he entered the room, Jason pinned his hazel eyes on Miriam. He ignored Phoebe completely, walking past her without a second glance. Jason was about Marcus's height—perhaps an inch shorter—and of a similarly compact, muscular build.

"Miriam." Jason kissed Phoebe's maker on both cheeks. The greeting was respectful and affectionate, but by no means warm.

"Jason." Miriam studied her mate's son. "You look well."

"As do you. Motherhood suits you," Jason replied drily.

"I'd forgotten how hard it is to raise a vampire," Miriam said with a sigh. "Phoebe, this is Bertrand's son Jason."

Jason turned toward Phoebe as if noticing her presence for the first time. Phoebe stared at him with open curiosity even though she knew this was the height of rudeness. She took in his open, honest expression, the slight bump on the bridge of his nose, the streaks of gold in his brown hair.

"Forgive her. She's still a child," Miriam said disapprovingly.

Phoebe remembered that she was supposed to be good and bit back a defensive retort. Instead, she extended her hand. Phoebe had been imagining this moment for days. She knew it would not be possible to walk toward him—she might run him over in her excitement. Even so, could she behave like a human, and simply shake hands without crushing Jason's fingers?

Jason stood before her, eyes slightly narrowed in appraisal. Then he whistled.

"For once in his life, Marcus didn't exaggerate," he said softly. "You are as beautiful as he promised."

Phoebe smiled. Her hand was still extended. She lifted it slightly. "Pleased to meet you."

Jason took her hand, raised it to his lips, and pressed a kiss upon her fingers.

Phoebe withdrew her hand as if she'd been slapped.

"You're supposed to shake it, not kiss it." Phoebe's voice trembled with fury, though she didn't know why the innocent gesture angered her so.

Jason stepped back, a grin on his face and both hands raised in a gesture of surrender.

Once the tension in the hall subsided, Jason spoke.

"Well, Miriam, she didn't accept my overture, nor did she strike me, bite me, or run out the open door." Jason nodded with approval. "You've done well."

"*Phoebe* has done well," Miriam said, her voice tinged with something Phoebe had not heard in it before. *Pride.*

"I just provided the blood," Miriam continued. "Freyja and Françoise have done the rest. And Phoebe herself, of course."

"That's not true." Phoebe was startled to hear herself contradicting Miriam. "Not just blood but history. Lineage. An understanding of my duty as a vampire."

"Very well done indeed, Miriam," Jason said softly. "Are you sure she's only thirty-one days old?"

"Maybe Freyja's modern parenting ideas aren't as ridiculous as they seem," Miriam mused. She shooed Phoebe and Jason in the direction of the front door. "Go. Get out of my sight. Come back in an hour. Maybe two."

"Thank you, Miriam," Phoebe said, already headed out of the room.

"And for God's sake, stay out of trouble," Miriam called after them.

THE STREETS OF THE 8TH arrondissement were by no means empty at this late hour. Couples were returning from their suppers at favorite restaurants. Pairs of lovers strolled arm in arm along the wide boulevards. Through illuminated windows, Phoebe could see night owls watching television, the canned laughter and gloomy newscasters forming a strange chorus. Snatches of conversation traveled through open bedroom windows as warmbloods took advantage of the June air.

And everywhere there was a low, constant drumming.

Heartbeats.

The sound was so mesmerizing that Phoebe barely registered when Jason stopped, hands tucked into his pockets. He had been speaking to her.

"Sorry?" Phoebe said, focusing her attention back on her stepbrother.

"Are you okay?" Jason's eyes were more green than brown, Phoebe noticed on closer inspection. There were faint creases at the corners of his eyes, too, even though he looked no older than she did. Phoebe had seen lines like these before, on friends who sailed and spent lots of time on the water.

"Where are you from?" Phoebe asked.

"You shouldn't ask," Jason said, his feet moving forward. "Never ask a vampire their birthplace, age, or real name."

"But you're not any vampire. You're family." Phoebe caught up with him easily.

"So I am." Jason laughed. "Still, you need to be careful. The last creature who asked Miriam her age is buried on the bottom of the Bosporus. Your maker's fierce. Don't cross her."

Phoebe had crossed her. In Freyja's dining room.

"Uh-oh. Your heart rate just spiked," Jason observed. "What did you do?"

"Challenged her."

"Did you end up wishing you'd never been born?" Jason's expression was sympathetic.

"Miriam hasn't mentioned it since." Phoebe bit her lip. "Do you think she's forgiven me?"

"No chance." Jason smiled cheerfully. "Miriam has the memory of an elephant. Don't worry. She'll make you atone. One day."

"That's what I'm afraid of," Phoebe said.

"Miriam will wait until your guard is down. It won't be pleasant. But at least then it will be over." Jason turned to face her. "If there's one thing everybody knows about Miriam, it's that she doesn't hold grudges. Not like Marcus's father."

"I still don't feel I understand Matthew," Phoebe confessed. "Ysabeau, Baldwin, Freyja—even Verin—I feel somehow connected to all of them, but not to Matthew."

"I doubt Matthew understands himself," Jason said quietly.

Phoebe was chewing on that tidbit of information when they turned off the Avenue George V and onto the banks of the Seine. The Palais Bourbon across the river was brightly illuminated, as were the bridges that spanned the river. Beyond the Pont Alexandre III, the spokes of the Roue de Paris glowed blue and white.

Phoebe moved toward the bright colors, mesmerized.

"Hang on, Phoebe." Jason's hand was on her elbow, his weight an anchor holding her back.

Phoebe tried to shake him off, dazzled by the prospect of all that light. Jason's hand tightened, his fingers exerting a painful pressure.

"Too fast, Phoebe. People are watching."

That stopped her in her tracks. Phoebe's breath was ragged.

"My mother used to say that." Phoebe's past and present collided. "When we were out at the ballet. Or the theater. Or playing in the park. *'People are watching.'*"

Jason said something, his voice sounding far away and muffled by the loud drumming of hearts and made inconsequential by the brilliant hues that surrounded them. He spun Phoebe around. She snarled as the lights and color fused into a dizzying whorl.

"You're lightstruck." Jason's eyes were pinwheels of green and gold. He swore.

Phoebe's knees crumpled and she sagged toward the pavement.

"Too much champagne, darling?" A woman laughed. White. Middle-aged. American, based on the accent. A tourist.

Phoebe lunged.

The tourist's eyes widened in sudden terror. She screamed.

Passersby—those strolling lovers, seemingly lost in their mutual adoration—stopped and turned.

"*Qu'est-ce que c'est?*" A National Police officer, fully kitted out in navy and white, was on patrol alone. She planted her feet wide and put her hands to the belt that held her communications device and weapons.

But the question came too late. Phoebe was already at the tourist's throat, her hands grabbing at her thin sweater.

A flashlight shone directly into Phoebe's eyes. She winced and let the struggling woman go.

"Are you all right, madame?" the officer asked the tourist.

"Yes. I think so," the American said, her voice shaking.

"This is outrageous. We were walking back to our hotel when that woman attacked us," the tourist's companion said. Now that the danger had passed, he was full of bluff and swagger.

A wave of contempt flooded Phoebe. *Pathetic warmbloods.*

"She's high on something," the woman said. "Or drunk."

"Probably both," her friend said, a nasty edge to his voice.

"You wish to file a report?" the police officer asked.

There was a long pause while the tourists weighed their umbrage against the inconvenience of spending the rest of their night and most of tomorrow filling out paperwork and answering routine questions.

"Or, you could leave this with me." The officer's voice dropped. "I'll make sure she doesn't trouble anyone else. Give her time to sober up."

The flashlight was no longer moving across Phoebe's eyes. Instead, it was a steady beacon. Phoebe's attention remained fixed on it, unwavering.

"Lock her up," the man recommended. "A night in a cell will sort her out."

"Leave it to me, monsieur," the police officer replied with a chuckle. "Enjoy the rest of your evening."

"I'm sorry," Jason said to the couple. He pressed something into the man's hand. "For the sweater."

"Keep your girlfriend on a tighter leash." The man pocketed the money. "I find it does wonders for their disposition."

Phoebe snarled at the insult, the light keeping her where she was. Had the flashlight not been there, Phoebe would have ripped the man's tongue out so that he could never say something so demeaning again.

"I'm her brother," Jason explained. "She's visiting. From London."

"Come on, Bill," the woman said, her feet shuffling against the stones. "The police will take it from here."

The officer didn't switch off her flashlight until the couple's footsteps and conversation had faded into silence.

"That was close," Jason said.

"Too close. And too soon. Thirty is too young to be out at night," the officer said.

"Freyja?" Phoebe blinked, bringing her eyes into better focus. There, standing in front of her, was Freyja de Clermont in a navy all-weather jacket, her tactical trousers tucked into heavy black boots, and a cap set on her head at an angle. Her hair was scraped back into a tight ponytail.

"I promised Marcus I would take care of you." Freyja slid the flashlight into a loop on her belt, anchoring it near a formidable-looking gun.

"Where did you get the costume?" Phoebe was intrigued by the possibilities for freedom and adventure this implied.

"Oh, it's no costume," Freyja said. "I've been in uniform since they first let women serve on the National Police force as assistants in 1904."

"How do you explain why you never . . ." Phoebe was distracted by a passing ambulance's blaring siren and flashing red lights.

"I don't explain. I'm a de Clermont. Everybody in Paris who is in a position to question me knows exactly what that means," Freyja said.

"But we're supposed to be a secret. I don't understand." Phoebe was tired and hungry, and her eyes stung. If she weren't a vampire, she would swear she was getting a migraine.

"We are, Phoebe dear." Freyja put a hand on Phoebe's shoulder. "It just happens to be a secret that many people share. Come. Let's get you home. You've had enough excitement for one night."

Back at Freyja's house, Phoebe was given a pair of oversize Chanel sunglasses, a cup of warm blood, and a pair of slippers. Françoise steered her to a seat in front of the fire, unlit on this June evening.

Miriam was reading her e-mail. She looked up from her phone when Phoebe and her entourage entered the room.

"Well?" Miriam smiled like a cat. "How was your first taste of independence?"

⇥ 24 ⇤

The Hidden Hand

15 JUNE

"Remind me never to host another birthday party." It was late afternoon and I was in the kitchen, decanting a bottle of red wine. The family was in the garden, where the tables were set and the candles were waiting to be lit, sitting in deep wooden chairs or reclining on chaise longues under bright umbrellas. Matthew's brother-in-law, Fernando Gonçalves, had joined us. Even the head of the de Clermont family, Matthew's brother Baldwin, was in attendance.

Fernando was in the kitchen with me, helping Marthe to arrange trays of food. He was, as usual, barefoot. His jeans and open-necked shirt emphasized his casual approach to most things in life, one that was strikingly different from that of Baldwin, whose only concessions to a family celebration had been to take off his jacket and loosen his tie.

"His lordship is calling for more wine." Marcus strode into the kitchen carrying an empty carafe, his blue eyes sparking with dislike. Normally, he and Baldwin got along, but the news from Paris had soured things. Vampires might be immune to all sorts of human illnesses, but they seemed to be plagued by other conditions, including blood rage and ennui, and being lightstruck.

"I'm working on it," I said, wrestling with the corkscrew and the bottle.

"Here. Let me do it." Marcus held out his hand.

"How is Jack?" I asked, dumping a tub of yellow cherry tomatoes on the platter of crudités. Agatha had designed it, and the thing was worthy of a wedding reception at the Ritz, adorned with curls of cabbage, kale, and mulberry leaves, which provided a colorful backdrop for trimmed carrots, bright yellow tomatoes, strips of pepper, radish rosettes, and cucumber sticks. A celery root in the middle of the tray sent up leafy stalks that resembled a tree.

"He's sticking close to Matthew." With one deft twist, Marcus freed the cork from the bottle.

"And Rebecca?" Fernando said, his sharp eyes belying his casual tone.

"She's on Baldwin's lap, perfectly contented." Marcus shook his head in amazement. "He dotes on her."

"And Apollo is still in the potting shed?" I wanted to break the news of Philip's familiar to Baldwin in my own way and at a moment of my choosing.

"So far." Marcus decanted the wine into a pitcher. "I'd bring out some blood, Marthe. Deer or human if you have it—just in case."

On that cheerful note, Marcus returned to the garden. Marthe picked up the platter of vegetables and followed. I sighed.

"Maybe Matthew is right. Maybe these family birthdays aren't a good idea," I said.

"Vampires do not, as a rule, celebrate birthdays," Fernando said.

"Not everybody in this family is a vampire," I retorted, unable to keep the frustration from my tone. "Sorry, Fernando. Things have been unusually—"

"Challenging?" Fernando smiled. "When have they been anything else between de Clermonts?"

We got through the hors d'oeuvres and chitchat with flying colors. It was when we sat down for dinner that the seams of our togetherness began to fray. What started the unraveling was Phoebe.

"Thirty days is much too soon to be gadding about in Paris after dark," Baldwin said disapprovingly. "Of course Phoebe got into trouble. Miriam's laxity doesn't surprise me, but Freyja knows better."

"I wouldn't say *trouble*, exactly," Ysabeau said, her tone dagger-pointed.

"Miriam's children have endured some terrible situations in the past. Do you remember Layla's mating, Ysabeau? What a poor choice," Baldwin said. "And Miriam let her make it."

"Layla ignored her mother's warnings," Fernando said. "Not all children are as cowed by their makers as you were, Baldwin."

"And just because you're older than dirt doesn't mean you know everything." Jack was toying with the stem of his wineglass, which still contained the last of a strong mixture of blood and red wine.

"What was that, pup?" Baldwin's eyes narrowed.

"You heard me," Jack muttered. "Uncle." His final word came a bit late to qualify as a title of respect.

"I'm sure Miriam considered Phoebe's night out carefully and thought it was for the best," I said, hoping to pour oil on the water before we were engulfed in waves.

Sarah, who was sitting next to Jack, took his hand. The gesture was not lost on Baldwin. My brother-in-law had reservations about letting Matthew establish his own recognized branch of the family—a branch that had not only witches in it, but blood-rage vampires, too. He had made me promise that I would do anything in my power to keep other creatures from realizing that the de Clermonts were harboring family members with the illness. I had even promised to spellbind Jack, if need be.

Jack poured himself another hefty measure of blood from the pitcher in front of him. Like Matthew, Jack found that ingesting blood helped to stabilize his mood when he was struggling with the disease's symptoms.

"You're hitting the blood rather hard tonight, Jack." Baldwin's remark got a strong reaction from the younger members of the family.

Marcus sat back in his chair, eyes rolling heavenward. Jack went on to pour so much blood into his glass that the contents reached the brim and sloshed over the side. Philip scented the rich blood and reached both hands toward Jack.

"Juice," Philip said, tiny fingers flexing. "Pleeeease."

"Here. Have some of this instead." I quickly cut some nearly raw steak into small pieces and put them on the mat in front of my son, hoping to distract him.

"Want juice." Philip scowled and pushed the meat away.

"Juicy juice." Becca, who was sitting next to Baldwin, drummed her feet against her chair. As far as she knew, there were two marvelous elixirs in the world: juice (milk mixed with blood), and juicy juice (blood mixed with water). Becca preferred the latter.

"Aren't they feeding you enough, *cara*?" Baldwin asked Becca.

Becca scowled at him, as if the idea that there was enough food in the world to satisfy her appetite was completely preposterous.

Baldwin laughed. It was a rich, warm—and entirely unfamiliar—sound. In nearly three years of knowing him, I had never heard him so much as chuckle, never mind laugh out loud.

"I'll trap a pigeon for you tomorrow," Baldwin promised his niece. "We'll share it. I'll even let you play with it first. Would you like that?"

Matthew looked a bit faint at the prospect of Baldwin and Becca going hunting together.

"Here, *cara*. Drink this," Baldwin said, holding his blood and wine to her lips.

"There's too much wine in it," I protested. "It's not good—"

"Nonsense," Baldwin said with a snort. "I grew up drinking wine at breakfast, lunch, and dinner. And that was before Philippe sired me. It won't harm her."

"Baldwin." Matthew's voice sliced through the rising tension in the air. "Diana doesn't want Rebecca to drink it."

Baldwin shrugged and put his cup down.

"I'll mix her some blood and milk. She can have it before she goes to bed," I said.

"That sounds revolting." Baldwin shuddered.

"For God's sake, leave it alone." Marcus threw his hands in the air. "You're always meddling. Just like Philippe."

"Enough, both of you." Ysabeau was in the unenviable position of sitting between the two feuding vampires. I had warned her in advance that she had drawn the short straw and would be placed between Marcus and Baldwin, but neither protocol nor prudence would permit any other arrangement.

"Nunkle!" Philip cried out at the top of his lungs, feeling left out.

"You don't have to shout to get my attention, Philip," Baldwin said with a frown. He clearly held his nephew to a different standard than his niece, who had spent most of the afternoon making noise. "You shall have pigeon tomorrow, too. Or is hunting forbidden as well as wine, sister?"

The room held their breath at Baldwin's challenge to me. Jack shifted in his chair, unable to bear the weight of the tension in the room. His eyes were inky and huge.

"Agatha. Tell them about your plans in Provence," Sarah suggested, still holding Jack's hand. She shot me a look across the table as if to say, *I'm doing my best to save this party, but no guarantees.*

"Jack!" Philip now tried to get Jack's attention by blaring out his name like a klaxon.

"I'm okay, flittermouse," Jack said, trying to soothe Philip's agitation by using his pet name for him. "May I be excused, Mum?"

"Of course, Jack." I wanted him as far away from this brewing storm as possible.

"You need to keep him better regulated, Matthew." Baldwin cast a critical eye over at Jack as he stood to go.

"I will not have my grandson declawed," Ysabeau hissed. For a moment, I thought she might strangle Baldwin—which was not a bad idea.

"Thirsty." Philip's voice was high, piercing, and very, very loud. "Help!"

"For God's sake, can someone give him a drink!" Jack snarled. "I can't bear to hear him beg for food."

Marcus was not the only one struggling with his past. Jack was, too, his memories of starvation on the streets of London returning with Philip's cries.

"Calm down, Jack." Matthew had Jack by the collar in a blink.

But Jack was not the only creature to be distressed by Philip's call for help. A tawny animal bounded in our direction wearing the frame from the potting shed window around its throat like a necklace.

"Oh, no." Agatha tugged on Sarah's sleeve. "Look."

Apollo felt the tension that surrounded his small charge. He shrieked before launching himself at Philip so that he could protect him from harm.

Sarah flung a handful of seeds into the air, which rained down on the griffin, stopping him in his tracks. She then removed a long chain from around her neck. Hanging from it was a golden stone that nearly matched the color of Apollo's fur and feathers.

Apollo shook his head in confusion, scenting the air with caraway. Sarah slipped the chain around his neck. The stone rested on the griffin's breast. He quieted down straightaway.

"Amber," Sarah explained. "It's supposed to tame tigers. Caraway seeds keep my chickens from straying. I thought it was worth a try—and I thought Peace Water might leave spots on the table."

"Good thinking, Sarah." I was impressed by her creativity.

Baldwin, alas, was not.

"When did my nephew acquire a griffin?" Baldwin asked Matthew.

"Apollo came when *my son* uttered his first spell," Matthew said, emphasizing his greater claim to Philip.

"So he takes after his mother." Baldwin sighed. "I had hoped he would be more vampire than witch, like Rebecca. We can still hope, I suppose, that time will change him."

Becca, who knew a good opportunity to make mischief when she saw it, took advantage of the distracted adults by reaching for Baldwin's cup of blood.

"No," Baldwin said, moving it out of her reach.

Becca pouted, her lower lip quivering. But tears would not dissuade her uncle.

"I said no, and I meant no," Baldwin said, shaking his finger. "And you can blame your mother if you're still hungry."

Even at the best of times—which this was decidedly not—Becca was not interested in complicated assignments of responsibility and blame. As far as she was concerned, Baldwin had betrayed her trust and he deserved to be punished for it.

Becca's eyes narrowed.

"Rebecca," I warned, expecting a tantrum.

Instead, Becca lunged, embedding her sharp teeth in Baldwin's finger.

The finger of her uncle. The man who was the head of her vampire clan. The creature who expected her complete obedience and respect.

Baldwin looked down at his niece, astonished. She responded with a growl.

"Still sorry Philip takes after his mother's side of the family?" Sarah asked Baldwin sweetly.

"BECCA DIDN'T MEAN to do it," I assured Baldwin.

"Oh, she most certainly did," Ysabeau murmured, sounding impressed and a trifle envious.

We had withdrawn to the parlor. The children were asleep, both of them exhausted from the day's excitement and the copious tears that had been shed in the wake of Rebecca's behavior. The adults were drinking whatever they required in order to stabilize their nerves, be it blood, wine, bourbon, or coffee.

"There." Sarah finished placing a superhero bandage over Baldwin's already-healed wound. "I know you don't need it, but it will help Becca connect actions with consequences when she sees it on you."

"This is what I feared might happen when the two of you announced your wish to strike out on your own, Matthew," Baldwin said. "Thank God I'm the first creature Rebecca bit."

I looked away. And, just like that, Baldwin knew.

"I'm not the first." Baldwin looked at Matthew. "Did the tests I ordered show blood rage?"

"Tests?" I stared at my husband. Surely he wouldn't have tested the children's blood for genetic anomalies—not without telling me.

"I don't take orders from anyone when it comes to my children." Matthew's voice was cold, his face impassive. "They're too young to be poked and prodded and labeled."

"We need to know if she inherited your mother's disease, Matthew, as you did," Baldwin replied. "If she has, the consequences could be deadly. In the meantime, I want her kept away from Jack in case his symptoms make hers worse."

I glanced at Ysabeau, who looked dangerously calm, and at Jack, who looked devastated.

"Is it my fault she's behaving badly?" Jack asked.

"I'm not talking to you, Jack." Baldwin turned to me. "Need I remind you of your promise, sister?"

"No. *Brother*." I was trapped in a web of my own weaving. I had promised him that I would spellbind any member of our family whose blood rage threatened the well-being and reputation of the de Clermont clan. It had never occurred to me that I might be forced to do so to my own daughter.

"I want both Jack and Rebecca spellbound," Baldwin announced, "until their behavior stabilizes."

"She's only a baby," I said, numb with the implications this might have for her. "And Jack—"

"I forbid it." Matthew's voice was low, but there was no mistaking the warning in it.

"Not on my watch, Baldwin." Marcus crossed his arms. "The Knights of Lazarus won't allow it."

"Here we go again." Baldwin jumped to his feet. "The Knights of Lazarus are nothing—*nothing*—without the support of the de Clermont family."

"Do you want to test that theory?" Marcus's question was quietly challenging.

Doubt flickered in Baldwin's eyes.

"You could, of course, say the same about the de Clermonts: They would be nothing without the brotherhood," Marcus continued.

"You cannot raise a vampire without discipline and structure," Baldwin said.

"The way we were raised won't work for Rebecca or Philip." Matthew, in the unlikely role of peacemaker, stood between his son and his brother. "It's a different world now, Baldwin."

"Have you forgotten how modern methods of child rearing failed Marcus?" Baldwin said, striking back. "I cannot believe you would want them to suffer as Marcus did in New Orleans. When young vampires determine the course of their own lives, they leave death and chaos in their wake."

"I was wondering when you'd bring up New Orleans," Marcus said.

"Philippe would not have allowed you to compromise Rebecca's future—nor will I," Baldwin continued, his attention focused on Matthew.

"You're no Philippe, Baldwin," Marcus said softly. "Not by a long shot."

Every creature in the room held their breath. Baldwin's only reaction was to twist his lips into a smile that promised retribution. Philippe's son had not survived the Roman army, the Crusades, two world wars, and the ups and downs on Wall Street by being hasty when it came to revenge.

"I'm going back to Berlin. You have two weeks to run the tests, Matthew. If you don't, I'm going to hold Diana to her promise," Baldwin said. "Sort your family out—or I will."

"WHY ON EARTH DID PHILIPPE choose him for a son?" Sarah asked when Baldwin was gone.

"I've never understood the attraction," Ysabeau admitted. Marthe gave her a sympathetic smile.

"What will you do, Matthew?" Fernando asked quietly. Tabitha sat in his lap, purring like a motorboat while he scratched her ears.

"I'm not sure," Matthew said. "I wish Philippe were here. He would know how to manage Baldwin—and Rebecca."

"Oh, for fuck's sake!" Marcus exclaimed. "When is this family going to stop holding Philippe up as the perfect father?"

Sarah gasped. I, too, was surprised by the outburst. It was difficult to think of Philippe as anything but a hero.

"Marcus." Matthew looked at his son in warning, then slid his eyes in Ysabeau's direction. But Marcus would not be silenced.

"If Philippe were here, he would have determined the course of Becca's entire future by now, and to hell with what you, or Diana, or even his own granddaughter might have wanted," Marcus said. "And he would be doing the same with Phoebe, interfering in every decision we made and managing every aspect of her life."

Philippe materialized in the corner, his outlines hazy. He was substantive enough, however, that I could see the proud expression on his face, and the respect with which he regarded his grandson.

He always was unfailingly honest, Philippe said, giving Marcus an approving nod.

"Philippe was a meddling old busybody who tried to control everything and everyone," Marcus continued, his voice rising along with his anger. "The hidden hand. Isn't that what Rousseau called it? Lord, Grandfather loved *Emile*. He would quote passages from it all day if you let him."

"Your grandfather was the same way when it came to Musonius Rufus's notions of how to raise virtuous children," Fernando said, taking a sip of his wine. "All you had to do was mention the fellow's name, and Hugh would groan and leave the room."

"I thought I was trading a life of powerlessness for one of freedom when I became a vampire," Marcus continued. "But I was wrong. I simply exchanged one patriarch for another."

⇥ 25 ⇤

Depend

JANUARY 1782

"Swords at the ready!" Master Arrigo stepped away from Marcus and Fanny. "*En garde!*"

Fanny flourished her rapier, cutting the air so cleanly that the blade sang. Marcus tried to imitate her but only succeeded in nearly impaling the Italian swordsman and slashing his own sleeve from elbow to wrist.

It was an unseasonably warm January afternoon on the rue de Saint-Antoine, and Fanny had relocated Marcus's fencing lesson from the house's grand ballroom, with its slippery parquet floor, to the wobbly-cobbled courtyard. Madame de Genlis was seated out of harm's way in an upholstered chair carried down from the dining room, basking in the watery winter sunshine.

"*Pret!*" Master Arrigo said.

Marcus tightened his hold on his rapier and held it at the ready.

"No, no, no," Master Arrigo said, stopping the proceedings with a frantic wave. "Remember, Monsieur Marcus. Do not grip the hilt like a club. You must hold it lightly but firmly—like your cock. Show it who is master, but do not squeeze the life out of it."

Marcus shot a horrified look at Madame de Genlis. She was nodding enthusiastically at the vivid analogy.

"*Exactement.*" Madame de Genlis rose from her chair. "Shall I demonstrate, *Maître?*"

"Good Lord, madame," Marcus protested, waving his rapier in hopes of persuading her to come no closer. The tip wiggled and quivered. "Stay where you are, I beg you."

"Stéphanie is not troubled by your puritan morals, Marcus," Fanny said. "Unlike you and Matthew, she has no fear of flesh."

Marcus took a deep breath and readied himself once again to attack his aunt with a lethal blade.

"*Pret!*" Master Arrigo barked, adding, "With care, monsieur, with care."

Marcus tried with all his might to imagine his sword into a cock, and to handle it with just the right blend of discipline and gentleness.

A niggle of awareness ran along his spine, distracting Marcus from his fencing lesson. Someone was watching him. His eyes swept the windows that overlooked the courtyard. A shadow moved past the glass in an upstairs room.

"*Allez!*" Master Arrigo said.

Someone twitched at the drapes. Marcus strained to see who was there. He felt a small prick on his shoulder, no more annoying than a bee's sting. Marcus waved it away.

"Touché, Mademoiselle Fanny!" Arrigo St. Angelo clapped his hands.

"*Zut.* He barely noticed." Fanny pulled the rapier's point free from Marcus's shoulder, disgusted. "What's the point of fighting blade to blade if you don't even wince when I pierce your flesh, Marcus? You're taking all the joy out of combat."

"Let us try again," Master Arrigo said, gathering his patience once more. "*En garde!*"

But Marcus was across the courtyard and up the stairs, already in search of his quarry. When he reached the upper stories of the house, there was a faint scent of pepper and wax, but nothing else to indicate anyone had been there at all. Could he be seeing things?

But the uncanny feeling Marcus experienced in the courtyard didn't leave him over the next few days. It accompanied him to the opera when Marcus escorted Madame de Genlis to a performance of *Colinette à la cour*. He borrowed her opera glasses and peered through them at the members of the audience, all of whom were similarly more interested in the other attendees than they were in Monsieur Grétry's latest masterpiece.

"Of course you are being examined!" Madame de Genlis retorted when Marcus complained of feeling scrutinized during a burst of applause. "You are a de Clermont. Besides, why else does one go to the opera, except to see and be seen?"

Marcus's survival instinct, which had been honed to a fine edge during the years he'd lived under Obadiah's tyrannical rule, had grown even sharper since he'd become a vampire. He would have liked to ask his grandmother about the prickling sensation that washed over him in the market when he was studying the types of waterfowl that might tempt his appetite with Charles, or outside the Hôtel-Dieu, which he didn't dare enter again in case the scent of blood drove him insane, or in the bookstores where he read snatches from the newspapers while waiting for Fanny to make her purchases of the latest novel and imported copies of the Royal Society of London's *Transactions*.

"Perhaps music is too passionate for such a young vampire," Madame de Genlis mused the morning after their disastrous second trip to the opera, her feet crossed on a low, padded stool and a cup of chocolate in her hand. Marcus had been so uncomfortable, and so convinced someone was spying on them, that they left after the first act.

"Nonsense," Fanny protested. "I was on the battlefield, ax in hand, within seven hours of my transformation. It was a baptism by blood and fire, let me tell you."

Marcus leaned forward in his chair, more eager to hear Fanny's story than he was to retreat to the library and conjugate more Latin verbs, which was his assignment that day.

Before Fanny could begin her tale, however, Ulf arrived, ashen faced and bearing a silver salver. On it was a letter. Ulf had arranged it so that its wax seal was on top—a distinctive swirl of red and black. Nestled in the pool of color was a small, worn, silver coin.

"*Merde*." Fanny took the letter.

"It is not for you, Mademoiselle Fanny," Ulf said in a sepulchral whisper, his long face grim. "It is for Le Bébé."

"Ah." Fanny waved Ulf toward Marcus. "Put it in your pocket."

"But I don't know what it says." Marcus studied the address on the outside. It was penned in dark, distinctive strokes. "*To Monsieur Marcus L'Américain, of the Hôtel-Dieu and Monsieur Neveu's shop, who now resides at Mademoiselle de Clermont's house, a reader of newspapers and a student of Signore Arrigo.*"

Whoever had written the letter seemed to know a great deal about Marcus's business, not to mention his daily routine.

"I do." Fanny sighed. "It says '*attend on me at once.*'"

"It was only a matter of time, *ma cherie*," Madame de Genlis said, trying to comfort her friend.

Marcus cracked the seal and freed the coin. It dropped toward the ground. Fanny caught it in midair and deposited it on the table next to him.

"Don't lose this. He'll want it back," she warned.

"Who will?" Marcus unfolded the paper. As Fanny had divined, the letter contained only a single line—brief, and exactly as she had predicted.

"My father." Fanny rose. "Come, Marcus. We are going to Auteuil. It's time to meet your *farfar.*"

FANNY AND MADAME DE GENLIS packed Marcus, protesting all the way, into a carriage. This one was equipped with better springs than the one that had brought him from Bordeaux to Paris, but the rough city streets were not conducive to a smooth ride. Then they reached the rutted dirt path that stretched out into the countryside to the west of Paris, and Marcus knew he was going to be violently ill if the bouncing and swaying didn't stop. He'd crossed the Atlantic with nothing more than a touch of seasickness, but carriages, it seemed, utterly defeated him.

"Please just let me walk," Marcus begged, feeling as green as the wool hunting jacket they'd found in an upstairs cupboard, discarded by one of Fanny's lovers after he discovered she was a vampire and fled the house in the middle of the night. The coat almost fit him, though it was too snug in the shoulders and too long in the arms, which made Marcus feel both pinched and drowning. Marcus had ruined the only coat that fit him properly at the hospital and was forced to make do with this secondhand garment.

"You are too young, and it is broad daylight," Fanny said briskly, the feathers in her hat swaying this way and that with the movement of the carriage. "It will take too long to walk there at human speed, and *Far* does not like to be kept waiting."

"Besides," Madame de Genlis added, "what if you meet with a maiden—or a cow—and are overtaken with a pang of hunger?"

Marcus's stomach flopped over like a fish.

"*Non*," Madame de Genlis said with a decided shake of her head. "You must direct your thoughts away from your discomfort and rise above them. Perhaps you could compose your remarks to Comte Philippe?"

"Oh, God." Marcus covered his mouth with his hand. He was expected to perform for his grandfather, like the trained monkey outside the Opéra who tumbled and danced for a fee. It reminded him of being dragged to Madam Porter's house when he was a child.

"You should begin, I think, with a few verses," Madame de Genlis advised. "Comte Philippe greatly admires poetry, and has such a memory for it!"

But Marcus, who had been raised in the fields and forests of western Massachusetts, where verses that were not found in the Bible were suspect, knew no poetry. Madame de Genlis did her best to teach him some lines from a poem called "*Le mondain*," but the French words refused to stick in Marcus's memory, and his constant retching kept interrupting the lesson.

"Say it after me," Madame de Genlis instructed. "'*Regrettera qui veut le bon vieux temps, / Et l'âge d'or, et le règne d'Astrée, / Et les beaux jours de Saturne et de Rhée, / Et le jardin de nos premiers parents.*'"

Marcus obediently did, over and over again, until Madame de Genlis was satisfied with his pronunciation.

"And what comes next?" his martinet of a schoolmistress demanded.

"'*Moi, je rends grâce à la nature sage,*'" Marcus managed to get out between belches. His sense of the poem's meaning was hazy at best, but Fanny assured him it was entirely appropriate to the occasion. Ulf, who was accompanying them to Auteuil, looked unconvinced. "'*Qui, pour mon bien, m'a fait naître en cet âge / Tant décrié par nos tristes frondeurs.*'"

"And do not forget the final line! You must say it as though you mean it, Marcus, with conviction," Fanny said. "'*Ce temps profane est tout fait pour mes moeurs.*' Ah, how I miss our dear Voltaire. Do you remember our last evening with him, Stéphanie?"

At last the carriage slowed to pass through the wide gates of a house that stretched along the hilltop. It was vast and made of pale stone, flanked by gardens that were more impressive than anything Marcus had ever seen. Though they were largely empty at this time of year, he could imagine what they would look like in summer. Marcus looked at Fanny in amazement.

"They belong to Marthe," Fanny said. "She is uncommonly fond of gardening. You will meet her, no doubt."

But it was not a woman who waited for them at the base of the wide staircase in the forecourt, but a dignified vampire with silver-flecked hair. Like the rest of the house, the forecourt was grand in scale and neat as a pin. There was a quiet hum of industry coming from the kitchens, as well as appetizing aromas. Grooms led fine horses out of their stalls. Servants and tradesmen shuffled in and out of a warren of offices and rooms in the service buildings that were tucked behind a stone wall.

"Milady Freyja." The man bowed. "Monsieur Marcus."

"Alain." It was the first time Marcus had seen Fanny looking anything less than confident.

"Pepper." Marcus recognized the vampire's scent. "You're the one who has been watching me."

"Welcome to the Hôtel de Clermont. *Sieur* Philippe is expecting you," Alain said, stepping aside so they could enter through the central, arched door and into the hall.

Marcus crossed the threshold and entered a house that was far grander than the one he had promised to own one day. The black-and-white marble floors of the hall were polished to a high sheen that reflected the light and made the entrance glimmer. A stone staircase curved up to a broad landing before spiraling up to another floor, and then another. A forest of white pillars added substance and style to the airy space, creating an arcade between the doors through which Marcus had entered and the doors opposite them, which led to an expansive terrace that provided a prospect over the river and beyond.

Marcus's sense that he was being watched returned, stronger than before. Bay leaves and sealing wax and a fruit Marcus had no name for tangled with the aroma of pepper from Alain, Madame de Genlis's musky scent, and the sweet hint of roses that always hung around Fanny. There were other, fainter notes as well. Wool. Fur. And something slightly yeasty that Marcus had detected in some of the older patients at the Hôtel-Dieu. It was the scent of aging flesh, he supposed.

Marcus took careful inventory of what his nose noticed, but he kept returning to the laurel and sealing wax. Whoever belonged to them was the center of gravity in this house. And he was behind him, where Marcus was most vulnerable.

His grandfather. The man called *Far* by Fanny, and *Comte Philippe* by Madame de Genlis, and *sieur* by Alain. Marcus wished that Gallowglass— or even the disapproving Hancock—were there to give him advice on what would be expected of him. He had learned much about how to wash clothes, make medicines, and handle horses since arriving in France, but Marcus had no idea how to properly greet a vampire except for the hand-to-elbow grip that Gallowglass and Fanny used.

And so Marcus fell back on his Massachusetts upbringing. First, he gave his most polished bow. Now that Marcus was a vampire, any ragged edges or infelicities of line had been smoothed into a perfect, graceful movement that would have made his mother proud. Then he plumbed the depths of his conscience and reached for the honesty that had been drilled into him from pulpit and primer.

"Grandfather. You must forgive me, but I do not know what I am supposed to do." Marcus straightened and waited for someone to rescue him.

"Already the son eclipses the father." The voice was velvet and stone, both controlled and clear. It belonged, Marcus surmised, to a man who had made music his whole life. His grandfather's command of English was perfect, but it was impossible to identify the accent that colored his words.

"You needn't worry. There isn't any aggression in him, *Far*." Fanny appeared from one of the many doors off the main hall, and Madame de Genlis with her. She was carrying two pistols, both of them cocked and ready to be fired at Marcus.

"He is nothing but curiosity, Comte Philippe," Madame de Genlis confirmed. She smiled at Marcus encouragingly. "He has prepared a poem for you."

Sadly, Marcus couldn't remember a single word of "*Le mondain.*" Once again he dipped into his memories of Hadley for reinforcements.

"'*Children's children are the crown of old men; and the glory of children are their fathers,*'" Marcus said, with all the conviction Madame de Genlis could have wanted.

"Oh, well done." The voice of praise was scratchy and nasal, with a bit of a wheeze at the end that might have been a chuckle. There was another man on the stairs. "Proverbs. Always suitable—especially when the sentiment is sincere. A very sensible choice."

The man descending the stairs had a balding head slightly too large for his body, and a waistline that rivaled Colonel Woodbridge's. The sweet scent intensified, and along with it came the iron-rich tang of black ink. He peered at Marcus over a set of spectacles. There was something familiar about him, though Marcus was sure they had never met.

"And what do you say to that, Marthe?" His grandfather was now close enough to see the trembling of his limbs as Marcus's nerves got the better of him. Marcus closed his hands into fists and took a deep breath.

A small, wizened old woman with glimmering eyes and a maternal air came from the shadows. Here was the woman Fanny had promised he would meet—Marthe.

"Madame." Marcus bowed. "My mother would have been envious of your gardens. Even in winter, they are impressive."

"A man of faith—and charm, too," said the man on the stairs with another wheezing chuckle. "And it would seem he knows something of *jardins* and *potagers*, and not just medicine."

"His heart is true, but there is a shadow in it," Marthe pronounced, scrutinizing Marcus closely.

"Matthew would not have been drawn to him otherwise." His grandfather's quiet sigh floated around Marcus.

"Put him out of his misery, my dear comte," the man on the stairs advised. "The poor boy reminds me of a fish caught between cats. He is certain of being eaten, but does not know which of us will have the honor of picking over the bones."

Heavy hands came to rest on Marcus's shoulders and swung him around. Philippe de Clermont was a giant of a man, as muscular as his elderly friend was soft and doughy. He had thick, burnished golden hair and tawny eyes that saw—everything. Or so Marcus suspected.

"I am Philippe, your grandmother's mate," his grandfather said, his voice soft. Philippe waited the space of a human heartbeat and then continued. "It is a sign of respect, among our people, to turn your eyes away from the head of the family."

"Respect is earned. Sir." Marcus kept his gaze on his grandfather. Staring into the eyes of a man so ancient and powerful was not an easy task, but Marcus forced himself to do it. Obadiah had taught him never to look away from anyone older and stronger than you were.

"So it is." The corners of Philippe's eyes creased with something that, in a lesser being, might have been amusement. "As for this darkness we all feel, you will tell me about it one day. I will not take the knowledge from you."

It had never occurred to Marcus that someone other than Matthew might learn of his past through bloodlore. Philippe's words, which appeared to be tender and paternal, sent a chill through Marcus's bones.

"You have done well with him, daughter. I am pleased," Philippe said, turning to Fanny. "What shall we call him?"

"He is called Marcus, though he tried to get me to call him Galen, and Gallowglass called him Doc," Fanny said. "He slept for a moment the other day, and cried out for news of Catherine Chauncey."

So Fanny was spying on him, too. Marcus's eyes narrowed at the betrayal.

"Marcus. Son of war. And Galen—a healer. I cannot fathom where the name Chauncey came from or what it might mean," Philippe said, "but it must be precious to him."

"Chauncey is a Boston name." The bespectacled man studied Marcus carefully. "I was right, Comte Philippe. The man is not from Philadelphia at all, but from New England."

The mention of Philadelphia brought the man's face into sharper focus, and Marcus realized who he was.

"You're Dr. Franklin." Marcus looked at the elderly gentleman with the stooped shoulders and ample belly with something akin to reverence.

"And you're a Yankee. I'm surprised the Associators took you in," Franklin said with a slow smile. "They're a clannish bunch, and don't usually accept anyone into their ranks who was born north of Market Street."

"What was your father's name, Marcus?" Philippe asked.

"Thomas," Marcus said, thinking of Tom Buckland.

"Don't ever lie to me," his grandfather said pleasantly, though the glint in his eye warned Marcus that this lapse into falsehood—like a challenging stare—was a serious matter.

"The man whose blood I once carried in my veins was called Obadiah—Obadiah MacNeil. But there is nothing left of him in me." Marcus's chin rose. "Thomas Buckland taught me how to be a surgeon. And a man. He is my true father."

"Someone has been reading Rousseau," Franklin murmured.

Philippe considered Marcus for a long moment. He nodded.

"Very well, Marcus Raphael Galen Thomas Chauncey de Clermont," his grandfather at last pronounced. "I accept you into the family. You will be known as Marcus de Clermont—for now."

Fanny looked relieved. "You won't be disappointed, *Far*, though Marcus still has much to learn. His Latin is abominable, his French deplorable, and he is clumsy with a sword."

"I can shoot a gun," Marcus said sharply. "What need do I have for swords?"

"A gentleman must *carry* a sword, at least," Madame de Genlis said.

"Give Stéphanie and me another month—perhaps two—and we will have him ready for Versailles," Fanny promised.

"That is perhaps a matter for Ysabeau to decide," Philippe said, casting a fond glance on his daughter.

"Ysabeau! But I—" Fanny was indignant. She turned her head away from her father. "Of course, *Far*."

"And what do I call you, sir?" Marcus didn't mean to sound insolent, though the horrified look on Fanny's face told him he might well have been.

Philippe merely smiled.

"You may call me Grandfather," he said. "Or Philippe. My other names would not suit your American tongue."

"Philippe." Marcus tried it out. It had been months, and he still couldn't think of the chevalier de Clermont as Matthew, never mind Father. It was definitely too soon to call this terrifying man Grandfather.

"Now that you are part of the family, there are a few rules you must obey," Philippe said.

"Rules?" Marcus's eyes narrowed.

"First, no siring children without my permission." Philippe raised a single, admonishing finger.

Having now met more members of the de Clermont family, Marcus had no desire to increase its size. He nodded.

"Second, if you receive a coin from me, like the one on the letter I sent to Fanny's house, you must return it to me. Personally. If you do not, I will come looking for you myself. Understood?"

Once again, Marcus nodded. Like adding to the de Clermont family, he had no wish for Philippe to show up at his door, unannounced.

"And one more thing: no more hospitals. Not until I think you're ready." Philippe's steady gaze traveled from Marcus to Fanny. "Am I clear?"

"Crystal clear, *Far*." Fanny flung her arms around Philippe's neck. She turned to Franklin. "Stéphanie and I discussed all the possible risks, Dr. Franklin, as well as the rewards. We didn't think anyone was in real danger. Certainly not Le Bébé."

"Tell me how you came up with the idea to let him ring the bells at Notre-Dame. What a coup—and something I have longed to do myself," Franklin said, steering Fanny through the doors and onto the terrace outside. Madame de Genlis went with them.

Marcus was left alone with Philippe.

"Your grandmother is waiting for you in the salon," Philippe said. "She is eager to see you again."

"You know about our meeting?" Marcus said, his throat dry.

Philippe smiled once more.

"I know most things," Philippe said.

"MARCUS!" HIS GRANDMOTHER OFFERED HIM her cheek for a kiss. "It is a delight to see you here."

Ysabeau was seated in a deep chair by the fire, which was lit in spite of the open windows.

"Grandmother," Marcus said, pressing his lips to her cool flesh.

Marcus sat quietly in Ysabeau's salon, listening to the banter taking place around him as Fanny, Madame de Genlis, and Franklin joined them. He understood about a quarter of what was said. Without Dr.

Franklin, who periodically translated in an effort to draw Marcus into the conversation, it would have been far less.

But Marcus was content to remain quiet. It allowed him to try to absorb his present situation, which was both dazzling and bewildering. He studied his surroundings, which were more lavish and elegant than anything he had seen through Philadelphia windows. Books lay on tables, thick carpets were underfoot, and the scent of coffee and tea hung in the air. The fire was a roaring blaze, and everywhere there were candles.

Philippe sat within arm's reach of Ysabeau in the only chair in the room that was not upholstered. It was wooden, painted blue, and had the curved, spindled back and saddle-shaped seat that were common to Philadelphia furniture. Marcus felt a pang of homesickness. The foreign speech, which had seemed pleasant and musical, became loud and dissonant. Marcus struggled to draw a breath.

"I see you have noticed my chair," Philippe said, claiming Marcus's attention.

Marcus felt his panic drop a notch. Then another. He felt able to breathe again.

"Dr. Franklin gave it to me," Philippe explained. "Does it remind you of all you left behind?"

Marcus nodded.

"With me it is scents," Philippe observed softly. "When the sun falls on pine boughs, warming up the resin, it takes me immediately back to my childhood. Moments of dislocation—of feeling out of place and time—happen to all of us who have been reborn."

Davy Hancock had nearly pummeled Marcus into the ground when he asked him about his youth and how long he had been a vampire. As a result, Marcus knew better than to ask any of the de Clermonts their age or their true name. Still, Marcus couldn't help but wonder just how ancient Philippe and Ysabeau were.

The air grew heavy around him, and Marcus found that Ysabeau was studying him. The expression on her face suggested she knew exactly what he was thinking. Her power was so different from that of her husband. Philippe was all civilization, a keen-edged sword in an elegant scabbard. Ysabeau, however, had a wild, untamed edge that could not be completely cloaked in satin or softened with lace. There was something feral and dangerous about his grandmother, something that caught at Marcus's throat and made his heart thud in warning.

"You are very quiet, Marcus," Ysabeau said. "Is there something wrong?"

"No, madame," Marcus replied.

"You will get used to us, I promise," Ysabeau assured him. "And we will, in turn, get used to you. It is too much, I think, to meet your new family all at once. You must come again—alone."

Philippe was watching his wife closely.

"You must do it soon," Ysabeau continued. "And when you return, you can share your news of Matthew. Philippe and I would like that. Very much."

"I would like that, too, madame." Perhaps he and Ysabeau could organize a trade—a piece of information about Matthew and what was happening in the colonies in exchange for some intelligence on vampire customs and de Clermont history.

A family tree would be useful, for a start.

⇥ 26 ⇤

Babel

OCTOBER 1789–JANUARY 1790

Veronique tossed her white cap, festooned with the red, white, and blue ribbons of revolution, onto the table next to the bed. She flung herself onto the rumpled sheets, nearly upsetting the pot of coffee that was perched on a stack of books. Flushed with victory and triumph, she shared her news.

"The march on Versailles was a success. Thousands of women were there. King Louis and his brood are all in Paris now," she said. "Marat is a genius."

Marcus looked over his copy of *L'ami du peuple*. "Marat is a daemon."

"That, too." Veronique trailed a finger along the outline of Marcus's leg. "It's only right that creatures should have a voice. Even your Lafayette believes that."

"You know that's against the covenant." Marcus put the newspaper aside. "My grandfather says—"

"I don't want to talk about your family." Veronique propped herself up on one shoulder. Her shift slid, exposing the soft curve of her breast.

Marcus moved the coffee and the books. His blood rallied at Veronique's scent, that heady mixture of wine and woman that he could not seem to get enough of.

Veronique rolled over onto the scattered pages of Marat's latest edition. Marcus lifted the hem of her shift, exposing shapely legs. Veronique sighed, her body opening to his touch.

"Lafayette brought the guards with him, though he waited long enough to do it," she said as Marcus teased her breast with his mouth.

Marcus's head lifted an inch. "I don't want to talk about the marquis."

"That will make a nice change," Veronique replied, arching her body toward him with a giggle.

"Vixen," Marcus said.

Veronique nipped him on the shoulder with sharp teeth, drawing beads of blood. Marcus pinned her to the bed with his body, entering her in a single thrust that brought a cry of pleasure. Marcus moved within her, slowly, deliberately, incrementally.

Veronique bared her teeth, ready to bite again. Marcus pressed soft lips to her throat.

"You're always telling me to be gentle," Marcus said, teasing her flesh with his teeth and tongue. Veronique was far more experienced than Marcus, and happy to guide him as he explored her body and discovered the best ways to please her.

"Not today," she said, pressing his mouth closer. "Today, I want to be overthrown. Like the Bastille. Like the king and his ministers. Like—"

Marcus stopped her from sharing any more revolutionary sentiments with a fierce kiss and applied himself to meeting her every desire.

IT WAS ALREADY DARK OUTSIDE when Marcus and Veronique emerged from their attic on the left bank of the Seine. Veronique's red, curling hair tumbled freely about her shoulders, the patriotic ribbons on her white cap fluttering in the breeze. Her striped skirts were hitched up at the side, showing plain petticoats and a hint of ankle along with sturdy clogs that protected her feet from both the hard cobblestones and the deep Parisian muck. She was buttoning her blue coat under her breasts, which accentuated her curves in ways that had Marcus longing to return to the bedroom.

Veronique, however, was intent on getting to work. She owned a tavern, one that Marcus still frequented along with his friend and fellow physician Jean-Paul Marat. There, Marcus and Marat talked about politics and philosophy while Veronique served up wine, beer, and ale to the students of the nearby university. She had been doing so for centuries.

Veronique was that rarest of all creatures: a family-less vampire. Her maker had been a formidable woman named Ombeline who had struck out on her own when the family she was serving didn't return from their crusade to the Holy Land. Ombeline made Veronique a vampire a century later during the chaos of the first plague epidemic in 1348, plucking her out of an infected hostelry near the Sacré Coeur. Paris's vampire clans had seen the opportunity the disease presented to dramatically increase their numbers; humans desperate to survive were quick to take any hope of survival that was offered.

Ombeline had met her end in August 1572 when she was killed by a rampaging Catholic mob who mistook her for a Protestant during the melee that erupted when Paris celebrated the marriage of Princess Margaret to Henry of Navarre. Veronique was not, as a result, a great believer in religion. It was something she and Marat had in common.

Though many of the city's vampire clans had attempted to fold Veronique into their ranks—first by persuasion, then by coercion—she had resisted all efforts at subjugation. Veronique was content with her tavern, her attic apartments high above the street, her loyal clientele, and her enjoyment of life itself, which, even after more than four centuries, still seemed precious and miraculous to her.

"Let's stay in tonight," Marcus said, catching her hand in his and pulling her back toward the door.

"Insatiable fledgling." Veronique kissed him deeply. "I must make sure that all is well at work. I am not a de Clermont, and cannot stay abed all day."

Marcus could not think of a single member of his family that did so, but had learned to steer conversation away from the sore subject of aristocratic privilege.

Sadly, it was the only topic of conversation in Paris, so it dogged them in overheard snatches all the way to the rue des Cordeliers, where the slump of Veronique's tavern awaited them, its roofline bent with age and the windows listing this way and that. Light streamed out onto the street in sharp angles, refracted by the panes of glass as though they were involved in one of Dr. Franklin's optical experiments. An ancient metal sign creaked on its pole overhead. The cutout shape of a beehive gave the place its name, La Ruche.

Inside, the conversation was deafening. Veronique's arrival was greeted with cheers. These turned into catcalls when Marcus appeared behind her.

"Late to work, citizen?" her patrons teased. "Up at the crowing of the cock, Veronique?"

"What's wrong with you, boy?" someone called out of the smoky gloom. "Why not keep her in bed, where she belongs?"

Veronique sailed through the room bestowing kisses on the cheeks of her favorites and accepting congratulations on the successful march on Versailles that she had helped to organize.

"Liberty!" a woman called from the counter where drinks were served.

"Fraternity!" the man next to her chimed in. This earned him a good-natured shove from his neighbor, which sent his coffee sloshing over the brim of the cup. Veronique served every kind of liquid refreshment a creature could desire—wine, coffee, tea, ale, chocolate, and even blood. The one thing she refused to serve was water.

Her customers began to bang their drinking vessels—dented tin and heavier pewter, fine glass and glowing copper, rough pottery and delicate porcelain—on tables, windowsills, the counter, walls, the backs of chairs, stools, and even on the skulls of nearby patrons.

Marcus grinned. He was not the only one drawn to Veronique's fire and passion.

"Equality!" Veronique cried, holding her fist in the air.

Marcus watched the crowd swallow her up, everyone eager to hear what she had seen at the palace, and how the royal family had responded, and whether it was true that Veronique spoke to the queen.

Marcus no longer panicked when his skin prickled and his hackles rose to alert him that that there was another predator nearby. He had been a vampire for eight years and was now a fledgling, capable of feeding himself and moving like a warmblood. The sleepless hours no longer weighed on him. He spoke French like a native, could converse with his grandfather and Ysabeau in Greek, and debated philosophy with his father in Latin.

"Hello, Matthew." Tonight, however, Marcus spoke in English, a language that he and his father shared but that was beyond the reach of the ordinary Parisians who filled La Ruche. He turned.

Matthew was sitting in a dark corner, as usual, sipping wine out of Veronique's finest glass. His waistcoat was the color of soot and embroidered with paler gray and silver thread. The plain white shirt he wore underneath was immaculate, as were the silk hose that extended from knee to polished shoes. Marcus wondered how much the ensemble had cost, and reckoned it would be enough to feed a family of eight for a year or more in this part of town.

"You're overdressed," Marcus said mildly, approaching his father's bench. "You should have donned your leather apron and brought a hammer and chisel if you wanted to blend in."

The man next to Matthew turned, revealing a face that was strangely twisted, the angles of cheek and mouth set in a fleshy imitation of the tavern's windows. Dark, deeply set eyes studied Marcus from under a thatch of black hair. Like Marcus, he wore no wig and his clothes were simple and made of thick, serviceable fabric.

"Jean-Paul!" Marcus was surprised to see Marat sharing a drink with his father. He wasn't aware they knew each other.

"Marcus." Marat moved along the bench, making room for him. "We are talking about death. Do you know Dr. Guillotin?"

The doctor inclined his head. He was dressed in somber black, though the material was expensive and the coat well cut. Guillotin's dark eyebrows and the shadow at his jawline suggested there was dark hair under his powdered wig.

"Only by reputation." Marcus wished he had ordered a drink first. "Dr. Franklin always spoke highly of you, sir."

Guillotin extended his hand to Marcus. Marat eyed them both suspiciously and then buried his nose in his tin cup.

Marcus took the doctor's hand and felt the shifting pressure in his grip that confirmed what Marat suspected: Guillotin was a Freemason, like Marcus. Like Matthew. Like Franklin. That meant that Guillotin knew about creatures, and about vampires in particular.

"Marcus often assisted Dr. Franklin in his laboratory," Matthew said. "He is a surgeon, and interested in medical matters."

"Like father, like son," Guillotin said. "And you are a physician, too, Dr. Marat. How fortunate that I came upon my old friend the chevalier."

No one came upon Matthew de Clermont by chance. Marcus wondered what constellation of influences had placed Matthew in Guillotin's path.

"The doctor is trying to reform medicine." Marat's voice echoed strangely in his contorted nasal cavities. "He has picked the oddest place to begin. Dr. Guillotin wants to give criminals a quicker, more humane death."

Marcus parted the tails of his coat and sat on the bench. God, he needed a drink. The pleasant hours he'd had with Veronique faded into memory as he prepared to navigate the tricky waters of this conversation.

"Perhaps, Doctor, we could get rid of death altogether. The chevalier de Clermont could make us all immortal, if he wanted." Marat, who was a daemon and should know better than to bait Matthew, pressed the matter further. "But true equality wouldn't suit the vampires. Who would be their *serviteurs de sang*?"

"Oh, I think we would always keep a few daemons around—for amusement if not nourishment," Matthew said quietly. "Like the fools and jesters of old."

Marat flushed. He was sensitive about both his small stature and his appearance. Marat's fingers scratched at his neck, where a rash bloomed red and pink.

"I oppose capital punishment, as you know, Monsieur Marat," Guillotin said. "But if we must put criminals to death, let it be quick and painless. And let it be done in a regular, reliable fashion."

"I'm not sure God means death to be painless," Marcus said. He searched the room for someone who might bring him a drink. Veronique caught his eye, and her mouth dropped open in astonishment at the company he was keeping.

"Improvements need to be made to these mechanical executioners," Guillotin continued, as if Marcus had not spoken. His real audience was Matthew, who was listening attentively. "They have engines of death in England and Scotland, but the axes are crude and crush the spine and tear the head from the body."

Marat's fingers dug deeper into his skin, vainly searching for relief from the itching. Matthew's nostrils flared as blood rushed to the surface, and Marcus watched as his father pushed back the appetites that plagued all vampires. The chevalier de Clermont was famously self-controlled. Marcus envied him that. Even though Marat was his friend, and a daemon, the metallic tang of his blood still made Marcus's mouth water.

"I need to speak to you." Matthew was suddenly next to him, his lips close to Marcus's ear.

Reluctantly, Marcus left Marat and Guillotin. It was not the conversation that made him want to stay, but the prospect of slaking his sudden thirst. Matthew led him to the stained wooden counter, where Veronique was watering down blood with wine. She handed a tall beaker to Marcus.

"Drink," she said, looking worried. Marcus was still too young to be fully trustworthy in a crowd of warmbloods.

Matthew waited until Marcus had swallowed down half the liquid before he spoke.

"I think you should stay away from Marat. He's trouble," Matthew advised.

"Then so am I, for we share the same views," Marcus retorted, his temper flaring. "You can order me around, make me study the law, restrict my funds, and forbid me from holding a job, but you cannot choose my friends."

"If you persist, you'll be summoned to an audience with Philippe." Once again, Matthew had switched to English. It was a common de Clermont practice, moving from one language to another in an attempt to speak more privately.

"Grandfather doesn't care what I do." Marcus took another sip. "He has bigger fish to catch than Jean-Paul or me."

"There is no such thing as a small fish during a revolution," Matthew replied. "Any creature who causes a ripple, no matter how seemingly insignificant, can change the course of events. You know that, Marcus."

Maybe, but Marcus had no intention of conceding to his father's demands. This city was his home now. Marcus felt comfortable among the working poor of Paris in a way he never did perched on a silk-covered chair in Ysabeau's salon or attending an aristocratic ball with Fanny.

"Go back to the Île de la Cité where you belong," Marcus told Matthew. "I'm sure Juliette is waiting for you."

He did not like Matthew's companion, whose soft, generous mouth said one thing and whose hard, dangerous eyes said something else.

Matthew's eyes narrowed. Marcus felt a sense of satisfaction that his shot had reached its target.

"I can take care of myself," Marcus insisted, turning his attention back to his drink.

"That's what we all thought—once," Matthew said softly. He slid a sealed letter across the counter. Embedded in the red-and-black marbeled wax was an ancient coin. "You can't say I didn't try. I hope you enjoyed your liberty, equality, and brotherhood, Marcus. In the de Clermont family, it never lasts for very long."

MARCUS WAS IN THE BACK room of La Ruche, dabbing at his wounds, wearing torn and filthy clothing. It was a frigid day in late January, and he had spent most of it running for his life.

"Have you forgotten what this means?" Philippe tossed the worn, ancient coin in the air and caught it as it dropped.

Marcus shook his head. The coin was a summons. He knew that. Every de Clermont knew that. Answer it, or face the consequences. Before, Marcus had always obeyed his grandfather's commands. Now he was going to find out what happened when you ignored them for months.

"We are winning, Grandfather. We've taken over the old convent," Marcus replied, hoping a diversionary tactic would work.

Philippe was a battle-hardened general, however, and unlikely to be impressed by something so minor as the conquest of a moldering old religious building in a seedy part of Paris. He wrapped one hand around Marcus's neck, while the other still held the coin.

"Where is Marat?" Philippe demanded.

"I'm surprised you don't already know." Even now, Marcus couldn't resist baiting his grandfather, even though he was stronger, older, quicker, and could flatten him in a moment.

"Then he is probably in the first place they will look for him." Philippe swore. "The attic above Monsieur Boulanger's bakery, where you and Veronique have lodgings."

Marcus gulped. Philippe was correct, as usual.

"I am disappointed in you, Marcus. I would have credited you with more imagination." Philippe turned and stalked out.

"Where are you going?" Marcus asked, hurrying after him.

Philippe didn't reply.

"I'll get Marat out of Paris—into the countryside," Marcus assured his grandfather, struggling to keep up while remaining within the normal parameters of human locomotion. Philippe's legs were longer than Marcus's, however, which made this difficult.

Philippe still paid him no notice.

The assault of sound that met them on the rue de Cordeliers hit Marcus like a blow. Even though it was winter, the streets were filled with vendors and market stalls. Gulls cried overhead before they swooped down to search for food. People called out to one another, advertising what they had for sale, the latest news and gossip, and the price of their wares.

"I swear, Philippe. On my honor," Marcus said, hurrying along in his grandfather's wake.

"Your honor is not worth much these days." Philippe whirled around. "You will do as I tell you and take Monsieur Marat to London. Gallowglass will meet you at Calais. He has been waiting there since Christmas, and will be glad to be rid of France."

"London?" Marcus stopped. "I can't go to London. I'm an American."

"If a vampire were to abstain from traveling to places occupied by his former enemies, there would be nowhere on earth left to go," Philippe replied, resuming his brisk walk to Boulanger's bakery. "Monsieur Marat is familiar with the place. So is Veronique. You may take her with you, if you like."

"Jean-Paul will not want to go," Marcus said. "He has work to do here."

"Monsieur Marat has done enough, I think," Philippe replied. "No meddling in human politics or religion. Those are the rules."

"But not for you, it seems," Marcus retorted, furious. His grandfather conducted French affairs as though they were an orchestra, and had a spy stationed on every corner in Paris.

Philippe didn't deign to respond. Nevertheless, he and Marcus were beginning to attract sidelong glances from the humans who filled the streets and alleys. Marcus wanted to believe that it was the presence of an aristocrat in this revolutionary neighborhood that drew the attention, but feared it was because they were both vampires.

"The comte de Clermont," one woman whispered to her friend. The comment was carried on the wind, from mouth to ear.

"Inside," Philippe said, pushing Marcus through the door to Monsieur Boulanger's shop. He nodded to the bakers as they passed through, most of whom had heavily muscled torsos and bandy-legs from shoveling massive loaves into the ovens.

"There you are," Veronique said in greeting, flinging open the door. She sounded relieved. The draft drew the scent of yeast and sugar up the staircase.

Then Veronique saw Philippe.

"*Merde*," she whispered."

"Indeed, *madame*," Philippe replied. "I am here to see your houseguest."

"Marat's not—oh, very well." Veronique stood aside to let them pass. She glared at Marcus. *This is your fault*, her expression said.

Marat, who was huddled in a chair by the window, leaped to his feet. He was not suited to the life of a fugitive, and was nothing but skin and bones. Worry and the need to keep moving from bolt-hole to bolt-hole had taken their toll on his health. Marcus, who still remembered what it was like to be on the run, always looking over your shoulder and never able to close your eyes for fear of discovery, was overcome by a wave of sympathetic fury at his friend's plight."

"Monsieur Marat. I'm delighted to have found you before the guard. The scholars at the university talk of nothing but how you have taken refuge with the fair Veronique and *Le Bébé Américain*," Philippe said, tossing his gloves on the table. The legs were uneven, and the weight of the supple leather was enough to give it a perilous tilt.

"You have nothing to fear, Jean-Paul," Marcus assured his friend. "Philippe is here to help."

"I do not want his help," Marat said, spitting on the floor in a show of bravado.

"And yet you will take it anyway," Philippe said cheerfully. "You are going into exile, sir."

"I am staying here. I am no peasant, bound to do his lord's bidding," Marat said with a sneer. "Paris needs me."

"Alas, your actions have made it impossible for you to remain in the city, or even France, monsieur." Philippe studied the dregs of wine in a pitcher and decided against it. "To London you will go. You will still have to hide, of course, but you will not be killed on sight as you will be if you step outside this door."

"London?" Veronique looked from Marat to Marcus to Philippe and back to Marcus.

"At first," Philippe replied. "Marcus will meet his father there. Matthew will take Monsieur Marat to the house of Mrs. Graham, a friend of Dr. Franklin who will be sympathetic to his revolutionary passions."

"It is out of the question," Veronique replied, her eyes sparking with displeasure. "Jean-Paul must remain in Paris. We are depending upon his vision, his sensibility."

"Monsieur Marat may not be able to see very far from a prison cell—which is where he is headed if you persist in this madness," said Philippe.

"This is Lafayette's doing," Marat snarled, his mouth contorted. "He is a traitor to the people."

A sword appeared at Marat's throat. Philippe was at the other end of it.

"Softly, Marat. Softly. The only things standing between you and utter oblivion are your friendship with Marcus and the marquis's decision not to pursue you today because of it. Lafayette sent the guard scurrying in a different direction, even though he knew where you were and could have set his hounds upon you," Philippe said.

Marat breathed heavily, his eyes lowered to watch the tip of the sword. He nodded. After a moment, Philippe withdrew his blade.

"You will all refrain from involving yourselves any further in the affairs of humans," Philippe said, sheathing the sword. "If you persist, I will let the Congregation have their way with you. Their punishments are far less civilized than Dr. Guillotin's methods of execution, I assure you."

Marcus had only a dim knowledge of the Congregation and its tactics. The organization was terribly far away—in Venice—but Marcus had learned from his experiences with Philippe that a creature did not have to be close at hand to thwart your plans.

"The Congregation's rules have little power over the creatures of Paris," Veronique said. "Why shouldn't we have a voice? Do we not have to live in this world the humans are making?"

"Pierre and Alain will see you to the coast," Philippe continued, as if Veronique hadn't spoken. "Be ready in an hour."

"An hour?" Marat's mouth dropped open. "But I must write to people. There is business—"

"Are you going with them, madame, or will you stay here?" Philippe was losing his temper, though no one who didn't know him well would have recognized the signs: the slight hitch in his right shoulder, the flutter of the last finger on his left hand, the deepening crease at the corner of his mouth. "I am not sure if I can keep you from harm if you remain in Paris, but I will do my best."

"So long as I behave like a good girl?" Veronique snorted at the impossibility of the notion.

"I am a practical man," Philippe purred. "I would never be so foolhardy as to ask for the moon and stars."

"Come with us, Veronique," Marcus urged. "It won't be for long."

"No, Marcus. You may have to obey Philippe, but I am no de Clermont." Veronique's scornful glance at his grandfather made it clear what she thought of Marcus's family. "Paris is my home. I rise and fall with her. My heart beats with hers. I will not go with you to London."

"Think of what might happen if you stay," Marcus pleaded, trying to reason with her.

"If you loved me, Marcus, you would be more concerned with what would happen to me if I go," Veronique replied sadly.

⊰ 27 ⊱

Incense

To be in England while winter gave way to spring, Marcus discovered, was to swing like a pendulum between opposing poles of misery and delight. Gallowglass had ferried them safely across the channel in January and shepherded them on to London, which was a sprawling monster of a city larger than Paris and dirtier, too. The filth running through the streets and floating in the river Thames froze, but it still gave off a scent that turned Marcus's stomach.

So, too, did the sight of so many Redcoats strutting around St. James's Palace and its nearby park. One night Marcus had fed off a drunken sot of an officer and found him both self-pitying and unappetizing. The experience did nothing to improve Marcus's opinion of the British army.

Unlike Marat, who adored London and had many friends there, Marcus couldn't be rid of the place quickly enough and was happy to leave the city for the countryside of Berkshire, where Mr. and Mrs. Graham would give them shelter. On the way, he had gawped like a bumpkin at the bulk of Windsor Castle. Marcus found the ancient fortress more imposing than Versailles, and had also admired the spires of Eton standing crisp and clear against a dusting of winter snow and the piercing winter-blue sky.

While London had failed to capture his heart, Berkshire's twisting lanes, patchwork fields tipped with frost, and sprawling farmhouses brought to mind his home in Hadley. The familiar sights sparked his memories of living according to the cycles of nature rather than measuring the passage of time with ticking clocks and changing dates on newspapers.

Matthew escorted Marat and Marcus to the house of Mrs. Graham—who turned out to be the most notorious woman in England, and one of the cleverest, too. Catharine Sawbridge Macaulay Graham had almost as many names as a de Clermont and just as much confidence. An autocratic lady near sixty with a high, domed forehead, a punctuation mark of a nose, ruddy cheeks, and a no-nonsense way of speaking, Mrs. Graham had scandalized polite society by marrying a surgeon less than half her age after the death of her first husband. William Graham was young, short, stout, and Scots. He doted on his wife and relished both her radical opinions and bluestocking tendencies.

"Fancy a walk, Marcus?" William said, poking his head into the library where Marcus was availing himself of the household's impressive collection of medical books. "Come on. Some country air will do you good. Those books will still be here when you get back."

"I'd love to," Marcus said, closing the illustrated anatomy text. Now that it was April, Marcus could hear and smell the earth coming alive again after its winter sleep. He liked to listen to the frogs by the stream and measure the slow leafing out of the trees.

"We could always . . ." William moved his hand up and down in a gesture that suggested there would be drinking involved.

Marcus laughed. "If you'd like."

They set out on what had become their customary route, putting Binfield House behind them and traveling south toward town. Ahead of them were the gates of an older and far grander residence than the new, redbrick build that the Grahams were renting.

"Matthew remembers staying there last century," Marcus commented as they strolled past the E-shaped building with its tall, leaded windows and crooked chimneys. The Grahams were fully apprised of the way the world really worked, and Catharine had been a friend of both Fanny and Ysabeau for years, so Marcus was free to speak of such things with his hosts.

"Full of rot and woodworm, and birds nesting in the eaves." Graham sniffed. "I'm glad to be living in a modern house, with sound windows and doors, and a chimney that won't catch fire."

Marcus made a noise of agreement, but truthfully he liked the charming old pile with its zigzag rooflines and exposed timberwork. His father had explained how the house was constructed from a mixture of wood and narrow bricks with stone casements for the windows. One of the unforeseen benefits of their forced exile was that Matthew was far more relaxed in England than he had been in either America or Paris.

Marcus and William circled west toward Tippen's Wood. This was the vampires' preferred hunting ground, though the wildlife was sparse at this time of year, and the bare branches didn't provide much cover from curious human eyes. As a result, most of Marcus's sustenance came from red wine and bits of raw game birds, supplemented with blood from the butcher. Marcus had grown accustomed to a more varied—and tastier—diet in Paris.

"How is Mrs. Graham this morning?" Marcus asked William. Catharine was suffering from a cold that had settled in her chest. William and Marcus had consulted on a cure and sent her to bed with one of Tom Buckland's tisane recipes and a chest plaster made with mustard and herbs to ease her congestion.

"Better, thank you," William replied. "I wish they'd taught me something half as useful in Edinburgh as what your Tom taught you in America. If they had, I'd be a prosperous surgeon by now."

William may have attended the finest medical school in Europe, but he had lacked the connections and resources to establish his own practice. His older brother, James, had completely overshadowed him with his controversial cures in London and Bath—the most famous of which was the Celestial Bed. For married couples trying and failing to conceive—which was their patriotic duty, according to James—Graham's contraption (complete with turtledoves, scented bedclothes, and a tilted mattress to put husband and wife at the most propitious angle while they made love) renewed their procreative hopes. James made a fortune from desperate couples, but William's medical prospects were jeopardized because of it. Fortunately, Catharine Macaulay was one of his brother's childless patients, and William's future was assured when they fell in love and married.

"What was Edinburgh like?" Marcus asked. Matthew still promised to send him there one day, as soon as Marcus was mature enough to withstand the anatomy lectures.

"Gray and damp," William replied with a laugh.

"I meant the university, not the city," Marcus said, grinning at his friend. He had missed having someone his own age to swap insults and banter with. Marcus and William were both born in 1757. William was now in his early thirties. Whenever Marcus looked at William, he was reminded of what he would be like today if Matthew hadn't made him a vampire.

"It was tedious and exciting as all courses of study are," William said, clasping his hands behind his back. "When you go, which I pray will be soon, you must make a point of attending Dr. Black's chemistry lectures, even though Dr. Gregory will want you on the wards seeing patients."

"And the lectures in anatomy?" Marcus knew that he must master a wider body of medical knowledge, but surgery remained his first love.

"Dr. Monro has a limitless curiosity and courage when it comes to surgical experimentation. You would be wise to attach yourself to him, and learn all that you can from his methods and discoveries," William advised.

The prospect of doing so almost made Marcus wish he could remain in England, though of course he must return to France and the Revolution as soon as he could. And there was Veronique to consider.

Marcus and William emerged from the wood and cut east across the fields along Monk's Alley. Once, the tree-lined lane led to a religious house owned by Reading Abbey, but that house was a crumbling ruin now. William had painted a watercolor of it based on Matthew's recollections of what it had once looked like, tucked into its green pastures and providing a bucolic retreat for the clerics of the nearby city.

"I suspect your teachers will all be dead and buried by the time I arrive," Marcus said, elbowing William. "Who knows? You might be a member of the faculty by then."

"My place is with Catharine," William replied. "Her work is far more important than mine could ever be."

At present, Catharine was writing histories of both the successful American, and the budding French, Revolutions. Since Marat's arrival, Catharine divided her time between asking him questions about what was happening in Paris, and perusing the papers given to her by General Washington when she and William visited Mount Vernon in 1785. Catharine had even interviewed Marcus and Matthew to better understand the events of 1777 and 1781, and had been fascinated by Marcus's reports of Bunker Hill.

"How did you know that Mrs. Graham was . . ." Marcus trailed off, embarrassed by his own boldness.

"The one?" William smiled. "It was fast—instantaneous, even. People think Catharine is a vain old woman and I am a fortune hunter, but from the moment we first met, I never wanted to be anywhere but by her side."

Marcus thought of medical school in Edinburgh, and Veronique in Paris. Perhaps she would consider setting up a business in Scotland.

"I've heard you talk about the woman you left behind in Paris—Madame Veronique," William continued. "Do you think she might be your soul mate?"

"I thought so," Marcus said, hesitant. "Think so."

"Such a weighty decision must be difficult for a long-lived vampire," William said. "It is a long time to remain faithful."

"That's what Matthew says," Marcus replied. "He and Juliette have been together for decades, but my father hasn't mated with her. Yet." Marcus worried that Juliette might persuade Matthew to take this irrevocable step, though Ysabeau assured him that if they were going to mate, they would have done so by now.

"Monsieur Marat says that Madame Veronique is quite the revolutionary," William said as they approached the Kicking Donkey, their last stop before returning home. "You have that in common at least."

"She is," Marcus said proudly. "Veronique and Mrs. Graham would get along famously."

"None of the rest of us would get a word in edgewise, I warrant," William said, holding the door for Marcus. Warm air beckoned them inside, redolent with hops and sour wine.

Marcus ducked his head to enter the low-ceilinged space. It was dark and smoky, filled with farmers talking in low murmurs about the price of wheat and exchanging tips for the best livestock coming up for auction. Marcus relaxed into the familiar sounds and smells of the rural tavern—something he was never able to do in Veronique's establishment in Paris, where the cacophony of voices and the press of bodies were so overwhelming.

William acquired two pints of foamy ale and carried them to the farthest corner of the room. The two of them settled into high-backed wooden chairs with stout arms for resting their tankards in between sips. Marcus sighed with contentment and clinked his cup against William's.

"To your health," Marcus said before taking a sip. Unlike wine, ale sometimes soured in his stomach, but it was worth it for the taste, which like everything else about Binfield reminded him of home.

"And to yours," William said, returning the courtesy, "though if we're to continue taking our daily walks, we're going to have to come up with something else. Your safety perhaps?"

The escalating conflict in France was the topic of every dinner conversation.

"My father worries too much," Marcus said.

"Monsieur de Clermont has experienced much war and strife over the course of his life," William replied. "And Monsieur Marat calls for the death of all aristocrats—even your friend the Marquis de Lafayette. It is no wonder your father is concerned about where all this might lead."

Last night, Catharine had drawn Matthew and Marcus out about what they thought of the current situation in France, and how it compared to what they had witnessed in the colonies. Marat had erupted into the conversation, waving his arms and crying out for greater equality and an end to social distinctions. Matthew had excused himself from the table rather than allow himself to be attacked by Jean-Paul or appear rude to his hostess.

"Do you agree with your father that the revolution in France will be far bloodier and more destructive than what happened in America?" William continued.

"How could it be?" Marcus said, thinking back to the stained fields at Brandywine and the winter at Valley Forge, to the surgical tents with their amputation saws and the screams of dying men, the hunger and filth, and the horrors of the British prison ships anchored off the coast of New York.

"Oh, humanity is marvelously creative when it comes to death and suffering," William said. "We'll come up with something, my friend. Mark my words."

MARCUS AND MARAT RETURNED to Paris in May. Matthew was called away from Binfield House on some business for Philippe, and, left without a supervisor, Marat hatched a plan for their escape. It was complicated, and expensive, but between Marcus's allowance (which had increased due to his good behavior in England), Marat's cunning (which was limitless), and Catharine's help as co-conspirator when it came to logistics, the plan succeeded. Marcus tucked himself back into Veronique's life and her new lodgings at the heart of their increasingly radical neighborhood. Veronique had given up her old apartments in the attic of Monsieur Boulanger's bakery so that a lumpen fellow named Georges Danton and his political cronies could use it as a base of operations for their new political club, the Cordeliers.

His father, who had returned to Binfield only to discover empty rooms and a triumphant Mrs. Graham, wrote a furious letter demanding Marcus return to England at once. Marcus ignored it. Ysabeau sent a basket of strawberries and some quail eggs to the Cordeliers along with a request that he call on them in Auteuil. Marcus ignored that, too, though he would have dearly liked to see his grandmother and tell her about Catharine and William. When Veronique complained that the de Clermonts were trying to interfere in their lives, Marcus promised that the only thing he would respond to in future was a direct summons from Philippe. But that never came.

Marat had now embarked upon a dangerous, clandestine life, one tilted more toward wild flights of fantasy and daemonic outbursts with each passing day. He resumed publishing his newspaper, *L'ami du peuple*, shortly after he arrived, seemingly working out of a shop on the rue de l'Ancienne-Comédie. During the day, he hid in plain sight, protected by Danton and the other neighborhood bullies while a citywide network of printers, booksellers, and newsagents put their own lives at risk to get the newspaper into the hands of its eager readers. At night, Marat secreted himself in the basements, lofts, and storerooms of his friends, jeopardizing their safety as well as his own.

Marat's lack of a fixed address, along with the high anxiety caused by the concerted efforts of the police, National Guard, and National Assembly to capture him, did nothing for his fragile mental and physical state. His skin, which had improved during their time away in England, flared into an agony of itchy, red sores. Marcus prescribed a vinegar wash to quiet the inflammation and prevent infection. It stung like the devil, but it brought Marat relief—so much so that he began to wear a vinegar-soaked cloth around his head. The sharp tang announced his presence long before he appeared, and Veronique dubbed him Le Vinaigrier and aired out her back room whenever Marat slept there so as not to tip off the authorities.

While Marat hid, Marcus spent late May and June digging out the Champs de Mars and ferrying wheelbarrows of dirt to the side of a vast oval arena so that Paris could properly celebrate the first anniversary of the storming of the Bastille come July. Marat was the only creature of their acquaintance who did not participate in the excavation, pleading a bad back and sore hands due to the many hours he spent crouched over newspaper copy and writing screeds against his political rivals.

With Marat increasingly convinced that there were vast conspiracies at work to undo the Revolution, and Veronique busy recruiting new members of the Cordeliers Club for Danton, Marcus found himself spending more time with Lafayette. As head of the National Guard and author of France's new draft constitution, the marquis was up to his neck in plans for the July celebrations. He had ordered troops from all over the country into Paris—one of Marat's conspiracies argued that Lafayette did so to proclaim himself king—and now had to find housing, food, and amusements for them. At the same time, Lafayette was called upon to greet the visitors who were arriving to join in the festivities. Even the royal family was slated to attend the fete.

Given the presence of the king, queen, and heir to the throne, as well as hundreds of thousands of intoxicated Parisians, foreign dignitaries, and armed soldiers, Lafayette was understandably concerned about safety. His anxiety mounted when Marat announced his opposition to the planned spectacle, bringing the simmering animosity between Marcus's two friends to a vitriolic boil.

"'*Blind citizens whom my cries of pain cannot penetrate—sleep on, on the edge of the abyss*,'" Lafayette read aloud from the newspaper. He groaned. "Is Marat trying to cause a riot?"

"Jean-Paul doesn't think people are listening to his calls for equality," Marcus said, trying to explain Marat's position.

"He publishes one shrill call to tear society apart after another. We have no choice but to listen." Lafayette tossed *L'ami du peuple* on his desk.

They were seated in Lafayette's private cabinet, the doors to the small balcony open to the heavy July air. Lafayette's house was luxurious, but not as large as the Hôtel de Clermont. The marquis had deliberately chosen a residence that was less ostentatious than those of most aristocrats, and decorated it with simple, neoclassical elegance. He and Adrienne, along with their children Anastasie and Georges, had gladly left Versailles to enjoy life as a family on the rue de Bourbon.

Lafayette's page entered, a letter in his hand.

"Monsieur Thomas Paine," the page announced. "He is waiting for you in the salon."

"There is no need for such ceremony," Lafayette said. "We will greet him here."

Marcus leaped to his feet. "*The* Thomas Paine?"

"There is only one, alas." Lafayette straightened his waistcoat and his wig while his servant fetched his American visitor.

After what seemed like an eternity to Marcus, the servant returned. With him was a man who looked like an English country parson, dressed in severe black from shoulder to foot, his simple white cravat the only thing to provide a dash of contrast apart from his hair, which was gunmetal gray. Paine's nose was long and bulbous, the end of it angled slightly to the right. The left side of his mouth drooped slightly, which gave him the odd appearance of someone whose features had been fashioned out of soft modeling clay.

"Ah, Mr. Paine. You found us. Adrienne will be sorry to miss you. She is with her family at the moment."

"Monsieur." Paine bowed.

"But I have some consolation, as well as some refreshment," Lafayette said. More servants appeared with tea and melted away again without uttering a word. "This is my dear Doc, who treated me at Brandywine. He is a great admirer of your writing, and can recite *Common Sense* chapter and verse. Marcus de Clermont, my friend Thomas Paine."

"Sir." Marcus returned Paine's polite bow, but was then overcome with emotion. He rushed to him with an extended hand. "Allow me to express my thanks for all you have done to bring liberty to America. Your words were the greatest comfort to me, during the war."

"I have done nothing, except cast a light on self-evident truths," Paine replied, taking Marcus's hand in his own. Somewhat to Marcus's surprise, it was a perfectly ordinary handshake. He had long suspected Paine was a Freemason like the rest of them. "Marcus de Clermont, you say? I believe you knew Dr. Franklin."

"Marcus and Dr. Franklin spent many happy hours experimenting together," Lafayette said, ushering Paine to a chair. "His death was a blow to all who believe in freedom, not least to his friends who could sorely use his advice in these troubled times."

News of Franklin's death reached Marcus a few days after he and Marat returned to France. His friend had died of pleurisy, the infection causing an abscess that had made it impossible to breathe. Marcus had always imagined Franklin would live forever, so powerful was his personality.

"A great loss indeed. And what would you ask Dr. Franklin, if he were here?" Paine inquired gently of Lafayette, taking a cup of tea with thanks.

Lafayette pondered the question, struggling over his answer, while he fiddled with the teapot and strainer. He preferred coffee, and was not as familiar with the equipment as he should be. Marcus, who had been trained in the proper handling of it by his mother, rescued the marquis from certain disaster and poured his own cup of tea.

"The marquis is troubled by Monsieur Marat," Marcus explained as he poured. "Jean-Paul does not like insincerity, and feels that the Bastille celebration is frivolous."

"Insincere! How dare he?" Lafayette cried, putting his cup down on its saucer with a clatter. "I can be accused of many failings, Doc, but not my devotion to liberty."

"Then you have nothing to fear," Paine said, blowing on his tea to cool it so that he could take a sip. "I have heard that Marat opposes all attempts at reconciliation between those who support his views, and those who are more moderate."

"Marat is a menace," Lafayette said. "I do not trust him."

"Perhaps that is why he does not trust you," Paine replied.

Another servant interrupted them, murmuring in his master's ear.

"Madame de Clermont has come," Lafayette announced, face wreathed in smiles. "How wonderful. She will not want tea. Fetch wine for her, at once. Madame will be exhausted, having come all the way from Auteuil."

Marcus had not seen his grandmother since he returned from London, and did not know what to expect from the encounter given how many of her invitations he had refused in order to please Veronique. He stood, nervous, as Ysabeau de Clermont sailed into the room, ribbons and ruffles fluttering. Her primrose dress was striped with white and adorned with sprigs of blue forget-me-nots. Her hair was lightly powdered, which made her green eyes and the touch of color in her cheeks more evident. And the tilt of her broad-brimmed hat was decidedly playful—not to mention flattering.

"Madame!" Lafayette went to Ysabeau, bowing and then kissing her familiarly on each cheek. "You have brought the summer gardens inside with you. What a happy surprise that you came today. Marcus and I are talking with Monsieur Paine about the fete. Will you join us?"

"Marquis." Ysabeau beamed at him. "I could not resist calling on you, when Adrienne said you were home alone. I have just come from the Hôtel de Noailles. How the children have grown. Anastasie is more like her mother every day. And Georges—what a rascal he is."

"Hello, *Grand-mère*." Marcus sounded as awkward as he felt. He tried to cover his nerves by taking her hand and kissing it. He had missed her more than he had realized.

"Marcus." Ysabeau's tone was cool, as if a stiff breeze had blown across the Seine. Happily, no one but Marcus noticed. She turned to Paine. "Mr. Paine. Welcome back. How is your leg? Does it still swell in the mornings?"

"It is much better, madame," Paine replied. "And how is our dear comte?"

"Busy with his affairs, as usual," Ysabeau said. "As you know, he takes a keen interest in how America fares during its youth." She slid a glance in Marcus's direction.

"You must thank him for sending me a copy of Mr. Burke's letter to Monsieur Depont," Paine replied.

"Philippe felt sure that you would want to know what was being said in the clubs of London." Ysabeau lowered herself into a waiting chair. It was deep, as chairs needed to be in order to support the birdcages women wore around their waists, not to mention all the silk and satin that was draped over them. Veronique might make do with a straight-backed stool and a cushion, but not Ysabeau.

"I am crafting my reply to Burke now, madame," Paine said, his body angled toward her. "He intends to publish the letter, and I wish to have an answer at the ready. There is no reason France cannot become a republic, as America did. May I impose on the comte further, and visit your house to discuss it with him? There is no man whose opinion I value more."

Marcus looked from Ysabeau to Paine and back to Ysabeau.

"Of course, Mr. Paine. The doors of the Hôtel de Clermont are open to all with serious political views." Ysabeau's green eyes fixed on Paine as though he were a plump raven she was considering for her next meal. "What are your thoughts on the marquis's celebration?"

"It is not mine, madame," Lafayette protested. "It belongs to the nation."

Ysabeau held up her hand, stopping his words. "You are too modest, Gilbert. Without you there would be no nation. We would still be living in the kingdom of France, and the peasants would still be paying their tithes to the church. Isn't that right, Marcus?"

Marcus hesitated, then nodded. Veronique and Marat would not agree, but Lafayette had drafted the new constitution, after all.

"I think the people need to see what they are being asked to believe in—democracy, in this case," Paine said. "What harm can there be in a parade?"

"Exactly!" Lafayette said, nodding his head enthusiastically. "It is not a 'vain spectacle,' as Monsieur Marat claims. It is a ceremony of harmony, a ritual of fraternity."

The clock on Lafayette's mantel struck four. Marcus leaped to his feet, shocked to see so much time had passed. He was late.

"I must go," he said. "I have an appointment with friends."

"My carriage can take you," Lafayette said, ringing a bell that rested by his elbow.

"My appointment is just down the road, and I'll be faster on foot." Marcus was strangely reluctant to leave Paine, and for a moment he considered changing his plans, but his loyalty prevented it. "Good-bye, Mr. Paine."

"I hope our paths cross again, Monsieur de Clermont," Paine said. "At the marquis's celebration, if not before."

"I'd like that, Mr. Paine. *Grand-mère*." Marcus bowed to Ysabeau.

"Don't be a stranger," his grandmother said, the corners of her mouth lifted into the shadow of a smile.

Marcus headed for the door as quickly as he could without alarming Mr. Paine.

"Marcus?" Ysabeau called after him.

Marcus turned.

His grandmother had picked up the red wool hat that Marcus had left on his chair in his haste to get away. It was a visible sign of Marcus's allegiance to the ideals of the Revolution.

"Don't forget your cap," she said.

CAFÉ PROCOPE WAS PACKED with hot, sweating bodies. There was barely room to stand, and Marcus was like a salmon swimming against the current as he tried to make his way from the door to the back corner where his friends were waiting.

"Marcus? Is that you?" Fanny waved her hand in greeting. She was wearing a plain silk gown in revolutionary white. Her unpowdered hair was tumbling around her shoulders in the new style being adopted by all the finest ladies, and she wore a version of Marcus's distinctive red hat—hers made by one of the most expensive milliners in town.

"Fanny!" Having successfully avoided his family for almost two months, Marcus could not seem to avoid them today. "You're far from home."

"This is the Quartier Latin, not Africa," Fanny replied, making rapid progress toward him through a series of deft moves that included treading upon others' feet, throwing elbows into ribs, and batting her eyes at the men. "The traffic through town is terrible, of course, so I abandoned my carriage on the Pont Neuf and walked the rest of the way. What brings you here?"

"I live here," Marcus said, his eyes searching the room for Veronique.

"With Danton and his band of murderers and thieves?" Fanny shook her head. "Charles said you and Veronique were crammed into a tiny attic with six other creatures. It sounded dreadful. You should move back into my house. It's far more comfortable."

"Veronique and I moved out of the attic." Marcus gave up searching for

Veronique with his eyes and tried using his nose and ears instead. "We're living in a second-floor apartment now. One closer to the Sorbonne."

"Who is your tailor these days?" Fanny wondered, looking him over. "Given the cut of that coat, you look as if you belong in Lafayette's salon, not the Cordeliers Club. Except for the cap, of course."

Marcus's eyes narrowed at her mention of the marquis. "What are you and Ysabeau up to, Fanny?"

"Ysabeau?" Fanny shrugged. "You're spending too much time with Marat. Now you think there are conspirators behind every door. You know perfectly well that we don't get along."

It was true that his grandmother and his aunt were usually shooting conversational barbs into each other at family dinners, but Marcus couldn't help but feel he was being managed.

"Liberté! Égalité! Fraternité!"

The chant of the Cordeliers Club echoed through the room. It had started in the back corner, where Marcus had agreed to meet Marat.

The crowds parted and Jean-Paul emerged from them, the soft tip of his red cap falling over one eye, holding a fist of paper in his hand. Georges Danton was behind him, ready to escort the daemon to whatever underground lair he would occupy tonight. With them was Veronique.

"Marcus!" Veronique's cheeks were flushed. She was wearing the authentic revolutionary dress on which Fanny's fashionable version was modeled. "We expected you hours ago."

"I was delayed," Marcus apologized. He moved to kiss her.

Veronique sniffed his coat.

"You've been with Ysabeau," she said. "You promised—"

"Ysabeau was visiting Lafayette," Marcus said, interrupting Veronique in his haste to reassure her that he had not broken his word. "I had no idea that she would be there."

"Lafayette! You see, I told you he cannot be trusted," Marat muttered to Danton. "He is a de Clermont, and like all aristocrats, he would rather slit the belly of your wife and rip out the heart of your infant son than give up one of his privileges."

"You know that isn't true, Jean-Paul." Marcus couldn't believe what his friend was saying.

"Come away," Fanny murmured, tugging on his sleeve. "There's no point in arguing with him."

A knot of spectators was gathering around them, roughly dressed and well into their third or fourth drinks. Most of them were filthy, rags tied around their necks to absorb the sweat and grime as though they had come straight from doing menial labor at the Champs de Mars.

"Wake up, Marcus," Marat said, his tone vicious. "Those people are not your true family. Lafayette is not your friend. They want only to use you for their own purposes, to further their own designs. You are a de Clermont puppet, jerking every time one of them pulls your strings."

Marcus looked mutely at Veronique, waiting for her to defend him. But Veronique did not jump to his rescue, and Fanny did.

"You're very brave, Marat, so long as you're hiding in the sewers, or behind your newspaper, or surrounded by your friends," Fanny said calmly, linking her arm through Marcus's elbow. "When you're on your own, though, I bet you piss yourself when a bug farts."

There were laughs from some of their audience. Not from Marat, though. Nor Veronique.

"You're all traitors," Marat hissed, his eyes wild. He was every inch a daemon now, and the human patrons began to draw away from him as if they could sense his strangeness. "Soon you'll all be forced to flee, like rats."

"Maybe, Jean-Paul." Fanny shrugged. "But like the rats, Marcus and I will survive long after you are nothing but bones and dust. Remember that, before you insult my family again."

WEEKS AFTER THE ARGUMENT at Café Procope, Marcus trudged home from the Marquis de Lafayette's grand anniversary ceremony covered in mud, his clothes soaked through to the skin. A positively biblical deluge had rained on the parades, the military exercises, the royal family, and the Parisians who flocked to the Champs de Mars.

In spite of the weather, it had been a triumph. No one had been accidentally shot. The king had behaved. More importantly, the outspoken queen Marie Antoinette had played her role to perfection, holding the dauphin and promising to honor the ideals of the Revolution. Lafayette had sworn an oath to defend the constitution. All of Paris cheered, even though the only creatures in attendance who could hear everything that was said were vampires like Marcus.

Most in Paris would have agreed that Lafayette's celebration convinced the nation that the worst was behind them and that progress had been made. Unfortunately for Marcus, Veronique and Marat were not among them. They had refused to attend the events.

"I am on strike," Veronique pronounced. These were words that struck terror in a Parisian heart, for they suggested a disruption of normal routines that would go on for some time.

"Go away! I have a newspaper to print," Marat shouted when Marcus came to urge him to go and celebrate a revolution that he had helped to create. "You are an overgrown child, Marcus, playing with toys instead of occupying your time with serious work. It will be all over for us, if we let creatures like you take charge. Now leave me be."

Marcus had decided not to press matters with Jean-Paul. It never worked—not when he was in this kind of mood. So he went alone to the celebrations, and enjoyed eavesdropping on conversations between Paine and the king about what constituted freedom and what was instead a sign of anarchy.

When Marcus pushed open their apartment door—dry and cracked on one side, and swollen with moisture from a dripping balcony on the other so that it was difficult to budge—he discovered that Veronique was waiting for him.

So was his grandfather.

"Philippe." Marcus stood, frozen, in the entry.

The presence of the de Clermont patriarch in their small flat only served to emphasize its shabbiness and discomfort. Philippe dwarfed most people, and his size made it seem as though he occupied more space in the room than one person should. At the moment, he was perched on the edge of a low stool, his legs stretched out and his ankles crossed. Instead of his usual fine clothes, Philippe was wearing brown linen, and if not for his size he might have been mistaken for a *sans-culotte*. His hands were clasped behind his head, and he was staring into the flames that were burning in the fireplace as though he was waiting for an oracle.

Veronique moved to the window, and stood biting at her nails and fuming.

She whirled around to face him. "Where have you been?"

"The Champs de Mars," Marcus said, stating the obvious. "Is something wrong with Ysabeau?" He could think of nothing else that might make Philippe show up here, unannounced, alone.

"You must choose, Marcus." Veronique put her hands on her hips and adopted a challenging posture. "Them, or me."

"Can we have that argument later?" Marcus was tired, and sodden, and he wanted something to eat. "Tell me what you want, Philippe, then go. You're upsetting Veronique."

"Madame Veronique summed it up quite nicely, I think." Philippe's hands dropped to his lap. He pulled a clutch of paper from his pocket. "Your friend Marat is violating the covenant by fomenting rebellion among the people of Paris. This would be reason enough for concern. Now, however, he plans to print this call to murder hundreds of aristocrats in order to purge the nation of potential traitors. Marat will place this call to arms on every wall and door in Paris."

Marcus snatched the papers from his grandfather. His eyes raced over the lines, which were in Marat's unmistakable, spidery script, complete with thickly ruled-out corrections and changes made between the lines and in the margins.

"How did you get this?" he asked Philippe, dazed.

"And you call yourself a defender of liberty and freedom," Philippe said softly. "You just read Marat's demand that we decapitate five or six *hundred* aristocrats in the name of peace and happiness, and your only reaction is to ask me where I got it. At least you did not insult me by pretending it was a forgery."

Marcus, like Philippe and Veronique, knew it was genuine.

"Marat would have your friend Lafayette—a man of honor, who fought and shed blood for the freedom of your native land—executed. He would execute the king, and the dauphin, though he is only a child. He would kill me, and your grandmother, and Fanny." Philippe let his words sink in before continuing. "Have you no loyalty, no pride? How can you defend such a person? Either of you?"

"You are not my father, and I owe you no allegiance, *sieur*." Veronique used the ancient term for the head of a vampire family. It was a sign of the seriousness of the situation—and its potential deadliness—that she would rely on such a courtesy now. "You have no right to come into my home and question me."

"Ah, but I do, madame." Philippe smiled at her amiably. "You forget, I am the Congregation. I have every right to question you, if I feel that you pose a danger to our people."

"You mean you are one of the representatives *on* the Congregation," Veronique said, though she sounded unsure.

"Of course." Philippe grinned, his teeth showing white in the dimming light. "My mistake."

But Philippe de Clermont did not make mistakes. It was one of the insights into his grandfather that Fanny had been at pains to share with Marcus, back when he was younger and still getting to know the family and how it operated.

"I think you are ready to attend the university in Edinburgh, Marcus. The anatomy lectures there cannot possibly be more bloodthirsty than the company you are keeping in Paris." Philippe handed Marcus a key. "Matthew is in London, and will be expecting you."

Marcus stared suspiciously at the ornate metal object.

"The key to your house. It is near St. James's Palace. Outside the city walls, where the air is less polluted and where you can have more privacy than you do here. There is a park nearby for hunting," Philippe continued, still holding out the key. "Mrs. Graham and her husband have a house nearby. She is not well, and you will be a comfort to William when she dies. When classes resume, you will travel north to Scotland. You will be useful to me there."

Marcus still didn't take the key. There were, he felt sure, more strings attached to it than assisting William in the hour of Catharine's death.

Philippe tossed the key in the air, caught it, and placed it on the corner of a nearby crate that was serving as a chair or a table, as the occasion warranted.

"I trust you are old enough to find your own way to London. Take Fanny with you, and make sure that she stays away. Paris is no longer safe." Philippe stood. His hair brushed the low ceiling. "Don't neglect to write to your grandmother. She will worry if she doesn't hear of you. Thank you for your hospitality, Madame Veronique."

Having laid out the terms of Marcus's surrender, Philippe vanished in a flash of brown and gold.

"Did you know about this, Veronique?" Marcus held up the papers.

His lover's silence said more than words could.

"Jean-Paul is calling for a massacre!" Marcus cried. This was not his idea of liberty.

"They are enemies of the Revolution." There was something fanatical in Veronique's flat tone and fevered eyes.

"How can you say that? You don't even know whom he plans to kill," Marcus retorted.

"It doesn't matter," Veronique shot back. "They are aristocrats. One is much like another."

"Lafayette was right," Marcus said. "Marat only wants to stir up trouble. There will never be enough equality to satisfy him. His revolution cannot be won."

"*Marat* was right," Veronique said angrily. "You're a traitor, just like the rest. I can't believe I let you inside me—that I trusted you."

Something dark and terrible had been unleashed in Veronique with all this talk of death and revolution. Marcus had to get her out of Paris, too.

"Gather your things," Marcus said, thrusting Marat's manuscript into the fire. "You're coming to London with me and Fanny."

"No!" Veronique dug into the flames with her bare hands to retrieve the pages. They were curling and blackened, but not yet totally destroyed.

Her hands, however—her beautiful, slender, agile fingers and soft palms—were a blistered, charred mess. Horrified, Marcus went to her.

"Let me see," he said, reaching for them.

"No." Veronique snatched them away. "No matter where I say it—in my bed, or in my tavern, or in my house, or in my city—you respect it as my final word, Marcus."

"Veronique. Please." Marcus held out his hand.

"I will not be told what to do by you, or your grandfather, or any man." Veronique was shaking, her body consumed with shock and anger.

Marcus could see her hands beginning to heal as her powerful blood repaired the damage the fire had wrought. "Go, Marcus. Just go."

"Not without you," Marcus said. He couldn't leave her here, where she might fall further under Marat's spell. "We belong together, Veronique."

"You chose the de Clermonts," Veronique said bitterly. "You belong to Philippe now."

Forty-Five

26 JUNE

A plump woman in her midfifties walked along the path by the Seine. She wore stout walking shoes, a flowing cardigan, and a brightly colored scarf knotted around her neck. A heavy bag was slung over one shoulder. Every few steps, she took out a sheet of paper and held it at arm's length to make out the words on it, then looked at the nearby landmarks and took a few more steps.

"She needs glasses," Phoebe observed.

"It's not important that she spots *you*," Jason replied. "You're here to spot *her*."

"How could I miss her, with that scarf?" The lengthy June twilight provided sufficient illumination for Phoebe's vampire senses to take in every detail of the woman's appearance—the long silver earrings with turquoise stones, the oversize watch, the black leggings and crisp white shirt.

"The scarf was part of the agreement, remember," Jason said, trying to be patient.

Phoebe bit her lip. The agreement had been more than a week in the making. Freyja had conducted interviews in the salon, and half a dozen middle-aged white women trooped through the house, cooing over the decor and asking questions about the gardens.

In the end, Freyja had selected the woman who asked the fewest questions and seemed least interested in the house. Curiosity, Freyja noted, was not an important quality in one's food.

"Take note of her habits," Jason said. "How fast does the woman walk? Is she on the phone? Is she distracted with a map, or a shopping list? Is she carrying bags, and therefore an easy target? Is she smoking?"

"Do smokers taste bad?" Phoebe asked him.

"Not necessarily. It depends on your palate. But smokers are often looking for a light—or are willing to share one with you. Always carry cigarettes," Jason advised. "It makes approaching complete strangers perfectly acceptable."

Phoebe added that to her mental list of all the things she should carry—moist towelettes, bribe money, a list of nearby hospitals—and all those things she shouldn't—credit cards, a cell phone, and any type of identification.

For a few minutes, Phoebe and Jason watched the woman in silence. Every time the woman looked at her notes and then squinted up to orient herself, she either bumped into someone or tripped on an uneven stone. Once, she did both and narrowly avoided a dunking.

"She's terribly clumsy," Phoebe said.

"I know. Freyja really knows how to pick them," Jason said, sounding pleased. "But remember, she may know you will be hunting her, but she still doesn't know where, how, or when you will strike. Margot will be surprised and afraid—you'll hear it in her heartbeat, and smell it in her blood. Fight or flight kicks in no matter what. It's instinctive."

The woman stopped again, seemingly to study the fading light on the water and stones.

"Okay, this is the moment," Jason said, nudging Phoebe with his elbow. "She'll be right in front of us in another sixty seconds. Hop down and get to it."

Phoebe remained glued to the stone wall that was providing an impromptu seat.

Jason sighed. "Phoebe. It's time you started feeding yourself. You're ready, I promise. And this woman knows exactly what she's doing. Freyja already fed from her, and her résumé is really quite impressive."

The woman—her name was Margot and she was an Aries, Phoebe recalled—had fed half the vampires in Paris, according to the references she'd provided during her interview. Margot's unassuming appearance masked the fact that she lived in a lavish apartment in the 5th and had extensive real estate investments throughout the city.

"Can you do it?" Phoebe asked. "I'd like to watch, and make sure I have all the moves worked out in my head."

The only way to approach feeding from a human, Phoebe discovered, was to treat it as though it were a ballet. There were specific steps, foot positions, facial expressions, and even costuming considerations.

"No. You've watched me hunt three humans already," Jason replied.

She and Jason had ventured forth several times since the disastrous night she attacked a tourist. Miriam went with them the first time, keeping watch over Phoebe while Jason took down a fit, attractive jogger in the Jardin du Luxembourg. It had piqued her appetite, not to mention her startling desire to run and chase things down. At that early hour of the morning, the only creatures available save joggers were squirrels and pigeons, but Miriam let Phoebe entertain herself with them until the sun rose. Jason dared her to snack on a squirrel, which was just as revolting as she had imagined it would be.

Since Phoebe comported herself without embarrassing her maker on that occasion, she and Jason were allowed to go out on their own. Dawns and twilights were designated as safe times for hunting, as the shadows were lengthening but the bright lights of the Parisian night were not yet likely to dazzle Phoebe's lightstruck eyes.

"Phoebe." Jason gave her a shove this time.

Had Phoebe still been a warmblood, she would have tumbled fifteen feet onto the path below. Because she was a vampire, she was merely irritated and gave him a shove back.

"Margot is walking past," Jason said, urgent.

"Maybe I'll wait and then bite her from behind," Phoebe prevaricated.

"No. That's not safe. Not when you're this young. Were she to run, and you gave chase—which you wouldn't be able to resist doing—humans would notice." Jason watched Margot disappear around the bend in the river. "Damn."

"Freyja's going to be cross, isn't she?" Phoebe didn't want to disappoint Marcus's aunt—or Miriam. But she just didn't feel ready to feed off a *person* yet. "Sorry, Jason. I'm just not hungry."

Phoebe was, in fact, ravenous. She needed to spend some quality time with Persephone and a bottle of Burgundy.

A group of women walked down the path, arm in arm. They were laughing and had clearly been out enjoying themselves that afternoon, based on their rollicking steps and the number of shopping bags they carried.

Phoebe sniffed the air.

"No, Phoebe," Jason said. "Those women are not suitable. They haven't been paid, for a start. You can't just—"

"Phoebe?" Stella stared at Phoebe in astonishment.

"Stella!" Phoebe whipped off her dark glasses, blinking in the dark light as though it were midday and the sun were shining. She hopped down to greet her sister, but was stopped by Jason.

"Too fast. Too soon," Jason whispered.

Freyja cautioned her day in and day out to slow down. But this was her sister, and Phoebe hadn't seen or talked to her for almost two months.

"I hardly recognized you." Stella took a step back as she approached. "You look—"

"Fantastic!" one of Stella's friends chirped. "Is that a Seraphin jacket?"

Phoebe looked down at the leather coat she'd borrowed from Freyja. She shrugged. "I don't know. It belongs to a friend."

"Your voice—" Stella remembered they were not alone, and stopped herself.

"How are Mum and Dad?" Phoebe was starved for news of the family. She missed their casual weekend suppers, and the exchange of stories about all that had happened the previous week.

"Dad's been tired, and Mum's worried that he's not sleeping. But how could he since—you know . . ." Stella drifted off into silence.

"Who's your friend?" one of the women asked, casting a seductive glance at Jason, who was standing a few feet away.

"Oh, that's my stepbrother. Jason." Phoebe beckoned him over. Jason strolled in their direction with an affable smile.

"You didn't tell us you had a brother," the other woman murmured to Stella, "never mind one who looked like that."

"He's not—I mean he's more of a close family friend," Stella said brightly. She glared at Phoebe.

Normally, that look of outrage and blame would have had Phoebe scrambling to apologize and make amends. Phoebe was the good girl in the family, the one who could be relied upon to give in, give up, and give way to keep the peace.

But Phoebe was a vampire now, and far less worried about her sister's feelings than she had been before Miriam's blood entered her veins. Her lips curled and her eyebrows rose. She returned Stella's glare, matching her in outrage and replacing the blame with scorn.

Not my problem, Phoebe said silently.

Based on Stella's dumfounded expression, she got the message. It was not like Phoebe to challenge her. But Stella, unaccustomed to conceding so quickly, fought back.

"What happened to Marcus?" Stella asked. "Does he know you're out with another man?"

Phoebe reacted as though she'd been bitten by a poisonous snake. She recoiled, horrified at the suggestion that she was being unfaithful.

"Let's go, Phoebe." Jason took her arm.

"Oh, I see." Stella's look was triumphant. "Couldn't bear the time apart, so you thought you'd have a little fun on the side?"

Stella's friends laughed, a bit nervously.

"He calls Mum and Dad every few days, you know," Stella reported. "Asks after them, after you. Even after me. I'll let him know that you're doing just fine—without him."

"Don't you dare." Phoebe was inches away from Stella, with no memory of how she'd gotten there. That wasn't good. It meant that she'd forgotten to move like a warmblood.

"What are you going to do?" Stella asked softly. "Bite me?"

Phoebe wanted to. She also wanted to wipe that superior expression from her sister's face and scare the piss out of her friends.

"You're not my type," Phoebe replied.

Stella's eyes widened.

"Don't fuck with me, Stella," Phoebe warned her sister, dropping her voice. "As you can see, I'm not the same good girl I used to be."

Phoebe turned her back on Stella. It felt freeing, as though she were saying farewell to the ways of the past in favor of a new, shiny future.

She walked away, the sky-high heels of her boots clicking on the pavement. Jason caught up with her and slowed her walk to what felt like a crawl.

"Easy there, Phoebe," Jason said.

They walked in silence for hours, until the moon had fully risen and the lights of Paris came on full blast, forcing Phoebe to put her sunglasses back on.

"Tonight didn't go very well, did it?" Phoebe asked Jason.

"You were supposed to hunt and feed from a live human," Jason said. "Instead, you fought with your warmblooded sister in full view of her friends. On balance, I'd say it was mildly disastrous."

"Miriam is going to be furious."

"She is," Jason agreed.

Phoebe caught her lip in her teeth, anxious. "And I'm still hungry."

"You should have had Margot while you had the chance," Jason commented.

A middle-aged white woman strolled by, texting madly on her phone. She stopped, and dug in her purse.

"Do either of you have a light?" she asked, barely looking up from the screen.

"Sure," Jason replied, tossing his lighter to Phoebe with a smile.

⇥ 29 ⇤

Their Portion of Freedom

I began to unravel a few days after Matthew's birthday party. As with most crises, I didn't notice the warning signs. It was not until the first of July that I knew I was in trouble.

The day began well enough.

"Good morning, team!" I said brightly to Matthew when I finished showering and dressing. I slipped my feet into my waiting sneakers. "Time to rise and shine!"

Matthew glowered and then pulled me back into bed.

Our latest family project—managing two Bright Born children entering the terrible twos slightly ahead of schedule, one with a griffin and one who liked to bite—had proved far more difficult than finding Ashmole 782 and its missing pages, or facing down the Congregation and its ancient prejudices. Both of us were utterly exhausted.

After an energizing tussle under the canopy, Matthew and I went to the nursery to rouse the twins. Though the sun had barely risen, the rest of Team Bishop-Clairmont was awake and ready for action.

"Hungry." Becca's lower lip trembled.

"Sleeping." Philip pointed to Apollo. "Shh."

The griffin had abandoned the fireplace and somehow managed to climb into Philip's cradle. His weight caused it to list alarmingly, his long tail spilling out over the side. The cradle swayed gently in time to his snores.

"I think we should consider making the switch from cradle to cot," Matthew said, lifting Philip free of his blanket and the griffin's wings.

Apollo opened one eye. He stretched and then sprang into the air. Just when I thought he might hit the ground with a thud, he spread his wings and gently glided the remaining distance to the floor. Apollo pecked at his chest feathers and shook his wings into better order. His long tongue lapped around his eyes and mouth as if he were washing the sleepy dust away.

"Oh, Apollo," I said, unable to stifle a laugh at the griffin equivalent of the twins' morning routine: hair smoothing, pajama straightening, face washing.

Apollo bleated out a plaintive sound and hopped toward the stairs. He was ready for act two—breakfast.

Becca was chattering amiably to her spoon while pushing blueberries into her mouth with her fingers when Philip began to fuss.

"No. Down." He was twisting and thrashing in his booster seat while Matthew tried to clip him securely into place.

"If you would stay put while you eat, we wouldn't have to tie you to your chair," Matthew said.

With those words, something inside me snapped.

It had been well hidden, twisted tight in a dark part of my soul that I chose not to notice.

The pottery bowl containing my breakfast of cereal and fruit fell from my hands. It shattered when it hit the hard flagstone floor, sending ceramic shards and berries flying.

A chair. Small. Pink. There was a purple heart painted on the back of it.

"Diana?" Matthew's face was creased with concern.

Marthe entered the room, alert as ever to any change in the household. She located Becca, sitting in her chair with spoon aloft and eyes round. Philip had stopped thrashing and was staring at me.

"Uh-oh," Philip said.

Shaking extended up my arms. My shoulders trembled.

Something happened in that chair. Something that I hadn't liked. Something that I wanted to forget.

"Sit down, *mon coeur*," Matthew said gently, resting his hands on my back.

"Don't touch me," I said, twisting and thrashing like Philip.

Matthew stepped back, his hands rising in a gesture of surrender.

"Marthe, go get Sarah," he said, his gaze fixed on me.

Fernando appeared in the kitchen doorway as Marthe rushed past.

"Something's wrong," I said, my eyes filling with tears. "I'm sorry, Matthew. I didn't mean—"

I didn't mean to fly.

"The tree house," I whispered. "It was after Dad built that tree house in the backyard."

I stood on the platform that stretched between the stout limbs. It was autumn, and the leaves were the color of fire and iced with a coating of frost. I stretched out my arms, feeling the touch of air all around me, whispering. I knew I wasn't supposed to be up there without an adult. That had been drummed into me, over and over and over.

"What happened?" Fernando asked Matthew.

"I don't know. Something triggered her," Matthew replied.

My arms rose.

"Oh, shit." Sarah had arrived, pulling her kimono around her. "I thought I smelled power."

Don't lie to me, Diana. I can smell it when you do magic.

"What does it smell like?" I wondered, then and now.

The room was filling up with creatures—Marcus and Agatha, Marthe and Sarah, Fernando and Jack. Becca and Philip. Apollo. Matthew. They were all watching me.

I didn't care if my mother could smell my magic or not. I wanted to play with the air. I dove headfirst into it. Something jerked at my arm. Fear gripped my belly, held fast, twisted me around.

"Go away," I shouted. "Just leave me alone. Stop watching me."

Philip burst into tears, confused by my outburst.

"Don't cry," I pleaded. "Please don't cry, baby. I'm not mad. Mommy's not mad."

Becca joined in, sobbing along with her brother as her surprise gave way to something else.

Fear.

Past and present hit me in terrifying, bruising waves. I did the only thing I could think of to escape.

I rose into the air and flew away, up the stairs and out onto the top of the tower where I dove, headfirst, into the whispering air.

This time no one tried to stop me from flying.

This time, I didn't hit the ground.
This time, I used my magic.
This time, I soared.

MATTHEW WAS WAITING on the battlements when I returned from my unscheduled flight. Though it was a bright, sunny day, he had lit a fire and thrown green wood on it to create a plume of smoke, as if he wanted to make sure I could find my way home again. I could see it as I approached, a thick gray feather rising into the blue sky.

Even after my feet touched down on the wooden deck, Matthew didn't take a step toward me, tension and worry making his body a tight spring. When I came to him, slowly at first and then in a rush, Matthew folded me into arms that had the gentle strength of an angel's wings.

I sighed against him, my body cleaving to his. Exhausted, emotionally drained, and confused, I let him hold me up for a few moments. Then I drew away and met his eyes.

"My parents didn't spellbind me once, Matthew," I told him. "They did it over and over, little by little, month after month. They started small, with tiny leashes and weights to keep me here, to keep me from flying, to keep me from starting fires. By the time Knox came to the house, they had no choice but to tie me up in so many knots I couldn't escape them."

"I triggered your memories, trying to buckle Philip into his chair." Matthew looked devastated.

"That was just the final straw," I said. "I think it was Marcus's stories about Philippe, and the hidden hand that guided his every action that broke through the walls I built around those memories."

In the grass below, the children chattered while they played with Apollo. Soft *plonks* suggested that Marcus was fishing in the moat. Hushed conversations among the adults provided a quiet, steady background melody. But there were vampires among them—young and old—and I had no wish to be overheard.

"The memories aren't the worst of it. It's the fear—not just mine, but my parents', too. Even though I know it happened long ago, it *feels* as though it's still happening now," I said, keeping my voice low. "I have this terrible sense that something awful is about to happen. It's as if my anxiety attacks are back, only they're worse."

"That's how memories of trauma surface," Matthew said, also quiet.

"Trauma?" The word conjured up images of cruelty and violence. "No, Matthew. That's not it. I loved my parents. They loved me. They were trying to protect me."

"Of course they meant to help, to protect, to guide," Matthew said. "But when a child finds out later that her parents have been choosing her life path all along, it's impossible not to feel betrayed."

"Like Marcus." I had never thought of my parents as having anything in common with Philippe de Clermont. They were so different, and yet in this they were so alike.

Matthew nodded.

"This family tradition stops here and now," I said, voice rough. "I won't tie up my children. I don't care if Becca bites every vampire in France, and Philip gathers a squadron of griffins. No more leashes. Baldwin is just going to have to deal with it."

Matthew's smile was slow, but wide.

"So you aren't going to be angry with me when I tell you that I destroyed all of the children's blood and hair samples without running tests on them?" he asked.

"When?" I asked.

"Just before Christmas," Matthew replied. "When we were at the Old Lodge. It seemed to me the best present I could give Rebecca and Philip was uncertainty."

I flung my arms around my husband and held him close. "Thank you," I whispered in his ear.

For the first time in my life, I was absolutely thrilled not to have all the answers.

LATER THAT DAY, I was watching the children sleeping on the rug in the library. Since I'd returned from my unscheduled flight, they had been clingy and wanted to stay close to me. I wanted to be near them, too.

I watched the threads that surrounded them shimmer and flicker with each deep breath they took. The twins had spent months in the womb together, and even now there were threads that seemed to bind them. I wondered if it was always this way with twins and whether anything would be strong enough to snap their close bonds, or if they would simply loosen and stretch with the passing of time.

Becca flung her arm over her head. An iridescent strand of silver dripped off her elbow. I followed it as it snaked over the sides of her cradle, coiled around the leg, and proceeded across the floor to—

My big toe.

I wiggled my foot, and Becca's arm jerked slightly, then relaxed again.

A cold stare settled on me. Feeling guilty that Matthew had discovered me interfering with our daughter's autonomy, I turned.

But it was Fernando who was watching me, not my husband. I got up and left the room, leaving the door open a crack so that I could keep my eye on the twins.

"Fernando," I said, drawing him away from the door. "Is there something you need? Is Jack all right?"

"Everyone else is fine," Fernando said. "Are you? I know how much you admire Philippe."

A green shade flitted down the corridor. Even dead, my father-in-law couldn't leave matters alone.

"I knew that Philippe was watching me in the past, and that he kept watching me until the day he died," I said. "Nothing Marcus said was a surprise, exactly. I just hadn't drawn the connection between what he did and what my parents did."

"Believing you are being manipulated and having proof of it are very different things," Fernando said.

"I wouldn't say 'manipulated,' exactly." Like "trauma," "manipulation" sounded so negative and malicious.

"To give him credit, Philippe was uncommonly good at it," Fernando continued. "When I first met him, I thought he must be part witch to be able to predict the actions that others would take with such accuracy. Now I know that he was just an expert judge of a creature's ethics—not just their moral sense, but the habits of thought and body that inform every action."

Even now, though Philippe was a ghost, I could feel his eyes upon me. I glanced across the landing.

There he stood, clothed in the dark robes of a medieval prince, his arms crossed before him and a slight smile on his face.

Watching.

"I know he's there. I can feel him, too." Fernando jerked his head toward the corner. "Ysabeau might drive his spirit away with her need, but not I. I would have liked Philippe's acceptance, of course, but I have never needed anything from him."

Hugh was always Philippe's favorite, you see," Fernando continued. "That never changed—not even after Hugh mated with a man with skin too dark to pass as white, a man who could not be useful to the family except as a servant or a slave. I could never sit down at the table next to Hugh, or join him in the corridors of power where Philippe was so at home."

Whatever hurt Philippe had caused Fernando had been tempered with bitterness over the course of many centuries, and his voice remained steady and even because of it.

"Do you know why Hugh was so special to his father?" Fernando asked.

I shook my head.

"Because Philippe could not figure him out," Fernando said. "None of us could. Not even me, though I drank from his heart vein. There was something mysterious and pure in Hugh that could never be touched or known. One felt it nonetheless, always waiting to be discovered. Without possessing that missing piece of Hugh, Philippe could never be sure of him or what he might do."

I thought of Matthew's decision not to probe into the twins' DNA for genetic markers of magic and blood rage. Fernando's story made me even more confident that it was the right one.

"You remind me of Hugh, and have that same aura of holding a secret you are not yet ready to share," Fernando mused. "I think Philippe would have had a devil of a time keeping up with you. Perhaps that is why he made you his daughter."

"You're saying Philippe took me as his blood-sworn daughter because he was bored?" I said with a hint of amusement.

"No—it was the challenge. Philippe loved a challenge. And there was nothing he admired more than someone who stood up to him," Fernando replied. "It is why Philippe was so fond of Marcus, too—although he figured out what made Matthew's son tick faster than a clockmaker. He proved that in 1790, and after that, too."

"New Orleans," I said, thinking ahead to the revelations that were yet to come.

Fernando nodded. "But only Marcus can tell that story."

MARCUS'S ROOM AT LES REVENANTS was, like most of the bedrooms, tucked into one of the round towers. Because I had wanted all of Matthew's family to feel welcome and at home here, I'd consulted each of them on what we could do to make the space comfortably and uniquely theirs. Marcus wanted nothing more than a bed with plenty of pillows so he could read in it, a deep chair by the window for watching the world go by, some thick rugs to keep the room quiet, and a television. Today the door to his room was slightly ajar, and I took it as a sign that he was receiving visitors.

Before I could rap on it to request entry, Marcus opened it.

"Diana." Marcus ushered me in. "We thought you might come."

Matthew and Ysabeau were with him.

"You're busy," I said, withdrawing slightly. "I'll come back later."

"Stay," Marcus said. "We're talking about heresy and treason. Typically cheerful subjects for members of the de Clermont family."

"Marcus is telling us what it was like for him after Philippe sent him away." Ysabeau was watching her grandson closely.

"Let's not mince words, *Grand-mère*. Grandfather banished me." Marcus had *Common Sense* in his hand. He held it up. "I left with this book, Fanny, and a sack of letters for Matthew. And I wasn't asked to come back again for half a century."

"You made it clear that you didn't want us to interfere in your life," Ysabeau said, her face stony.

"But you did interfere." Marcus paced the edges of the room like a caged animal. "Philippe was still directing my life. Grandfather spent most of the next hundred years dogging my footsteps. Edinburgh, London, Philadelphia, New York, New Orleans. No matter where I was, or what I was doing, there were always reminders that he was watching. Judging."

"I didn't realize you knew," Ysabeau said.

"You can't have thought I was that oblivious," Marcus said. "Not after those last days in Paris, with you turning up at Gil's house—with Tom Paine, no less. Then Fanny appeared at the Café Procope. Finally, Philippe himself appeared in Veronique's flat. It was all a bit orchestrated."

"Not Philippe's finest moment," Ysabeau agreed, her eyes glittering strangely. It looked as though there was a red film over them.

Ysabeau was crying.

"That's enough, Marcus," Matthew said, concerned for his mother's well-being. She had still not fully recovered from Philippe's death, nor had she stopped grieving.

"When did this family decide the truth was unacceptable?" Marcus demanded.

"Honesty was never part of our family code," Ysabeau said. "Right from the very start, we had so much to hide."

"My contracting blood rage didn't make the de Clermonts more open," Matthew said, accepting part of the blame. "I often think of how different everything would be, had I not been susceptible to it."

He sounded wistful.

"You wouldn't have Becca and Philip, for a start," Marcus retorted. "You've got to stop with this regret, Matthew, or you are going to damage your children in ways that you won't be able fix, like you did for me in New Orleans."

Matthew looked startled.

"I knew, Matthew," Marcus said wearily. "I knew Philippe sent you, and that you would have let me sort it out myself if left to your own devices. I knew that he ordered us all dead—Philippe wouldn't have made an exception for me, or for anyone else, not if our existence would put Ysabeau in danger. You disobeyed Grandfather's orders, even though Juliette was right at your elbow, egging you on to do the 'right thing' and put me down."

I had wanted to know about New Orleans and thought it would be hard to get Marcus to talk about that terrible time. It seemed he was ready to revisit what had happened there.

"Philippe was always more ruthless with those he loved than those he pitied," Ysabeau said. Something in her expression told me she knew this firsthand.

"Father wasn't perfect, you're right," Matthew said. "Nor was he all-knowing and all-seeing. He never dreamed you would go back to America, for a start. Philippe did everything he could to make England attractive to you—Edinburgh, the house in London, William Graham. But there were two things he just couldn't control."

"What?" Marcus asked, genuinely curious.

"The unpredictability of epidemic disease and your gifts as a healer," Matthew replied. "Philippe was so busy trying to keep you away from Veronique and the Terror in France that he forgot the ties you had to Philadelphia. After Marat was assassinated, Philippe gave notice to the captain of every ship that they were not to transport you across the channel for any reason. If they did, they would find their business affairs in ruins."

"Really?" Marcus looked impressed. "Well, to be fair, only a lunatic would have chosen to go to Philadelphia in 1793. The guillotine was less terrifying than yellow fever. Quicker, too."

"There was never any question in my mind which path you would choose." Matthew gave his son a fond, proud look. "You did your duty as a physician and helped others. That's all you've ever done."

Morning Chronicle, *London*
24 October 1793
page 2

The execution took place on Wednesday the 16th.

. . .

Nothing like sorrow or pity for the Queen's fate was shewn by the people, who lined the streets, through which she had to pass. On her arrival at the Place de la Revolution, she was helped out of the carriage and ascended the scaffold with seeming composure. She was accompanied by a Priest, who discharged the office of Confessor. She was in a half-mourning dress, evidently not adjusted with much attention. Her hands being tied behind her, she looked around, without terror; her body being then bent forward by the machine, the axe was let down, and at once separated the head from the body. After the head was displayed by the Executioner, three young women were observed dipping their handkerchiefs in the streaming blood of the deceased Queen.

⇥ 30 ⇤

Duty

Marcus had lived in England for years and had gotten used to searching through newspapers for news from abroad. The first page was always dominated by playbills, advertisements for medical cures, real estate notices, and the sales of lottery tickets. News from America was usually on page three. Marat's assassination back in July had warranted mention only on page two.

Still, he was surprised to find the story of the trial and execution of Queen Marie Antoinette relegated to the same spot that Marat had once occupied on the second page, the two of them becoming strange bedfellows in death.

"They executed the queen," Marcus told Fanny quietly. It had become part of their morning routine to sit together and drink coffee and read the papers. "They called her a vampire."

Fanny looked up from her copy of *The Lady's Magazine.*

"Not in so many words," Marcus hastened to add. *"Marie Antoinette, widow of Louis Capet, has, since her abode in France, been the scourge and the blood-sucker of the French."*

"Widow Capet." Fanny sighed. "How has France come to this?"

Every bit of news coming from France told a fresh horror story of death, terror, and betrayal. Philippe and Ysabeau had fled Paris months ago, taking refuge at the family château, Sept-Tours. They did so to avoid the mounting violence. The Jacobins pledged to give a guillotine mounted on a wagon to each regiment of the army so that they could execute aristocrats as they progressed across France.

"Do not worry. The family has weathered worse storms within these walls,"

Ysabeau had written to him in one of the last letters he had received from his grandmother. *"No doubt we will survive this, too."*

But it was not just his grandparents who were in danger. So, too, were Lafayette and his family. The marquis was a prisoner in Austria, his wife and children under house arrest in the countryside. Thomas Paine was back in Paris, and stood against Robespierre and the other radicals in the National Convention.

And there was Veronique, about whom Marcus could discover nothing.

"We should go back," Marcus said to Fanny over the wide expanse of mahogany that dominated the dining room at Pickering Place.

"*Far* doesn't want us back," Fanny observed.

"I need to know Veronique is safe," Marcus said. "It's as though she has utterly disappeared."

"That is how vampires survive, Marcus," Fanny said. "We appear, we disappear, we transform ourselves into something else, and then we emerge, phoenixlike, from the ashes of our former lives."

John Russell burst into the room. He was wearing an extraordinary buff leather coat he'd bought from a trader in Canada, decorated with brightly dyed porcupine quills and glass beads. It almost covered his long, gaitered linen trousers, which marked him as a man who had utterly abandoned decency and tradition.

"Did you hear? They've killed that Austrian girl after all. I knew they would, in the end," John said, flourishing a newspaper of his own. He paused a moment and took in his surroundings. "Good morning, Fanny."

"Do sit, John. Have some coffee." Fanny gestured across the table's gleaming surface. Since Marcus left Edinburgh and returned to London a proper doctor, she had become the de facto lady of the house on Pickering Place, hosting card parties and receiving visitors in the afternoon.

"Much obliged." John dropped a familiar kiss on her cheek as he went past, and tugged gently on a flaxen strand that had escaped from the intricate pile on her head.

"Flirt," Fanny said, returning to her reading.

"Hoyden," John said fondly. He took one look at Marcus and knew something was wrong. "Still no word from Veronique."

"None." Every day Marcus expected a letter to come. When it didn't, Marcus searched the newspaper for a notice of her death, and took solace that he didn't find it—even though the fate of such a woman would not be newsworthy to anyone but him.

"Veronique has survived plague, famine, war, massacres, and the unwanted attention of men," Fanny said. "She will survive Robespierre."

Marcus had been enmeshed in revolution before, and knew the course of liberty could take sudden, disastrous turns. In France, the situation was made more complicated as vain and self-important men like Danton and Robespierre fought over the soul of the nation.

"I'm going out," Marcus said. He drank the last of his coffee. "You coming, John?"

"Hunting or business?" Russell asked, hedging his bets.

"Bit of both," Marcus replied.

MARCUS AND JOHN HEADED EAST from London's fashionable residential neighborhoods, through the bordellos and theaters of Covent Garden, and into the twisting thoroughfares of the ancient City of London.

When they reached Ludgate, Marcus rapped on the carriage roof to remind the driver to pay the toll to the lame beggar who was there at all hours of the day and night. The ruler of this part of London insisted that all creatures entering the square mile of his territory pay tribute in order to have safe passage. Marcus had never clapped eyes on the man, who was known as Father Hubbard and seemed to occupy a place in the civic imagination that was roughly akin to that of Gog and Magog, the ancient giants who guarded London from her enemies.

Their tribute paid, Marcus and John got stuck in traffic (one of the chief hazards of London life) and proceeded on foot to Sweetings Alley. It was narrow and dank and smelled like a piss pot. They found Baldwin in New Jonathan's, trading futures and cashing in his chits with the rest of the stockjobbers and bankers.

"Baldwin." Marcus took off his hat. He had stopped bowing, but when faced with one of the elder de Clermonts, it was impossible for him not to make some sign of respect.

"There you are. What kept you?" his uncle replied.

Baldwin Montclair was the last surviving full-blooded son of Philippe de Clermont. He was ginger-headed, with a temper to match, and underneath his forest-green stockbroker's suit he had the muscular, athletic body of a soldier. Whether marching across Europe or marching across bank accounts, Baldwin was a formidable opponent. Fanny had warned Marcus never to underestimate his uncle—and he had no intention of ignoring this piece of advice.

"Always a pleasure to see you, Baldwin," John said, his voice dripping with insincerity.

Baldwin looked John over from the tip of his fur-trimmed cap to the heels of his boots and made no reply. He returned his attention to his table, which was covered with empty wine jugs, inkpots, account books, and scraps of paper.

"We've heard about the queen's execution," Marcus said in an effort to capture his uncle's attention. "Do you have any more news from France?"

"No," Baldwin said shortly. "You must focus on the work to be done here. The brotherhood's estates in Hertfordshire are in need of attention. There are two probate cases to settle, and the surveys are years out of date. You will go at once, and see to them."

"I don't understand why Philippe bothered to send me to Edinburgh to study medicine," Marcus grumbled. "All I do is write reports and draw up writs and affidavits."

"Father is breaking you in," Baldwin said. "Like a new horse, or a shoe. A de Clermont must be adaptable and ready for any need that arises."

Russell made a rude gesture, which thankfully Baldwin missed as his nose was buried in a ledger.

Baldwin noticed an entry in the account book. "Ah. I wish I caught this before Gallowglass left for France."

"Gallowglass was here?" John asked.

"Yes. You just missed him." Baldwin sighed and scribbled some notes in his book. "He arrived from America last night. It really is too bad he left so soon. Matthew might have made use of this debt in his efforts to blackmail Robespierre."

"Matthew's in the Netherlands," Marcus said.

"No, he is in Paris. Father needed another set of eyes in France," Baldwin said.

"Christ's bones," John said. "Paris is the last place on earth I'd want to see. How many deaths can one man witness before he goes mad?"

"We can't all bury our heads in the sand and pretend the world isn't coming apart, Russell." Baldwin was nothing if not direct. "As usual, that means the de Clermonts must step to the fore and take charge. It is our duty."

"Good of your family to always think of others before yourselves." John didn't like Baldwin's sanctimony any more than Marcus did, but where Marcus was expected to remain silent and obedient, John was free to speak his mind. Sadly, Baldwin had no ear for sarcasm and took his words as a genuine compliment.

"Indeed," Baldwin replied. "Your mail is on the table, Marcus. Gallowglass brought some newspapers for you, as well as a letter that looks as though it was written by a madman."

Marcus picked up a copy of the *Federal Gazette* from the last days of August.

"Gallowglass usually makes better time coming from Philadelphia," Marcus noted, flipping through the pages.

"He stopped in Providence on the way here to take in supplies," Baldwin said, "on account of the fever."

Marcus began flipping through the paper.

. . . services at this alarming and critical period . . .

Words leaped out at him from the smudged newsprint.

Nothing so good to stop the progress of the yellow fever as the firing of cannon.

"Christ, no," Marcus said. Yellow fever was a terrible disease. It spread like wildfire in the city, especially in summer. People turned jaundiced, and spit up black and bloody vomit as the fever poisoned their bellies.

The College of Physicians having declared that they conceive FIRES to be very ineffectual, if not dangerous means of checking the progress of the prevailing fever . . .

Marcus scrambled through the rest of the mail looking for a later Philadelphia paper, but that was the only one. He did, however, locate a copy of Providence's *United States Chronicle* that bore a later date, and scoured it for an update on the situation to the south.

"*We are all much alarmed by the rapid progress a putrid fever is making in this city,*" Marcus read aloud. "*There is no accounting for it.*"

Marcus had grown up under the shadow of smallpox, had fought cholera and typhus in the army, and had grown accustomed to the febrile perils of urban life in Edinburgh and London. As a vampire, he was immune to human disease, which made it possible for him to treat the sick and observe the progress of an epidemic even after his warmblooded colleagues had sickened, abandoned their charges, or died. These accounts in the American newspapers marked the beginning of a cycle of death with which Marcus had grown familiar. There was little chance that matters in Philadelphia had improved. The city would have been ravaged by yellow fever between late August and the present moment.

He picked up the letter. *To Doc, in England or France.* The letters bobbed up and down like the waves.

It was from Adam Swift, and contained only one line.

I've left you my books, so don't let those bastards take them for taxes.

"Which way did Gallowglass go?" Marcus said, gathering up the newspapers and the letter.

"To Dover, of course. Here, take these, too." Baldwin held out some ledgers. "You'll need them in Hertfordshire."

"I'm not going to bloody Hertfordshire," Marcus said, halfway out the door. "I'm going to Philadelphia."

PHILADELPHIA'S STREETS WERE QUIET when Marcus arrived in early November. As usual, the westward crossing took far longer than the voyage from America to England. Marcus had driven Gallowglass and his crew mad with constant questions about speed and distance, and how much longer it was going to take.

When they arrived, Gallowglass ordered all the warmbloods to remain on the ship, and left the ship itself anchored well outside the harbor. It had been months since Gallowglass had last been in Philadelphia; there was no telling in what state they would find the city. Gallowglass rowed the distance from where he'd dropped anchor to the Old Ferry Slip between Arch and Market Streets. The wharves were empty, the only ships barren of crew and sails.

"This doesn't look good," Gallowglass said darkly as they tied up the skiff. As a precaution, his cousin took one of the oars and slung it over his shoulder. Marcus had a pistol and a small bag of medical supplies.

"Jesus and his lambs," Gallowglass said, pinching his nose shut as they turned down Front Street. "What a stench."

This was Marcus's first time back in Philadelphia since he had become a vampire. The city had always smelled bad. But now—

"Death." Marcus gagged. The odor of rotting flesh was everywhere, replacing the more familiar fumes from the tanneries and the everyday filth of urban life. There was a strange, sharp tang in the air as well.

"And saltpeter," Gallowglass said.

"Please." A waif approached them wearing nothing but a smock and one shoe. It was impossible to tell whether the child was male or female. "Food. I'm hungry."

"We have none," Gallowglass said gently.

"What's your name?" Marcus asked.

"Betsy." The child's eyes were huge in a face that was miraculously pink and white, with no sign of yellow fever. Marcus put his pistol in his belt and picked up the child. There was no scent of death on her.

"I'll get you some," Marcus said, heading toward Dock Creek.

Like the area around the wharves, the busy streets were strangely empty. Dogs ran wild, and there was the occasional snuffle of a pig. Piles of manure rotted on corners, and market stalls were abandoned. It was so quiet that Marcus could hear the creaking of the rigging on the masts of the ships. There was a steady clop of horses' hooves on cobbles. A wagon came into view. The driver had pulled his hat low, and wore a kerchief over his nose and mouth. He looked like a highwayman.

The wagon carried dead bodies.

Marcus turned the child away from the sight, though he suspected she had seen worse.

As the driver came closer, Marcus saw that his skin was black and his eyes weary.

"Are you sick?" the man called out, his voice muffled.

"No. We've just arrived," Marcus said. "Betsy needs food."

"They all do," the man said. "I'll take her to the orphanage. They'll feed her there."

Betsy clung to Marcus.

"I think I'll take her to German Gerty's instead," Marcus said.

"Gert's been gone for years." The driver's eyes narrowed. "You seem to know a lot about Philadelphia for someone who just arrived. What did you say your name was?"

"He didn't," Gallowglass replied. "I'm Eric Reynold, captain of the *Aréthuse*. This is my cousin, Marcus Chauncey."

"Absalom Jones," the driver said, touching his hat.

"Is the fever gone?" Marcus asked.

"We thought so. There was some frost a few days ago, but the weather turned warm again and it's back," Jones said. "The shops were just opening and people coming back to their houses. They even flew the flag over Bush Hill to show there weren't any more sick people in it. There are now."

"The Hamilton estate?" Marcus dimly remembered the name of the mansion outside the city.

"Been vacant for years," Jones replied. "Mr. Girard took it over when the fever struck. This is one of his wagons. But these folks aren't going to the hospital. We're headed to potter's field."

Marcus and Gallowglass sent him on his way. They settled Betsy down on the street, each taking one of her small hands. She skipped between them, crooning a song, a testament to the resilience of children.

The tavern that Marcus had known as German Gerty's was still on the corner of Front and Spruce Streets. Dock Creek, however, had been paved over and was now a narrow, twisting alleyway that jutted off at an angle across Philadelphia's regular street plan.

The door was open.

Gallowglass gestured to Marcus to stay where he was and stuck first his oar, then the rest of him, inside the dark interior.

"It's all right," Gallowglass reported, sticking his head out a window. "Nobody here but some rats and someone who died long before August."

To Marcus's astonishment, the skeleton was still sitting in the front window, though he had lost his left radius and ulna. His left hand was perched rakishly atop his head.

They searched high and low for food, but found none. Betsy's lips started to quiver. The child was famished.

Marcus heard a *snick*.

"Stop there."

He turned, his hands up in the air.

"We're not here to rob you," Marcus said. "We just need some food for the girl."

"Doc?" The man standing before them holding a musket in his trembling hands looked like something out of a cartoon, a caricature of a human being with yellow skin, blackened lips, and red-rimmed eyes.

"Vanderslice?" Marcus lowered his hands. "Christ, man. You should be in bed."

"You came. Adam said you would." Vanderslice dropped the gun and began to weep.

THEY GOT VANDERSLICE UPSTAIRS, where they found stale bread that had not yet gone moldy, a bit of cheese, and some beer. They settled Betsy in a corner as far away from Vanderslice's bed as possible. It was covered with vomit and flies. Marcus stripped the bed and tossed the sheets and blanket out the window.

"He's better off on the floor," Marcus said tersely when Gallowglass started to lower Vanderslice onto the mattress.

Gallowglass and Marcus used their coats to make a pallet, and Marcus cleaned up his friend as best he could.

"You look good, Doc," Vanderslice said, his eyes rolling around with fever. "Death suits you."

"I'm not dead, nor are you," Marcus replied. He held some of the beer up to Vanderslice's lips. "Drink. It will help with the fever."

Vanderslice turned his head. "Can't. It burns going down, and it burns worse coming up."

Gallowglass shook his head at Marcus. *This is hopeless*, his expression read.

But Vanderslice had been the first to make room for Marcus beside a campfire when he was frozen and starving and on the run from his ghosts. It was Vanderslice had shared food with him, and his blanket, at Trenton. Vanderslice had whistled Christmas songs when he was on patrol duty, no matter the season, and told bawdy jokes when Marcus's spirits were low. When Marcus had been utterly alone in the world, afraid and without kith or kin, Vanderslice had accepted him like a member of his family.

Marcus might have killed his own father, but he had no intention of losing Vanderslice. He'd lost enough—his home, his mother and sister, countless patients, Dr. Otto, and now Veronique.

Marcus wanted someone to belong to again. Someone who would restore his faith in family after Obadiah and the de Clermonts had made him doubt the bonds of blood and loyalty.

"I can make the burn go away," Marcus said. He crouched down next to his friend—his brother.

"No, Marcus," Gallowglass said.

"It will hurt like hell at first, but you won't feel much pain after that," Marcus continued, as if his cousin hadn't spoken. "It takes a bit of getting used to, but you'll have to drink blood to survive. And you'll have to learn to hunt. You never could bait a fishhook, never mind bring down a deer, but I'll teach you."

"Have you lost your fucking mind?" Gallowglass grabbed Marcus by his collar and hauled him to his feet. "You're too young to start a family."

"Let go of me, Gallowglass." Marcus's voice was even, but he was prepared to strangle the man if his cousin refused. The more time that passed, the more obvious his choice became and the more resolute he was to save Vanderslice's life. "I've ripened now, you see, and I may not be your equal in size, or strength, or age, but that's been true my whole life."

Marcus's intentions must have been clear in his expression. Gallowglass dropped him with a blistering oath that had Vanderslice wheezing with appreciation.

"He reminds me of that French *kakker*," Vanderslice said. "What was his name? Beauclere or du Lac or something like that."

"De Clermont," Matthew and Gallowglass said in unison.

"That's it. De Clermont. Wonder whatever happened to him?" Vanderslice said. "Probably got his head chopped off in France, along with his friend."

"They're both still alive, actually," Marcus said. "The chevalier de Clermont saved me at Yorktown. I had a fever, like you."

Vanderslice looked at Marcus skeptically. "Not even you can save me, Doc. I'm too far gone."

"Yes I can," Marcus said.

"Wanna bet?" Vanderslice was always up for a wager.

"Don't do it, Marcus," Gallowglass warned. "For the love of God, listen to me. Matthew was never supposed to make any more children, and you've promised not to do it, either. Granddad said—"

"Bugger off, Gallowglass," Marcus said pleasantly. He was watching Vanderslice closely, and though he was lucid now, his heartbeat was skipping faster than Betsy had on her way to the tavern, and his breath was shallow. "Take Betsy with you."

"If you break your word to Philippe, you'll regret it," Gallowglass said.

"He'll have to find me first," Marcus replied. "No man's reach is indefinite, Gallowglass."

"I thought that—once. We all believed it, once." Gallowglass told him. "And we all learned better."

"Thank you for bringing me to Philadelphia. Please tell Ysabeau where I am." Marcus knew that so long as his grandmother knew where he was, Matthew would find out. And if Matthew knew, then he would inform Veronique—if she were still alive, that is. Marcus could do nothing to save Veronique, but Vanderslice was another matter.

"And that's it. Thanks, and don't let the door hit you on the arse on your way out?" Gallowglass snorted. He beckoned to Betsy, who was listening to their conversation with interest. "Come, lass. Let's let these two brew up their cup of disaster and drink from it, while we take a walk and look for your mam."

"Mumma's sleeping," Betsy said.

"We shall see if we can rouse her," Gallowglass said, taking her by the hand. "You best wake up, too, Marcus. You can't be turning everybody you love into *wearhs*. It's not how the world works."

"Good-bye, Gallowglass." Marcus looked over his shoulder. "And I meant what I said. Thank you for bringing me to Philadelphia."

Fever or no fever, this was where Marcus was supposed to be. Here, in this familiar place where he had saved some lives and been saved by Dr. Otto's faith in him and the Associators' friendship. Here, in Philadelphia, where he had drunk in the atmosphere of liberty and freedom in that heady summer of 1777.

When the sounds of Gallowglass's heavy footsteps and Betsy's piping voice had faded, Marcus looked down to discover that Vanderslice was studying him.

"You look exactly as you did fifteen years ago," Vanderslice said. "What are you, Marcus?"

"A vampire." Marcus settled back against the edge of Vanderslice's filthy bed. "I drink blood. Animal blood. Human blood, too. It keeps me from aging. It keeps me from dying."

Vanderslice's eyes flickered with fear.

"Don't worry. I'm not going to drink yours—unless you want me to take it all, so that I can give you back some of mine in exchange." Marcus was determined to do a better job of explaining what was about to happen to Vanderslice than Matthew had done with him, and drew on what Gallowglass had told him on board the *Aréthuse*. "Humans aren't the only creatures in the world, you see. There are vampires, like me, who drink blood. There are also witches, who wield unspeakable power. They can die, though, just like humans. So can daemons. They're really clever. I thought you might be a daemon, but you don't smell like one."

Marat had smelled like fresh air and electricity, as if one of Dr. Franklin's experiments had come to life.

"Daemon?" Vanderslice's voice was faint.

"I like daemons," Marcus said fondly, still thinking of Marat. "You would, too. Never a dull moment when there are daemons around. Vampires can be a bit unimaginative."

Vanderslice wiped the back of his hand across his mouth. It came away black and bloodied. He examined it for a moment, then shrugged.

"What have I got to lose?" Vanderslice said.

"Not much," Marcus admitted. "You're going to die either way. The only difference is that if I take your life before the fever does, you can drink my blood and probably survive. No guarantees, though. I've never done this before."

"That's what you said to Cuthbert when you cut that wire out of his thumb," Vanderslice said. "He did all right, as I remember."

"If you come out of this alive, you'll have to tell me all about Cuthbert, and Adam's last days, and even Captain Moulder," Marcus said. "Deal?"

"Deal," Vanderslice replied with a hint of his old grin. "But only if you return the favor and tell me stories of France."

"I met Franklin, you know," Marcus said.

"No!" Vanderslice began to wheeze again. This time, the laughter turned to coughing, the coughing to vomiting, and the vomit was blackly red.

"You sure, Claes?" Marcus had never called Vanderslice by his given name, but this seemed like the moment to do it.

"Why not," Vanderslice replied.

"I've got to bite you first, to take your blood," Marcus explained, just as he had once explained inoculation to the soldiers at Trenton. "Then I'll drink every drop of it."

"Won't you get sick with the yellow fever if you do?" Vanderslice asked.

Marcus shook his head. "No. Vampires don't get sick."

"Sounds good to me," Vanderslice said wearily.

"You might get scared when I bite you, but try not to fight me. It will be over before you know it," Marcus said, using his best bedside manner. "Then I'll ask you to take my blood. Drink as much of it as you can. You'll see things—all sorts of things. Betsy and Gallowglass, my voyage here on the ship, the chevalier de Clermont. Don't let that stop you. Just keep drinking."

"Any pretty girls?" Vanderslice said.

"A few," Marcus said. "But one of the prettiest is your great-grandmother, so no lewd thoughts."

Vanderslice crossed his heart with trembling fingers. "Then what happens?"

"Then we figure out how we're going to survive in a city full of dead people until it's safe to move you somewhere else." Marcus figured there was no point in being anything less than honest. "You ready?"

Vanderslice nodded.

Marcus took his friend into his arms. He held him close, like a lover. Like a child. He hesitated. What if Gallowglass was right? What if he regretted this?

Vanderslice looked up at him, quiet and trusting.

Marcus bit into his friend's neck. He tasted sour and dirty, bitter with fever and the sickly taste of imminent death. It was all Marcus could do to continue, to keep drawing Vanderslice's blood into his mouth and then swallow it down.

He kept going, though. He owed Vanderslice that.

When there was nothing more to take, and Vanderslice's veins were dry and his heart on the verge of stopping, Marcus bit into his own wrist and held it up to Vanderslice's mouth.

"Drink." Marcus's voice had the same note of calm concern that it did when he was seeing a patient, or working on a hospital ward. *Trust me*, was the unspoken message.

Vanderslice did. He latched on with teeth and tongue, instinctively thirsty for what would bring him back to life.

Marcus had to stop Vanderslice—his son, he reminded himself—before he passed out from loss of blood. He couldn't take care of an infant if he were out cold. Gently, he drew away. Vanderslice snarled at him.

"You can have more," Marcus told him. "Just let that settle for a moment."

Vanderslice covered his ears. "Why are you shouting?" he whispered.

"I'm not. Your senses are sharper, that's all," Marcus explained.

"I'm thirsty," Vanderslice complained.

"You will be. For weeks," Marcus said. "Tired, too. But you won't be able to sleep. I didn't sleep for nearly two years after Matthew made me a vampire. Lie back and close your eyes. It's best if you don't try to do too much too fast."

That was one of the things that Marcus learned when he and Matthew had run from Yorktown to Pennsylvania to New York to Massachusetts. He was glad he got to share his hard-won knowledge with someone, instead of being the one always asking questions from older, more experienced vampires. So far, Marcus liked being a father.

"While you rest, I'll tell you about France. About your new family." Marcus felt a bit delirious himself, after all the exertion. He closed his eyes, too, pleased that it had all gone so well.

"I TOLD YOU not to do it," Gallowglass said, hauling Vanderslice out of the water.

"I had to. He deserved a second chance," Marcus said. "It was my duty—"

"No. Saving the world is *not* your duty. I know that's what Matthew tries to do, but it's going to get us all killed one day." Gallowglass shook the water off Vanderslice. "Your duty is to listen to Philippe and do precisely what he tells you and nothing more. You are supposed to be in Hertfordshire, counting sheep. Instead, you're in Philadelphia making babies."

"I'm not a baby," Vanderslice snarled, snapping his teeth at Gallowglass.

"Have you ever seen a toothless vampire?" Gallowglass asked Vanderslice.

"No," he replied.

"There's a reason for that," Gallowglass growled. "Try to bite me again and you'll learn what it is."

"Why is he so . . ." Marcus waved his hands in the air, unable to put Vanderslice's behavior into words. Being an infant wasn't easy, but Vanderslice was behaving like a lunatic, running after dogs in the street and stealing meat from the butchers in the market house. If he wasn't more careful, he'd get himself killed or, even worse, arrested.

"Because you're too young to be a father, Marcus. I told you as much," Gallowglass said. "There are good reasons why Philippe forbade you from siring children."

"What are they?" Marcus demanded.

"I can't tell you." Gallowglass dropped Vanderslice on the slimy cobblestones of Front Street. They were coated with bits of rotten fish, seaweed, and manure. "You need to ask Matthew."

"Matthew isn't here!" Marcus shouted, at the end of his tether.

"And you can thank your lucky stars for that, lad," Gallowglass said. "Take my advice. Dry out young Claes and leave Philadelphia. He's known here. You may be, too. Go to New York. That's a city that will swallow you both up whole, and nobody will notice."

"What do I do in New York?" Marcus said.

Gallowglass looked at him with pity.

"Whatever you fancy," his cousin said. "And you better enjoy it, because it will be the last taste of independence you get after Matthew and Philippe find out what you've done."

MARCUS AND VANDERSLICE ARRIVED in New York the following January. The two of them started out at the wharves and warehouses of the lower tip of Manhattan, scratching out a living helping unload and load ships. The waterfront felt familiar, like Philadelphia but on a smaller scale. What New York lacked in size it more than made up for in violence, however. Gangs of humans roamed the streets, and there was a thriving black market in contraband and stolen goods. Marcus and his son participated in this marginal economy, helping themselves to unattended cargo and reselling it. Slowly, they began to accumulate some money—and a reputation for outliving most of their competitors. Vanderslice earned the nickname "Lucky Claes" because of it, but most people just called him Lucky, just as most called Marcus "Doc."

It was only a matter of time before Marcus grew tired of the thieving and the drinking that Claes enjoyed and instead devoted more time to his medical work. Like Philadelphia, New York had its fair share of yellow fever outbreaks, and Marcus found healing the sick was more satisfying than amassing a fortune. Between epidemics, Marcus tended to the problems of poverty among the city population and fought the constant scourges of typhus, cholera, and worms.

Vanderslice felt differently. He liked the pleasures that money brought. When Marcus encouraged him to pursue his own business interests, Vanderslice fell in with the wrong business partners, a pair of vampires newly arrived from Amsterdam with money to burn and no scruples. The Dutch vampires destroyed their rivals without a second thought or a pang of guilt, convinced that survival was the only evidence of valor. Vanderslice was soon spending more time with them than he was with Marcus, and the distance between them grew.

Marcus, who knew nothing about how to raise a child and even less about how to raise a man, failed to stem Vanderslice's rush toward inevitable disaster. Marcus's approach to fatherhood had none of Obadiah's violence, or Philippe's watchfulness, but was composed instead of Tom Buckland's unquestioning support, Dr. Otto's cheerfulness, and Matthew's benign neglect. This gentle concoction gave Vanderslice enough freedom to indulge in serious mischief with drunken whores and endless high-stakes card games without having to face any serious consequences.

One March morning in 1797, just days after John Adams was inaugurated as president, Marcus found Vanderslice at the foot of the stairs that led to their rented rooms, his throat cut from ear to ear, lying in a pool of his own blood, a victim of a risky gamble or a business deal that turned sour. Marcus used his own blood to seal the wound and tried to force more of it down Vanderslice's throat to revive him, but it was too late. His son—his family—was gone. No amount of vampire blood could bring back a lifeless corpse.

Marcus held Vanderslice and wept. It was the first time he had cried since he was a child, and what fell from his eyes this time was not salt water but blood. Gallowglass was proved right: Marcus did regret making Claes a vampire. Marcus erected a stone marker over Vanderslice's grave and swore he would abide by his promise to Philippe. He would never make another child without his grandfather's permission.

After Vanderslice's death, Marcus devoted himself entirely to medicine, working in the hospitals at Belle Vue and on Second Avenue. The practice of medicine seemed to change daily, with inoculation giving way to vaccination and physicians abandoning bloodletting in favor of other treatments. Marcus's Edinburgh education served him well, providing a solid foundation on which to build his skills. With a scalpel in one hand and his medical chest nearby, Marcus focused on his profession instead of his personal life.

Marcus was in New York, alone, when George Washington died in December 1799. A few weeks later, the century in which Marcus was born drew to a close. The events of the Revolutionary War were fading into memory for most Americans. Marcus wondered where Veronique was, and if Patience had had more children, and if his mother was still alive. He thought of Gallowglass, and wished his cousin were in New York to celebrate with him. Marcus wrote a letter to Lafayette, but did not know where to send it and so burned the paper in the fireplace so the wind might carry his good wishes to his absent friend. Marcus remembered his only child, Vanderslice, and felt regret for the ways he had failed him.

Revelers outside his house in the village of Greenwich, just on the outskirts of the city, welcomed the new century with enthusiastic shouts and dancing. Inside, Marcus poured himself a glass of wine, opened the worn covers of his copy of *Common Sense,* and remembered his youth.

The birthday of a new world is at hand. Marcus read the familiar words over and over, like a prayer, and hoped that Paine's prognostication would be proven true.

⇥ 31 ⇤

The True Father

We didn't usually celebrate Independence Day. But we had a Revolutionary War veteran in the house this year—two, actually, if one counted Matthew's service. I asked Sarah what she thought we should do in honor of the occasion.

"Are you sure Marcus would want to remember the war, and everything that came before and after?" Sarah looked doubtful. "He can't even eat flag cake. What's the point?"

The Bishop contribution to every Madison bake sale had been a vanilla sheet cake, with white frosting and rows of strawberries for stripes and blueberries for the blue field of stars.

"He's had a difficult few days, it's true," I said. Marcus's account of Philadelphia and what had happened there was on everyone's mind. No matter where our conversations started this summer, they always seemed to end with a tale of rebirth and the complications that followed.

Phoebe seemed both with us all the time and very far away as a result. I couldn't imagine how difficult the strange push and pull between past, present, and future felt to Marcus.

In the end, Marcus took Independence Day on himself.

"I've been thinking," Marcus said on the morning of the Fourth of July, "what about you and me put on a fireworks display tonight?"

"Oh, I don't know . . ." I couldn't imagine how Hector and Fallon would react to all that banging and booming—never mind Apollo and the twins.

"Come on, it will be fun. The weather is perfect," he insisted.

This was the Marcus I remembered from Oxford—irrepressible,

energetic, and full of charm and enthusiasm. With every shared memory, and as each passing day brought him closer to his August reunion with Phoebe, a little more of his hope and optimism returned. Marcus was less tangled in the strands of time that surrounded him. There were still red strands in a snarl of pain and regret, but there were hints of green for balance and healing, as well as twists of black and white for courage and optimism, along with Marcus's signature, sincere blue.

"What do you have in mind?" I asked with a laugh.

"Something with lots of color. It has to sparkle, of course, or Becca won't like it," Marcus said with a grin. "We can use the moat's reflections to make it seem like there are fireworks on the ground as well as in the sky."

"This is beginning to sound like a fireworks display at Versailles," I said. "I'm surprised you don't want illuminated fountains and arcs of water, accompanied by something by Handel."

"I'm up for that if you are." Marcus surveyed me over his coffee cup, a twinkle in his eye. "Though to be honest, I've never been much for all the trappings of monarchy—which definitely includes Handel."

"Oh, no." I warded him off with my hands. "If we are going to do fireworks, they're going to be normal, everyday fireworks—the kind that you buy in a stand at the side of the road. No magic. No witchcraft."

"Why?" Marcus asked.

We stood in silence for a moment. Marcus's blue eyes held a definite note of challenge.

"I don't see the point of doing something ordinary, when it could be extraordinary," he said. "I know it's been a crazy, fucked-up kind of summer. You weren't expecting to have me here the whole time, for a start. Nor did you think you'd have to relive the events of my past with me."

"But that's been the best part of it," I interrupted. "Far better than getting my grades in, or dealing with the Congregation, or even my research."

"I'm glad that my constant presence pales in comparison with Gerbert and Domenico," Marcus teased. "Still, we could all use a little bit of leavening in the lump. The summer hasn't exactly been a vacation thus far."

"What an expression!" I laughed. "Where did you learn that? It sounds like something Em would have said."

"The Bible." Marcus picked a blackberry out of the big bowl Marthe had left on the counter and popped it in his mouth. "You're not very well versed in your proverbs and parables, Professor Bishop."

"Guilty of being a pagan, your honor," I said, raising my hand high. "But I bet you don't know the names of all the sabbats witches observe and their dates, either."

"True." Marcus held out his hand. "So, do we have a deal?"

"I don't even know what I'm agreeing to," I said, reaching for it.

Marcus withdrew his hand slightly. "Once we shake, there's no backing out of it. A deal's a deal."

"Deal." I shook Marcus's hand.

"Don't worry," he said. "What could possibly go wrong?"

"Good lord." Matthew stood, mouth open, and surveyed our work with amazement.

Marcus was hanging from a tree branch like a possum, a string of lights in his teeth. I was drenched and sunburned, and one of my eyebrows was a trifle singed. Bales of hay studded the field on the far side of the moat. We'd rowed two of the wide-bottom boats around from the boathouse and tied them to the shallow dock that Marcus and Matthew used for fishing. I'd decorated the boats with garlands of red and white flowers to make them look more festive.

I threw my arms around Matthew and gave him a kiss. "Amazing, isn't it?"

"I had no idea we were in for such an extravagant production," Matthew said, grinning down at me. "A few sparklers, maybe, but this?"

"Wait until you see the fireworks," I told him. "Marcus went to Limoges, and bought all the leftovers from the Fêtes des Ponts in June."

"We've got something special planned for afterward," Marcus said, draping the lights over the end of the branch. He dropped his legs, swung for a moment by one hand like a monkey, and then plummeted thirty feet straight down.

"And when is this all starting?" Matthew asked.

"Ten thirty—sharp," Marcus said. "Are the twins taking naps?"

"I left them—and Apollo—sleeping soundly," Matthew said.

"Good, because I don't want them to miss this." Marcus gave me a salute and went off smiling. As he walked, his smile turned to whistles.

"I haven't seen him like this for months," Matthew said.

"Me, neither."

"We're just passing the halfway point in his separation from Phoebe," Matthew said. "Maybe realizing that so much time has already gone by accounts for his change of mood?"

"Possibly. Telling his tale has helped, too." I looked up at Matthew. "Do you think he'll be ready to talk about New Orleans soon?"

A shadow crossed Matthew's face. He shrugged.

"Speaking of time," Matthew said, deliberately changing the subject. "Have you heard from Baldwin? His two-week deadline came and went without a word."

"No, I haven't talked to him." I didn't even have to cross my fingers. It was the absolute truth.

That didn't mean Baldwin hadn't left me a dozen messages, in both my voicemail and my e-mail. He'd also written me a letter, which bore a Japanese postmark. I'd dropped it in the moat without reading it, comforted by the fact that he was halfway around the world.

"Odd. It's not like Baldwin to let something like that slip," Matthew mused.

"Maybe he changed his mind." I took Matthew's hand in mine. "I'm going to weave a spell around Apollo. Want to come and watch?"

Matthew laughed.

"Wait, I have an even better idea. You'll have to catch me if you want to find out what it is." I crooked my finger at him. Then I took off at a run.

"That is the best invitation I've had in some time," he said, strolling after me.

I kept running, knowing this was just part of the chase, knowing Matthew would catch me, still surprised when he tackled me to the ground, his arms cradling me from impact, a few yards from our secret hideaway.

At some point in the late nineteenth century, Philippe had constructed a small boathouse inside a curve of the moat that looked over the estate's open fields and forests. The structure was typical of its time, made out of wood rather than the castle's stone, and decorated with all manner of gingerbread trim.

It had fallen into a state of romantic ruin, the original yellow paint on the outside faded and peeling, and the inside dusty with disuse. Matthew had fixed the roof to make it weathertight again, and had big plans to restore it to its former glory. Now that he'd widened and deepened the moat, and stocked it with fish, these plans no longer seemed as ridiculous as they once had. I could imagine us all enjoying a paddle around on the moat as the children got older—though the moat was never going to provide me with enough room to ply the oars on a racing scull.

Matthew and I often fled to the boathouse when we needed some privacy. There was a sturdy, welcoming chaise longue inside, which we had grown fond of during our stolen moments away from the twins. This summer, with all that was going on with Marcus, not to mention Agatha and Sarah visiting, we hadn't spent as much time here as we had hoped.

We made use of the chaise and lingered to watch the clouds through the skylight. The puffs of white came into view against the bright blue background, changed their shapes, and moved on in a never-ending parade.

We stayed at the boathouse for as long as we thought we could get away with before someone would come to look for us. When we could postpone it no longer, Matthew helped me to my feet and we returned to the house, hand in hand, relaxed and happy.

But I felt the tension the moment we stepped into the kitchen.

"What's wrong?" I said, looking around the kitchen for signs of fire, flood, or other natural disasters.

"You've got a visitor," Sarah said, munching her way through a bowl of popcorn. "Marcus told him to go away—well, he told him to bugger off, but that's the same thing."

A bloodcurdling shriek came from upstairs.

"Apollo really doesn't like your brother, Matthew," Sarah said. "He's flying around in the stairwell, carrying on as if it's the end of the world."

Matthew gave a sniff and turned to me with an accusing stare. "You said you hadn't heard from Baldwin."

"No, I said I hadn't talked to him," I said, feeling that it was important to draw the distinction. "Not the same thing at all."

"Where are the children?" Matthew demanded.

"Jack and Marthe are with them. Marcus and Agatha are with Fernando in the great hall, trying to talk Baldwin down off the mountain," Sarah said around another mouthful of popcorn. "I volunteered for lookout duty. Baldwin makes me nervous."

Matthew stalked off in the direction of the hall.

"Should you call Ysabeau?" Sarah asked.

"Already on her way," I said. "We invited her to come for the fireworks."

"Guess we won't have to wait until dark for the excitement to start after all." Sarah dusted the salt off her hands and hopped off the stool. "Let's go. We don't want to miss anything."

When we arrived in the hall, Matthew and Baldwin were facing off across the carpet while Marcus and Fernando urged them both to see sense. Agatha's contributions to the negotiations involved pointing out that this whole family drama smacked of male privilege.

"You need to take a deep breath and realize that this isn't all about you," Agatha said. "You're behaving like these children are chattel."

"God, I love that woman," Sarah said, beaming. "Down with patriarchy. Right on, Agatha."

I had had it, too. I turned my hands heavenward and splayed my fingers wide. Brightly colored strands appeared, snaking down each finger, across my palms, and around my wrists.

"With knot of one, the spell's begun," I said.

"This is what happens when you don't answer your e-mail!" Baldwin said, shaking his finger at me.

"With knot of two, the spell be true." I touched the tips of my thumb and little finger together. A silver star emerged from where the two met.

"Don't speak to Diana like that, Baldwin," Matthew warned.

"With knot of three, the spell is free," I said, releasing the star into the sky.

"Cool," Sarah said, watching my every move.

"With knot of four, the power is stored." My ring finger glowed with an inner, golden light, and the silver star grew in size, floating toward the knot of men in the hall.

"Does anyone smell something burning?" Marcus wrinkled his nose.

"With knot of five, the spell will thrive." I touched the green thumb on my right hand to my middle finger, uniting the energy of the goddess as mother with the spirit of justice.

"Well, well," Fernando said, looking at the five-pointed silver star that was hovering above him. "I don't believe anyone's ever put a spell on me."

"With knot of six, this spell I fix."

The star descended in a *whoosh*, tangling Matthew, a startled Baldwin and Marcus, and a bemused Fernando in its loops and twirls. With a flick of my fingers, I tightened the star so that it held them fast. Then I gave it an extra twist so that the more they struggled against the bonds, the more snug they would become.

"You lassoed us!" Marcus exclaimed.

"Diana went to camp in Montana one summer," Sarah said. "She wanted to be a cowgirl. I had no idea they taught her how to do *that*."

"You wanted to talk to me, Baldwin?" I said, advancing slowly on the group. "I'm all ears."

"Let me go," Baldwin said through clenched teeth.

"Not fun, is it, to be all tied up?" I asked.

"You've made your point," my brother-in-law said.

"Oh, come on," I said. "Since when has it been that easy to change your mind? As you see, Baldwin, I'm not against tying people up when they deserve it. But this branch of the family is done with turning their children into puppets and wrapping them in knots."

"If Rebecca has blood rage—"

"If Becca has blood rage. If Philip is a weaver. If, if, if," I interrupted. "We'll just have to wait and see."

"I told you to run tests," Baldwin said, trying to grab Matthew. The movement forced the bindings tighter, just as I intended.

Ysabeau arrived with a wicker hamper filled with bottles. She surveyed the scene and smiled.

"How I've missed family gatherings," she said. "What have you done this time, Baldwin?"

"All I'm trying to do is keep this family from self-destructing," Baldwin shouted. "Why is it so impossible for the rest of you to see the trouble Rebecca might cause? The child cannot go around biting people. If she has blood rage, she could give it to others."

Jack entered the room with Becca in his arms. Her eyes were red-rimmed, and her arms were wrapped tightly around Jack's neck. She had been crying.

"Stop it. All of you, just stop it," Jack said fiercely. "You're upsetting Becca."

Jack's voice was rough with emotion, but miraculously there was no sign of blood rage in his eyes. The children were often stabilizing influences on Jack, as though being responsible for their well-being trumped any other emotions or concerns he might have.

"Becca is a *baby*," Jack said. "She couldn't hurt anybody. She's soft, and sweet, and trusting. How could you think Becca needs to be punished for being who she is?"

"Well said, Jack." Agatha was beaming with pride.

"Dad keeps telling me what happened to me as a child wasn't my fault. That the man who was supposed to take care of me didn't hurt me because I was bad, or evil, or a whore's son, or any of the things that he told me," Jack continued.

Becca looked up at Jack as though she understood every word he said. She reached out with one of her small, fragile fingers and touched him lightly on the lips.

Jack took the time to give her a reassuring smile before resuming.

"Mum and Dad *trust* me," Jack said. "Which means for the first time in my life, I feel like I can trust myself. That's what families are supposed to do—not order each other around and make promises nobody should have to keep."

I was so moved by Jack's speech that I forgot to hold on to my binding spell. It fell to the floor, making a bright and gleaming star around the feet of the de Clermont men.

The youngest male in the family, on whose small shoulders so many hopes and expectations already rested, toddled down the stairs, holding on to Marthe with one hand and Apollo's tail with the other. The three of them made a small but united pack.

"Nunkle!" Philip said, delighted to see Baldwin.

"We have a celebration planned for Independence Day," I said. "Are you staying for the fireworks, Baldwin?"

Baldwin hesitated.

"You and I could take a ride while we wait for the fun to start," Matthew said to his stepbrother. "It would be like old times."

Becca squirmed to be put down. Once Jack placed her feet on the floor, she ran straight to Baldwin, her steps sure and her face determined as she trod on the fading remains of my spell.

"Horsey?" she said, looking up at her uncle with a winsome smile.

Baldwin took her hand in his. "Of course, *cara*. Whatever you wish."

BALDWIN WAS DEFEATED, and knew it. But the look he gave me promised that our struggles over the children weren't over yet.

At 10:37 P.M.—for it turned out that our fireworks display, like all others, was not ready precisely on time—the show began.

Marcus and I had devised a perfect division of labor. I provided the fire. He provided the work.

As the family climbed into the waiting boats so that they could drift on the moat and watch the display from every angle, Marcus dashed around the field making sure all of the man-made fireworks were ready. He plugged the string of lights into an extended line of cords that led back to the house. Once they were lit, the trees sparkled as though a hundred fireflies had settled onto the branches. Then he turned on the music. It was a rousing combination of Handel and military tunes from the American Revolution as well as the French.

"Ready?" Marcus asked, coming up behind me.

"As I'll ever be," I said.

I stood on a stack of hay bales and took the stance of an archer, tall and straight. I extended my left arm forward and drew my right arm back. A shimmering bow appeared, along with a silver-tipped arrow.

From the moat, only those with vampire sight would be able to detect my outline in the darkness. The rest would see only a bow and arrow, illuminated against the night sky.

I released my fingers and the arrow shot forth, traveling in a blazing arc toward the first of Marcus's fireworks: a set of spinning Catherine wheels mounted on long poles in the ground. The arrow went straight through them, lighting each one in turn. They began to spin and spit fire, their colors bright and cheerful.

Oohs and aahs of delight as well as the enthusiastic clapping of the twins provided the backdrop while Marcus sped among his Roman candles. Each one shot into the air and burst into a thousand stars with a mild pop that didn't seem to bother Apollo or the children. I'd put a silencing spell on them to keep the noise down and the animals calm.

At last it was time for the finale. Marcus and I had decided to use my power over fire and water to create something that would amaze not only the children, but the adults as well. I nocked another bolt of fire and pointed it straight above me into the sky.

The ball of flame climbed higher and higher. As it flew, a fiery green tail appeared. The tail stretched and grew, and the ball began to take the form of a firedrake.

I set up another arrow made from witchfire and launched it into the air. This one was golden and burnished, morphing and twisting into a young griffin who chased the firedrake across the heavens.

My magic almost depleted, I took my final fiery arrow and sent it into the moat. The surface hissed and popped as the magical flames traveled through the water, past the two boats of astonished spectators. Fish, sea-beasts, and mermen and mermaids leaped into the air like sculpted soap bubbles, shimmering and dancing before they popped and disappeared like dreams.

The firedrake and griffin faded and then disappeared. The Catherine wheels spun to a stop.

Matthew broke the silence that followed with an unscripted addition to our fireworks display.

"*We are such stuff / As dreams are made on,*" Matthew said softly, "*and our little life / Is rounded with a sleep.*"

ONCE THE CHILDREN WERE PUT to bed, the adults gathered in the kitchen.

"I don't remember spending this much time in the kitchen before," Baldwin said, looking around as though the space were unfamiliar to him. "I must say, it's a pleasant room."

Sarah and I exchanged smiles. The domestication of Baldwin had begun.

"You should sleep in tomorrow, *mon coeur*," Matthew said, rubbing the small of my back. "You expended a lot of energy tonight."

"It was worth it." I raised my glass of champagne. Ysabeau was right. Hers was much better than what we normally drank. "To life, liberty, and the pursuit of happiness."

The family joined in the toast, and I saw even Fernando touch his wineglass to Baldwin's, a definite hint that the de Clermont family might one day form a more perfect union.

"I wonder what they're doing in Hadley to celebrate," Marcus said. "It's funny. I go for decades without ever thinking of home, and then something happens to bring it all back. Tonight, it was the smell of the hay bales and the flickering light from the fireworks."

"When was the last time you saw Hadley?" Sarah asked.

"When I left America in 1781. I almost returned—once. But I went to New Orleans instead," Marcus replied. "Ever since I met Phoebe, though, I think of going back. I imagine taking her there, after she finds out about Obadiah. If she still wants me after that."

"She'll still want you." Of this, I was certain.

"As for Hadley, you can go back anytime you want," Matthew said. "The house is yours."

"What?" Marcus seemed confused.

"Obviously you haven't waded through all of the Knights of Lazarus's real estate transactions," Matthew said drily. "I bought it from your mother, just before she and the rest of the family moved to Pennsylvania. Patience's husband received a war pension, and they took it in the form of a land grant."

"I don't understand," Marcus said numbly. "How could you have known then that I would ever want to return?"

"Because it's your home, the land where you were born," Matthew said. "Terrible things happened to you there, and you suffered as no child should have to suffer."

I thought of Matthew, who, like Marcus, had chosen to end Philippe's life rather than let his father live a broken man. These were not empty words to him. He spoke from the heart—and from experience.

"Time has a way of healing these old wounds," Matthew continued. "Then a day comes when they no longer pain us as they once did. I hoped that would be the case with you. I saw how much you loved Hadley even when the memories of your father were still fresh and sharp, in 1781."

"So you bought the farm," Marcus said carefully. "And kept it."

"And took care of it," Matthew said. "The land has been worked ever since. I leased it to the Pruitts for as long as I could."

"Zeb's family?"

Matthew nodded.

Marcus buried his face in his hands, overcome with emotion.

"The hidden hand need not always be a crushing grip," Ysabeau said gently, looking at Matthew with love. "The touch we feel as a restraint when we are younger has a way of bringing us comfort later in our lives."

"We all chafed under Philippe's rules, Marcus," Baldwin said. "It just never occurred to us that it should—or even could—be any other way."

Marcus thought about his uncle's words for a moment.

"I blamed Matthew for what happened, at first. He seemed like the latest in a long line of patriarchs trying to take my freedom away," Marcus said. "It took me a long time to see that he was caught in the same trap of loyalty and obedience that snared me in Hadley. And it took me even longer to admit that Matthew was right to come to New Orleans and put a stop to what I was doing."

I could see from his expression that this was news to Matthew.

"I was too young to have children of my own. I should have learned my lesson from Vanderslice. But I kept making more. If you hadn't come to New Orleans when you did, Matthew, there's no telling what might have happened. But it would have been even bloodier—that I know for sure."

Marcus leaned on the kitchen island, his fingers tracing the rough scars and gouges in the wood.

"Whenever I think of that time in my life, what I remember are the funerals. My journey to New Orleans began with one, and I left the city after a hundred more had taken place," he said quietly. "Other people think of bright colors and laughter and parades when they think of New Orleans. But it has a darker side now—and it did then, too."

⇥ 32 ⇤

Future

Marcus was returning home in the small hours of a frigid January morning when he came upon a wizened old man fending off a mob of boys at the normally quiet intersection of Herring and Christopher Streets. The wooden houses and shops were shuttered, and there were no passersby to intervene. The man's long coat was covered in muck, as though he'd been knocked down and hauled back onto his feet only to be knocked down again.

"Gettaway," the man said, waving a pottery jug at the boys. His slurred speech indicated that he had been drinking. Heavily.

"Come on, grandpa. Where's your patriotism?" one of the boys jeered. "We're all entitled to some happiness, aren't we?"

The rabble joined in with catcalls, and the circle around the man tightened.

Marcus shoved the young men aside, elbows pushing to the left and right in rapid succession. The crowd parted. The old man was cowering against a brick wall, his stance unsteady and his eyes unfocused. The acrid smell of fear and piss surrounded him. He flung both hands in the air, a gesture of surrender.

"Don't hurt me," the man said.

"Mr. Paine?" Marcus stared at the man. Under the smudges of dirt and beneath the frowsy, disorderly gray hair was a familiar face.

Paine squinted at Marcus, trying to ascertain whether he was friend or foe.

"It's Marcus—Marcus de Clermont." He extended a hand in friendship. "From Paris."

"Hey, mister, you'll have to wait your turn," one of the boys said. His fists were bloody and his nose was running with the cold.

Marcus turned on him and bared his teeth. The boy stepped back, eyes wide.

"Find some other source of entertainment," Marcus growled.

The boys stood their ground, uncertain of what to do next. The pack leader, a burly thug of a teenager with a bad complexion and no front teeth, decided to take Marcus on. He stepped forward, fists raised.

Marcus flattened him with a single blow. The boy's friends dragged him off, casting anxious looks over their shoulder.

"Thank you, friend." Thomas Paine was shaking, his limbs trembling from exposure to the elements and strong drink. "What did you say your name was?"

"Marcus de Clermont. You know my grandparents," Marcus explained, plucking the jug of rum from Paine's hand. "Let's get you home."

Paine gave off a distinctive scent of alcohol, ink, and salt beef. Marcus followed his nose and tracked the combination down to the source: a clapboarded boardinghouse set in the middle of a block of Herring Street just to the south. Inside, candles illuminated the slats in the shutters.

Marcus knocked on the door. An attractive woman in her late thirties with eyes the color of brandy and brown curls threaded through with silver flung open the door. Two boys stood with her, one of them bearing the poker from the fireplace. "Monsieur Paine! We have been so worried!"

"Might I bring him inside?" Marcus said. Paine hung, lifeless in his arms. He had passed out on the short journey. "Madame . . . ?"

"Madame Bonneville, Monsieur Paine's friend," the woman explained in accented English. "Please, bring him in."

The moment Marcus crossed over the threshold of the boardinghouse on Herring Street, he traded in his life of isolation and work for one of lively debate and familial concern. The Bonneville family took care not only of Paine—who was a drunk and prone to apoplexy—but Marcus, too. It became his habit to return to Herring Street after working in the hospital, or after a busy day of attending private patients in his home on nearby Stuyvesant Street. France had rejected Paine, and Marcus's fellow Americans now ridiculed the elder statesman's radical ideas about religion. But Marcus liked nothing more than to sit with Paine by the south-facing window on the ground floor, the sash raised so that they could eavesdrop on the conversations in the street, and discuss their reactions to the day's news. There were always books on the table before them, as well as Paine's spectacles and a decanter of dark liquid. Once they'd exhausted current events, they reminisced about their time in Paris, and their shared acquaintances, like Dr. Franklin.

Marcus brought along his copy of *Common Sense,* so well-read that the paper felt plush and soft to the touch, and would sometimes read passages aloud. He and Paine talked about the failures of their two revolutions, as well as the successes. The colonies' separation from the king had not resulted in greater equality, as Paine had hoped. There was still hereditary privilege and wealth in America, just as there had been before the revolution. And it was still possible to enslave negroes, in spite of what the second paragraph of the Declaration of Independence stated.

"My friend Joshua Boston told me I was a fool to believe that Thomas Jefferson was thinking of people like him or the Pruitts when he wrote that all men were created equal," Marcus confessed to Paine.

"Well, we mustn't rest until America lives up to its ideals," Paine replied. He and Marcus often discussed the evils of slavery and the need to abolish it. "Are we not all brothers?"

"I think so," Marcus said. "Perhaps that's why I carry your words with me wherever I go, and not the Declaration of Independence."

As the weeks passed, Marcus got to know Marguerite Bonneville, Paine's companion. Madame Bonneville and her husband, Nicholas, had known Paine in Paris. Bonneville had published Paine's works, and when the authorities tried to shut his press down the man fled. When Paine returned to America in the autumn of 1802, he brought Madame Bonneville and her children with him. Marcus's friendship with Madame Bonneville deepened after they started conversing with each other in French. Not long after that, the two became lovers. Still, Madame Bonneville remained devoted to Paine, managing his farm in the country and his affairs in the city as well as his engagements, his correspondence, and his declining health.

Marguerite and Marcus were both at Paine's bedside when the man who had given voice to a revolution quietly passed on from the world of men on a hot and humid day in June 1809.

"He's gone." Marcus gently crossed Paine's hands over his heart. The year Paine spent in Paris's Luxembourg Prison in 1794 had left him frail, and Marcus had known that his friend's devotion to strong drink would hasten his end.

"Monsieur Paine was a good man, as well as a great one," Madame Bonneville said. Her eyes were swollen with tears. "I do not know what would have happened to us, had he not brought us to America."

"Where would any of us be, without Tom?" Marcus closed the front of his wooden medicine case, the time for balsams and elixirs now over.

"You know he wished to be buried at New Rochelle, among the Quakers," Madame Bonneville said.

They both knew where Paine kept his final testament: behind a thin panel of wood in the back of the kitchen cupboard.

"I'll take him there," Marcus said. It was more than twenty miles, but he was prepared to honor his friend's last wishes no matter the cost or distance. "Wait with him, while I find a wagon."

"We will go, too." Madame Bonneville laid a hand on Marcus's arm. "The children and I will not abandon him. Or you."

THEY REACHED NEW ROCHELLE DURING the lingering summer twilight. It had taken all day. Two black men drove the wagon carrying Paine's body. They were the only team Marcus could find who were willing to haul a dead man nearly as far as Connecticut in the summer heat. The first three men that Marcus approached had laughed in his face when he proposed the journey. They had plenty of work in the city. Why should they take a rotting body up the coast?

Marcus rode alongside the wagon, and Marguerite and her eldest son, Benjamin, accompanied them in a carriage. Once they arrived in New Rochelle, they checked into an inn, for it was too late to bury Paine at this hour. Marcus and the Bonnevilles shared a room while the drivers, Aaron and Edward, slept with the horses in the barn.

The next morning, Marcus and Marguerite were turned away from the Quaker burying ground.

"He was not our brother," said the elder who barred them from entering the low stone walls.

Marcus argued with the man, and when that didn't work, he tried to arouse the fellow's patriotism. That failed, as well, as did Marcus's attempts to stir his pity and his guilt.

"So much for brotherhood," Marcus fumed, banging on the carriage door in frustration.

"What do we do now?" Marguerite asked. She was sheet white with exhaustion, and her eyes were circled with hollows of grief. "I'm not sure how much longer we can keep the hired men."

"We bury him on the farm," Marcus said, giving her hand a reassuring squeeze.

Marcus dug the grave himself under the walnut tree where Paine had sat on summer days gone by, the thick canopy of leaves providing shade from the sun. It was the second time Marcus had dug a grave between the roots of an ancient tree. This time, his vampire strength and his love for Paine made short work of the task.

There was no minister present, no one to say God's words over the body as Aaron, Edward, Marcus, and Benjamin Bonneville lowered Paine into the ground. Marguerite held a bouquet of flowers she picked from the garden, and placed it on the shrouded figure. The drivers left as soon as their business was done, and returned to New York.

Marcus and Marguerite stood by the grave until the light began to fade, her sons Benjamin and Thomas standing quietly between them.

"He would want you to say something, Marcus." Marguerite gave him an encouraging look.

But Marcus could think of nothing appropriate to say over the body of a man who did not believe in God, or the church, or even the afterlife. Thomas Paine had come to believe that religion was the worst form of tyranny because it pursued you through death and into eternity—something no king or despot had yet managed to do.

At last, Marcus settled on repeating something Thomas himself had written.

"'My country is the world, and my religion is to do good.'" Marcus took a handful of earth and sifted it into the grave. "Be at peace, friend. It is time for others to continue your work."

The death of Thomas Paine cut Marcus's final ties to his former life in ways the close of the last century, symbolic though it was, had failed to do. Marcus had walked the earth for more than half a century, and during that time he had always felt the retrograde pull of Hadley, his family, and the War for Independence. Now that Paine was gone, there was nothing left to look back upon but a chronicle of loss and disappointment. Marcus needed to find a future that did not have so much of the past in it, and wondered how long the search would take.

MARCUS FOUND HIS FUTURE at the southern boundary of America, in the sultry city of New Orleans.

"When did you arrive?" Marcus asked his patient, a young man of eighteen who had come from Saint-Domingue. Refugees continued to flood into New Orleans from the island that they had once called home, driven away by war between Spain and France.

"Tuesday," the man replied. It was now Friday.

"Have you been vaccinated for smallpox?" Marcus asked, feeling his patient's neck and examining the inside of his eyelids for signs of jaundice. Jenner's new, safer method of preventing smallpox, which used a strain of cowpox to prevent the disease, had revolutionized medicine. Marcus felt sure this was the beginning of a brighter age for patients, with more effective cures based on stimulating the body's responses to disease.

"No, monsieur."

After examining him, Marcus didn't think the man had smallpox, or yellow fever, or any of the other highly contagious diseases that struck terror into the hearts of the city's residents. Instead, the man's watery diarrhea and vomiting suggested cholera. With New Orleans's poor drainage, poverty, and crowded housing, cholera was endemic.

"I'm pleased to tell you, sir, that it's cholera, not smallpox," Marcus reported, noting the diagnosis in his ledger. He was tracking his patients by age, which ships they had arrived on, where they were living in the city, and whether or not they had been inoculated or vaccinated. In New York, medical records like these had helped Marcus react swiftly when new outbreaks of fever occurred, and here in New Orleans they were already a resource for city officials.

"Cholera? Will it kill me?" The young man looked frightened.

"I don't think so," he replied. The man seemed young and healthy. It was children and the aged who seemed to be hardest hit by the illness—though Marcus would have to wait and see whether that pattern held true for New Orleans.

As Marcus gathered the herbs and tinctures he needed to concoct a medicine for his new patient, he had the unpleasant, uncanny feeling he was being watched. He looked up from his medical formulary, where he noted down his cures and their success. A man stood across the street from Marcus's small apothecary shop. He was of an ordinary height and build, and dressed in a well-made though ill-fitting suit. He was shuffling cards and watching Marcus's every move. Even from a distance, Marcus was struck by his mesmerizing green eyes.

"Here. I've made you a packet of medicine." Marcus had mixed spearmint, camphor, and a bit of poppy together to help with the nausea and cramps. "Put a spoonful in boiling water, and sip it while it's warm—not hot. Don't drink it down all at once, or it will just come up again. Try to rest. You should feel better in a week or so."

Once the patient paid for his services, Marcus went out onto the street.

Marcus was sure the fellow watching him wasn't a vampire, but there was no telling what his grandfather might do to keep an eye on him, even if it meant employing a warmblooded spy. Marcus had hoped it would take the de Clermonts years to find him in New Orleans, but perhaps Philippe was more powerful than Marcus knew.

"Do you have some business with me?" Marcus demanded.

"You're awfully young to be a doctor, ain't you?" The man spoke with the slow, rollicking speech of the southern colonies, tinged with a touch of a French accent and a twang of the local dialect that was too forced to be natural. Whoever this man was, he was hiding something.

"Where are you from?" Marcus asked. "Not here. Virginia would be my guess."

The man's eyes flickered.

"Do you need medical help?"

"No, Yankee. I do not." The man spat out a stream of tobacco. It scuttled a bit of eggshell bobbing on a sea of filth in the gutter.

Marcus leaned against the peeling doorframe. There was something intriguing about this man. His combination of brash insincerity and honest charm reminded Marcus of Vanderslice. Even after nearly two decades, Marcus still missed his old friend.

"Name's Chauncey," Marcus said.

"I know. Young Doc Chauncey is the talk of the town. The women are all in love with you, and the men swear that they feel healthier and more virile than they have in years after seeing you. Quite a racket, if you ask me." The man smiled disarmingly. "Ransome Fayreweather, at your service."

"You shuffle those cards like a man who likes to gamble," Marcus said. Ransome's swift fingers reminded him of the way Fanny handled a deck.

"Some." Fayreweather never stopped shuffling, the cards moving smooth and quick through his hands.

"Maybe we could play sometime," Marcus suggested. He had learned a few tricks playing with Fanny, and felt he could hold his own against this Fayreweather fellow.

"We'll see." Fayreweather tipped his hat with exaggerated courtesy. "Good day to you, Doc Chauncey."

MARCUS FELT SURE he would see Fayreweather again, and he was right. Two weeks later, he spotted him in the Place d'Armes, peddling medicine from a small table draped in a black cloth that was weighted down with a human skull. The residents of New Orleans—brown, black, red, white, and every shade in between—milled around the square, speaking French, Spanish, English, and tongues that were unfamiliar to Marcus.

"Have you been vaccinated?" Fayreweather said in a fair imitation of Marcus.

"Yes, sir," his prospective female patient replied. "At least, I think it was a vaccination. One of the witches scratched my arm with a chicken's foot and spat on it."

Marcus was horrified.

"I'm pleased to tell you, madame, that you have cholera. And I have just the treatment for you. Chauncey's Elixir—my own receipt." Fayreweather held up a green bottle.

Marcus continued to watch as Fayreweather performed the role of Doc Chauncey, the medical marvel from the north, recently arrived in New Orleans. After a few more patients, the trickster noticed his attention. When Fayreweather looked up, Marcus tipped his tall hat.

Fayreweather began to pack up. He looked in no hurry, but Marcus could smell a whiff of fear about him and heard his heart speed up.

"Doctor Chauncey, as I live and breathe," Marcus said, strolling in Fayreweather's direction. "What made you leave your storefront and take to the streets?"

"The smell of money," Fayreweather replied. "There is more of it here than on Chartres Street."

"Congratulations on passing the Cabildo's examination and becoming certified to dispense medicines." Marcus picked up the piece of paper tucked under the skull. It resembled the document Marcus had hanging on his shop wall to show he was a reputable physician and not a quack. He glanced at a knot of Garde de Ville standing nearby. Fayreweather had brass balls to fleece people within arm's reach of the city police. "I hear the test takes three hours."

"So it does." Fayreweather snatched the paper from Marcus's fingers.

"Listen," Marcus said, dropping his voice. "I have no wish to deprive you of your liberty, or your livelihood, but please impersonate someone else." He tipped his hat and walked away.

Marcus had taken only a few steps when Fayreweather's voice caught up with him.

"What's your game, friend?" Fayreweather called.

Marcus turned. "Game?"

"I know humbug when I see it," Fayreweather said.

"I don't know what you're talking about," Marcus said smoothly.

"You don't want to tell me, that's fine." Fayreweather smiled. "But I'll discover your secret. You can count on it."

After their encounter in the Place d'Armes, Fayreweather kept cropping up in the crowded city. Marcus spotted Fayreweather playing cards in the back of his favorite coffee shop. He heard Fayreweathers's honeyed tones on Chartres Street as he tried to seduce a young widow. Fayreweather had a fiddle, and played it on street corners, drawing crowds of rapt listeners. Everywhere Fayreweather went there was life and laughter. Marcus soon envied the man.

Marcus began to look for Fayreweather as he went about his daily business, and to be disappointed when he didn't catch the man's sardonic green eyes or have a chance to greet him in the market. One day, Marcus shared a table with Fayreweather at his favorite drinking establishment, the Café des Réfugiés on Rue de St. Philip.

"I think you should call me Ransome," Fayreweather suggested after they clinked glasses. "And I think you need to have some fun, Doc. Otherwise, you're going to get old before your time."

Marcus was swept up into Ransome's seductive world of gamblers and whores, surrounded by men and women who were all trying to craft a new life for themselves in the bustling port that was welcoming the whole world. Ships put in at the mouth of the Missisippi from every place imaginable, some carrying passengers and others cargo.

Inch by inch, Marcus began to shed the layers of himself that had been bruised by childhood and revolution, and toughened by war and adversity. Surrounded by Ransome's friends, Marcus often remembered his time among the Brethren—odd though it was to think of Johannes Ettwein and Sister Magdalene in a seedy bar or a whorehouse—and the way that these unlikely allies lived side by side. Marcus began to laugh at Ransome's jokes, and to share gossip as well as political news when he sat down with his cup of coffee at Lafitte's tavern.

It was in one of these easy moments that Ransome finally extracted Marcus's secret from him.

They were smoking cigars and drinking wine at a gambling parlor on St. Charles Avenue. The thick red velvet drapes gave everything a lurid air, and the haze of anxiety rising from the players and the fumes from the tobacco were so thick they practically choked you.

"I'm calling your bluff, Doc." Ransome threw a handful of tokens into the center of the table.

"You've caught me a bit short." Marcus was out of cash, out of tokens, and out of luck.

"Of course, you could tell me your secret and I'd call us even," Fayreweather said. It was his standing offer whenever Marcus lost a game of chance.

Marcus laughed. "You never give up, do you, Ransome?"

"Not if death himself was staring me in the face," Fayreweather said cheerfully. "I'd simply challenge him to a game of monte and sucker him like I do all the others."

Fayreweather had been teaching Marcus some of the tricks he used on the deep-pocketed visitors to New Orleans. Fanny would adore Ransome, Marcus thought wistfully, remembering his aunt's bustling household and exuberant spirit. Marcus got lonelier and more nostalgic with every passing year.

"That's a strange look for a successful man such as yourself," Fayreweather said. Like all cardsharps, Ransome was a keen observer. "You look positively blue, Doc. Isn't there something you can prescribe that will cure your doldrums?"

"Just thinking of the folks I left behind."

"I hear you." Ransome's eyes flickered. "We all lost something on our travels here."

"I lost my life, and got it back again," Marcus said, staring into the depths of his wine. "I left my home, and returned to it, and left it again. I sailed the seas, and met Ben Franklin, and buried Thomas Paine. I studied at university, and learned more in the streets of Paris in one night than I did in a year in Edinburgh. I loved two women, and had a child, and here I am, alone in New Orleans, drinking sour wine and losing money hand over hand."

"Ben Franklin, you say?" Ransome chewed on his cigar.

"Yep," Marcus replied, taking another slug of wine.

"Son, I think he died before you were born." Fayreweather put his cards on the table. A straight. "If you want to pass as something you're not, you've got to be more careful with your fabrications. For a moment, I almost believed you. But your mention of Franklin—"

"I was born more than fifty years ago," Marcus said. "I'm a vampire."

"One of those bloodsuckers Madame D'Arcantel and her friends are always going on about?" Ransome asked.

"They're witches," Marcus said. "You can't believe a word they say."

"No," Ransome said, his eyes narrowing. "So why is it that I believe you?"

Marcus shrugged. "Because I'm telling you the truth?"

"Yes, I believe you are—and for the first time, too."

After that night, Marcus told Ransome more about what it was to be a vampire than he probably should have. He took Ransome hunting in the bayou and demonstrated how he sometimes applied a bit of vampire blood to a wound in order to save a life even though he wasn't really supposed to. Once again, Marcus had found an unlikely brother, someone like Vanderslice who accepted him for who and what he was.

"Why don't you just make us all vampires, like you?" Ransome had wondered.

"It's not as easy as it sounds," Marcus explained. "I made one child—a son—but he fell in with the wrong crowd, and ended up dead."

"You need to pick smarter children," Ransome said, eyeing Marcus with open speculation.

"I see. And you think you have what it takes to be a vampire?" Marcus laughed.

"I know I do." Ransome's eyes flashed with sudden desire, then returned to normal. "Together, we could make a family that would rule this city for centuries."

"Not if my grandfather catches wind of it," Marcus said.

But that didn't deter Ransome. He offered to pay Marcus to transform him into a vampire. He threatened to expose Marcus to the authorities unless he was made immortal. When Ransome was dying of malaria, that scourge of the city's watery location, he offered Marcus his gambling den, substantial fortune, and a private house Marcus didn't know he owned in exchange for his blood. Ransome Fayreweather had, through grift and deceit, amassed enough money to open his own establishment in the old quarter of the city devoted to drinking, gambling, whoring, and other pleasures of the flesh. On a bad day, Ransome brought home a small fortune in revenue. On a good day, he pocketed more money than Croesus. When Ransome showed him a ledger outlining his various properties and investments, Marcus had been stunned—and then admiring.

Against his better judgment, Marcus decided to try fatherhood for a second time. Marcus had no desire to return to life as it had been before Ransome arrived in it: quietly productive with little laughter and much reading of *Common Sense.* Instead, Marcus wanted to take part in Ransome's plans to further develop the bar that was known as the Domino Club, and to gather with New Orleans's spirited citizens at dinner tables and in music halls to celebrate the pleasures of youth.

Marcus administered his blood to his dying friend in the opulent upstairs bedroom in Ransome's grand new house on Coliseum Street.

Unlike Vanderslice, Ransome took to being a vampire like sucking the blood from humans was second nature. Marcus discovered in Ransome's bloodlore that he'd been swindling people since he was a boy of eight, taking money from innocents by maneuvering three walnut shells and a kernel of corn atop a cellar door.

Marcus's medical practice continued to grow after Ransome's transformation. The city had swollen considerably in size thanks to the continued influx of refugees from the Caribbean, the slave traders who unloaded their captives on the wharves, and the speculators and land developers who arrived in pursuit of their fortune. Such a plan had certainly worked for Ransome, who was now one of the richest men in New Orleans and planned on remaining in that enviable position for the rest of his days.

Ransome's future depended on him having his own children. He started with a mixed-race man called Malachi Smith—a small, agile fellow who clambered up the sides of houses and broke into bedrooms to steal women's jewels. Marcus became a grandfather, and with that title came new worries about the family's increasing notoriety.

Then Ransome adopted Crispin Jones, a young British fellow newly arrived in New Orleans with a head for business and a taste for young men.

"You can't keep making vampires, Ransome. If you do, we're going to get caught," Marcus warned him one night when they were hunting in the swamps outside the city for something to feed to Ransome's latest project, a Creole prostitute named Suzette Boudrot who had been run down by a wagon near the cathedral.

"So what," Ransome said. "What are they going to do if they find out we're vampires—shoot us?"

"A piece of gunshot between the eyes will kill you, vampire or not," Marcus replied. "So will hanging."

"They only hang runaway slaves and felons in the Place d'Armes. Worst I'd get is a day in the pillory with a placard around my neck," Ransome retorted. "Besides, we wouldn't have any trouble with the law at all if you would just let me make a few of the police into vampires."

"You're too young," Marcus said.

"I'm older than you are," Ransome observed.

"In human terms, yes," Marcus replied. "But you're still not ready to have more children of your own." Marcus stopped himself before he could utter more de Clermont logic.

"Anyway, it's too risky," Marcus continued. "We're not supposed to gather in packs. Humans notice when we do. We make them nervous, you see, and as soon as something goes wrong—"

"And it always goes wrong," Ransome said with the voice of experience.

"Indeed," Marcus agreed. "That's when the humans start looking around for someone to blame for their troubles. We stick out from the crowd, just like the witches do."

"In this city?" Ransome guffawed. "Lord, Marcus. With all the odd bodies in this town, a few vampires more or less won't make any difference at all. Besides, aren't you tired of saying good-bye to friends?"

The city was plagued with disease, and every month Marcus seemed to lose someone to the latest illness sweeping through the streets. Reluctantly, he nodded.

"I thought so," Ransome said. "Besides, all I'm doing is making good on the promise of the revolution you fought to win: liberty and fraternity. Equality Isn't that what it's all about?"

Encouraged by Ransome's conviction that no one would notice, and spurred on by his own need to belong, Marcus began to take note of young people who seemed destined for something greater than their sad lot in life. One by one, he started to save them.

Marcus began with Molly, the Choctaw who worked in one of Ransome's upstairs rooms and had the voice of an angel. Was it really fair that such a beautiful young woman lose her life, not to mention her looks, because one of her customers had given her syphilis? Marcus felt having a daughter would bring respectability to the family, provide him and Ransome with a hostess in their fine house, and stop the wagging tongues of neighbors. None of these dreams came true.

He tried again with One-Eyed Jack, who ran with Lafitte's gang of thieves before he fell down drunk onto a wrought iron finial shaped like a fleur-de-lis. The point went straight into his eye. Marcus removed the spike, but not the eyeball, and all of his blood. Then Marcus gave One-Eyed Jack enough of his own blood to bring the man back to life, though the eye never recovered. Instead, the iris turned a hard, flat black that made his pupils seem permanently dilated, and he couldn't see out of it afterward.

After One-Eyed Jack came Geraldine, the French acrobat who could swing between balconies on Bourbon Street even before she became a vampire, and then Waldo, who dealt the cards at Ransome's new gambling hall and could spot a cheat quicker than anyone in New Orleans. Myrna, Ransome's neighbor, who kept too many cats and donated her clothes to the poor—even if that meant stripping down on Rue Royale and giving her bloomers to a beggar—had a heart of gold and a quixotic mind that kept them all entertained, even when the slaves revolted and the British threatened to invade the city. Marcus couldn't let her die, though her delicate mental state wasn't improved once she began to drink blood.

One by one Marcus's family grew larger and more boisterous. It happened so incrementally that Marcus took no notice of it, though Marguerite D'Arcantel and her coven surely did, as did the city officials.

By the time yellow fever hit the city hard in the summer of 1817, Marcus had generated a family of two dozen men and women of all backgrounds, religions, colors, and languages in his charge, as well as three distilleries, two brothels, and Ransome's Domino Club, which had been shut down several times only to come back to life, vampire-like, as a members-only dining establishment. Since the mayor was the first to join, it seemed unlikely that the card games and sexual liaisons that took place before and after meals would get them into trouble.

It was at the height of the epidemic that New Orleans residents began to ask questions about Marcus and his family. Why did none of them ever get sick? What was keeping them healthy, when everyone else was dying of the fever? There were rumors of voodoo, which Marcus laughed off. He was feeling comfortable in New Orleans now. Marcus liked the city, and its inhabitants. He was well-fed, happy with his work, and enjoyed his family and their fast-paced life. Sometimes Marcus worried that he and Ransome were drawing too much attention to themsleves, but it was easy to shrug off those concerns and focus instead on another game of cards or a new woman in his bed.

He and Ransome were at the Domino Club, counting the night's take while Geraldine recorded the sums in the club's ledger, when a woman arrived at the door. She was beautiful—not just pretty, but jaw-droppingly perfect. Her mixed-race heritage showed in her saftly curled hair—most of which was piled on her head while the rest fell in tendrils that clung to her neck in the humid air—her café au lait skin, and her high cheekbones.

"Marcus de Clermont." The woman smiled like a cat.

Ransome pulled a pistol out of the desk drawer.

"Juliette." Marcus's heart jumped, and Geraldine looked from him to the woman at the door, curious about her effect on him.

"Hello, Marcus." His maker, Matthew de Clemont, joined the woman. "I told you he would remember you, Juliette."

"What are you doing here?" Marcus asked Matthew, dazed by the sudden intrusion of past into present.

"I've come to meet my grandchildren. They're the talk of the town." His voice was calm, but Matthew was clearly furious. "Will you introduce me—or should I do it myself?"

"I TRUST YOU KNOW my son." Matthew poured a glass of wine for the aristocratic vampire who sat across the table. It was so polished that you could see the dark reflections in the mahogany surface.

"Everybody knows him." The vampire, like Matthew, spoke French. Marcus's French was excellent thanks to Fanny and Stéphanie, and living in New Orleans kept him fluent.

"I am sorry for that." Matthew sounded genuinely regretful.

"Louis." Juliette sailed into the room, a silk turban wrapped around her head that nonetheless allowed a few curls to escape and tumble around her delicate face and neck. Her dress was also silk, caught under her breasts in a way that accentuated her slim figure and the curve of her shoulders and bosom.

"Juliette." Louis stood and bowed. He kissed her on both cheeks in the French manner and pulled out a chair.

"So you've met Matthew's problem child." Juliette pushed out her lower lip in a seductive pout. "He's been very naughty, I hear. What shall we do with him?"

Matthew looked at Juliette fondly. He poured her a glass of wine.

"Thank you, my love, but I would prefer blood," Juliette said. "Would you like a slave, Louis, or are you content with wine?"

"I have all that I require at present," Louis said.

"We have no slaves." Marcus had been told not to speak unless he was directly addressed by one of his elders, but he detested Juliette Durand.

"You do now." Juliette snapped her fingers and a vacant-looking black girl walked into the room. She stumbled and nearly fell.

"Juliette. Not here," Matthew said, a note of warning in his voice.

But Juliette ignored him.

"I've told you not to be so clumsy." Juliette pointed at the floor before her. "Kneel. Offer yourself to me."

The girl did so. There was a look of panic in her eyes, quickly shuttered. She tilted her head to the side, and once again nearly toppled over.

"How much blood have you taken from her?" Marcus leaped out of his chair and pulled the girl away. He examined her eyes, and felt the pulse at her wrist. It was weak, and stuttering.

"Do not touch what's mine." Juliette's nails dug into his scalp as she grabbed Marcus by the hair. "This is the problem with your *son*, Matthew. He has no respect for age and power."

"Put him down, Juliette," Matthew said. "As for you, Marcus, don't interfere in Juliette's affairs."

"This is my house!" Marcus shouted, keeping hold of the girl. "I won't have a child abused in it—not for food, and not for sport."

"We all have different tastes," Louis said softly. "In time, you will learn to accept that."

"Never." Marcus looked at Matthew in disgust. "I expected better from you."

"I've never touched a child," Matthew said, his eyes darkening.

"No, but you'll stand by and let your whore do it."

Juliette launched herself at Marcus, her fingers raised in claws.

The child, who was caught between them, screamed in terror, her weakened heart skipping beats, slowing, then stopping. She slumped to the floor, dead.

Myrna flew into the room, wearing nothing but a corset and a pair of high-heeled slippers. Her hair was in disarray, and she held a bread knife aloft in one hand.

"The child. The child." Myrna sobbed, her eyes wild. She began slashing at the air, left and right, slaying whatever ghosts had accompanied her into the room.

"Hush, Myrna. You're safe. No one will harm you." Marcus shielded Myrna from the view of the other vampires. He took off his coat and draped it around Myrna's shaking shoulders.

"Get out of this house. All of you." Ransome appeared, carrying a gun. One of his friends had modified the barrel, and it carried a ball and charge so large it could blow off half of a vampire's head. Ransome called his gun "my angel."

"I think, Monsieur de Clermont, that the time has come to do more than talk," Louis observed with a superior sniff.

THE DEATHS BEGAN WITH MOLLY. Her body was found in the bayou, her neck savagely torn.

"Alligators," the city coroner said.

Juliette smiled, her teeth hard and white.

Within a few days, Marcus knew that it wasn't alligators who were disposing of his family, one by one. All died in mysterious circumstances that suggested the Chauncey family of Coliseum Street was experiencing a colossal streak of bad fortune.

Marcus knew it wasn't Lady Luck who was doing this evil work. It was Juliette. And Matthew.

Marcus could tell which kills belonged to which creature. Juliette's showed an element of savagery, with gaping wounds and signs of a struggle. Matthew's were surgical, precise. One fast, quick cut from ear to ear across the throat.

Like Vanderslice.

"There will be no more children," Matthew told Marcus, when only a handful of his children, including Ransome, remained. All were in hiding, most of them far out of town. "Philippe gave you strict orders on this subject."

"Tell grandfather his message was received." Marcus sat, head in his hands, at the same table that he had gathered around with his family, telling tales and swapping insults, long into the New Orleans night.

"Tragic," Juliette said. "Such a needless loss of life."

Marcus snarled at her, daring her to continue. Wisely, she turned away. Had she not, Marcus would have ripped her heart out and let Matthew feast on his bones if he wished.

"I will never forgive you for this," Marcus promised Matthew.

"I don't expect you to," Matthew said. "But it had to be done."

⇥ 33 ⇤

Sixty

Finally, after two months, Miriam's vampire blood was beginning to take root in Phoebe's body. Some of the physical and emotional changes were subtle—so much so that Phoebe herself wasn't always able to perceive them right away. There were moments, like the night she met Stella by the Seine, when her altered blood had been obvious. Most days, however, Phoebe looked into the mirror and saw the same face she'd always seen looking back at her.

As she approached the fledgling stage of vampire development, however, it was becoming increasingly clear that she was no longer a warmblood. Her five senses had all become laser sharp and precise. There was no such thing, for example, as background noise for a vampire. She could hear a cricket as loudly as though it were a brass band. Conversations held on mobile phones, all of which seemed to be undertaken at maximum volume, infringed on her sanity so much that she had to resist the impulse to rip the devices out of people's hands and stomp on them. But music— oh, music was a delight. No one had told her how music would become something so utterly enrapturing. When Phoebe heard a song of any sort—classical, pop, it didn't matter—she felt as though the notes had replaced the blood in her veins.

Phoebe could now classify the information coming through her nose into the same five categories that warmbloods used for tastes: sweet, salty, sour, bitter, and savory. Phoebe knew simply from smelling an animal or a person what they would taste like, and whether or not she would enjoy feeding from them. It was far more humane to sniff than to bite, and raised fewer human eyebrows.

Witches, Phoebe discovered while walking along the rue Maître Albert with Jason, smelled almost saccharine. Though she had a sweet tooth, and still enjoyed standing outside the window at Ladurée to smell the macarons and see the beautiful colors, the scent of witches turned Phoebe's stomach. She wasn't sure how she was going to endure spending time with Diana. Perhaps one became less sensitive to such a powerful odor, or became more aware of its top and bottom notes, like a fine perfume?

Phoebe's memory had changed along with her senses. Instead of becoming sharper, however, it had grown fuzzier and more fragmented. Once she could recall precisely what color she wore on her birthday ten years ago, how much every handbag she owned had cost, and the titles (in accepted chronological order) for every canvas Renoir ever painted. Now she couldn't remember Freyja's mobile number from one hour to the next.

"What is wrong with me?" Phoebe had asked Françoise after she couldn't find her glasses. "I want to take Persephone into the garden and it's too bright out."

It was eight in the morning and overcast, but Phoebe still found the light hurt her eyes.

With Françoise's help she located the glasses, but then misplaced Persephone. The two of them were reunited in the laundry room, where Persephone napped in a basket full of Miriam's dirty clothes.

"All *manjasang* have trouble with their memories," Françoise said. "What did you expect? You have too many now for one brain to hold. It will get worse the longer you live."

"Really?" Nobody had told Phoebe that. "How am I supposed to go back to work?" A sharp memory was crucial for someone working with fine art. You had to be able to recall stylistic differences, changes in techniques and materials, and more.

Françoise gave her a pitying look.

"I *am* going back to work," Phoebe said firmly.

"So you say." Françoise tucked one of Miriam's T-shirts around Persephone like a blanket. It read COUTURE IS AN ATTITUDE, a sentiment with which Freyja did not agree.

Phoebe was finding that being a vampire, like most things in life, was a delicate balance of gains and losses. With every loss, be it temporary like her job or permanent like the taste of ice cream, there were gains.

One day, Françoise found Phoebe studying the latest mark she'd made on the doorframe. To Phoebe's relief, she had grown a full inch.

"Your teacher is here," Françoise said, delivering a freshly laundered pair of ballet tights and a leotard.

"I'll be down in a minute," Phoebe replied, noting the date on the doorframe in red ink. Freyja had asked her to stop scratching the wood in favor of a felt-tip marker that smelled of cherries and unidentifiable chemicals. "I've grown, Françoise."

"You still have a long way to go," Françoise replied.

"I know, I know," Phoebe said with a laugh. Françoise was not talking about her height. Even so, Françoise's criticisms did not sting as they once had.

"Do you need help?" Françoise asked.

"No." Phoebe could manage dressing herself now without popping all the buttons off her blouses and buggering up the zippers.

She peeled off her pajamas and bathrobe. Both were silk and kept her from waking up at night itchy and raw-skinned. Phoebe was still uncommonly sensitive, even when compared to other young vampires. Fabric, light, sound—they all had the potential to make her irritable. But Phoebe was now aware of these triggers and was able to manage them most days.

Phoebe slid the tights over her legs, keeping her fingernails free of the mended patches that reminded her of previous attempts to wrestle with the slippery nylon and Lycra. This time she got the blush-colored hosiery on without a snag, a hole, or a wrinkle. Next came the black leotard with its skinny straps that went over her shoulders. They'd snapped in two several times and been replaced. Phoebe adjusted them so that the neckline of the leotard fit properly. Then she checked her silhouette in the mirror and picked up her toe shoes.

She'd been taking classes with a tiny Russian vampire with long legs and big eyes for several weeks now. Phoebe and Madame Elena practiced in the mirrored ballroom, which had excellent acoustics and a resilient wooden floor. Madame Elena's son, Dimitri, a mousy-looking vampire who appeared to be in his early thirties, accompanied them, pounding on the keys of Freyja's grand piano with a determined air.

Ballet had been an important part of Phoebe's childhood, but she hadn't touched a tutu for more than a decade. Though she had adored the music and the calming rituals of getting ready and doing warm-up exercises at the barre, followed by the exhilaration of jumping and turning, her teachers hadn't thought she showed much promise as a dancer. Both Phoebe and Stella liked to excel at their activities, and Phoebe had moved on to tennis instead. At the time, she felt there was no point spending so much time on something she would never be good at. Now she had nothing but time.

After the incident with Stella, Freyja had thought that Phoebe needed a wider social circle and more exercise to smooth out her volatile moods. To everyone's surprise, Madame Elena had a passing acquaintance with Phoebe's childhood ballet mistress, Madame Olga.

"Good arms, terrible feet," Madame Elena had said with some regret.

In Freyja's ballroom, inscribing delicate circles with her toe and stretching out her vampire limbs, Phoebe was able to work her body to the point where it almost felt like she'd done some exercise. After a steady ninety minutes of controlled movement combined with the grandest of jetés and an exhilarating series of fouetté turns, Phoebe was pleasantly relaxed and her muscles ached. The aches and pains, she knew, would disappear in a matter of minutes.

"You are making progress, mademoiselle," Madame Elena told her. "Your timing is still abominable, and you must remember to turn out from the hips, not the knees, or you will break your legs in two."

"Yes, madame." No matter what Madame Elena said, Phoebe agreed with her so that the woman would return.

She waved Madame Elena and Dimitri off, remaining safely in the shadowed confines of the front hall where the light would not reach her. All that time among the mirrors with Madame Elena had given Phoebe a headache, and she put on her dark glasses again.

"How was your lesson?" Freyja asked.

"Wonderful," Phoebe said, riffling through the mail on the table. There was no mail for her. There wouldn't be until after ninety days had passed. Still, it was her habit to check. "Where's Miriam?"

"At the Sorbonne. Some conference," Freyja said, airily dismissive. She linked arms with Phoebe, and the two strolled toward the back of the house, where Phoebe had taken possession of a room that overlooked the garden.

Freyja felt every female vampire should have a space of her own in the home that was set apart from the boudoir where she slept, bathed, and entertained intimate visitors. With twenty-four hours to fill, it was important to develop routines that moved one about and gave structure and substance to the day. At Freyja's insistence, Phoebe had gathered up some of her favorite things in the house and taken them down to the old morning room, now known to all as "Phoebe's study." The Roman vase was there that used to be in the front hall, as well as a particularly nice Renoir that reminded her of how she felt when she was with Marcus. It was soft and sensual, and the dark-haired woman picking roses looked a bit like her.

"You finished your painting!" Freyja exclaimed, looking at the canvas propped on the easel.

"Not quite," Phoebe said, casting a practiced, critical glance over the work. "The background needs adjusting, and I think the light is still too strong."

"You think all light is too strong, Phoebe, and yet you are drawn to it in your art as well as in your life." Freyja inspected the painting closely. "It's really quite good, you know."

Like ballet, painting was something Phoebe was pleased to pick back up.

"What I'm learning will be a huge help when I go back to work. To Sotheby's." Phoebe tilted her head this way and that to change her perspective on the piece.

"Oh, Phoebe." Freyja looked sad. "You know you will never work at Sotheby's again."

"So you all say. But I'm going to have to do something other than paint and dance, or I'll go mad," Phoebe said. "You may have been a princess, Freyja. I never was."

"We shall find you some good causes," Freyja said. "They will occupy your time. You can build schools, join the police, take care of widows. I do all of those things, and they make me feel useful."

"I don't think I'm police material, Freyja," Phoebe teased. She was growing fonder of Marcus's aunt with each passing day.

"You didn't think you'd remembered how to plié," Freyja reminded her. "You never know where the path of your life will take you."

"There's always Baldwin's collection to catalog, I suppose," Phoebe replied. "Not to mention making an inventory of Pickering Place. And Sept-Tours."

"You can make a list of everything in my house when you are finished with those. And don't forget to take a look Matthew's house in Amsterdam. The attics are filled with the most enormous canvases covered with dead white men in ruffs."

Having seen some of the places where Matthew kept his art, which included the downstairs loo at the Old Lodge, Phoebe wasn't surprised.

"But you must do more than hunt for treasure, Phoebe dear," Freyja warned. "You cannot save the world or everyone in it, but you must find a way to make a difference. My father always said that was what vampires were put on earth to do."

⊰ 34 ⊱

Life Is But a Breath

We were just finishing up with the twins' baths when Marcus rocketed into the room. Marthe was steps behind, looking concerned.

"Edward Taylor's in the hospital," Marcus said to Matthew. "Freyja says it's a heart attack. She won't tell me where he is, or his condition."

Matthew handed Philip's towel to Marcus before taking out his phone.

"Miriam?" Matthew asked when it connected. He put it on speaker so we could all listen in.

"Freyja shouldn't have called you, Marcus," Miriam said sourly.

"Where is Edward now?" Matthew asked.

"The Salpêtrière," Miriam replied. "It was closest to the flat."

"His condition?" Matthew said.

Miriam fell silent.

"His condition, Miriam," Matthew repeated.

"It's too early to say. It was a major episode. Once we know more, we'll decide whether or not to tell Phoebe," Miriam said.

"Phoebe has a right to know that her father is gravely ill!" Marcus said.

"No, Marcus. Phoebe has no rights when it comes to her human family—and I have a responsibility to make sure that my daughter is not a danger to herself or others. A hospital? She's sixty days old!" Miriam replied. "And she's still lightstruck. The Salpêtrière is lit up like a Christmas tree at all hours of the day and night. She wouldn't be safe there."

"Can Edward be moved?" Matthew was thinking outside of the box of ordinary warmblooded medical options. If need be, he would transform Freyja's house into a clinic, outfit it with the finest equipment, hire the most advanced cardiac surgeon in the world, and make Edward the facility's sole patient.

"Not without killing him," Miriam said bluntly. "Padma already asked. She wanted him moved to London. The doctors refused."

"I'm coming to Paris." Marcus tossed Philip's towel aside, leaving the baby standing, naked and pink after his bath, holding a plastic duck. Marthe hurried toward him and helped him into his pajamas.

"You're not welcome here, Marcus," Miriam said.

"Story of my life," Marcus replied. "But Edward is Phoebe's father, so you can imagine how little a warm reception from you matters at this moment."

"We'll be there in four hours," Matthew said.

"We?" Miriam swore. "No, Matthew. That's not—"

Matthew disconnected the call and looked to me. "Are you coming, *mon coeur*? We might need your help."

I had finished getting Becca into her pajamas, and handed her off to Marthe.

"Let's go," I said, taking Matthew by the hand.

MARCUS'S CONCERN FOR PHOEBE, and Matthew's steady foot on the accelerator carried us to the outskirts of Paris in a little over three hours. Once there, Matthew zipped along streets that no tourist ever found, taking every shortcut until we reached the ancient university quarter near the Sorbonne and the Salpêtrière hospital. Matthew turned off the engine and spun around to face his son in the backseat.

"What's the plan?" he asked.

We'd had none up to this point—other than reaching Paris as quickly as possible. Marcus looked startled.

"I don't know. What do you think we should do?"

Matthew shook his head. "Phoebe is your mate, not mine. It's up to you."

I loved Matthew with all my heart, and was often proud of the quiet perseverance with which he handled the many challenges that faced him. But I had never been so overwhelmed with pride as I was in this moment, idling on a Paris street in the 13th arrondissement, waiting for his son to make his own decision.

"Freyja called me because I'm a doctor," Marcus said, staring up at the bulk of the hospital. "So are you. One of us should go check on Edward, and make sure that he is being taken care of properly."

I thought it unlikely that a British diplomat, taken by ambulance to one of the finest hospitals in the world, would be treated *improperly*, but held my tongue.

"And I don't give a toss what Miriam thinks. Phoebe needs to know what's happened. And she needs to be here, at her father's side," Marcus said, "just in case."

Still, Matthew waited.

"You deal with the doctors," Marcus said, hopping out of the backseat. "Diana and I will tell Phoebe."

"Wise decision," Matthew said, yielding his place behind the wheel to his son.

Matthew circled the car. I pushed the button, and the window went down.

"Take care of him," Matthew murmured before he pressed his lips to mine.

MIRIAM WAS WAITING FOR US on the front step when we arrived at Freyja's house. I had never been there before, and was struck by its grandeur as well as its privacy.

"Where's Phoebe?" Marcus asked, cutting right to the heart of the matter.

Miriam stood her ground before the door. "This breaks all the rules, Marcus. We had an agreement."

"Edward falling ill wasn't part of the plan," Marcus replied.

"Warmbloods get sick and die," Miriam said. "Phoebe needs to learn she can't go running to hospital every time they do."

"Edward is Phoebe's *father*," Marcus said, his fury evident. "This isn't just any warmblood."

"It's too soon to expose her to that kind of loss." Miriam's eyes were filled with warnings that I didn't understand. "You know that."

"I do," Marcus said. "Let me in, Miriam, or I'll break down the fucking door."

"Fine. If there's a disaster, it will be on your conscience—not mine." Miriam stepped aside.

Françoise, whom I had not seen since leaving sixteenth-century London, opened the door. She bobbed a curtsy.

Phoebe was waiting in the foyer, Freyja at her side with an arm around her in a protective arc. Phoebe looked pale, and there were streaks of pink on her cheeks from her blood tears.

She already knew about her father. There had been no need for us to rush to Paris to tell her. Our only reason for speed was to reunite two lovers as quickly as possible.

"You knew Marcus would come," I said softly to Miriam.

Miriam nodded. "How could he not?"

Marcus rushed toward Phoebe, then stopped, remembering that it was the female who must choose and not the male. He gathered his composure.

"Phoebe. I'm so sorry," he began, his voice raw with emotion. "Matthew is with Edward now—"

Phoebe was in his arms with a speed that proved just how young and inexperienced she was. Her arms tightened around Marcus as she sobbed out her worry and fear.

It was the first time I'd seen such a young vampire, and the sight was dazzling. Phoebe was like a freshly minted coin, strong and shining. There was no way a human wouldn't stop and stare if she passed by on a Parisian catwalk, let alone a hospital corridor. How were we going to get her into Edward's room, glowing with so much life and vitality?

"If he dies, I don't know what I'll do," Phoebe said. Her blood tears flowed once more.

"I know, sweetheart. I know," Marcus murmured, his fingers laced through her hair and her body cradled against his.

"Freyja says I can go and see him, but Miriam doesn't think it's a good idea." Phoebe sniffed back the tears. For the first time, she seemed to realize that I was there. "Hello, Diana."

"Hello, Phoebe," I said. "I'm sorry about Edward."

"Thank you, Diana. I'm sure there's something I ought to do or say, meeting you for the first time since I became a vampire, but I don't know what it is." Phoebe sniffed, then burst into tears again.

"It's okay. Let it out," Marcus said, gently rocking her in his arms, his face ravaged with concern. "Don't worry about protocol. Diana doesn't care."

No, but I was pretty sure that the staff of the hospital would care if someone showed up with blood streaming out of her eyes.

"You see why Phoebe can't go to the Salpêtrière and sit at her father's bedside," Miriam said with her habitual bluntness.

"That's up to Phoebe." Marcus's tone held a sharp warning.

"No, it's up to *me*. I'm her sire," Miriam retorted. "Phoebe cannot be trusted around warmbloods yet."

What did they think Phoebe was going to do—siphon the blood out of Edward's IV and snack on his bones? I was far more worried about the reaction warmbloods would have to her appearance.

"Phoebe," I said, wading into the conversation, "would you mind very much if I worked a bit of magic on you?"

"Thank God," Françoise said. "I knew you would think of something, madame."

"I was thinking of a disguising spell, the kind I wore after my powers came in," I said, studying Phoebe as though I were making her a new outfit. "And I think you should go with her to the hospital, Françoise, if that's all right."

"*Bien sûr.* You did not think I would leave Mademoiselle Phoebe to fend for herself? But you will need something very dull," Françoise said, sizing up her charge, "if you wish her to pass as human. It was easier to make you look like an ordinary person. You were still a warmblood, after all."

Françoise had kept me from making hundreds of mistakes—large and small—during my time in the sixteenth century. If she could keep a twenty-first-century feminist from causing an uproar in Elizabethan London and Prague, she could surely manage a young vampire in a hospital. Feeling more optimistic simply because of her stolid presence, I proceeded.

"Everyone will be focused on Edward," I said. "Perhaps we can get away with something easier to wear, more like a veil than a burlap sack?"

In the end, it was a heavy weaving that was more like a shroud. It not only dimmed Phoebe's appearance, it also slowed her down. She still didn't look ordinary, but she would no longer draw every eye.

"One last thing," I said, touching her gently around the face. Phoebe winced as though my touch was searing.

"Did I hurt you?" I withdrew my hands immediately. "I was just making sure that, if you cry, the tears will appear clear rather than red."

"Phoebe is quite sensitive," Freyja explained.

"And we haven't done the full range of tests to determine those sensitivities." Miriam shook her head. "This is not a good idea, Marcus."

"Do you forbid me from taking her to the hospital?" Marcus asked.

"You know me better than that," Miriam retorted. She turned to Phoebe. "This is your decision."

Phoebe was out the door in a flash, Françoise on her heels.

"We'll be in touch," Marcus said, following her.

MATTHEW WAS IN THE HALL with Edward's chart when we arrived at the hospital. A flock of physicians and nurses were in conference nearby. Through the door, I could see Padma and Stella sitting by Edward, who was connected to machines that monitored his heart and helped with his breathing.

"How is he?" I asked, putting my hand on Matthew's arm.

"His condition is critical but stable," Matthew said, closing the chart. "They're doing everything possible. Where's Phoebe?"

"On her way with Marcus and Françoise," I replied. "We thought it would be better if I came ahead, in case . . ."

Matthew nodded. "They're discussing surgical options now."

The elevator doors opened. Phoebe was inside, with Marcus on her right and Françoise on her left. She was wearing dark glasses, her hair dull instead of glossy, and she appeared to be wrapped in an unflattering olive drab coat.

"Disguising spell," I murmured to Matthew. "A heavy one."

"Phoebe," Matthew said as she approached.

"Where's my dad?" Phoebe's eyes were streaming with tears. Thankfully, they left nothing but wet traces on her cheeks.

"In here. Your mother and sister are with him," Matthew said.

"Is he . . ." Phoebe searched Matthew's face, unable to finish her sentence.

"He's in critical condition, but stable," Matthew replied. "His heart sustained considerable damage. They're discussing surgery now."

Phoebe took a shuddering breath.

"Are you ready to go in?" Marcus asked gently.

"I don't know." Phoebe was gripping Marcus's hand with such power that it became mottled with bruises, from blue to purple to green. She looked at Marcus in panic. "What if Miriam is right? What if I can't handle this?"

"I'll be with you," Marcus said, trying to reassure her. "So will Françoise and Diana. And Matthew is here, too."

Phoebe gave a shaky nod. "Don't let go."

"Never," Marcus promised.

Padma's tearful face looked up as we entered. Stella rushed toward her sister.

"He's dying!" Stella's features were swollen with tears, her eyes red and raw. "Do something!"

"That's enough, Stella." Padma's voice was shaky.

"No. She can make this better. Fix him, Phoebe!" Stella was distraught. "He's too young to die."

The fast approach of a warmblood—sister or no sister—was more than any young vampire could handle. Phoebe's lips curled into a snarl.

Matthew whisked Stella out the door. She was still begging for somebody—anybody—to do something for her father.

With Stella out of the way, Phoebe was able to regain control. She searched for her father amid the machines that were keeping him alive.

"Oh, Mum."

"I know, Phoebe." Padma patted the empty seat next to her. "Come and sit with me. Talk to him. He's missed you so these last few months."

Marcus guided Phoebe to the chair. He cast a long look at Padma as if to make sure that she was bearing up under the strain.

"This is my fault, isn't it?" Phoebe whispered. "I knew he wasn't feeling well. But I just wanted to be married before—before—"

"Your father's heart has been weak for years, Phoebe," Padma said, tears welling up. "This has nothing to do with your decision."

"But the stress," Phoebe said, turning to her mother. "He never wanted me to become a vampire. We argued over and over about it."

"There's no point in second-guessing yourself, or engaging in magical thinking—that if only we hadn't gone to Mumbai for that vacation, then your father wouldn't have caught that virus, or he should have retired sooner and had a proper rest like the doctor wanted," Padma replied.

"Your mother is right, Phoebe. I knew as soon as I met him that Edward's heart was fragile, and that he wasn't taking good enough care of himself. Remember? We talked about this." Marcus waited for his mate's response.

Reluctantly, Phoebe nodded.

"You are in no way responsible for the choices your father made in his life," Padma said. "You're here now. Don't waste this precious time. Tell him you love him."

Phoebe reached over and took her father's hand.

"Hey, Dad," she said, sniffing back her tears. "It's me. Phoebe. Marcus is here, too."

Her father lay unconscious and unresponsive. Phoebe's mother gave her other hand an encouraging squeeze.

"Miriam and Freyja think I'm doing well, with, you know, the change." Phoebe wiped at her eyes and gave a shaky laugh. "I grew a whole inch. You know how much I hoped for some more height. I've started dancing again. And painting."

Phoebe's father had always wanted her to go back to sketching and painting. He still had one of her teenage attempts, a portrait of her mother in the garden, hanging in his office at home.

"That's wonderful, Phoebe," Padma said. "I'm happy for you."

"I'm still not very good," Phoebe said, not wanting her mother to get her hopes up. "I'm just a vampire, not Van Gogh."

"You don't give yourself enough credit," Padma said.

"Perhaps," Phoebe said. Taking credit was Stella's department.

"I don't think you have to be worried about being bored during de Clermont family gatherings, Dad," Phoebe continued. Her father wasn't responding to her small talk, but she felt as if he was listening and liked to hear about her life. He always had, no matter how minor the event or insignificant the concern. "Freyja and Miriam tell the most amazing stories. It's like living with a pair of Scheherazades."

Before she could say anything else, Phoebe was distracted by Stella's conversation with the doctors out in the corridor.

"What do you mean he needs surgery?" Stella demanded.

"Is something wrong?" Padma asked Phoebe, noticing her wandering attention.

"They can save him," Stella told the doctors. Through the window, Phoebe saw her point to her and Marcus. "They can give him their blood, and it will all be fine."

"Your father doesn't need blood," one of them replied. "Of course, if we do surgery—"

"No, you don't understand," Stella cried. "Their blood can save him!"

"Let me talk to her," Matthew said. "She's in shock." He took Stella by the elbow and steered her away from the doctors and into their father's room.

"I can't save Edward," Matthew said. "I'm sorry, Stella. It doesn't work that way."

"Why not?" Stella demanded. She turned on Phoebe. "You do it, then. Or are you too selfish to share your good fortune with the rest of us?"

One of Edward's machines made a high-pitched sound, then another. Medical personnel flooded into the room, reading machines, having urgent conversations, and checking Edward's vitals. Marcus drew Phoebe into the corner, where she would not be in the way.

"Let the doctors do their work," Marcus said when she protested.

"Is he . . ." Phoebe stopped, unable to say the words.

Padma let Matthew lead her slightly away from the bed. She trembled, and he put his hand on her shoulder, lending her what little comfort she could. Padma turned in to his arms, her shoulders shaking with grief.

"If you let him die, I'll never forgive you, Phoebe," Stella said, her voice filled with fury. "Never. His death will be your fault."

But Edward did not die. The doctors were able to save him with a long and arduous surgery, though the damage to his heart was significant and his prognosis was still guarded. Though it took some convincing, we managed to get the Taylors to leave the hospital once Edward was out of recovery and into the cardiac ICU. We took them back to Freyja's, rather than to their hotel, so that they could all be together.

Matthew had advised a mild sedative for Padma, who had not slept in days.

Freyja put Padma and Stella in a suite that overlooked the gardens. Miriam sent Phoebe up to her own rooms to rest. She'd taken one look at her daughter, given Marcus a good sniff, and informed Phoebe that this was neither a request nor open to further discussion. Phoebe, exhausted by all that had happened, put up a minor protest but was in the end persuaded by Françoise.

Charles fussed over Marcus, but he refused blood and wine. Matthew took both.

"It's always the same," Matthew said. "Every warmblood thinks that a second chance at life is the answer to their prayers."

"Of course it's not," Miriam said. "It's just another opportunity to do everything wrong all over again."

"I learned that the hard way—in New Orleans." Marcus stood by the empty fireplace, staring at the door through which Phoebe had left.

"What happens now?" Miriam asked Matthew. "There's no point in pretending we've stuck to the rules. Marcus might as well stay."

"Phoebe's not staying here," Marcus said flatly. "I want her at home. Away from Stella. Edward is stable. The doctors will tell us if there's any change."

"Pickering Place is too small," Freyja said. "And there's nowhere to hunt—not even a garden—unless you are willing to have Phoebe roam Piccadilly Circus."

"Marcus is thinking of Sept-Tours, Freyja." Matthew took out his phone. "I'll call *Maman*. If that's all right with you, Miriam?"

Miriam considered her options. I was used to her quick reactions. This thoughtful side of Miriam was unexpected—and welcome.

"If Phoebe wants to go with you, I won't oppose it," she said at last.

WE TRAVELED DOWN TO SEPT-TOURS that night, hoping that the darkness would make the journey more bearable for Phoebe. She and Marcus sat together in the backseat, her head on his shoulder, their hands knotted together. Françoise sat next to them like a Victorian chaperone, though she spent most of her time looking out the window rather than at her charges.

Ysabeau was waiting for us, as we knew she would be. She had heard the car's approach, the sound of the engine and the crunch of tires on gravel the only early warning system she needed.

She helped Phoebe out of the car.

"You must be tired," Ysabeau said, kissing her on both cheeks. "We will sit quietly together, and listen to the birds as they wake. I always find that very restful, in times like these. Françoise will draw you a bath first."

Marcus came around the car with a small case of Phoebe's clothes. "I'll get you settled."

"No." Ysabeau looked at her grandson with a forbidding expression. "Phoebe is here to see me, not you."

"But—" Marcus looked at Phoebe, wide-eyed. "I thought . . ."

"You thought you would stay here?" Ysabeau snorted. "She does not need a man fussing over her. Go back to Les Revenants—and stay there."

"Come," Françoise said, drawing Phoebe gently toward the stairs. "You heard Madame Ysabeau."

Phoebe looked conflicted between her desire to be with Marcus and her respect for the de Clermont matriarch.

"It won't be much longer now," she whispered to Marcus, before letting Françoise lead her away.

"I'm not far," Marcus said.

Phoebe nodded.

"That wasn't fair, *Grand-mère*," Marcus said. "It's too soon for Phoebe to have to make a choice like that. Especially after how Stella behaved."

"Too soon? There is no such thing," Ysabeau said. "We are, all of us, asked to grow up too quickly. It is the way the gods remind us that life, no matter how long, is still but a breath."

⇥ 35 ⇤

Seventy-Five

26 JULY

Phoebe was on her hands and knees, digging in the soft garden soil. The sun had barely crested over the surrounding hills. Nevertheless, she was wearing a wide-brimmed hat to protect her from its rays, as well as the Jackie O–style sunglasses that had become an essential part of her wardrobe.

Marthe was working in the next bed, weeding around the leafy tops of carrots and the pale green stalks of celery. She had come from Les Revenants, where she had been helping Diana and Matthew with the children. Sarah and Agatha were still there, along with Marcus and Jack, so they didn't need her assistance as much as they had when they first arrived, jet-lagged and exhausted, from America.

Phoebe wiped a dirty hand across her cheek. There was a tiny fly there, and it was driving her crazy. Then she resumed digging.

The sun was warm on her back, and the ground underneath her hands smelled fresh, like life. Phoebe plunged her trowel into the soil, breaking it up, readying it to be planted with the seedlings Marthe wanted them to move from the greenhouse.

Phoebe was sure there was some lesson to be learned from her work with Marthe, just as there were lessons to be learned from Françoise and Ysabeau. Now that she was at Sept-Tours, lessons were woven into every activity.

Since her father had been hospitalized, everything around Phoebe had shifted. Miriam had gone back to Oxford, placing her entirely in Ysabeau's care. Freyja had not wanted to spend these weeks before Phoebe made her decision under her stepmother's roof, though she planned on coming down for the day itself. In just two more weeks Baldwin would be here, and the next stage of Phoebe's life would begin. She would be a fledgling vampire then.

Within Ysabeau's household, the four women coexisted with remarkably few outbursts and little fuss. This was not how things had been in Phoebe's house growing up, where the three Taylor women had always been jockeying for position and control. Françoise and Marthe were a formidable pair, both of them forces of nature, neither of them yielding an inch of their own power to the other, each respecting the other's carefully delineated sphere of influence. Phoebe still didn't understand what all the divisions of responsibility were, but she could sense adjustments to them whenever Marthe appeared in the family apartments to look after Ysabeau, or when Françoise bustled through the kitchen on the way to mend a shirt.

Authority. Power. Status. These were the variables that shaped a vampire's life. One day, Phoebe would understand them. Until then, she was content to watch and learn from two women who clearly knew exactly how to not only survive, but thrive.

But it was from the castle's chatelaine that Phoebe was learning the most about how to be a vampire. According to Françoise, Ysabeau was the oldest and wisest vampire left on earth. Whether or not this was true, Ysabeau made Freyja and even Miriam seem young and inexperienced by comparison. As for Phoebe, she felt every bit the infant whenever she was in the woman's presence.

"There you are." Ysabeau glided across the garden, her feet making no sound on the gravel, her movements smoother and more elegant than even Madame Elena's. "You two do know that you can't really dig to China, as the ancients hoped."

Phoebe laughed. "There go my morning plans, then."

"Why don't you walk with me instead?" Ysabeau suggested.

Phoebe stuck her spade in the ground and hopped to her feet. She loved Ysabeau's walks. Each one took her through a different part of the castle or its grounds. Ysabeau told her stories about the family as they strolled through the courtyard or the house, pointing out where the laundries had been, and the candlemaker, and the blacksmith.

Phoebe had been to Sept-Tours before, back when Matthew and Diana were timewalking and Marcus had wanted her close. She'd returned after the couple came home, too, and a few times since the babies were born. But something had changed in Phoebe's relationship to the house. It was more than the fact that she was a vampire. She was a true de Clermont now—or so Ysabeau said, confident that Phoebe's mind had not changed when it came to Marcus.

"The sun is rising fast today," Ysabeau observed, looking up at the sky. "And there are no clouds. Why don't we go inside, so that you can take off your hat and glasses?"

Phoebe linked arms with Ysabeau as they turned toward the castle. Ysabeau looked a bit startled by the familiar act. When Phoebe pulled away, fearing she had broken some rule, Ysabeau instead drew her closer. The two of them walked slowly indoors, drinking in the early morning scents.

"Monsieur Roux burned his croissants," Ysabeau said, giving the air a sniff. "And I do wish the priest would stop changing his laundry soap. I no sooner get used to the smell of one than he buys another."

Phoebe sniffed. The sharp, floral scent did not smell "springtime fresh," but of chemicals. She wrinkled her nose.

"Did you hear the fight last night between Adele and her new boyfriend?" Phoebe asked.

"How could I not? They were on the other side of our wall, and shouting at the top of their lungs." Ysabeau shook her head.

"Madame Lefebvre—how is she doing?" Phoebe asked. The old woman was in her nineties and still went around to the shops every day on her own, pulling a wire cart to hold her groceries. Last week she'd fallen and broken her hip.

"Not well," Ysabeau said. "The priest went round yesterday. They don't expect her to live out the week. I will go and visit her this afternoon. Maybe you would like to come?"

"May I?" Phoebe asked.

"Of course," Ysabeau said. "I'm sure Madame Lefebvre would like to see you."

They were inside now, and making their stately way through the ground-floor rooms: Ysabeau's salon, with its gilded furniture and Sèvres porcelain; the formal dining room, with the statues that flanked the door; the family library, with its worn sofas and piles of newspapers, magazines, and paperback books; Ysabeau's warmly colored breakfast room that always looked as though the sun was streaming into it even on the cloudiest days; the great hall, with its high beamed roof and painted walls. In each room, Ysabeau revealed something about what had happened here, once upon a time.

"Diana's firedrake broke one of those," Ysabeau said, pointing to a large lion's-head vase. "Philippe commissioned a set of two. I must confess I was never very fond of them. If we are lucky, Apollo will break the other and we can find something new to take its place."

Another memory of Philippe popped up in the formal dining room, with its long, polished table and ranks of chairs.

"Philippe always sat here, and I sat at the other end. That way we could manage everyone's conversations, and make sure that war didn't break out between the guests." Ysabeau ran her fingers over the chair's carved back. "We had so many dinner parties in this room."

"Sophie's water broke on this sofa, on the day before Margaret was born," Ysabeau said when they reached the family library. She plumped one of the cushions. Though the rest of the sofa was covered in faded brown, this cushion was a rosy pink. "We did not have to replace the whole piece of furniture, as Sophie feared, only the cushion. See, this one does not match the others. I told Marthe not to even try, but to use something that would always remind us of Margaret's birth."

"Here, I tried to frighten Diana away from Matthew," Ysabeau said in the breakfast room, a smile turning up the corners of her lips. "But she was braver than I knew."

Ysabeau turned slowly around in the castle's lofty great hall, inviting Phoebe to do the same.

"This is where Diana and Matthew held their wedding feast." Ysabeau surveyed the large room with its suits of armor, weapons, and faux medieval decorations. "I was not there, of course, and Philippe did not tell me about it. It was not until Diana and Matthew returned from the past that I heard the tale. Perhaps you and Marcus will celebrate here, and fill the hall again with the sound of laughter and dancing."

Ysabeau led Phoebe to where a set of stone stairs climbed to the crenellated heights of the castle's square keep. Instead of climbing them, as they normally would, Ysabeau drew Phoebe toward a low, arched door in the wall that was always locked.

Ysabeau took a worn iron key from her pocket and fit it into the lock. She turned it and motioned Phoebe inside.

It took Phoebe's eyes a few minutes to adjust to the changing level of light. This room had only a few small windows fitted with colored panes of glass. Phoebe took off her sunglasses and rubbed her eyes to help bring them into focus.

"Is this another storeroom?" Phoebe asked, wondering what treasures it might contain.

But the stale air and faint scent of wax soon told her this room had a different purpose. This was the de Clermont chapel—and crypt.

A large stone sarcophagus occupied the center of the small chapel. A handful of other coffins were set into alcoves in the walls. So, too, were objects: shields, swords, pieces of armor.

"Humans think we live in dark places like this," Ysabeau said. "They are more right than they know. My Philippe is here, in the center of the room as he was once at the center of our family and my world. One day, I will be buried here with him."

Phoebe looked at Ysabeau in surprise.

"None of us is immune to death, Phoebe," Ysabeau said, as if she could hear Phoebe's thoughts.

"Stella thinks we are. She didn't understand why no one would save Dad," Phoebe said. "I'm not sure I understand myself. I just knew he wouldn't like it—that it would be wrong."

"You cannot make every person you love into a vampire," Ysabeau said. "Marcus tried, and it almost destroyed him."

Phoebe knew about New Orleans and had met those of Marcus's children who survived.

"Stella may have been the first human to ask you to save someone's life, but she won't be the last," Ysabeau continued. "You must be prepared to say no, again and again, as you did last night. Saying no takes courage— far more courage than saying yes."

Ysabeau took Phoebe's arm again, and resumed their walk.

"People wonder what it takes to become a vampire." Ysabeau gave Phoebe a sidelong glance. "Do you know what I tell them?"

Phoebe shook her head, intrigued.

"To be a vampire you must choose life—your life, not someone else's— over and over again, day after day," Ysabeau said. "You must choose it over sleep, over peace, over grief, over death. In the end, it is our relentless drive to live that defines us. Without that, we are nothing but a nightmare or a ghost: a shadow of the humans we once were."

⇥ 36 ⇤

Ninety

Phoebe sat in Ysabeau's salon, amid the blue and white porcelain, the gilded chairs, the silk upholstery, and the priceless works of art, and waited, again, for time to find her.

Baldwin strode into the room, his navy suit harmonizing with the room's color scheme. Phoebe had picked her dress to stand out, however, rather than blend in. It was a bright shade of aquamarine, a color that symbolized loyalty and patience. It reminded her of her mother's wedding clothes, and Marcus's eyes, and the color of the sea when it returned to the shore.

"Baldwin." Phoebe thought about rising and found she was already standing, offering a cheek to the head of her husband's family.

"You look well, Phoebe," Baldwin commented after he'd kissed her, his eyes surveying her from head to toe. "Ysabeau hasn't been mistreating you, I see."

Phoebe didn't acknowledge his remark with a response. After the past several weeks, she would walk across deserts for Ysabeau, and was keeping a silent record of every slight uttered against the matriarch of the de Clermont clan.

Phoebe intended to settle those accounts one day.

"Where are your glasses?" Baldwin asked.

"I decided not to wear them today." Phoebe was battling a headache, and every time the curtains blew she winced, but she was determined that her first long look at Marcus was going to be without any interference. When she'd seen him at the Salpêtrière, she had been too distracted by her father's condition to pay any attention to her mate.

"Hello, Phoebe." Miriam entered. She was not in her usual black leather and boots, but in a flowing skirt. Her long hair fell around her shoulders, and her neck, arms, and fingers were covered with heavy jewels.

"Excellent. We can get started," Baldwin said. "Miriam, do you consent to your daughter's decision to mate with Marcus, a member of my family and the Bishop-Clairmont scion, son of Matthew de Clermont?"

"Are you actually going to go through the entire betrothal ceremony?" Miriam demanded.

"That was my plan, yes." Baldwin glared at her. "You wanted it to be official."

"Wait. Don't we need Marcus to be here before we go any further?" Phoebe asked. "Where is he?" Her anxiety rose. What if Marcus had had second thoughts? What if he decided he didn't want her now?

"I'm right here."

Marcus stood just over the threshold, wearing a blue shirt, blue jeans, and sneakers with a hole in one toe. He looked handsome and slightly mischievous, as he always did. And he smelled divine. Freyja was with him, though Phoebe had to tear her eyes away from her mate to give his aunt a proper hello.

"Hello, Phoebe," Freyja said, beaming. "I told you we would make it."

"Yes," Phoebe said, her eyes fixed on Marcus. Her throat felt dry, and she had to struggle to get that single word out.

Marcus smiled. Phoebe's heart thumped in response.

Her senses clicked into overdrive. All she could hear was the sound of his heart beating. All she could smell was his distinctive scent. Her thoughts were only of Marcus. Her skin yearned for his touch.

And just like that he had her in his arms, his lips pressed to hers, the clean scents of licorice and bee balm and pine surrounding her along with a hundred other notes she couldn't yet recognize or name.

"I love you, sweetheart," he murmured in her ear. "And don't even think about changing your mind. It's too late. You're already mine. Forever."

There were congratulations and champagne and laughter after Phoebe formally chose Marcus to be her mate. None of it made much of an impression on her, however. Phoebe had waited for ninety long days to announce her intention to irrevocably attach herself to another creature.

When it came time to do it, however, all she could do was stare at Marcus with rapt attention.

"You have a bit of red in your hair," Phoebe said, removing a strand from his shoulders. "I've never noticed it before."

Marcus took her hand and kissed it, his touch electrifying. Phoebe's heart skipped a beat and then felt like it was going to explode. Marcus smiled.

That tiny crease at the side of his mouth—she'd never noticed that before, either. It wasn't a wrinkle, exactly, but a light depression in the skin as though it remembered precisely how Marcus grinned.

"Phoebe. Did you hear me?" Miriam's voice penetrated Phoebe's consciousness.

"No. That is, I'm sorry." Phoebe tried to focus. "What did you say?"

"I said it's time I left," Miriam replied. "I've decided to go back to New Haven. Marcus isn't going to be much use as a research partner for the next few months. I might as well be useful."

"Oh." Phoebe didn't know what she was supposed to say. A horrifying thought occurred to her. "I don't have to go with you, do I?"

"No, Phoebe. Although you might want to sound a little less anguished at the prospect of spending time with your maker." Miriam looked at Ysabeau. "I'm trusting you with my daughter."

Seeing Miriam and Ysabeau facing each other, one light and one dark, was like watching two primeval forces of nature struggling to achieve balance.

"I have always looked after her. She is my grandson's mate," Ysabeau assured her. "Phoebe is a de Clermont now."

"Yes, but she will always be *my* daughter," Miriam replied with a touch of fierceness.

"Of course," Ysabeau said smoothly.

Finally, Miriam and Baldwin left. Their hands tightly twined, Phoebe and Marcus saw them to their cars.

"How much longer do I have to wait to get you alone?" Marcus whispered, his mouth pressing lightly into the sensitive skin behind her ear.

"Your grandmother is still here," Phoebe said, struggling to remain composed even though her knees felt bendy and after their separation she wanted nothing more than to spend the next ninety days in bed with

Marcus. If it felt that good to have him kiss her neck, what was it going to be like to make love?

"I paid Freyja to take Ysabeau and Marthe to Saint-Lucien for lunch."

Phoebe giggled.

"I see that meets with your approval," Marcus said.

Phoebe's giggle turned to laughter.

"If you keep laughing like that, they'll suspect we're up to something," Marcus warned before swallowing her laughter in a kiss that left her gasping for air.

After that, Phoebe was pretty sure Ysabeau and Marthe did more than suspect what would happen when they descended the hill to Madame Laurence's restaurant.

By the time she and Marcus were finally, completely alone, Phoebe had had time to get nervous about what was about to happen.

"I'm not very good at biting yet," Phoebe confessed as Marcus drew her toward his room.

Marcus gave her a kiss that left her dizzy.

"Do we exchange blood before or after we make love?" Phoebe asked once they were inside and the door was closed and locked. It was a very stout lock, she noticed, probably fifteenth century in date. "I don't want to do it wrong."

Marcus was on one knee before her, sliding her knickers out from underneath her dress.

"I'm so glad you didn't wear trousers," he said, shimmying the aquamarine linen up to expose bare flesh. "Oh, God. You smell even better than you did before."

"I do?" Phoebe stopped worrying about what she was *supposed* to do long enough to thoroughly enjoy what Marcus was *actually doing* with his mouth and tongue. She gasped.

Marcus looked up at her with the wicked expression that only she saw. "Yes. Which is completely impossible, because you were perfect before. So how could you be more perfect now?"

"Do I—taste—different?" Phoebe asked, her fingers threaded through his hair. She gave it a little tug.

"I'll have to do more research to be sure," Marcus said, giving her a grin before delving into her once more.

Phoebe discovered that, like most things in life, vampires had no need to rush when it came to pleasure. She could expand her being into every moment of their lovemaking, unconcerned about the time, never worried if she was taking too long or if it was her turn to please Marcus.

Time just—stopped. There was no *then*, no *soon*, only a bone-satisfying, endless *now*.

Every nerve in her body was tingling, seconds or minutes or hours later, when Marcus had finished reacquainting himself with her body and Phoebe had explored his with the enhanced touch, taste, smell, hearing, and sight that she now possessed. She had never imagined she could *feel* so deeply, or be so completely joined with another human being.

When Phoebe was moments away from climax, Marcus rolled them over so that Phoebe was balanced atop him. He was still inside her. Gently, Marcus cupped her face in his hands. He searched her face as though he was looking for something. When he found what he sought, Marcus drew her mouth toward his breast.

Phoebe picked up a scent—elusive, mysterious. It was unlike anything she had ever smelled before.

Marcus moved, slowly. Phoebe moaned as that maddening, alluring scent grew stronger. He put his hands on her hips, holding her tight to him, increasing the friction between them.

Phoebe felt her body begin to spiral toward completion. Her cheek was resting on Marcus's chest, and she heard his heart beat. Once.

Phoebe bit into Marcus's flesh, and her mouth was flooded with the scent-taste of heaven—of the man she loved and would always love. His blood sang within her, the notes echoed in his heart's slow cadence.

Evermore.

Marcus's thoughts and feelings coursed through her veins like quicksilver, a flash of light and fire that brought a kaleidoscope of images along with it. There were too many for Phoebe to acknowledge never mind absorb. It would take her centuries to understand the tales that Marcus's blood told.

Evermore, Marcus's heart sang.

But there was one constant in the endless changing barrage of information: Phoebe herself. Her voice, as Marcus heard it. Her eyes, as Marcus saw them. Her touch, as Marcus felt it.

Phoebe heard her own heart answer his, the harmony perfect.

Evermore.

Phoebe lifted her head and looked into Marcus's eyes, knowing that he would see himself reflected in hers.

Evermore.

A Fence Against the World

13 AUGUST

"My God, that's a griffin!" Chris Roberts stood in the doorway to the kitchen in New Haven, holding a birthday cake and staring at Apollo.

"Yes, he is," I said, taking a tray of roasted vegetables from the oven. "He's called Apollo."

"Does he bite?" Chris asked.

"He does, but I have some of Sarah's Peace Water in case he gets anxious." The bottle in my pocket was filled with layers of different-colored blue liquids. I took it out and gave it a shake. "Come, Apollo."

Apollo obediently bounded over.

"Good boy." I pulled the stopper on the bottle and dabbed a bit of liquid on the griffin's forehead and its breastbone.

Ardwinna stalked by with her bone. She gave Chris a sniff, then settled down to gnaw on it.

"And what the hell is that?" Chris demanded.

"A dog. She's my birthday present from Matthew—a Scottish deer-hound. Her name is Ardwinna."

"Ard—whatta? Willa?" Chris shook his head and studied the gangly puppy, who was all legs and eyes at the moment with tufts of gray hair sticking out all over her. "What's wrong with her? She looks like she's starving."

"Hello, Chris. I see you've met Ardwinna and Apollo." Matthew had Philip by the hand. The moment Philip saw Chris, he began to dance around him, babbling a mile a minute. Every third word was intelligible. Based on those I understood, he was telling Chris about his summer.

"Blocks. Granny. Boat. Marcus," Philip said, reeling off the high points while he hopped in place. "Jack. Griff'n. Gammer. Aggie."

"Deerhounds are supposed to look that way," I said, trying to answer Chris's question. "And don't you dare give her a nickname. Ardwinna is perfect, just as she is."

Ardwinna looked up from her bone when her name was mentioned, and thumped her tail before returning her attention to her treat.

"Chris!" Becca bellowed, barreling through the house like a Tasmanian devil. She flung herself at Chris's knees.

"Whoa. Easy there. Hello, Becca. Did you miss me?"

"Yes." Becca was squeezing Chris so tightly I was afraid she might cut off his circulation.

"Me, too." Philip bounced up and down like an energetic tennis ball. Chris high-fived him, which pleased my son to no end.

Matthew divested Chris of the cake, which made him an easy target for more of Becca's attention.

"Up!" Becca demanded, holding her arms in the air so Chris could do her bidding.

"Please," Matthew said automatically, reaching for the bottle of wine on the table.

"Pleeeeaaaassseee," Becca said in a wheedling tone.

I was going to go stark raving mad if she didn't stop doing that. Before I could say anything, though, Matthew kissed me.

"Let's settle for exaggerated courtesy tonight," Matthew said when he was through. "Beer, Chris?"

"Sounds good." Chris looked around at our new house. "Nice place. A bit gloomy, though. You could paint the woodwork, brighten it up a bit."

"We'd have to ask our landlord first. It belongs to Marcus," I said. "He thought it would be a good place for the twins, now that they're bigger."

Since Apollo arrived, it had become clear that our growing family would not fit into my old place on Court Street. We needed a backyard—not to mention better laundry facilities. Marcus had insisted we use his sprawling mansion near campus while we looked for a place that was a little farther away from the hustle and bustle of New Haven, somewhere the children and animals could run. It was not precisely our style. Marcus had bought it in the nineteenth century when formality had been in fashion. There was carved wood everywhere you looked, and more downstairs reception rooms than I knew what to do with, but it was fine for now.

"Miriam hates this house, you know." Chris's lips curved up at the mention of Phoebe's maker. The precise nature of their relationship was something that Matthew and I speculated about endlessly.

"She doesn't have to live here, then," I said tartly, feeling a bit defensive on behalf of our new home.

"True. If she does come back to the lab, Miriam can bunk with me. I've got plenty of room." Chris took a sip of beer.

I looked at my husband in triumph. Matthew owed me ten dollars and a foot massage. I planned on collecting it as soon as Chris left.

"Has anyone seen the box with the cutlery in it? I'm sure I labeled it." I rummaged around in the piles by the sink.

Chris reached into the box nearest to him and produced a spoon. "Ta-da!"

"Yay you! Magic!" Philip bounced up and down.

"No, sport, just an old Boy Scout trick: open boxes, look in boxes, find stuff. Simple." Chris handed Philip his spoon and looked at Matthew and me. "Isn't he a bit young to know that word?"

"We no longer think so," I said, stirring some bits of raw meat into Philip's beet puree.

"Short of spellbinding, there is no way to keep the twins away from magic, or magic away from the twins," Matthew explained. "Philip and Becca don't fully understand what magic is—yet—or the responsibilities that come with it, but they will. In time."

"Those children will be spellbound over my dead body," Chris said roughly. "And I'm one of their godparents, so you can take that as a serious threat."

"Only Baldwin thought it was a good idea," I assured him.

"That guy has got to learn to relax," Chris said. "Now that I'm a knight, and have to talk to him occasionally, I've learned he has no life outside of what he thinks is his duty to his father's memory."

"We talked a lot about fathers and sons this summer," I said. "And mothers and daughters, too. In the end, even Baldwin came around on the twins' spellbinding. As for the magic, well, story time is really fun at our house." I wiggled my fingers in the air in an imitation of how humans thought witches worked their magic.

"You mean—you're doing magic in front of them?" Chris looked shocked. Then he smiled. "Cool. So is the griffin yours? Did you conjure him up for the children to play with?"

"No, he belongs to Philip." I looked at my son with pride. "He seems to be an early bloomer, magic-wise. And a promising witch, too."

"And how did you get Apollo here?" Chris said, concerned only with the practicalities, not the bigger question of how a mythological creature came to be living in New Haven. "Does he have his own passport?"

"It turns out you can't send a griffin on commercial aircraft," I said, indignant. "I checked both cat and bird on the form, and they just returned it to me and told me to correct my mistakes."

"Sore subject," Matthew murmured to Chris, who nodded in sympathy.

"We could get Ardwinna onto a plane, and she's twice his size. I don't see why we couldn't just smuggle him on board in a dog carrier," I grumbled.

"Because he's a griffin?" Chris said. I glared at him. "Just a suggestion."

"I would have used a disguising spell, obviously." I lifted Philip into his booster seat and delivered the beets and beef to him. He tucked into his dinner with enthusiasm. Becca wanted only blood and water, so I let her have it in a sippy cup on the floor. She sat next to Ardwinna to drink it, watching the dog chew her bone.

"Obviously." Chris grinned.

"I'll have you know Apollo makes a convincing Labrador retriever," I said. "He's been a good boy in the dog park, when we've taken him with Ardwinna."

Chris choked on his beer, then quickly recovered.

"I imagine he's got good hang time, what with his wingspan. He might like a game of Frisbee." As usual, Chris took the idiosyncrasies of our family in stride. "I'd be happy to play with him, if you're too busy."

Matthew took a platter of steaks out of the fridge. He kissed me as he passed by, this time on the nape of my neck. "I'm headed outside to grill these. How do you like your steak, Chris?"

"Just walk it through a warm room, my friend," Chris replied.

"Good man," Matthew said. "My sentiments exactly."

"Walk a bit more slowly through that warm room with mine," I reminded him.

"Savage." Matthew grinned.

"So Phoebe and Marcus made it to the big day," Chris said.

"Their official reunion was three days ago," I said. "Though of course they had already seen each other."

"Sounds like things got a bit complicated for a while, what with her father's illness," Chris commented.

"We were all sure it would work out," I replied.

"You two seem good," Chris said, gesturing with his beer in Matthew's direction.

"On balance, it was a lovely summer," I said, thinking back over all that had happened. "No work got done, of course."

"No, it never does," Chris said with a laugh.

"But otherwise, it was perfect." To my surprise, I meant it.

"And you're happy," Chris observed. "Which makes me happy."

"Yeah," I said, looking around me at the chaos of unpacked boxes and pureed beets, children and animals, stacks of unopened mail that had been collecting all summer, books and laptops, toys that squeaked and toys that didn't. "I really am."

That evening, after Chris left and the children were put to bed, Matthew and I sat out on the wide porch that wrapped around the corner of the house and overlooked the fenced garden. The sky was filled with stars, and the night air held a welcome note of coolness to balance out the heat of the day.

"It feels so protected here," I said, glancing over the yard. "Our own private paradise, hidden away from the world, where nothing bad can happen."

The slanting moonlight glanced off Matthew's features, silvering his hair and adding lines and shadows to his face. For a moment— just one moment—I imagined him an old man, and me an old woman, holding hands on a late summer evening and remembering when our children slept safely inside and love filled every corner of our lives.

"I know it can't stay this way," I said, thinking back over the events of the past summer. "We can't stay in the garden forever."

"No. And the only true fence against the world and all its dangers is a thorough knowledge of it," Matthew said as we rocked in silence, together.

⇥ 38 ⇤

One Hundred

20 AUGUST

Marcus drove through the center of Hadley, along the village green that preserved the town's colonial layout. Stately houses with carved doorways clustered around the leafy space with an attitude of determined persistence.

He swung the car onto a road that led west. Marcus slowed slightly as they passed a graveyard, then pulled up in front of a small, wooden house. It was far more modest than those in the center of town, with no extensions or additions to alter the original footprint: two rooms downstairs and two rooms upstairs arranged around a central chimney made of brick. The house's façade sparkled with casement windows on the ground and first floor, and Phoebe adjusted her glasses to lessen their glare. There was a single stone step leading up to the door. Outside, a small garden in the front was filled with sunflowers that stood out against the white painted clapboards like polka dots. Like the house, the white picket fence had been freshly painted, and the wood was in surprisingly good condition. An old-fashioned, sprawling rosebush filled the space under the windows on one side of the door, and a tall shrub with dark green, heart-shaped leaves was on the other. Fields surrounded the house in every direction, and two ramshackle barns added a romantic note.

"It's beautiful." Phoebe turned to Marcus. "Is it how you remember?"

"The fence wasn't that sturdy when we lived here, that's for sure." Marcus put the car in park and turned off the ignition. He looked uncertain and vulnerable. "Matthew's been busy."

Phoebe reached over and took her mate's hand.

"Do you want to get out?" Phoebe asked quietly. "If not, we can always keep driving, and stay somewhere else."

It wouldn't be surprising if Marcus wanted to wait a bit longer. Returning to the home of his childhood was a major step.

"It's time." Marcus opened his door and came around to open hers. Phoebe fished around in her purse and found her mobile. She took a picture of the house and sent it to Diana, as she had promised.

Phoebe held tight to Marcus's hand as they walked through the garden gate. Marcus closed it securely behind them. Phoebe frowned.

"Habit," Marcus explained with a smile. "To keep the Kelloggs' hog out of Ma's garden."

Phoebe caught him in her arms when he returned. She kissed him. They stood, arms locked around each other, noses touching. Marcus took a deep breath.

"Show me our house," Phoebe said, kissing him again.

Marcus led her down the short, gravel path to the stone threshold. It was rough-hewn and uneven, a massive piece of rock that was weather-worn and had a dip in the center from the tread of hundreds of feet. The door had a split in the top panel, and its dark red paint was peeling. Phoebe scratched at it, and the paint underneath was the same color, as was the paint beneath that.

"It's as though time stood still, and everything is just as I left it," Marcus commented. "Except the lock, of course. Mr. Security strikes again."

When they turned the modern brass key in the substantial mechanism and pushed the door open, the air that met them smelled old and stale. There was a touch of damp, too, and a slight scent of mold.

Phoebe searched for a light switch. To her surprise, she couldn't find one.

"I don't think there's any electric," Marcus said. "Matthew refused to wire Pickering Place until about twenty years ago."

Phoebe's eyes adjusted to the dim light coming through the ancient casement windows. Slowly, the house's interior came into focus.

There was dust everywhere—on the wide pine floorboards, on the chamfered summer beam that spanned the width of the house, on the shallow sills that held the diamond panes on the casement windows, on the round newel post that punctuated the end of the banister.

"Christ." Marcus sounded shaky. "I half expect my mother came out of the kitchen, wiping her hands on her apron, to see if I was hungry."

They walked together through the four rooms of Marcus's childhood. First the kitchen, with thickly boarded walls that ran horizontally around the room. They were painted with a mustardy yellow paint that had turned black around the fireplace where Catherine Chauncey had cooked meals for her family. A long hook was all that remained of the iron equipment that once would have filled the brick enclosure—the trivets and griddles and deep pots. The beams that held up the rooms above were exposed, and cobwebs clung to the corners. There were a few pegs driven into the walls, and a rickety chair sat in the corner. A brighter yellow patch on the wall indicated where there had once stood a cupboard.

They crossed the entrance hall and into the parlor, where another fireplace shared the same wall with the one in the kitchen. This room was grander, with rough plastered walls that had been whitewashed. Bits of plaster had fallen off here and there, and the dust was visible in the air thanks to the slanting rays of the afternoon sun. A long table sat in the center of the room, its dark wooden surface cracked and split. Pulled up to it was a small chair with holes in the back slat.

Marcus touched the hooks over the fireplace.

"This is where we kept my grandfather's gun," Marcus said. He rested his hands on the mantel. "My mother's clock sat here. She was probably buried with it, or else she left it to Patience."

Phoebe slid her arms around Marcus's waist from behind and rested her forehead against his back. She could feel her mate's pain, but she could also hear the bittersweet note in his voice as Marcus remembered and remembered some more. She pressed a kiss against his spine.

Marcus placed an old book on the mantel, slender and bound in brown leather. His fingers caressed the covers for a moment. He turned to face her, and was distracted by something in the nearby corner.

"Philippe's chair," he said in a tone of disbelief.

Phoebe recognized the old, blue-painted chair with the curved, frond-like volutes at the ends of the crest rail, the gracefully tapered legs, and the substantial saddle seat. It was always in the same spot in Philippe's study at Sept-Tours, and Phoebe had never seen anyone sit in it, in spite of its sturdy construction. The paint on the arms was worn through to the bare wood, a sign that it had once been in constant use.

An envelope addressed to Marcus was propped against the finely turned spindles.

Marcus frowned and reached for the letter. He slit the top with his finger and pulled out the single page.

"*Philippe would want you to have his chair,*" Marcus read aloud. "*So would Dr. Franklin. Remember we are not far away, if you have need of us. Your father, Matthew.*"

Diana had made sure Phoebe knew exactly how to get to their house in New Haven, which parts of the route were likely to be difficult in snowy weather, and every phone number where she and Matthew could be reached—just in case.

"I'm not sure I have the nerve to sit in it." Marcus sounded slightly awed by his new possession.

"If you don't, I will," Phoebe said with a laugh. "Ysabeau told me Philippe thought it was the most comfortable chair in the world."

Marcus smiled and ran one finger along the arm rest. "I must say it suits this house better than it ever did Sept-Tours."

Phoebe thought it suited Marcus, too.

Back in the front hall, Marcus stared at the newel post at the bottom of the stairs, where faded black ink delineated a jagged coastline. They climbed the stairs, which were narrow and swayed slightly under their weight. The two rooms upstairs were unfinished, with simple boards laid across beams to make the floor, and neither plaster nor wooden paneling to hide the walls' construction. Between the clapboards you could see a few glints of sunlight.

"Which room was yours?" Phoebe asked.

"This one," Marcus said, pointing to the room over the kitchen. "Ma insisted we sleep here, because it was warmer."

The room was empty, except for an old brass rooster that looked as though it belonged to a weather vane.

"It's much smaller than I remember," Marcus said, standing next to the window.

"Do we need more than this?" Phoebe was already imagining the house with fresh paint on the inside, the panes of glass clean and gleaming, a fire crackling in the kitchen hearth and filling the house with homely sounds and scents.

"Neither of these rooms have doors." Marcus's eyes darted around the room. "I'm not sure we could even get a bed up here."

"What does that matter?" Phoebe laughed. "We don't sleep, remember?"

"That's not the only thing beds are good for," Marcus said, his voice lower and more intense than usual. He pulled Phoebe into a kiss that was deeply possessive. Had she still been a warmblood, it would have left her breathless.

But there was no rush for them to make love. They had hours and hours left in the day, and no need to look for food or shelter or warmth or light. They had each other, and that was enough.

"Let's go look at the barn," Phoebe said, drawing away and leading him back toward the stairs.

They stepped outside the kitchen door that led out back—it would need to be planed at the bottom to make it easier to open and close, Phoebe noted. And it was a good thing they were vampires, and impervious to cold, because the wood wasn't thick enough to keep out the chill for much longer. How had Marcus's family survived a Massachusetts winter with only that thin door between them and the snow and the wind?

Marcus stopped in his tracks.

Phoebe looked back at him. She recognized this spot. It was etched in Marcus's blood, just like the coastline of America was on the newel post on the stairs.

"You made the only choice you could," Phoebe said, returning to his side. "It had to be done."

"Hey!" A woman waved from the road. Her hair was iron gray and she was wearing an apricot-colored shirt and white cropped trousers as though she were about to go on holiday in the Caribbean. "You two are trespassing. Get out of here, or I'll call the cops."

"I'm Marcus MacNeil. I own this place." His true name flowed smoothly off his tongue. Phoebe blinked, used to thinking of him as Marcus Whitmore.

"Well, it's about time you showed up. Every year people come and clear the snow, and mow the hay, and make sure the roof hasn't collapsed, but a house doesn't like to be empty." The woman peered at them through wire-rimmed spectacles. "I'm your neighbor. Mrs. Judd. Who's she?"

"I'm Marcus's fiancée." Phoebe tucked her hand into Marcus's elbow.

"Are you two planning on living here now?" Mrs. Judd looked them both over. "It would be awfully hard work to make this house habitable. It's not connected to the sewer, or the power grid, for starters. Of course, nothing worth doing is ever easy."

"You're right," Marcus said.

"There are lots of stories about this place, you know. Somebody found a human skull under that tree." Mrs. Judd pointed to the large elm tree. "They say the split in the door was made in one of the last Indian raids. And the cellar is definitely haunted."

"How enchanting," Phoebe said brightly, wishing this busybody would leave off the spooky stories until they got to know her better.

"You sound foreign," Mrs. Judd said suspiciously.

"English," Phoebe replied.

"I knew you were different." On this rather ambiguous note, Mrs. Judd decided that they had visited long enough. "I'm going to spend Labor Day at the Cape with my kids. If you are going to stay here, can you bring in my mail? Oh—and if you could feed my cat, I'd appreciate it. Just leave food out on the back porch. She'll find it if she's hungry."

Without waiting for a reply, Mrs. Judd trod off in the direction of home.

Marcus wrapped his arms around Phoebe and held her close. His heart was beating a bit fast, which put their bloodsongs out of sync. "I'm not sure if this is a good idea."

"I am." Phoebe sighed happily. "I choose you, Marcus MacNeil. I choose this place. I choose to wake up here tomorrow, next to you, surrounded by memories and ghosts, with no electricity and a falling-down barn."

Phoebe held Marcus until his blood stopped racing and their hearts were beating to the same rhythm.

Evermore.

"I'm sure you never dreamed we'd end up here," Marcus said. "It's not exactly a beach in India."

"No," Phoebe confessed, thinking of Pickering Place with its elegant furniture, and the grandeur of Sept-Tours. Then she looked back at the MacNeil house. She thought of all that had been lost within its walls, and all the joys that might be found there.

"I didn't realize how much this place still mattered to me," Marcus said.

They stood, hands entwined, and looked over the farm where Marcus had lived so many years ago, and which was now his. Hers. Theirs.

"Welcome home," Phoebe said.

Evermore, sang their two hearts.

Evermore.

ACKNOWLEDGMENTS

I don't know where to start, and so I find myself taking Hamish Osborne's advice: begin at the end.

To Laura Tisdel and the entire team at Viking: thank you for the many kindnesses shown to the author and the depth of expertise you all brought to this project in every department and at every stage of its production.

To my stalwart supporters, Sam Stoloff of the Frances Goldin Literary Agency and Rich Green of ICM Partners: I could not do this without the two of you.

To my publicist, Siobhan Olson of Feisty PR: thank you for taking on All Souls and reminding me to have fun.

To my operations manager, right arm, and co-conspirator, Jill Hough: I am so grateful for you every day and for all the many ways you make this possible.

To my gentle readers Candy, Fran, Karen, Karin, Lisa, and Jill: thank you for always saying *yes* when I asked if I could trouble you with another draft.

To my historical experts Karen Halttunen, Lynn Hunt, Margaret Jacob, and Karin Wulf: thank you for being so patient with an early modernist who drifted into the long eighteenth century. I pestered you with questions, peppered you with my reactions to the period, and in general made a nuisance of myself. You responded with generosity and lent your considerable expertise to this book when called upon to do so. You will all know better than anyone that the remaining mistakes are my own!

To the family and friends (two-legged and four-legged) who pick me up, dust me off, and carry me along—you know who you are: thank you for being part of my circus. My mom, Olive, can share in this experience and is a source of joy as well as inspiration. Thanks, Mom, for always being my biggest cheerleader.

To my Karen, no words could ever express how much your support and love make this all possible.

First, and last, this book is dedicated to the memory of my beloved father, John Campbell Harkness (1936–2015), whose roots extended down into the soil of Pelham and Hadley, who lived much of his life in Philadelphia, and who shared his love of history with me.